Silent Partners

A Novel by

ELIZABETH JEFFETT

ELTON-WOLF PUBLISHING

Silent Partners

Cover design by Beth Farrell and Paulette Eickman
Text design by Paulette Eickman
Edited by Jan Keeling

Publishers's Note: This book is a work of fiction. Names, characters, places,
and incidents either are the product of the author's imagination or are
used fictitiously, and any resemblance to actual persons, living or dead,
business establishments, events, or locales is entirely coincidental.

01 02 03 04 05   1 2 3 4 5

ISBN: 1-58619-032-6
LOC: 2001 090650

First Printing August 2001
Printed in the United States

Published by Elton-Wolf Publishing
Seattle, Washington

ELTON-WOLF PUBLISHING

2505 Second Avenue Suite 515   Seattle Washington 98121 (206) 748-0345
e-mail: info@elton-wolf.com   Internet: http://www.elton-wolf.com
Seattle • Los Angeles

DEDICATION

With deepest love to Austin, Katie, and Larry.

Beloved, let us love one another:
for love comes from God (1 John 4:7) —

ACKNOWLEDGMENT

My darling children, Austin and Katie, supported me from the very beginning, believing that "mom" could do anything. When they were tiny, they quietly played on the floor under the computer table. Thank you for your love, patience and support, and for being a constant reminder to never limit our dreams. Your love has kept me going through this long endeavor. This novel would not have been possible if not for the love, support and faith given to me by my loving husband Larry. You are a gift from God who has forever altered the landscape of my life. Thank you for being my soul mate. My beloved parents believed I could do anything and be anyone I chose to be. My mother, Nancy Jeffett, is the living example of the female entrepreneur who taught me how to build a business. Frank Jeffett, my father, blazed the trail and showed by example that authoring a book was possible. Thanks Mom and Dad. My faith in God has sustained me. Thank you Doug B.

I am indebted to the following friends whom I love deeply: Martha Jones Williams, Dianne Ingels Moss, Beth Huddleston, Margret Bennett, Marjory Joy Witham, Isabelle, and Kay F. Turner who loyally supported me through the last several years. Many thanks to Cindy Brinker, my former partner; Sally Giddens Stephenson, who helped organize the first drafts; Phil Pfeffer, former president of Random House, who never stopped supporting me and guiding the project; Jan Keeling, who brilliantly edited the manuscript; Lorretta Barrett, who believed in the story from the beginning; and Norman Brinker, who nurtured a lifelong friendship with our family.

Many others deserve recognition for their support and contribution: Beth Farrell and the team at Elton-Wolf Publishing; Marj Waters, publisher and editor of the *Park Cities News* who never wavered in her support; Rena Pederson, vice president of the *Dallas Morning News*; Mary Ann Smith for her encouragement; Marjorie Powers Currey, for her support; Margot Perot for offering to sponsor the first book signing.

Virginia Slims and the Maureen Connolly Brinker Tennis Foundation, which gave me the opportunity to work with and be mentored by some of the best and brightest women in the sport of tennis including Ellen Merlo, Billy Jean King, Peachy, Virginia Wade, Chris and Martina, Lucy Belknap, and Nancy Jeffett—"You've come a long way baby!"

Recognition must also be given to the following: The Denver Police Department, Vern Mallinen, Dr. Linda Norten, Planned Television Arts, Craig Doran, and the many other individuals who contributed their time and energies to make this book possible.

THE ROAD NOT TAKEN

Two roads diverged in a yellow wood,
And sorry I could not travel both
And be one traveler, long I stood
And looked down one as far as I could
To where it bent in the undergrowth;

Then took the other, as just as fair,
And having perhaps the better claim,
Because it was grassy and wanted wear;
Though as for that the passing there
Had worn them really about the same,

And both that morning equally lay
In leaves no step had trodden black.
Oh, I kept the first for another day!
Yet knowing how way leads on to way,
I doubted if I should ever come back.

I shall be telling this with a sigh
Somewhere ages and ages hence:
Two roads diverged in a wood, and I—
I took the one less traveled by,
And that has made all the difference.

— ROBERT FROST

PROLOGUE

Alex Sheridan saw herself plodding through the field again, in mud-caked hiking boots that weighed heavily against her stride. Warm, dark circles of perspiration bled through threadbare remnants of denim blue.

It was a familiar scene that she had come to know a hundred times or more. Sometimes it was in Far West Texas where the dust devils choked perpetually parched lips and short, brown desert tundra dominated the landscape. One time it was in the desert of Saudi Arabia. Most often she saw herself walking across a rolling field of freshly cut hay in the flatlands of what was surely Colorado. The scene was always the same . . .

Rusty oil field equipment was strewn in every direction. A field crew milled about performing mundane chores. It was a haphazard vision of pipe and steel and cable, with a drilling rig creaking and groaning in the background. The workers performed their duties in faded disarray. Then, without explanation, Chris would appear. She was always in white, a most unlikely color.

And the dialogue was always the same. "What's the status on the well, Alex?" Chris would casually inquire. It was a predictable inquiry from an interested partner.

"She's showing water, but there's oil down there," Alex always responded, as if she were reading from a script. "We just don't want to let it get away from us."

Sometimes the sun was bright. Once they appeared to be caught in a driving rainstorm. But Chris was always there, and there were always mounting feelings of anticipated success. "She's coming in now, Ms. Sheridan," yelled a disembodied voice. "Goddamn it, boys! She's coming in."

Alex ran by the trailer that served as a makeshift headquarters as the gusher came in. Wind blasted sand. Skin burned. Oil spewed. It wasn't what they wanted. Only in old movies was the drama of a gusher still desirable. They needed to keep the well under control and cap it without losing pressure. But this one was blowing right out of the ground. Panic swarmed over the crew like angry bees. The well was slipping through their gnarled fingers. "Get it under control!" Alex yelled. Why weren't the blow-out preventers operating? "Shut it off before we lose it!" But a rain of oil spewed from the severed artery inside the earth. Nearby, sludge pits holding the gooey mixture of oil and fracking chemicals, boiled with overflow. Everything was black.

They were losing it. Alex felt the thick, black crude covering her skin in a deathly slick. She wiped at the oil dripping down her temples, but the rain of blackness thundered down. There was no shelter. And Chris had vanished.

Alex looked at her hands as they turned crimson in her dream, drenched with blood. Blood covered her face and matted her long, dark hair as the gusher now spewed red, out of control. A guttural scream broke into the madness. There was no blue left in the sky. She heard her own violent cry. "Somebody cap it! Cap the well!" she pleaded to the wind. Dirty pools of crimson congealed around her feet. The field crew had mysteriously disappeared, and Alex was alone in a place where no one could hear her screams.

All that was left was the blood.

CHAPTER 1

Dallas, 1995

Alex jerked back to the world of the conscious and looked around her bedroom. Once again she found herself sitting board straight, chilled to the bone. The sweat dripping down her temples felt like blood, and the aching in her jaws reminded her to unclench her teeth. She wiped away the watery anguish from her head as an uncontrollable palsy rippled through her body. She blinked hot, burning eyelids, closing them tight as she tried to refocus.

She was grateful the dream had come to an end—until the next time. Finally she drew the courage to look at her hands. It was a ritual. They were long and thin and fine, and for the hundredth time they were covered in neither blood nor oil. A small sigh escaped into the silence. She ran her hands through her damp jet-black hair, then checked her palms again . . . no blood.

Click! The digital clock displayed 4:56 A.M. She was always thankful for the little things. The dream that plagued her like a dead carcass upwind had waited until nearly 5:00 A.M. to appear this time. Fortune was not always so benevolent.

Sleep never returned after the dream—but there was no room for sleep on this particular day anyway. She turned on the bedside table lamp, illuminating the ornate bedchamber. Levi's, pulled half inside out, lay rumpled across the settee at the foot of the poster bed. She wondered when and if the dream would ever go away for good.

Emptiness filled the chilly sheets beside her. Steve had long since gone to work out and then to have a power breakfast with someone important—that usually meant rich, which translated to powerful. Over the years he had tired of her nighttime outbursts, her screams and tears. It was good that he'd missed this episode. Alex had tried to will her problem away, but there was no exorcising the curse. If she admitted the frequency or intensity of the dream to anyone, they would probably think she was losing her mind. Everything from hypnosis to sleeping pills had been tried, but nothing was powerful enough to kill her demons. She just had to stay frantically busy, always hoping distraction would be the answer.

The shower's cold water pushed away the memory and brought reality and the morning in ahead of schedule. On the positive side, there would now be a few extra moments for coffee and a short glance at the newspaper before a final review of her to-do list for the evening's event.

She threw jeans and a sweatshirt on a lean frame and pulled her hair back in a tight, silky ponytail. She looked in the mirror for a quick check before heading downstairs. Subtle lines of stress were working their way across her brow. In black Italian loafers, she padded silently down the long hallway that led to the suspended spiral staircase.

Like the angel of death on its mission, the aroma of Starbucks Breakfast Blend worked its way through the cracks and crevices of the Texas mansion, announcing morning. She clanked open the bolt on the massive French doors and reached for the daily edition of the *Dallas Morning News*. Crisp cool air fought warm autumn-morning sunlight. The front page of the newspaper listed the juicy lead stories of the day, including the arrival from Washington of the First Lady of the United States, who would be making an appearance in Dallas with a coterie of Secret Service and press. Alex flipped to the inside page to scan the details—she had spent over two hours with the society writer in an attempt to make sure every detail was reported accurately. No matter how hard she tried to stay on the subject of breast cancer research, the journalist had persistently returned to his fundamental interest: who was coming to the elite charity dinner party. But she saw he had been diligent about recording most of the pertinent facts.

Throwing the paper aside, Alex strode to the solarium-turned-office and located a typed list of precise duties for the day, which Steve had dropped on her desk before leaving. It was almost 7:00 A.M., and Fran, her executive assistant and confidante, would be arriving soon to begin final preparations for the fundraiser. Fran's chameleonic duties included management of the Blake estate on Turtle Creek. The neighborhood was occupied by oil barons and millionaires—the city's billionaires, like Ross Perot, lived on even larger estates or ranches farther north of town.

Alex looked up from her desk as Fran walked in carrying a fresh cup of steaming coffee in an eggshell-white Hungarian china mug. "Good morning. Thought you might be ready for a fresh cup, Alex," Fran said cheerfully.

"You're an angel!" said Alex. "Hope you had your Wheaties this morning—Steve's got our work cut out for us again. But in twenty-four hours it will all be behind us."

"Don't worry. It will be perfect, Alex. We've checked and double-checked every arrangement. What we can't control is not worth worrying about."

"I just hate dealing with Washington and the Secret Service. It's so unpredictable."

"I faxed them a diagram of the house and grounds and requested their advance authorization of our layout," Fran informed Alex.

"Well done!" By this evening the house would be transformed into an enchanted palace.

"I hope everyone appreciates *your* efforts," said Fran.

"Whether they do or not, it's all worth it. Many people almost beg to give their money to a cause when they have a chance to be around powerful political leaders. Yesterday I had fifteen calls asking for seats . . . but we're already oversold. We're bursting at the seams."

"Is there anything we need to go over before you leave for

the day?"

"You've got everything so well organized, all I have left are some last-minute personal details."

"There are some vendors outside waiting for directions. Is there anything else before I go?" Fran asked.

"Just try to keep people out of my office until I've had a chance to clear the desk."

Fran noticed shadowy circles beneath her employer's young eyes. "No problem. Did you get any sleep last night, Alex?" Fran pried in a motherly tone. She was fifteen years Alex's senior and the signs of fatigue, plus something more, did not escape her.

"More than some nights. If Schaeffer calls, tell her to call me on the cell phone. I want to talk to her no matter what," Alex said, ignoring Fran's interest in her health.

"I'll take care of it." Fran had the skills and loyalty of a military officer. "Have you finalized the seating arrangements? The Secret Service wants the complete list of the guests and where they are all to be seated."

"I'm working on it now. Everyone and his mother wants to be near the first lady's table, including the mayor and the governor. You'd think they'd never met a celebrity before!"

The two women parted to complete the final details for the arrival of the most powerful woman in the free world—or rather, Alex corrected her thoughts, *the most influential wife in the world.*

CHAPTER 2

"There's a Detective Carter on the phone. He asked to speak with Alex Sheridan," Fran said, carrying in the portable phone. Curiosity lingered in her eyes. Few people used Alex's maiden name, which was a relic from a past life.

Fran saw the look of concern that clouded her employer's face as Alex sat rigid in her office chair. The past had an uncanny way of knocking at her door at the worst times. Fran waited for direction and Alex finally responded.

"Ask him to leave a number." Her hands gripped the side of the chair for support.

Fran did as requested, but the caller must have been persistent. "He says it's urgent."

"Okay. Tell him it will be a minute." Alex looked out the window into a bottomless sky as possibilities raced through her mind . . . then she picked up the extension. "Detective Carter, what a pleasant surprise," she said, making her best effort to appear cool and collected.

"Thank you for taking the call, Alex," the detective said in a familiar voice that catapulted her back to another time and place.

"I'm sorry, I can't talk now," she said in a harried tone.

"I'll make it brief," he said. "There's a new lead in the case, and it's imperative that I speak with you as soon as possible."

A larger-than-usual swelling formed in her throat and worked its way down to her stomach. This was the first time Carter had called in almost five years. For a moment she closed her eyes, envisioning the mountains.

Then she halted the indulgence. She couldn't let Colorado

memories interfere with her life now. For too many years she had both prayed and dreaded that she would hear from Carter again. She had systematically crammed those expectations back where they belonged. "I'm sorry I can't be of any help right now, Detective Carter. Please excuse me, but I have to go." She hung up abruptly—but he would call back, and then she would have to be emotionally armed.

༄

Alex entered the garage and jumped into her Range Rover. The car, a sentimental favorite that had been bought with the profits from the liquidation of her Denver oil company, was nestled between the black Mercedes she refused to drive and the parking space that had been vacated by Steve's silver Rolls Royce. Her insistence on driving the Range Rover with its original Colorado plates displayed in the back window was one of the few things she did that continued to drive Steve mad. Its British Racing Green exterior bore the scars of many off-road adventures. She pragmatically gave in to most of Steve's wishes, but driving her battleworn Range Rover and occasionally going out with old friends to drink beer and talk oil shop were a couple of habits she refused to give up.

She whipped off Mockingbird Lane into the Highland Park Village shopping center in the heart of the Dallas suburb, bringing the vehicle to a stop in front of the Dallas Hermès store. Three different models of Rolls Royces were meticulously parallel parked out front where they could not be missed. World-class vendors occupied commercial real estate in the city's oldest shopping center, a terra-cotta tile-and-stucco architectural legacy of the state's Spanish heritage. Here Chanel, Yves St. Laurent, and Escada vied for the money that flowed through the hands of the Texas rich.

Alex slammed on the emergency brake, bolted from the car,

handed a security guard ten dollars, and dashed into the famous French boutique. The phone call from Detective Carter reverberated in her head like a battle hymn.

"Good morning, Ms. Blake. The ties you ordered are ready," the store clerk informed her. "Would you care for a mimosa?"

"No, thank you, Connie," Alex smiled. "I feel as if the day is evaporating into thin air!" She fidgeted with her wad of keys, then stilled her hands so as not to appear too preoccupied.

"I read that you and Mr. Blake are hosting an event in honor of the first lady." The woman looked starstruck.

"It is for a very worthwhile cause." Alex glanced at the racing long hand of her wristwatch.

"You must be very excited," another clerk remarked.

"How do you think we can teach Mr. Blake to keep up with his ties?" Alex said gaily, changing the subject. "They keep disappearing." Then she signed a charge slip and headed for the door.

"Maybe he thinks they're disposable!" Connie called after her, laughing.

As the door closed behind Alex, the manager turned to the new sales clerk and barked an order. "Make note of her! That was Alex Blake, one of our best customers. She and her husband are two of the most prominent people in Dallas. She could buy the store with cash today if she wanted to."

"But she looks so young!" the clerk exclaimed.

"She is, but she's one of the most influential women in the city. And I want her to continue to patronize Hermès. Have flowers sent to her home with a note thanking her for her business and wishing all the best for the event this evening."

"I'll have an arrangement delivered right away. What does her husband do?" the doe-eyed clerk inquired.

"Investments of some kind. She's from an old ranching and oil family, but the scuttle is she made a lot of money on her own before she married Steve Blake—who has made millions in no telling what kind of deals. He's rumored to be a rogue of the first order. Kind of an odd couple. She's become a very active philanthropist. Last year she raised over five million dollars for some childhood cancer cause. Before that it was the Cattle Baron's Ball. Now it's breast cancer research."

"She seems so down-to-earth," the clerk observed.

Alex jumped into the Range Rover, grabbed the cell phone, and hit the speed dial for Fran. "Where are we?" she asked without introduction.

"Everything is in order. The video people just finished."

"What about the lighting people?"

"The chief electrician is staying throughout the evening just in case the orchestra's equipment overloads the system."

"That was mighty generous of him! And just where in relation to the first lady does he want to be seated?" Alex asked lightly.

"Next to you!" teased Fran. "The orchestra is not due here until five, but someone's dropping off the sound equipment in just a little while."

"Good! Has the Secret Service arrived?" Alex continued down her list of mental notes. She had once been accused of being an organizational machine, and it was true that she had no patience for overlooked details. She believed it was important to go over every detail that could be anticipated and controlled. When it came to the unanticipated, damage control and response time were essential.

"They are here now for an advance site check, and at least two men will be here from now until the guests arrive. A total of twelve agents will be on the grounds during the evening."

"Do you think that's enough protection? They must think we're fighting a war instead of cancer."

"I took the liberty of setting up a table with sandwiches and coffee for them in the pool house."

"You're ahead of me as always, Fran. Good job. What else?"

"Don't forget your dress for tonight is ready at Milano's. He wants you to try it on for a final fitting."

Alex winced. "He may be the best clothes designer in the city, but he's kind of a pain to deal with. Every time I'm in there he harps about my weight, and I'm getting tired of it."

"You have been looking rather thin recently," Fran remarked gently. Fran was a good, solid woman with keen senses and mature wisdom. After her beloved husband died prematurely of cancer, she entered the working world. A bright woman with limited business experience, she found her niche as a personal assistant to high-powered businesspeople who led hectic lives. Details were her forte, and little escaped her eye.

"You worry too much!" Alex deflected the issue as quickly as she had brought it up. Besides, she had no intention of stopping by Milano's, as she had no intention of wearing the conservative black Ungaro cocktail dress Steve had selected for her. "What time will the first lady be arriving?"

"The limousine will be here at 6:30. They say she'll want to say a few words, then dinner should be served promptly at 7:20."

"Has Steve called in?"

"Yes, he said to remind you about his ties, and his studs at Robert Whitestone's, and to remind you to wear the dress he bought for you in Paris. He says it photographs well," she said crisply.

Alex felt her stomach tighten. "Thanks, Fran. What time will he be gracing us with his presence?" she asked, making no attempt to hide her feelings.

"He said he was leaving the polo club, going to a short meeting downtown, stopping for a steam at the country club, and then coming home. He also said to remind you not to forget the name tags for the press, but I took care of that, along with everything else on his checklist."

"You're the best!" said Alex as she hung up. Then, to herself: *Screw Steve and his pompous, controlling attitude.* She couldn't wait for this event to be over and for Steve's pretentious guests to come and go.

Steve lived for social events, and he required that Alex at least pretend to be interested. She much preferred the behind-the-scenes fund-raising and the actual organizing of the events—those activities reminded her of the life she had known when she ran her own business. In particular, she shied away from seeing herself in the society pages of the local newspapers. Steve, on the other hand, had been salivating for days about the coming photo opportunity with the first lady. He would revel in the evening. Celebrities and media on all fronts with Steve Blake taking center stage!

At least this fund-raiser touched a personal chord for Alex. Alex was proud to contribute to helping find a cure for the devastating disease that afflicted almost one in eight women.

She folded and quartered her feelings, stuffed them into a mental file folder, and deposited them in a protected drawer deep in the back of her mind. She was determined to make a success of the evening. Steve would turn on his charm—the way he had during their whirlwind romance. The owner of the Highland Park newspaper would capture the appropriate high-profile guests and feature the evening all over the cover of the weekly edition's front page. *The results were all that mattered,* Alex reminded herself as she pulled in front of Robert Whitestone's boutique.

"It's wonderful to see you, Alex." Robert Whitestone familiarly embraced his favorite client. A gifted jewelry designer, he was a slight man with a big personality.

"Thanks for all you've done to help with this event," Alex said. "The bracelet you donated will raise a great deal of money for our cause."

"Anything for you, Alex," the craftsman offered extravagantly.

A jewel-encrusted timepiece behind Alex chimed the quarter hour.

"Here are the cuff links and something else Steve wanted you to have. He said this will look good with the dress you're wearing tonight." He handed her a silver suede jewelry box containing a conservative strand of cultured pearls, and his gaze retreated to the large window that overlooked Lover's Lane.

Alex took the box reluctantly. "They're lovely," she said, noting the fine quality.

"Mr. Blake was in yesterday and picked them out himself. I tried to show him something more to your liking, but he insisted they were precisely what he wanted you to wear."

"Thank you, Robert. See you tonight."

Alex walked out the door, which automatically locked behind her.

"That son of a bitch should be shot," Robert said bitterly in the general direction of his assistant. "When he was in yesterday, he also bought a diamond and ruby necklace for that woman he keeps. He made sure I wouldn't slip and mention it to Alex. Sometimes I think I should tell her, but then, it's none of my affair. Besides, it might be ruinous for business."

Alex slid back into the Range Rover and tossed the jewelry box carelessly into the empty backseat. She was suffering from sleep deprivation and continued to be frustrated with her husband's tentacle-like attempts at control. Steve never seemed to notice her fatigue, which was the legacy of an early-trimester miscarriage several weeks ago. She still wondered where Steve had been that terrifying night. When the pain was over she had been filled with relief and the guilt that went with it—it had been an unwanted pregnancy. She had once had dreams of a family and happy home, but her union with Steve had evolved into a business. Trust had evaporated, leaving only the barren dust of their marriage.

CHAPTER 3

Alex sat in the bedroom looking at the red cocktail dress that had been taken in at the waist and shortened to a seductive length. She saved it for very special occasions; memories seemed to emanate from its rich fabric. She had worn it the first time to the Carousel Ball in Denver years earlier, when she had been one of the guests at Marvin Davis's elite diabetes fund-raiser. The oil baron–turned–movie mogul had just completed his acquisition of Twentieth Century Fox and, along with the rest of Denver society, was celebrating in Hollywood style. Phantom music from that starlit evening sometimes still played in her head.

Not long after that night her life had taken an unexpected turn. The business partnership that had been her center and the substance of her every dream was over as suddenly as it had begun. Alex had left Denver to abort everything that had been important in her Colorado life. She returned to Dallas, where she had lived off and on for much of her life and which she thought would always be home in her heart.

Steve Harrington Blake had pursued her relentlessly, appearing to love the chase. Alex had been shell-shocked, dazed and vulnerable from her Denver experiences, and Steve was a strong, exciting man who seemed to find her independence challenging. At last she had found it impossible to turn down his charm. In search of some kind of stability, something grounded to hold on to, she married the powerful man and buried the wounds of the past as deep as was humanly possible. Now, on the surface at least, she had a neatly packaged life: an attractive husband, as well as wealth and the social responsibilities that went with it.

Alex never discussed the events that had brought her so abruptly back to Texas, and Steve was too absorbed with his own blue-sky deals to take much notice of the buried past. All the "right" people came to their wedding at the Presbyterian Church in Highland Park, a municipality in the heart of Dallas where the rich and famous played behind impenetrable walls. Their reception at the Dallas Country Club was one of the biggest events of the social season.

Not long after the ceremony, the couple moved into a large French Mediterranean house on Lakeside Drive along Turtle Creek. They settled into a luxurious life of Steve's design, one filled with self-made aristocrats and civic obligations. It was the happy ending many women dream of: sports cars, European vacations, a second home next to Coral Beach Club in Bermuda, servants, lunches at The Dallas Women's Club, and no worries about money. The business world that Alex had embraced so passionately faded into the horizon. Much like the dutiful wives she had observed from a distance during her working days, she set up house and went about the business of being a society wife and philanthropist, just as her husband directed.

Steve Blake was a power broker firmly rooted in Dallas. He spent weekends at The Dallas Hunt and Polo Club playing chukker after chukker on one of his prize ponies. When they were not at the polo matches, Steve and Alex would entertain friends at a Texas Stadium skybox, watching the Dallas Cowboys play on the Astroturf below while Dom Perignon flowed in magnum proportions. Steve and Alex talked politics and polo from the start. After a few months of marriage, Alex realized that was where their conversations stopped. She also began to realize that she had married a very smooth, very charming man who was ruthless in his business life and controlling in his personal life.

Steve's Lear Jet (my "relatively modest Lear Jet," he called it) was hangared nearby at Dallas Love Field, only fifteen minutes from their front door. Alex had wanted to learn to fly, and this had been a sore point between them. After the last painful argument on the subject, she never mentioned flying lessons again.

She felt as if she had left a large part of herself in Colorado. Her fond, intimate relationships with her Denver business associates had slipped into a memory. A few colleagues had tried to stay in touch, but her walls were high and dense. And it was clear that Steve, too, wanted that chapter in her life to be over.

Her only friend who knew all the details of the past was one of her former partners, Schaeffer London. Once in a while the two would reminisce over a glass of wine. Then memories would come flooding back, bringing the past into the present like a freight train. But Alex was determined to stay in Dallas in her neatly packaged life, however hollow it might be. At least in Dallas there was never anyone asking her prying questions.

∽

A deluge of caterers, contract employees, and reporters was descending on the normally quiet estate. Fran knocked on the dressing-room door, jolting Alex out of her memories. "There's a writer from *D Magazine* waiting to talk to you."

"I'll be right down. Is everything in order?"

"Schaeffer is downstairs handling the press, and the only thing we're waiting for is you. And, of course, the first lady."

Alex hurriedly slithered into her red cocktail dress. She was thankful for Schaeffer London, her staunch ally. Schaeffer, happily married, operated a small independent oil and gas company from a Park Cities office of glass and mirrors and computers. She raised the money and her rugged husband drilled the wells, a perfect alliance. She wanted Alex to get back in the oil business, but her prodding had been fruitless thus far.

Alex descended the winding marble stairs at the entry of the mansion.

Steve stared in amazement at the sight of Alex in the scarlet dress that accentuated her youthful figure, showing a million miles of slim leg. It was not what he had directed. At the sight of the simple gold chain around her neck his temper quietly ignited. He was already irritated by the presence of Schaeffer London, a woman he considered a bad influence on a headstrong wife. He blamed Schaeffer for Alex's refusal to wear the clothing and jewelry he had requested.

But for now it was more important to keep his social visage intact than to argue with Alex in front of guests. Steve approached Alex, hand outstretched, smiling as would any proud husband. Through his teeth and under his breath he hissed, "Are you *trying* to look like a slut?" Then he casually turned away to speak to a guest.

The guests began arriving at 6:30 P.M. Car attendants in tailcoats greeted the train of automobiles in the wide circular drive. A rainbow of water spewed from a Grecian fountain on the front lawn, and four violinists from the symphony played a medley of Andrew Lloyd Webber music.

It was early November, and the sun had left its handprint on the limitless Texas horizon. Exquisite landscape lighting illuminated the ornate gardens at the entry to the fourteen-thousand-square-foot Blake mansion. Flowers of every description filled huge oriental fishbowls in the massive entryway, and ivy accented with white roses snaked up the winding iron balustrade. The gentle sounds of a string quartet could be heard behind the rising din of excited party guests.

A stretch limousine pulled into the winding circular entry. Its door opened and a long, slender leg in a high-heeled pump twisted out from the rear seat. The woman who emerged was not extraordinarily tall, but her slight weight created the illusion of height. She was not dressed in formal evening attire as were the other guests, but she drew the most attention from the crowd milling at the front entrance. Her suit was black, like almost every other article of clothing she was wearing except for tortoiseshell glasses with polarized lenses and a leopard-print scarf wrapped stylishly around her neck. The driver unloaded a briefcase and slim hanging bag from the trunk of the limo.

Alex and Steve were speaking to each guest, welcoming them all to their home. None of the guests could detect the smoldering anger Steve masked, even when he murmured something to his wife through clenched teeth about the red dress and asked about the pearls Alex had "forgotten" to wear.

Schaeffer London, blonde, blue-eyed, and wearing a black sheath that could not disguise her curves, approached Alex, who was being distracted by the local society editor. The editor was desperately trying to make a list of the guests streaming through the entry hall. Nearby stood the controversial owner of the Dallas Cowboys, a good old Southern boy discussing politics with the mayor, who looked bored.

"Alex, there is a guest who would like to see you," Schaeffer ignored Steve's glare.

"Please excuse me for a moment," Alex said, thankful to dismiss the writer. She turned toward the door and came face to face with a piece of her past. The beautiful austere woman in the black suit, a friend of a lifetime, stood on the second marble step.

Alex ran through the door like a jubilant high-school girl in a display of warmth and affection. "Jeanne, my goodness, I thought you were in the middle of a research conference in Sweden!"

"I was . . ."

"How'd you get away?"

"I couldn't miss this event, Alex. And, of course, I wanted to be here to support you."

The two women hugged, then they ran into the house to join Schaeffer, who grabbed them both in a triumphant embrace. Remembering where she was, Alex turned to the throng of guests. "Let me have everyone's attention," she said loudly, mounting the staircase to quiet the cocktail-induced noise. "Everyone, please. I want to welcome our distinguished guest who has flown in from Sweden to be here tonight. Dr. Jeanne Gougon, the fore-most cancer research physician in the field of diagnostic breast cancer. Thanks to her work, we are closer to finding a cure!"

Everyone clapped politely, and Alex turned back to Jeanne, who was flushed with embarrassment. "I'll get even with you for that!" the doctor said with a smile. "You know how much I hate the spotlight."

"You deserve it, though!" Alex insisted.

"It's a near miracle I made the flight."

"I can't believe you are really here. We have to talk!"

"Let's go back to the library for a minute," Schaeffer suggested.

"You knew about this?" Alex accused Schaeffer affectionately.

"Of course!" Schaeffer looked pleased with her coup.

"When did you get here?" Alex asked Jeanne as she directed her friends to a small study away from the guests.

"I flew directly to DFW Airport from Stockholm. Schaeffer told me about the miscarriage, Alex," she said bluntly.

Alex shrugged, but Jeanne saw through the show of detach-ment. "I wish you had called." Schaeffer had told Jeanne that Alex felt alone and helpless the night it happened. With Steve out of town on one of his mysterious trips, she had driven herself to the emergency room. "You're thin!" the physician added.

"I've been busy—you look ravishing, Jeanne," Alex said, avoiding the physician's comments.

Alex was delighted to see her old friend, the brilliant doc-tor who had almost every square filled in her life: success, wealth, a cool Scandinavian-type beauty, and worldwide rec-ognition and acclaim from her peers. Only a relationship seemed to be missing; but then, the gifted doctor had always been mar-ried to her work.

"Thank you," she said humbly. Then, "How's Steve?" she asked politely.

"The same. How's your practice?"

"It's been a busy year. And it's been too long since we've

been together."

The three women looked at one another and fell silent. It always happened. The painful fact of Chris's absence was magnified when they all came together. The reunion instantly created a hole where Chris used to be. Alex fought back a well of emotion.

"I have to meet the first lady. See you outside." She left her two former associates to visit with each other while she performed her duties.

"I'm so thankful you came, Jeanne."

"How is she doing, Schaeffer, really?" Jeanne freshened her makeup as she tried to get the real story on Alex.

"I think she's depressed. She's smothered her feelings for so long. There's a mountain of unresolved anger and fear inside her. For you and me, it was different. You had your medical research and I had another business here in Dallas. But Alex was enmeshed in the Denver company. It was her lifelong dream to build a business—and not just any business, but a business with Chris. Chris was her mentor and closest companion. That kind of relationship couldn't be duplicated when it all came to an end."

"No one could have been prepared for the emotional fallout."

"I just wish I could shake her into feeling something. It's like there's a rock around her heart."

"I've felt that, too, even in short phone conversations."

"I have to think there's a chink in that armor . . . somewhere."

"We'll have a chance to talk with her after the party. We can go back to your place and have a glass of wine and really catch up."

"No way that will happen!" Schaeffer challenged. "Steve won't let her alone with us. You wait and see."

The doctor furrowed her brow. "Then we can have coffee in the morning before I leave."

"You're going back to Sweden tomorrow?"

"No, Paris. There's an afternoon flight, which will allow time for a good talk. I wish it could be longer, but the stars didn't line up this time."

"I hope you'll stay with us tonight." Schaeffer offered.

"Your guest room sounds perfect."

"It's not as grand as this, but there's pretty good coffee in the morning." Schaeffer lived in a charming cottage-style home in a more modest section of Dallas.

"That would be more comfortable. I don't want to hurt Alex's feelings, but Steve gives me the creeps," Jeanne said bluntly.

"I know. It's something in his eyes," Schaeffer's eyebrows shaped into a serious scowl. "I don't trust him!" she said emphatically.

Jeanne sighed. "A few months after their marriage, Alex asked me some questions about split personalities and pathological liars. It was very ominous. But then she never brought it up again—just like what happened in Denver. She has a defense against pain that is formidable."

"It's Steve!" Schaeffer blurted out angrily. "She has erected so many walls. We hardly ever talk about anything deep anymore. Steve keeps her virtually locked up."

"I know—she was so vulnerable when she met Steve. But she is still very strong way down deep inside. Something will give, Schaeffer. It's just a matter of time."

"She'll have to get rid of Steve for that to happen. He's a stone on her soul."

"Alex will figure it out in time," Jeanne assured Schaeffer.

"I hear them asking people to move outside. Maybe we should join the party."

"Are we seated together?"

"Yes. With the first lady."

"Oh, no! Schaeffer! What if I slip and say something offensive?" Jeanne rolled her translucent blue eyes.

"It wouldn't be the first time." Schaeffer smiled. "I'm sure she'll respect you for speaking your mind."

"I'll have to use the right fork and make serious conversation. Can't we sit someplace in the back?"

"Alex wouldn't hear of it. You know, she's still her same determined self in *some* ways—even if part of the old Alex is dead."

"I'm a great believer in reincarnation! After the first lady leaves, we can let our hair down."

∽

The soirée was a great success, especially with the first lady's appearances. Nancy Brinker, a national icon in the field of breast cancer fund-raising and awareness, was there, as rumors spread that Ross Perot was going to pledge ten million dollars. After dinner and a few words from the first lady, the Secret Service ferried her out a side entrance, leaving the rest of the guests to wind down the party.

In an obscure corner, Jeanne and Schaeffer reminisced about their days in Aspen and the all-too-brief life of their Denver oil company while Alex continued to work the remaining crowd. Finally, the last stragglers moved toward the entry hall, where hundreds of photos had been shot by a swarm of reporters who had left the party to meet deadlines for the next day. The perfect hostess was concealing a slow, smoldering anger, fanned by the under-the-breath insults delivered by her husband over the course of the evening.

After the last guest drove away, Schaeffer approached Alex. "Congratulations! You handled everything like a master, Alex."

"Thanks! I couldn't have done it without you."

"Just like the old days?"

Alex avoided the allusion to their past. "I thought it went well. No one insulted the first lady, and from my estimation, we raised more than eight hundred thousand dollars."

"Jeanne is going to spend the night at my place. We thought you would need a break after this one."

"It made it very special for us all to be together again. How long has it been?"

"Too long!" Schaeffer looked hard at Alex. "Come back to my place," she implored. "We can drink wine and stay up and talk all night the way we used to."

The words lingered in the cool night air. "I can't," Alex said quietly.

"Sure you can!" Schaeffer pressed. "Bill is out in West Texas . . . we'll have the place to ourselves."

But Alex bit her lip. "Steve's upstairs waiting," she said, "and I am pretty bushed." The comment was not convincing, not even to Alex.

"Are you sure?" Jeanne urged.

"Let's have coffee in the morning." *After Steve is gone*, Alex added silently.

"Come to the office as soon as you can," said Schaeffer.

"I can hardly wait! Jeanne, I am so honored and grateful that you came." Alex knew how her friends felt about her husband, but there was no point in trying to explain the relationship. She preferred to keep a distance between her close friends and her life with Steve.

Her two former business partners moved to the open entryway as an uneasy feeling filled Alex's heart. She tried to write it off as a letdown from the monumental evening that had finally come to an end. Part of her desperately wanted to walk out the door with them and never come back . . . but Alex let her friends disappear into the crisp Texas night.

"Y'all are the best," she called out as the massive doors closed. In the chill of the cavernous house, she wondered how she had arrived at this desolate place.

CHAPTER 4

Steve walked into their bedroom as Alex was preparing for the night.

"It was a successful evening, don't you think?" he inquired, carelessly tossing his gold studs next to the suede jewelry box on the antique English mahogany dressing table. He was strikingly handsome, although some women would think him a little too well groomed. The wet-look gel in his slicked-back, black hair had hardened to the texture of dried glue, and his collar and cuffs never seemed out of place, even when he had been drinking heavily. His icy blue eyes, set off by a year-round tan, seemed to be one-way mirrors. He glanced across the room, catching a moment of profile in the mirror—a habit his wife was beginning to find terribly annoying.

Alex abandoned her black pumps in a corner near the bed, then slid out of the tiny red dress into a T-shirt. "Yes, I think we raised over eight hundred thousand dollars." She thought about Schae and Jeanne. They would be having a glass of Chardonnay now and had probably already broken out Schaeffer's secret pack of Marlboro Lights, reserved for very special girls-only occasions.

"I expected it to be more."

Alex ignored the slight. She sighed. "I hope the press will remember to mention the purpose of the evening and not just who came to the party."

"It's all about money and power, Alex!" Steve lectured arrogantly. He glanced in the mirror again.

"Not if you're dying, Steve!"

"You can't believe these people were really here because they care about breast cancer!" He rolled his eyes toward the ceiling. "As long as the powerful, beautiful people are the party guests, you could be raising money to save endangered rattlesnakes and everyone would still come!"

"That's true of *some* people, but not *all*. I just don't see life through your filter, Steve."

"They were all here to rub shoulders with other rich and powerful people and to see their faces in print over morning coffee. Period! And you are a fool if you think any different."

"Let's drop the debate." Bored with the hopeless conversation, Alex sighed.

"What picture do you think they'll run in tomorrow's society section?" Steve asked, bringing the subject back to something of personal interest. His hand-tailored tuxedo landed aimlessly on the back of a French chaise, leaving his near-perfect body naked except for Ralph Lauren boxers. He looked in the full-length beveled mirror, studying his sculpted physique. *Not bad*, Alex could almost hear him thinking. He scrubbed his head vigorously with his smooth hands, trying to relieve the pressure from the sculpting gel.

"I couldn't care less," Alex said wearily.

"Well, I wish you cared enough to have worn something more appropriate. I don't want my wife featured in the *Dallas Morning News* looking like a whore," he said in an ugly tone. A little alcohol, and his tongue sharpened like a scalpel.

"That's the fourth time you've called me a whore tonight. That's enough!"

"You have my reputation to consider."

"I looked just fine. In fact, from the looks I got from your partner, I must have been ravishing," she jibed.

"If you'd wear something that covered more than your ass, you wouldn't have that problem."

"You are my only problem."

"I don't want to see you in that dress again!" he thundered.

"Don't you have enough people to humiliate and control besides me?" Alex shouted. "If you had your way, I'd look like a nun."

Steve grabbed the red dress, tearing it in half from its back zipper to the hem. He threw it on the floor in a heap.

"That's one of my favorite dresses!" she cried.

"Not anymore! And you'll not dress that way again, especially not next week for the polo tournament."

She bent to pick up the tattered garment, but he kicked it out of reach.

"I'm not one of your goddamn polo ponies, Steve," Alex screamed.

"I expect you to look and act the part of 'my wife,' no less! Do I make myself clear?" He pointed and jabbed his finger at her as if she were a naughty child.

"Perfectly," she said in a voice filled with loathing. Her attention landed on the gray box on the dresser. She moved to the dresser and grabbed the pearls. "You can keep these!" she spat and threw the expensive necklace at her husband.

He shook his fist in the air, angrily gripping the rejected pearls. "There are women who would get down on their knees and beg for a gift like this."

"I guess you're speaking from personal experience!" she shot back.

Her sharp remark pushed a red-hot button. Steve lost control and slapped Alex sharply across her cheek. Blindsided, they stared at each other in shock. Even Steve seemed stunned by his action. Thick rage hung between them. In slow motion Alex raised a hand to her stinging cheek. She was dazed by what had just happened.

"You shouldn't have done that!" she said defiantly.

Steve's eyes hardened to black ice. He started to retreat, but she stopped him.

"I hope you are going out of town this week," she said in a hollow voice. She hoped he would leave and give a break to the tension in their home.

"Yes, I'm leaving in the morning."

"Can I ask where?"

"Just to a couple of different places. There are several deals we are looking at. Call the office if you need me." He was speaking in the tone he used for employees and other help.

"I needed you before and you weren't here," Alex said in a small voice.

"I'm not going to discuss that again. I'm not going to report my every move to you or anyone, ever!"

"Then expect the same from me!" she retorted.

"You are such a bitch."

"Please, Steve, I'm too tired to do this anymore." And she was tired, tired of hurting and hiding feelings, more tired than even she had known. The years of anger had chipped away at her heart, one harsh word at a time.

Steve Blake calmly went to bed.

Alex lay in a fetal ball in a corner on her side of the bed, wondering again how she had arrived at this place. A roller coaster of memories raced in her head. She thought about the night she had driven alone to the hospital when she lost the baby. Steve had been nowhere to be found and she had been scared and alone. A few days later she had become angry. Her anger had metastasized into resentment and now a defiant rage. Yet she felt paralyzed to act.

When she first met him, Steve's control had been a comfort. He had taken firm control of their life, and she had followed willingly. Why not let someone else hold the reins?

Repeatedly she wondered why her celebrated instincts had not prevented her from making such an unhappy marriage. Most of the time she understood only too well that the tragic events in Denver had shut down the valuable instinctive parts of herself. After all, she blamed herself for the tragedy because she had not listened to her intuition. She still thought she could have prevented it somehow.

Now she felt like a prisoner in Steve's world. Fretful, thirsty and sleepless, she moved from the bed to the dressing room. The mirror offered a still-life portrait of a beautiful dark-haired woman she once knew. The mark on her cheek had paled, but the wound to her soul was deep. She couldn't remember exactly when her marriage had become emotionally abusive, but it had been before the first year was out. She had remained determined to work on the relationship, always believing Steve could change, always making excuses for his behavior. *He was under enormous pressure in his high-powered business world. She wasn't a traditional enough wife. She didn't anticipate his needs. She was too independent.* All these things he had told her and she in turn had told herself. She waited for a while as if the woman in the glass might give her some clear direction, but no offering came. She crept silently back between the cool silk sheets.

"Get some sleep, Alex," Steve said coldly, turning his back to her in the darkness. The bathroom light softly illuminated the shape of his body beneath the sheets. Alex was relieved that he hadn't forced her to "make love," a phrase he confused with copulating. He usually insisted they consummate a violent argument that way. After a series of painful confrontations, all intimacy between them had been lost. Sex had become a vacant, missionary event slotted in between the *Wall Street Journal* and a workout.

In another life and time Alex had known there could be more. Once in a while memories would emerge, bringing back misty passionate moments of how things could be . . . but there was no use trying to put smoke back in a bottle, and thinking about warm possibilities only sharpened the cold edges of the present. She accepted the lack of intimacy with Steve because it allowed her to keep a part of her protected. She still believed that in order for her to survive, everything about her Colorado experiences had to be erased. Her sanity had been based on creating an acceptable reality with Steve in Dallas . . . but now he had upped the ante. The anger and hurt from his increasing attempts at control kept her awake late into the night.

CHAPTER 5

Alex awoke to a sore cheek and welcome solitude on Monday morning. The redness had disappeared during the night and Steve had stealthily slipped out without disturbing her. For both these things she was grateful.

And, as always, thank goodness for Fran. She arrived dressed in a neat, beige cotton dress, very conservative and completely appropriate for her role as personal assistant and household manager. Her light brown hair was pulled back in a tight bun and she wore no visible makeup, just pale-pink lip gloss. She was carrying a portable phone and her ubiquitous clipboard with a to-do list for the day as she joined Alex in the sunroom.

Alex had poured a cup of coffee and sat down scanning the *Dallas Morning News* headlines about the first lady's visit to a prominent Park Cities home. Just as she was beginning the story, the telephone rang.

"Blake residence," Fran answered. "One moment, please. May I tell her who's calling?" Fran covered the receiver with one hand and nodded a warm good-morning to Alex, who was holding her hand to her right temple. "Are you all right?"

"Yes, just a bit tired."

Fran saw more in Alex's eyes than fatigue, but she knew it would be futile to try to discuss what was guarded inside. "The man who called yesterday, Carter, would like to speak with you. Should I take a message?"

So much had changed in twenty-four hours. The first lady had come and gone, and Steve had pushed Alex to the edge. She had tossed and turned throughout the night, fighting the side of her that wanted to make things work, finally realizing that she had to take some action. The slap had been the last straw, inflicting a potentially terminal injury on a marriage that was already fragile. When Steve was miles away, it was easy to be brave. But oh, how her confidence melted in the shadow of his anger.

"No, I'll take it in here. You did a superb job with the event, Fran," Alex complimented as she moved to her office phone. "Please call and get extra copies of today's papers for our records."

Alex's heart skipped a beat as she picked up the receiver. "Hello, Mike," she said less apprehensively than before.

"Good morning, Alex. I really do need to speak with you." Mike Carter was sitting at his desk in the Denver police headquarters, a steaming cup of coffee in one hand and a cream-filled pastry perched on top of his Chris Welbourne file.

"Sorry I was so busy yesterday."

"That's quite all right. It's been a long time, Alex."

Alex's heart picked up pace. His voice brought back every visceral memory as if it were yesterday. Mike Carter was a man she had initially loathed but gradually grown to trust. Her palms turned warm and sticky as she unconsciously held her breath. Then she choked out the question: "Has there been a break in the case?"

"Possibly . . . I know this is hard for you, but I need to speak with you again."

"Shoot."

"No, not over the phone. Face to face. We have a new lead, a reliable source, and we need some help that only you can give. It's hard with a murder case like this one that happened such a long time ago." Detective Carter had never given up on the case that had brought them together and torn Alex's world from its moorings.

To Alex, the phone receiver felt like a sledgehammer that could deliver a blow. She had just about reconciled herself to the possibility that the case might remain unsolved, a mystery without closure. "I don't know, Mike," she said weakly.

"We need your help, Alex," he said in a flat voice. "We need you to come to Denver as soon as possible."

Denver . . . the door had been slammed shut and sealed like a tomb. She always thought nothing could have made her return —until now, until last night. Now there was a small chink in her resistance.

A small one. "Can't the questions be handled over the phone?" she asked. She felt this would be a reasonable alternative.

"I'm afraid not, Alex. We need you in person and as soon as possible." he added cryptically.

"Detective Carter," she said in a new tone, one a little desperate. "I have a husband and friends who know virtually nothing about my past and the details of this case. I don't want this tragedy to keep playing forever." Silently she raised a hand to her cheek while the scene from the previous night played vividly in her mind.

"We'll try to make it as brief as possible, Alex."

Carter would never know the events that were working in his favor. Yesterday she wouldn't have considered going back to Denver, but with the fund-raiser over and her angry emotional state fueled by her confrontation with Steve, she was wavering. "If I agree to come to Denver, no one is to know where I am."

"Whatever you say," he paused. "I thought you, more than anyone else, would be excited about a new lead." He expertly delivered the dose of guilt.

"I am!" she said defensively. "It's just that I thought it was over, and my husband has no tolerance for intrusions. He's very busy and there are huge time demands on both of us."

"We wouldn't ask you to come if we didn't believe there's a good chance this lead could break open the case."

"It's hard for me to get my hopes up and believe it might be a real breakthrough when every other clue has led to a dead end." She was trying to fight a growing sense of excitement. Maybe this *would* be the clue that would solve the plaguing decade-old mystery.

"I hope this one will be different."

"Why is someone coming forward after so many years?" she asked.

"That's all I can say for now, but it's imperative you come as soon as possible. Can you be here for a meeting tomorrow morning?"

"Tomorrow? I don't know . . ."

She turned to her daily calendar. Nothing life-threatening stared back.

"I can fill you in on the details when you arrive." He wasn't going to let her back out.

Alex thought about Steve and what he would do when he found out she had left. But . . . *screw him!* He deserved a dose of his own medicine for a change.

"Yes, I'll be there," she said. "There are flights leaving hourly for Denver." As soon as she had acquiesced, her anxiety rippled into full excitement. Alex hung up, wondering when and how she would explain things to Steve. It would serve him right to come home and find her gone after he had been so vague about his own whereabouts. She called Fran to go over the details.

"Cancel my meetings for the rest of the day and please make an excuse for me." Civic obligations could wait.

"Yes, Alex. Is there some kind of emergency?"

"Not exactly. Well, yes, you might call it that," Alex allowed. "Please get a small carry-on suitcase from the storage closet. I have to take a short trip to Denver, but you don't know that, right?"

Fran's eyes widened but she remained silent. If Alex did not want to tell her any more than that, she knew there had to be a good reason.

Alex thought about Steve. An upcoming polo match between the United States and Argentina would serve as a significant distraction when he returned from his trip, wherever he was. He had never been known to miss a good polo match. The Dallas

Hunt and Polo Club was fielding a formidable team with several three- and four-goal players. Steve would be so distracted he might not even miss Alex.

"If Steve calls, please tell him something urgent came up. There's no need for alarm—it's related to an old business deal in Colorado. I won't be gone for more than a couple of days. I'll call you at home to check my messages." Alex did not want to put her employee in a compromising position by giving her too many details.

When Steve did call, he would be upset, but Alex would deal with that later. Her next call was to American Airlines to find out the day's flight schedule from Dallas to Denver. She had enough time to pack and make the next flight out of DFW, and she even had time to stop by the bank, say good-bye to Jeanne and Schae, and pick up some cash. She was determined to get out of the house and out of the city before Steve or his secretary called with a list of tasks, or with a peace offering. Steve's pattern following abusive episodes usually included phone calls and flowers and gifts, if not apologies. It wouldn't be long before he called looking for her.

Deep in her heart Alex had always known she would have to go back to Denver someday. There were too many loose ends, too much unfinished business.

She rummaged an old phone log out of the back of the desk in the office on the east wing of the house. She flipped to the Ws and dialed the number that had once been so familiar. No answer— the message machine came on and she listened to the male voice before she left her message. "Jake, it's me, Alex, sorry it's been so long. There's no good excuse. The reason I'm calling is to let you know I'm on my way to Denver. I'll be at The Brown tonight if there's any way you can meet me. It's about Chris!" She knew he would be there. She regretted that she had been unable to maintain the friendship for so many years.

She threw boots, jeans, black pants, and a few accessories

into her small leather carry-on bag along with makeup and a toothbrush. An exquisitely designed fur coat was hanging in the hall closet—all she would need for a few days. It was late fall, a cold fresh season in the Rockies.

Alex thought about another old friend, a ghost she had tried to exorcise over and over again. She thought about Denver in the moonlight and her lost life in the Mile High City. Then the familiar gut-wrenching pain of reality swept over her.

Life was in Dallas now her conscience argued. Chris was gone and Alex had cast her lot with Steve. She would go to Denver, take care of business, and return to face her husband and home. *What a strange world,* she thought—Dallas felt more like an overwhelming obligation than a home.

But she also suspected that the forces of destiny were moving again, on an uncharted course that not even Steve Blake with all his horses and all his money could control. She gave in to an urge to open the small wall safe next to her desk. Her fingers trembled as they rotated the combination lock. Left right left. At first the lock refused to cooperate. On the second attempt, it opened.

Inside the dark hole lay miscellaneous items, a rough will, the copy of the articles of incorporation of the Aspen Development Partners, an ancient yellow photo of her mother embracing a scrawny eleven-year-old Alex, her father's gold wedding band worn thin over more than thirty years—items worthless to anyone else but priceless to her.

Not smart, Alex told herself. She was disturbing old bones . . . but she couldn't help herself. Longing and desire were much more powerful than reason. And right now she was running full throttle on instinct again, following the daimon that held the reins of her destiny. She dug around in the back of the safe until her fingers found their mark. She crammed the familiar crinkled envelope into the inside pocket of her cluttered handbag, then reached in again for the clip file of articles she had kept—her nightmare detailed in chronological order.

Alex closed the safe and put the articles she had removed into her traveling bag. She carried the bag out to the Range Rover and set off for the Preston Center office of Schaeffer London. She dialed Schaeffer's number on the car phone as she approached the building.

"Hello, Schae," Alex said without introduction. "I'm on my way to the airport, but I wanted to come by and say good-bye to Jeanne. Oh, and if Steve or his secretary calls asking questions, you never heard a word from me . . ." Excitement dangled on the edge of Alex's voice.

"What's going on?" Schaeffer interrupted. "I thought you were going to meet us here for coffee. Jeanne's on the phone making calls in the conference room, waiting for you now."

"I'm pulling into the Park Cities Bank building right now. I'll be up in one minute after I get some cash."

Alex took the elevator upstairs to the beautifully decorated offices of London Enterprises, a small but profitable energy company. Most of the players had fallen by the wayside as the eighties brought business to a halt and the money stream dried up. But a few real oil men had survived, and Schaeffer, as tough as she was beautiful, was one of them.

"So tell me where you are going so secretively," Schaeffer ordered as her best friend and former partner entered the office. Schae stepped from behind an enormous partners desk in a skirt the size of a matchbox—standard business attire for her was the tiny skirt, a silk blouse, and three-and-a-half-inch black pumps. She wore no stockings on her sumptuous tanned legs and a shiny blonde cloud of hair framed her friendly blue-eyed face. Early in her career she had stopped trying to hide her voluptuous sex appeal. If the men in the business world had trouble working with a drop-dead beauty, she put that under the heading of Their Problem.

An eight-by-ten photo of Schaeffer, Alex, Jeanne, and Chris rested prominently on the corner of the leather-inlaid credenza.

Schaeffer had purchased the enormous mahogany office furniture from one of the real estate companies that bellied up during the real estate and savings and loan bust that had devastated Texas and Colorado. Alex picked up the photo, caressing it with her eyes before responding to Schaeffer—who immediately noticed a new spark in those eyes. The photo captured four gorgeous women on Ajax Mountain in Aspen with a bottle of champagne in one hand and the world by the tail in the other. When the picture was taken they had been on their way to take the gondola down the mountain after a magnificent day of waist-deep powder skiing. Alex delicately replaced the photo.

"I got a call from Detective Carter in Denver just an hour ago," she told Schaeffer. "They're reopening the case, or at least they think they have something new."

Jeanne walked out of the conference room in time to catch the tail end of Alex's revelation. "Alex, that's great news."

"This lead may be as useless as all the others, but he insisted I come to Denver."

"I'm glad you're going back," Jeanne said, embracing her friend. "Maybe this will help resolve your feelings about what happened. You can't hold yourself responsible forever."

"You have to quit torturing yourself for something that is beyond your control," Schaeffer added, choosing her words carefully.

"I'm not torturing myself" Alex said defensively. "I've tried putting it to rest but it isn't finished. Not a day goes by that I don't see Chris and that scene at her office. Not a day goes by that I don't regret where I was the night it happened. And I know I should have been there for her."

"And you think making yourself miserable by living half a life will change things?" Schaeffer had danced these steps a thousand times. "Jeanne, talk to her," she pleaded.

"Grief and anger can be insidious, Alex. They are always a by-product of death. I see it every day, each time with a new face. If you turn that energy inward, it will rot your soul little by little. It has the power to destroy you. Don't let it win, Alex. Go back to Denver."

"It won't be over until we find out what really happened," argued Alex.

"Find everything you're afraid of, why you're afraid to go back. You know it's more than the obvious. Don't return until you can get rid of the dream that harbors your pain. When it's gone, you'll find the peace that evades you."

Alex respected her two closest friends, both of whom were urging her to face the past. Maybe the journey to Denver would shake loose the stranglehold of guilt that had consumed her life.

❧

Margaret Pullman, Steve Blake's personal assistant, hung up from a short conversation with Fran and quickly dialed her boss's mobile pager. The call was returned instantly.

"What do you have?" he barked from the starboard side of the Lear. His sleek plane was leaving Houston, heading back to Dallas for a few hours before leaving for Memphis, where he would look at a hot new company in the initial stages of going public.

"The market's off fifty points, and I sent the flowers to the house, but I haven't located Alex."

Steve looked at his watch and noted there were still fifteen minutes before the market closed. "What do you mean?" he asked, a rough edge in his voice.

"Fran was evasive. She wouldn't tell me where Alex is . . . she said something vague about her needing to go somewhere on business. I thought you would want to know."

"Put me through to the house immediately."

Margaret followed the order, conferencing the call through to the Blake estate.

"Where's Alex?" Steve barked at Fran.

"I'm not really sure. She's left town for a few days."

"Left town! What for?" he demanded.

"I'm sorry, sir, she didn't say."

His temper flared. "She had to have told you more than that, goddamn it."

"I think she said Colorado. That was it."

"If I find out you're lying to me, you'll be fired!" Steve hung up angrily and continued his shouting at Margaret. She was a woman who had lasted with him longer than most because she knew how to follow orders, questioned nothing, and accepted verbal abuse.

"That fucking little bitch! Who does she think she is?"

"Yes, sir?"

"Colorado," he said aloud, letting the information set in. He knew he had been a little hard on Alex the night before, but he couldn't believe she would just leave. He would not tolerate this defiance. He wouldn't allow her to embarrass him. His voice thundered with rage. "Call the CEO at American Airlines and tell him I want to know what flight she is on, *now!* I'm sure she's headed to Denver. Then call every hotel until you locate her. I want to know where she is and what the hell is going on."

"Yes, sir."

"If she contacts you, I want her to call me immediately! We're supposed to be getting ready for the Argentinean polo team and its diplomatic entourage."

"Yes, sir."

"Tell her I expect her to be back home immediately and for everything to be perfect for this event. You can also tell her I am not one damn bit amused."

"Yes, sir."

"Hold on a minute, Margaret." His other phone was ringing. "Where's it trading? Yes, buy one hundred thousand shares. What are the rumors about the tobacco stocks? Eliminate our position. Is there anything else, Margaret?"

"Crystal called to check in. She wants to go by the jeweler and have the clasp on her new necklace adjusted." Margaret Pullman delivered the information like a computer-generated recording. She never made judgments regarding her boss's liaisons.

"Tell her to stay out of there. Have the necklace picked up and couriered over to Whitestone. And tell her to stay put, I may be stopping by the apartment." He hung up, studying the thunderheads forming to the north. He was suddenly uncomfortable in the luxurious seats of the jet. A big storm was blowing in. It was the only thing that ever frightened him about flying. The plane could be grounded for a few hours. It would be very inconvenient, but then again, he might get a fix with Crystal. He called the house again, but Fran let the answering machine do its job. He slammed down the cell phone. That she had left with no explanation, no permission, blinded him with rage.

CHAPTER 6

Alex Sheridan Blake looked out the window of the Boeing 737 at the remnants of last season's snow on the western range of the Rockies. She could see Pike's Peak in the distance on the south side of the plane. The landing gear locked into position as the flight attendant announced their approach to the Denver airport. Passengers on the north side of the plane could see the Denver International Airport that was under construction. DIA, a controversial project, with its marble concourses and billions in cost overruns, was a monument to the 1980s financial debacle. Nevertheless, it was a spectacular sight. Alex thought it looked like the billowing sails of an ancient ship.

The pain in her stomach abated with the sight of the snow-capped mountains. Memories of the city lights of Denver in the early morning and Boulder's Sunshine Canyon were pulling at her like an old habit. At last she let thoughts of Colton Forrester flood out of the neat compartment where she had tried to hide them for the last ten years.

She had left Denver with almost no good-byes. Colt had desperately tried to break through to Alex, but she had moved to Dallas, her old stomping grounds, and quickly married. After the wedding she told Colton it would be best if he stopped calling. Her husband was intensely jealous and wouldn't understand, she had painfully explained.

A card had arrived for Alex last Christmas in a discreet envelope in Schaeffer's post office box. The most recent evidence that he still cared, it read simply: "Time has changed nothing. I would love to see you, baby, anytime, anywhere. You tell me and

I'll be there." She had cried like a baby until there was nothing left to feel. Then she had pulled herself together, run six miles, and filed away thoughts of Colt again.

Now she was on her way back to Colorado, this time not in search of black gold fortunes and acquisitions but maybe something close to peace of mind. She pulled out the crumpled letter that had been hibernating in the office safe. It was a small piece of tangible evidence of a brief moment of paradise. She knew it was stupid to torture herself by unearthing echoes from the past, like watching old Super Bowl reruns—the game was played and nothing ever changed. But her trembling fingers groped at the delicate, rumpled blue paper, and she tenderly opened the envelope. The letter had been written six weeks after Chris's death in 1984. Years had passed since she had last let her eyes take in the haunting words.

To my dearest Alex,

What we have shared is beyond words, beyond explanation and understanding. I am writing this to try to tell you about the emotions you have evoked in me. Feelings that explode, pouring from within. No matter how much pain you are now feeling, nothing can change what we have, what we feel. Together we have peered into a corner of heaven, and we hold in our hearts a piece of eternity. Like the wind, nothing can hold us back. Somewhere deep in my soul is a hunger—a yearning like a frenzied beast trying to break free. I have tried to satiate the beast, make its yearning go away. The void is momentarily filled by distractions, but a deeper hunger always returns. With each reawakening the hunger intensifies. The hunger has only once in my life been nourished, nourished by you.

The road we have accidentally stumbled on may have many pitfalls and false turns, but nothing can alter its direction and destination.

To you, Alex, with deepest love. I am truly yours, Colton

At thirty-six, Alex Sheridan Blake was a stunning woman. With two lifetimes under her belt, she wondered what the next chapter would bring. She carefully refolded the letter and placed it back inside her handbag. She gazed out the window at a deep blue sky and thought about Robert Frost's poem *The Road Not Taken*. She decided she was too far along this journey to consider looking back.

Gazing out the tiny porthole window, Alex devoured the familiar horizon emerging in the distance, and thought it seemed like a million years ago that she had disembarked the old Frontier Airlines plane, grabbed a taxi, and headed into the city to The Brown Palace Hotel and then to the Aspen Development Partners office.

Back then, in the mid-eighties, Denver was booming, riding on the crest of a giant wave being fueled by speculators. Oil had touched forty dollars a barrel and real estate was doubling in value over ninety days. Growth appeared to be unending and Denver had the potential to become the central gateway for the United States. Every land speculator within five hundred miles was trying to get in on the feeding frenzy.

Now she was retracing old steps. Time stood still as she thought about her closest friend and partner, Chris Welbourne, who had enticed her to Colorado, where she began a love affair with oil and the Rockies that culminated in laying the foundation of their dream company. It had been a time of opportunity and mile-high dreams before destiny had interfered with a plan of its own. The ten years seemed like more than a lifetime ago, but even now the anger raged whenever she let her mind slip back in time.

CHAPTER 7

Aspen, Presidents' Weekend 1984

Alex Sheridan and Chris Welbourne stepped out of the sleek six-seat Lear Jet, followed by Schaeffer London and Dr. Jeanne Gougon. The four were planning to lock themselves up in the mountains for forty-eight hours of dreaming and brainstorming about the new company they planned to build.

The copilot took care of the luggage and skis and pulled the Jeep Wagoneer around to the front of the private aircraft terminal. He loaded the boot bags and briefcases, then piled four full-length fur coats, eight pieces of luggage, four black western hats sporting various feathers and rhinestones, and a mixed case of liquor into the rear of the four-wheel-drive vehicle.

Jeanne Gougon flashed a brilliant smile at her three comrades. "You know, doctors are famous for getting into bad business deals. But we're about to prove the critics wrong."

"I'm betting my life on that," Alex chimed in.

"Where's the house?" Jeanne inquired of Chris, who had leased the residence where they would be staying for the weekend.

"This time I rented a place on Red Mountain." Red Mountain maintained enormous multimillion-dollar secondary residences for owners from around the globe.

"You've always gotten great places for us before," observed Schaeffer.

"Well, you just may find this to be the most enchanting!" said Chris. "You'll feel as if you're on top of the world in a private sanctuary."

The Jeep lurched its way past rolling foothills and into the shadow of the Maroon Bells, picturesque, raw, carved mountains that loomed on the outskirts of town. It was only a matter of minutes along the much-traveled two-lane Highway 82 to the tiny mining town–turned–ski resort.

Picturesque Victorian houses flanked the main thoroughfare. Aspen was a charming chalet village which had made its name as a silver-mining town in the 1800s. Later, a few adventurous souls designed a pulley system to drag willing victims to the top of the mountain for quick downhill runs on wooden skis. Skiing took off not long after the silver mines burned out, and by the early seventies the postcard town of gingerbread houses had become a vacation area for the social elite. In the eighties, Aspen emerged as a playground for the rich and famous, including singer-songwriter John Denver, tennis stars Martina Navratilova and Chris Evert, and Hollywood stars like Kevin Costner and Jack Nicholson. Huge private jets lined the airport's runway. Saudi sheiks built over twenty-thousand-square-foot houses on the edge of the world overlooking the town, with Mount Sopris as a backdrop.

The Hotel Jerome was on Main Street, a historical legacy of the silver-boom years in Aspen. Its rusty-red brick façade had been preserved, as had its charming bar, a popular watering hole for both rich tourists and colorful locals.

"Let's stop here for drinks!" Chris spontaneously cried as they pulled in front of the Jerome. "I haven't had a cocktail here in years." Furs and hats were quickly discarded as the definitely not-local group paraded into the Jerome. They did not go unnoticed by the two local barflies hunched at the end of the long oak bar. Several shotglasses emptied of tequila rested next to half-full glasses of golden ale. It was not the first round of the day for either of the old characters.

"Where you lovely gals from?" one of the half-inebriated cowboys slurred.

"Dallas!"

"Denver!"

"Y'all sure do dress this place up."

Perceiving a threat to their privacy, the women moved to a more remote table. As soon as they sat down, the beeper at Dr. Gougon's waist vibrated. "Order a scotch and soda!" She pulled out a mobile phone and called the intensive care unit in the hospital in Houston.

"Nurse's station."

"This is Dr. Gougon."

"One moment, Carrie is with your patient. I'll tell her you're holding." Jeanne Gougon knew what was coming before it hit.

"Dr. Gougon, Mrs. Bradford didn't make it. I knew you would want to know." Carrie, the senior nurse, relayed the news with a quiver of sadness in her voice.

A dark cloud passed over the delicate features of Jeanne Gougon. "Is her husband there?"

"Yes, would you like me to say anything to the family?"

"No, let me speak with him."

Mark Bradford came to the phone, one of the many husbands who would lose their young wives to a near epidemic. One in eight women would develop breast cancer, and although more lives were being saved, not enough had yet been done to slow the ravaging disease.

"Hello, Mark. I'm terribly sorry we couldn't do more."

The voice at the other end of the phone was hollow and dull, truly the tone of death. "Me, too. She was so peaceful last night, and then today everything just fell apart. I thought she was napping. I left the room for only a moment to get a coffee . . . when I returned, she was gone—" his voice trailed off into a sob.

"I'm very sorry. Would you like to come by and see me on Monday? There are some wonderful counseling services we now provide for the families of cancer patients."

"Thank you . . . I might do that, Dr. Gougon."

"Mark, there was nothing more anyone could do."

It was a ghastly disease that she loathed, and she was determined to find the gene she believed was responsible for cancer. On Monday she would dive in again and redouble her efforts to find a cure.

Jeanne Gougon turned back to her friends. "I could use that drink now." She took a long gulp.

Alex noticed the dark circles beneath Jeanne's cobalt-blue eyes. There wasn't much room for rest in the doctor's life.

"It doesn't sound as if that was very good news." Chris asked.

"No. A patient died. I diagnosed her cancer, but it was far advanced. She was only thirty-four. She hadn't thought a mammogram was necessary, and the cancer devoured her like wildfire. That was her husband. We had become pretty close during her treatment."

Then, as if a curtain dropped, the edges of her mouth turned up into an impish grin. The three other women waited for the other shoe to fall. "So, girls, that just shows one thing." The doctor had quickly transformed her mood into a light one, as those who live close to death become accustomed to doing.

"And that one thing is? . . ." Alex questioned.

"We need to make this one count, 'cause you never know when your time's up." She raised her glass. "To Aspen Development Partners!"

They toasted the new company and their bright future.

They reviewed some of the tricky details of the partners agreement during the cocktail hour. Schaeffer was responsible for the marketing aspects of the business. Dr. Gougon was a passive investor, but her investment entitled her to come to the annual meeting in Aspen. To Jeanne, that annual trip alone was worth the price tag. She was a wealthy woman who could afford the investment risk, but more significant, she was a loyal friend and the investment was a bond between friends. Now the partners had an official excuse to meet in their favorite resort every year. Chris Welbourne was chairman and equal partner with Alex, who was president. Together they controlled the company and its future.

The company's goal was to roll the dice and reach out on some oil and gas deals that could hit big. Real-estate deals were not out of their scope either. If they could see a way to make money, it fell within the company's guidelines. Their personal portfolios included plenty of conservative business investments, but this endeavor was a high stakes play.

Then Alex thought of something. "We need a mission statement, don't you think?"

Chris winced. She did not believe in mission statements and had been heard to say they were not worth the paper they were printed on. "How about this?" she suggested. "To make a lot of money and have a really good time doing it!"

"Nothing wrong with that!" Schaeffer hooted.

"I like it!" Jeanne concurred. "How about if we add: *and to laugh a lot along the way?*"

They made a show of going over the "important" details of the wording of the mission statement.

"Should we say a lot of? Or tons of?"

"A really good time? Or a great time?"

They were frolicking with laughter as they played with the banal phrases. Finally Jeanne said with a smirk, "Let's go back to the first one, the one Chris suggested!"—and they voted unanimously to accept it.

Then they left for dinner at Pinion's, a charming restaurant on the second floor of one of Aspen's turn-of-the-century buildings, to celebrate their dream.

In the warm, low candlelight, patrons sipped on fine wine, waiting for their tables. The smell of rich meats and garlic sifted through the bar. The maître d' recognized the women and ushered them to a prime table.

"Ladies, what can we offer you this evening?" he asked the four handsome guests.

"Four vodka martinis," Alex ordered.

"Extra, extra dry!" Chris chimed in.

"With extra olives!" Schaeffer added. "We're here to celebrate."

"I can see." The waiter raised an eyebrow at the energetic group.

"Make one with a twist," Jeanne Gougon said, getting the last word.

"The special this evening is seared marinated antelope with our famous garlic mashed potatoes, complemented by a warm lobster salad." The waiter left the ladies to their menus and went in search of the martinis.

"I want to know what we're going to do with all the millions we're going to make from this company?" Schaeffer playfully asked the group.

"If I were you, I'd hold onto it with your life," said Chris. She had seen gold rush–real estate frenzies more than once in her lifetime. "This economy is overheated. I can feel the financial community coming unhinged," she said caustically.

"What's your forecast, Chris?" Alex asked the senior member of the group.

"I've seen this kind of hysteria before. People are flying high, too high. And no one wants to look at the past and think it can happen again. Real estate is moving fast, and when it decides to slow down, it's going to come to a screeching halt. But in the near term, there is money to be made—if we're not greedy. Let's not forget this is a short-term market!"

"I've never seen anything like the Dallas market," Schaeffer remarked, her blue eyes wide with amazement. "You can't get money fast enough, and land is slipping between people's fingers like molasses. It's a bidding war over raw land for new buildings that can't be built fast enough. The savings and loans just keep lending the developers money."

"It's happening in Denver, too," said Chris. "And the people in the industry are too close to the situation to be realistic about the future. Occupancy projections are bloated like a three-day-old carcass. They see big profits and little downside for the moment, and they're ignoring rising vacancies, which will be staggering if this continues. It's good for us now, but when the house of cards starts to crumble, heads will roll, and it won't be just the little guys who get hurt."

"So what's our strategy—to take advantage of the current market and not get caught in the maelstrom?" Dr. Gougon inquired in a serious tone.

"Our first order of business is to look at the property we currently own," Chris began. "We have the land rights and the mineral rights and some history of the area, which means we aren't operating blindly."

Alex picked up where Chris left off. They were a formidable business alliance with complementary skills. Like expert dancers, Chris and Alex presented the plan.

"The geology reports for the last year show nice oil wells producing in the area from a well-established formation," said Alex. "We have the capital we need to do one well right. I think we should plan to do more with investment dollars depending on the results. Oil and gas prices are extremely favorable, thanks to the embargo. If it's a successful well, Schaeffer can take over the promotion of the drilling program."

"This is a world-class opportunity," Schaeffer agreed. "Investors are ravenous for deals right now. It's a chance for people to get a piece of the pie without risking everything. There should be no problem raising money if we are even remotely successful with the first well."

"What will the first well cost?" Jeanne asked. This was her first foray into the oil business.

"We won't know until the engineer studies the geology reports. Most of the wells in the area produce from six to ten thousand feet out of the Black Sand Zone," Chris explained as a round of wine was poured. "If we are really lucky and hit pay dirt, then it will cost less."

"On the other hand, if we have to work the well or pull up to another zone and frack it several times, then it gets exponentially more expensive," Alex said.

"How do we improve our odds of making a well?"

"We spend time and money on the front end. We want the very best engineers and geologists in the business. They'll make the final call on where the well is drilled, how deep. And if it has to be fracked, they know what kind of explosive charges should be used," said Alex.

"Explosives?" the doctor asked.

"Engineers use controlled charges to crack the sand formations in the earth so that the oil can flow out," Alex explained. "In different parts of the world, the formations vary, and so does the viscosity of the oil. Some is very dense and has to be heated to flow in a pipeline. In contrast, Texas is famous for its free-flowing oil. There's only one man in Texas I'd use on our West Texas wells because he was a master. A true genius. It was as if he could feel the earth and know exactly what it would take to make a well. There's a lot of gut in this business."

"Will he come up here for this project?"

"No," Chris interjected. "He knows the geological formations in Texas like the back of his hand, but Colorado is different. We want someone who is intimate with our area. There's one person I would really recommend. But the decision will be up to Alex. She's the one who will be working directly with the engineer."

"You would think it would be an academic job, where the engineer studies reports and follows predictable calculations," mused Alex. "That's the irony of the engineering consultant. The best ones operate off a sixth sense. They have to have a working instinct about the land and the particular formation."

"I trust Alex with the gut-instinct issue. She's got the best sixth sense I've ever seen! Sometimes it's scary," Schaeffer remarked. "Remember that time she predicted the stock market adjustment?" she said to Jeanne, who nodded.

"I just try to pay attention to my feelings," said Alex. "If I listen and have the sense to follow, I find they are usually right."

"Alex, you begged me to get out of my long position on that stock, and I just didn't listen. It cost me dearly," said Jeanne ruefully.

"How about when she told us about that fire on the well in West Texas?" Schaeffer reminded Chris. "Alex predicted a major problem on a well we were thinking about investing in last year. They had a dynamite prospectus and great proven data on the area. But Alex insisted there was going to be a catastrophe."

"What happened?" Jeanne asked.

"Right when the well was about to come in, there was a terrible explosion. They lost several of the field crew and the well had to be shut down. Thanks only to Alex, we hadn't invested."

"You give me too much credit, Schae. I just smelled a rat in that deal. Nothing I could put a handle on, but it didn't feel right. Unfortunately for the crew, we were right," the young entrepreneur said. Alex was like someone who had already been through a dress rehearsal of life—the present was opening night.

Snow continued to fall through the twinkling lights as the four businesswomen formulated their plans for the oil company. After enjoying a splendid wild game dinner with a Stags' Leap Cabernet, the team headed up Red Mountain to their retreat on top of the world.

The Jeep wound its way up the dirt road and into the private drive which seemed to touch the snow-filled sky. Enormous homes looking new and out of place were nudged in between smaller, quaint cabins. The house Chris had leased for the group had a large redwood deck surrounding a log-and-stone structure in a horseshoe configuration. A hot tub at the center billowed a smokestack of steam into the frigid night air, and a warm yellow fire danced in the frosty glass of wide windows. A blanket of twinkling lights lay below them—Aspen. Across the valley town on Ajax Mountain, the tiny bright headlights of a snowcat plowed its way, grooming the ski runs for the morning. And the snow kept coming down as the four women built towering dreams late into the night. They were all young and free with relentless spirits. Nothing could stop their success.

CHAPTER 8

Denver, Late October 1984

Alex Sheridan's to-do list was two yellow legal pages of hen scratches and doodles that would have been indecipherable to anyone else. Her organization style would have driven organized list makers insane, but the system served her well. Plowing through the most urgent matters and working into the smaller brushfires allowed Alex to accomplish more in two hours than many thorough worker-bee sorts did in a standard eight-hour day. Then again, Alex Sheridan probably hadn't thought about an eight-hour day since she had counted the minutes on the clock ticking toward the end of some requisite class in "How to Be a Successful Businessperson 101" at the University of Texas.

How any of the institutions of higher learning could get away with calling their classes preparation for practical business had always astounded the young workaholic. If there could be a course in "Gut Instinct and Intuitive Business Sense," the students might learn something about the most important criteria for a shot at success in the cutthroat world of business.

With her to-do list in hand, Alex ran through the cold October rain into the Whitespot Diner on Colfax Avenue in downtown Denver. Not all of Denver looked like the city that was portrayed in the "Dynasty" television series, where mirrored-glass towers reached for the sky and ultramodern architecture loomed overhead. The diner was in the older section of town, not too far from the Capitol, and Jackson "Jake" Winston, one of Colorado's real estate dealmakers–turned–open space planners, had picked the meeting place. She was surprised he hadn't chosen the Petroleum Club or one of the many other posh power breakfast spots—she had heard he was connected to every significant person who made things happen in Colorado.

Jake Winston had left Boulder, Colorado, exactly one hour before his scheduled breakfast meeting with Alex Sheridan. Alex was a friend of Chris Welbourne, a woman he had long ago tried to quit loving, and he would never deny Chris a favor. He conveniently had other business in Denver, and he could be cordial enough to a stranger for thirty minutes.

Before he started Colorado Land Preservation, Inc., the nonprofit organization of which he served as president, he had been the most sought-after oil-and-gas-land man in the Rockies, but he had spent most of his leisure time at the Petroleum Club, drinking away a miserable marriage in between land deals. One day, at the bottom of his glass, Winston walked out of a beautiful home, leaving behind two small children, an empty marriage, and booze. His loyal friends and business associates stood by the rugged cowboy, but the rest of Denver society was thoroughly appalled, and he acquired a somewhat sordid reputation. Even if the midlife crisis had not occurred, there was something about his tall frame thrown into faded Levi's and size-thirteen Justin cowboy boots, topped off by salt-and-pepper hair and a slate-gray Stetson that had always bothered the social group. But what other people thought of him was one of those things Jake never gave a second thought.

Boots and Levi's were not his attire on this rainy morning. He had gotten out his suit for a meeting with the president of Denver's most powerful savings and loan, so he would also be wearing it to his breakfast rendezvous with Chris's friend, the Texas would-be oil and gas developer Alex Sheridan. In the rearview mirror he could see thunderheads not far above his home in Sunshine Canyon. A heavy rumble clapped as he passed the University of Colorado campus and picked up Highway 36 heading southeast to Denver.

His black Day-Timer with its meticulous lists of to-dos and appointments was tucked neatly in the console between the driver and passenger seats of the silver Jeep Cherokee. He knew exactly where and when his breakfast meeting would take place, but out of habit he glanced at the Day-Timer one last time. He checked that the car windows were all secured against the now-pounding rain, then walked into the Whitespot Diner. This was a good place for a short meeting. There would be no distractions or any temptation to linger too long.

As he waited for a table to clear, Jake pulled out a pipe from his right-hand coat pocket and a lighter from his left. He found himself looking through the first billow of blue smoke at what he hoped would prove to be Alex Sheridan.

Alex was wiping the rain droplets from her dark hazel eyes when she spotted Jake Winston. He was every bit the six-foot-six-inches-tall, lean former ballplayer she had seen pictures of and heard about, but she didn't take too much notice of his physical appearance at first, probably because of the two pages of pressing issues on her legal pad. First on the list was to secure the assistance of Mr. Winston. His government connections would be invaluable and he could give them information on the preservation side of the business. He was always aware of restrictions on development, and they needed this invaluable information. If he wouldn't help her, she would move ahead with other parts of the plan. But because of his great respect for Chris, the chances of his turning them down were slim. Besides, Alex wanted him on her side, and she usually got what she wanted.

He looked straight into Alex Sheridan's big hazel eyes. They were the rare kind of eyes that could penetrate a soul or light up like the Fourth of July when she was excited. Later he would know that they could be sorrowful, reflecting pain like gray mist in the lowlands at daybreak.

The diner was buzzing with morning energy. A waitress motioned for Jake to take any available seat. An abundance of starch-white face powder contrasted with her pink bubble-gum lipstick, and inside her transparent hair net was a neatly twisted bun of dyed red hair. The smell of frying bacon and grilled hash-browns permeated the small restaurant. Jake loved this place. And right now at 9:05 A.M., standing next to the pie-and-cake case, Alex Sheridan was the most beautiful creature Jake Winston had ever seen.

She was slight, no more than a hundred pounds, and her muscular, lean, athletic figure had not been apparent during their conversation. Winston laughed at himself, thinking he shouldn't be surprised that a stranger on the phone hadn't said, "and by the way, you won't have any trouble recognizing me when you get to the diner because I'll be the girl that walks in like a hundred pounds of sensual tiger meat strapped to a steel frame."

Alex reached forward with a firm energetic hand. "You must be Jake Winston. I'm Alex Sheridan." She was dressed in a black-fitted suit with an open V neckline, sheer black stockings, and suede pumps, all of which complemented her rich dark coloring. A simple gold necklace draped across her sculpted collarbones, and she wore a daytime onyx-and-pearl ring on her right-hand ring finger. Her straight black hair was pulled back in a French twist, adding height. The overall effect was sophisticated. "Thanks for coming all the way in from Boulder in this weather."

Winston shifted his pipe into his left hand and tried not to break her hand with his bearlike paw. "It wasn't much trouble. I have another meeting here in the city, with some very stuffed shirts." He looked contemptuously at his dark-blue suit. "That's why I'm in this ridiculous costume."

"Suits and Mercedes are the uniform of the day in Dallas," Alex said lightly.

"Well, *I* only wear one when absolutely necessary—which means when I'm groveling for money! Anyway, tell me what you've got up your sleeve and, more important, how did you meet Christine Welbourne?" The two moved to a nearby Formica-topped table and sat across from each other. They ordered coffee.

"Chris and I met some years ago at a Petroleum Club function in Dallas," Alex said. "She was the keynote speaker and a friend of one of my associates. We formed a friendship and eventually a working relationship . . . "

Jake was mesmerized by Alex's every move as she talked. His mind wandered with fantasies. Then he realized she had been talking for at least seven or eight minutes and he hadn't heard a word. He quit daydreaming about how he would entice Alex into his arms, shook off the drugged effect, shifted to his business mode, and tried to become interested in her business venture.

She was saying, " . . . Chris called me not too long ago about some property she had, which is located on the northeast side of Denver. It was partial collateral for one of her mortgage banking deals. When it was time for the guys to pay up, Chris ended up with the title to the land and the mineral rights. She knew my expertise was oil and gas and that I was looking for a new business opportunity. We decided to form a company. We are particularly interested in oil and gas ventures, but are by no means limiting ourselves to that area. In fact, at this moment we are looking at the possibility of developing some land to the south, with a golf course and country club."

"Chris mentioned that the initial project will be the well on the piece of land she put into the company?"

"Yes, and if we are successful, we'll expand the program. Primarily, I want to acquire some strong leases where we can drill proven wells, I hope from the same formations. We hold two additional lease options on a very attractive parcel of land. That's where we want to concentrate."

"Sounds exciting. Are you capitalized, or are you trying to raise money for the first project?" he asked.

"Chris and I and two minority investors have put our own money in to capitalize the company, but we're going to have to inject more financial resources as we build the business. We want to expand the program as quickly and prudently as possible. We do want to take calculated risks—no one's in this for their retirement! Bingo, there you have it."

"Chris said you have quite a track record in Texas. I read the article in *Forbes* on the company you sold in Midland," he said, referring to a small but flattering article that had recently appeared in the business magazine. "After meeting you, it's all even more amazing, since you still look wet behind the ears."

"I got a head start in the business," Alex said without cracking a smile. "They don't care if you are polka-dotted in Texas, just how good the wells are. It's a place that thrives on risk-takers and spawns entrepreneurs."

"Why Colorado instead of Texas where you know the game?" he inquired, trying to make sense of his enigmatic coffee partner.

Alex paused for just a moment and for a split second Jake thought he saw sadness in her eyes. Then the shadow was gone. "Chris and I wanted to work together. After the sale of my Texas company, I had some flexibility and some capital burning a hole in my pocket. It's time to build a substantial interest. We hope to eventually go public if we play our cards right."

"I would never have predicted Chris would take on a partner. But I can see she has met her match."

"We have a unique relationship. It just works. It's as if we each know what's going on inside the other's head at every moment. We complete each other's sentences and that sort of thing," the young maverick explained. "But enough about me—explain more about your organization. Is it a nonprofit company?"

"Yes, we, Colorado Land Preservation, that is, compete against the developers, attempting to preserve critical open space. We raise money from the private sector to acquire land that would otherwise be developed. Then it is deeded as open space. So you see, we are adversaries of sorts," he smiled.

"I always like a strong opponent," she said with a wink. She could hardly take her eyes from the cowboy's hypnotic gaze. She had seen him in many pictures and had conjured up her own visions of this man through Chris's stories. In a way it was like meeting an old, yet distant friend.

"CLP's charge is the protection of the beautiful environs from the sprawling growth of the cities," Jake said. "If we don't act to buy and preserve the remaining pristine areas for future generations, the encroaching vines of suburbia will reach from Colfax Avenue all the way to Aspen. It is a matter of *when*, not *if*."

Alex could see his passion in his eyes.

"Okay, end of lecture," he said. "So, where is Aspen Partners headquartered at the moment?" he asked, returning the ball to Alex's court.

"We just added an extra incoming line and took over an empty office in the Welbourne Enterprises suite where another associate from Dallas will work." Alex gave Jake a measuring look. "I hope that we can at least be *friendly* adversaries. You could tell me a lot about what is going on in this community."

Jake listened in awe to the woman whose ageless poise contrasted with her youthful beauty and enthusiasm. "What's your time frame, and what can I do to be of assistance?"

"As you can guess, I'm in a hurry to get things done. It's just the way we do things in Texas—and now Colorado." Alex winked again at Jake, thawing another protective layer. "That's the reason Chris wanted us to meet as soon as possible. The long-term deal really hinges on two issues: first, we must make a successful show on the initial well—that's my job! And second, we must raise the necessary capital to expand the program. We have a base of investors in Dallas, but we want to diversify here."

"I can't see anything stopping a team like the one you're putting together. What was the name of this new venture again?" He had pulled out a small notepad from his left breast pocket and was now scribbling furiously.

"Aspen Development Partners, Inc."

"Well, it seems as if you know this business and have a well-thought-out plan."

"Yeah, but it will make it a hell of a lot easier to promote the subsequent drilling programs if we hit pay dirt on the first well."

"That's the truth, especially with the number of prospectuses that are flying around town these days. There are a hundred wannabe small-time operators out there trying to raise money. But when word gets out who's behind *your* company, there's no question, you'll be a huge success."

"Thanks for the vote of confidence, but in this business you're only as good as your last successful deal. The good news is that there are quite a few proven oil and gas wells in the area. Our first one will be relatively conservative. We can eventually reach out as we gain a solid base of investors who want a shot at big returns. But we're starting out holding on to our skirts."

"So, what can I do?" Jake asked.

"What I really need is someone I can trust, someone I can bounce ideas off, and, specifically, someone who can help us stay abreast of limits on development," she said.

"Well, you've come to the right man! I would be interested in looking at your property and helping in any other way as long as there is no conflict with Colorado Land Preservation."

"Of course. I certainly appreciate your commitments, and I think there is plenty of room for both of us. But I know from our dealings in Dallas that it is really easy to, if you'll pardon my French, piss off the wrong people in one hell of a hurry. The last thing I want to do is go around stepping on some big toes before we've even gotten out of the starting gate. Chris knows all the ropes and the players in the financial circles, but she insisted that you and I meet. Your government connections would be invaluable to us."

Well, that's pretty Texan for you, thought Jake as he reflected on her bullet-straight approach. He wasn't sure if he could be of much help to Alex—his boundaries were firm—but he hoped they would have an opportunity to cross paths on many occasions. He was quite willing to be of assistance as long as he didn't compromise his own commitments—if he could just keep his hands in his pockets and his mind on business. She was different from the women he typically met. Alex was all business, beautiful and scalpel sharp, with fire in her gut. He hoped she and her associates wouldn't get caught in the riptide that was beginning to grip the real estate business. She was too young to have seen booms bust like locomotives into stone walls. She had no memories like that to dampen her contagious enthusiasm.

"Would you like some more coffee?"

"Please, and a fresh cup."

"I'll get the waitress. Excuse me while I make a quick phone call to the office," Jake apologized. As he walked away, he yelled, "I still want to know more about you and Chris Welbourne."

"I'll hold that thought!" Alex Sheridan studied him as he walked away, trying not to be too obvious as she scoped out his long, broad frame and the massive hands that had been gentle to the touch. He had to have been the model and inspiration for the original Marlboro Man ad campaign. Certainly some marketing guru in New York had been out West, seen Jake Winston, concluded he was the last of a dying breed of late great cowboys, and memorialized him on billboards and in magazine ads. Chris had described him as a gentle giant, and Alex was immediately drawn to her newest friend.

His expertise would be of value while maneuvering through the good-old-boy network that was still thriving in most sectors of the oil business. It was the kind of industry that had been dominated by men like Red Adaire, who had been immortalized in several tough-guy films. Alex Sheridan and her associates had a job ahead of them if they planned to break through and even surpass the inner circles of the male-dominated oil industry. To some extent, Chris Welbourne had already blazed her own trail, as evidenced by the fact that she was the only female member of Denver's prestigious Petroleum Club.

Jake Winston was currently investing tremendous energy competing against young hawk business entrepreneurs just like

Alex, but he was not going to turn her down flat. He was now contemplating the issue of how and why an exquisite twenty-six-year-old businesswoman from Dallas might be enticed into dinner with a forty-one-year-old graying real estate broker who looked like he just fell off his horse. Then again, she was a Texan, and they were a different breed, born dice rollers known for taking risks, so he might have a chance. Besides, she was probably used to cowboy boots.

Jake smiled at Alex as he returned to their table at the Whitespot. Despite her small stature, he already felt this woman had a big personality held together with steel-hard character. He could see she knew who she was and what she wanted, and she certainly made no bones about her aspirations. He looked at the strong, angular features and fine lips, wondering how a kiss would feel. Like an earthquake, he guessed. He had the perfect spot in his house in the living room where he could gently lift her up, placing her on the back of the sofa, and kiss tenderly above her eyes and all around the edges of her mouth, anticipating the tremors that would follow. He would have to wait.

Alex assumed there were important deals occupying the rest of Jake's day, so she wanted to make good use of their time before the meeting came to an end. He looked larger than life as he returned to their table. Except for the smoking, he obviously took care of himself.

The sweet scent of his pipe hung in the warm air. Raising his left hand gracefully, Jake placed pipe between teeth—a fresh pinch of tobacco had just been packed firmly in the bowl—igniting the chrome lighter and taking several deep, rapid puffs. Heron-gray smoke swirled around his head, climbing up toward the ceiling, then was gone in a whirl of the ceiling fan.

"Do you see much of Chris these days?" she asked, wanting to know his view on the status of their friendship.

"Not the way we used to. In our business lives we cross paths periodically. I'm glad she called to make *our* introduction," he said with a smile.

"Well, it is a pleasure to finally meet the famous Jake Winston. In fact, it's nice to know you really exist."

"You must know Chris is prone to exaggeration."

"I don't think so. As far as I can tell, you're living up to the bigger-than-life picture she painted." Her penetrating eyes pierced a soft spot in his heart.

He made a little awkward clearing of his throat. "I'll try not to disappoint you! What are your plans for the rest of the day?" he asked, looking at the stainless-steel timepiece on his right wrist.

"Just the usual rat race. I'll go by Welbourne Enterprises and then out south for a meeting. I spend about half my time at the office and the rest of the time I'm out looking at property."

"I know that drill! I have this blasted meeting with the chairman of Rocky Mountain Savings and Loan, which shouldn't take too long, if he cooperates. Unfortunately, I need to cut *our* meeting a little short. We might be able to talk in more specific terms when I don't have this other stuff hanging over my head."

Alex felt the morning slipping away. Her curiosity had been piqued—she wanted to know more about this man. What had really happened between Jake and Chris Welbourne? Why hadn't he fallen in love with such a beautiful, brilliant woman? Chris had described him at length. She had talked about his tender, passionate nature and the love of the mountains that he shared with Chris. She described how they had ridden horses in the high country and watched young bear cubs play quiet and alone in high-mountain meadows. He was the only man that Chris had seriously thought about marrying, the only one who had come close to getting under her skin. Like a skillful surgeon he had peeled back her layers of protective emotional coating, coaxing feelings out of their hiding places.

"Could we get together later this afternoon?" he inquired.

"Sure!" Alex responded with a flashing smile. Her heart pounded and her palms perspired as they always did when she was nervous or excited. She could feel her stomach tighten into a knot, and wondered why she found this cowboy so intriguing. Maybe it was because of what she had heard from Chris. Maybe in a remote way it was because he reminded her of her father. Her father had been challenging and mysteriously enigmatic, something Alex could not say about most of the men she had known.

"Have you ever been to Boulder?" Jake asked, trying to see into her dark eyes.

"No, but I've heard so much about it from Chris that I feel as if I've been there."

"It's a beautiful place, and not too far if you don't mind a short drive."

"She said you have a spectacular remote home in the mountains just above the town."

"I'm not sure spectacular is the way it should be described. But I like it. Chris and I spent a great deal of time there." A cloud shadowed his face for a fleeting second. "A long time ago," he added.

"What happened?" she asked boldly.

"We became great friends. But time and business make it difficult to keep up. So, what would be best for you?" He seemed to be making it clear that his past with Chris was a closed chapter.

"Any time after I finish my interview with the prospective engineering firm."

"I used to know most of the players in the industry—who are you considering?" he asked, trying to be helpful.

"Chris recommended Front Range Engineering. They're supposed to be the best in Colorado, so I'm hoping they live up to their reputation."

"They wouldn't be my choice—but then, Chris has a stellar track record unmatched by anyone in the business," he said.

"Why wouldn't you use Front Range?" Alex probed, wanting to understand his reservations.

"They're technically very good. I'm just more of a team

player, and Front Range is a real wildcatter operation. They like to do things their own way. Period."

"That doesn't sound bad for our business."

"It can be when they forget who pays the bills and who signs their paychecks," he said, revealing a chip on his shoulder.

"Thanks for the tip," she said, deciding to drop the subject. "Jake, I just know this is going to be a huge success. I'm sure you've seen hundreds of small firms come and go, but we're different. Who cares if we work ourselves to death? This is going to be the chance of a lifetime to build a major independent oil company."

Jake watched with delight as she talked about the fledgling business. The light in her eyes danced and played as she shared her dreams. He was entranced by her expressive face and hand gestures and the enthusiasm that reminded him of the fire he once felt for business when he was a young man. No posturing. No restraint. He was sure that if he held her hands down she would be rendered speechless. Although she was forthright and typically Texan in her speech pattern, the saucy businesswoman was surprisingly elegant. She displayed an economy of movement and regal style until she embarked on an exciting subject. Then it was as if a kaleidoscope of light erupted as animation and enthusiasm scampered across her face.

"The Boulder walking mall has a host of great restaurants. And perhaps I could show you my home," he added hesitantly. He was probably getting a little ahead of himself. "Just give me a call when you're ready and I'll pick you up," he said. "About 4:30?"

"That won't be necessary. I can take my car and follow you to Boulder." Alex liked being in control, no matter how nice a person Jake Winston appeared to be. She liked knowing she could leave on her own terms. After all, she would be going to another city with no way back to Denver except through the good graces of a man she had known for forty-five minutes.

"You should not be on the highway alone!" he said sharply. "And you've never made the drive at night." Jake caught a look of surprise on Alex's face and realized he sounded inappropriately concerned for a new acquaintance.

"I'm quite accustomed to looking after myself. But thank you for the offer," she said rather curtly. Surviving alone was a way of life for Alex. She embraced the unknown and relished the forbidden. It made her feel alive.

"I'm sorry, that sounded a little overbearing, didn't it? It's just that I don't think it's a good idea for you to drive alone, particularly since you've never been there before. I live up in a canyon. That can be a little tricky."

"And you're concerned that I can't drive in the mountains at night?" Astonishment vibrated on the edge of each word.

"Well, yes . . . it can be treacherous . . . it's the drive back to Denver that can be hazardous. They're predicting snow," he offered in a futile stutter.

"Have you ever made the drive from Lausanne to Genoa, Italy? Now, *that* will raise the hair on the back of your neck—but Boulder, I don't think so!" They both laughed and smiled, enjoying their verbal jousting.

"There are deer wandering around the area, and they can cause a nasty accident if you aren't expecting one in your headlights," Jake said, attempting to climb out of the hole he had accidentally dug for himself.

"I'm sure I can handle it, Jake, but I do appreciate your concern." There was no sarcasm in her voice. She appreciated the sincerity she would have been able to sense in him from a mile away.

"Besides, it would be fun to tell you something about what I do on the drive over from Denver." Jake hoped he wasn't skating on thin ice. This was one independent woman who he guessed wasn't used to being coerced or controlled. But the horse was out of the barn, as they say in Texas, so he thought he'd better keep going. "I'll pick you up. Where are you staying?"

Alex decided to relinquish a little control and accept the offer. Chris had said only wonderful things about this man.

Jake was a loner who lived on top of a mountain in Sunshine Canyon. This was not out of necessity—he wanted to be alone. More than a year had passed since he had last invited anyone to his secluded refuge. He had built and designed the house exclusively for himself, having no plans to share his space with another person in his lifetime. This had worked well, for no one had ever seemed able to cope with his periodic retreats into his private emotional cave.

Inside, Jake was wrestling with two warring emotions. One wanted Alex to come home with him, see his house, share a moment of his life. The other, darker side strained to keep the private places he had so carefully created hidden and alone. He rarely invited women into the mountain home; he didn't want their tracks in his private life. It was his sanctuary in Sunshine Canyon, and he preferred that memories of vacuous relationships not cloud his view. He wanted to awaken to the sun dustily filtering through crystal-light windows and muse in silence over steaming black coffee. Why should he expose himself, let an almost-stranger see, touch, and feel the things that were so precious to him? He was painfully aware of his idiosyncratic ways—he struggled with the feelings that made him want to retreat inside his private world and that had even made it difficult at times to spend enough time with his own children. Something about Alex had overcome the nagging emotions, and he had risked asking her to Boulder. He would deal with the consequences later.

"I am staying at The Brown Palace, commuting between Dallas and Denver, until I can make more permanent arrangements," Alex responded, and she noticed a distance in the smoky gray eyes focusing down on her.

"That's a charming old-world hotel."

"Chris offered her guest room, but we both tend to like our privacy."

"Yes, I too have been accused of liking my privacy . . . too much so, sometimes."

"I often work late into the night, which isn't conducive to being a polite houseguest . . . or living with anyone for that matter," Alex said flatly. An awkward silence crept between the two oddly matched loners.

"And what keeps that beautiful head of yours churning into the wee hours of the morning?" he asked lightly.

"Oh . . . it's when I'm most creative. I like to write sometimes," she said mysteriously, "but most of the time my thoughts are related to business." Rarely did she mention her writing, but something unquantifiable in Jake brought out a feeling of trust in her.

"What kind of writing?"

"Just personal thoughts. Poems and journals. Nothing for the *New York Times* list. And frequently, solutions to business problems reveal themselves in the hours before dawn. Turning off the rat race in my head these days has become a challenge."

"I will look forward to hearing more about your writing over dinner."

"Thank you for the coffee."

Jake extended his hand and again Alex noted his gentleness despite his rough, craggy appearance. He put his Stetson back in its rightful place, making it necessary for him to stoop to avoid the ceiling fan. He paid the check for the coffee, leaving a modest tip. "Wear some jeans or something casual. They'll run you out of Boulder if you show up looking like that." His eyes spanned her elegant apparel with playful disdain. He offered to walk Alex to her car, but she declined, hoping the rain would let up in a moment.

Alex knew Jake had studied her intently during the meeting, not taking his eyes from her during the entire conversation. She watched him run into the downpour that was falling from a lifeless sky and thought about the files she needed to pick up from the office before her meeting. It would be unpleasant driving way out south in the rain for the meeting at the engineering firm.

CHAPTER 9

Not everyone in Denver shared Alex's dream for drilling oil, but prices were at an all-time high, and Alex Sheridan wanted a piece of the pie. So did Chris Welbourne, one of Colorado's powerful business leaders. Wind whipped violently around the corners of giant high-rises as Alex headed down Seventeenth Street to Chris's office—also the headquarters of Aspen Development Partners—which had a spectacular view of the mountains.

The massive revolving doors of the Rocky Mountain Savings and Loan building led to modern elevators, which spirited Alex to the twenty-third floor. Here Chris Welbourne ran her multimillion-dollar operation, and this is where the two partners were making their plans to shake up the male-dominated oil and gas business.

Christine Dunne Welbourne's office was in the heart of Denver's financial district, two blocks north of The Brown Palace, Denver's most elegant hotel. The female entrepreneur had risen into the politically elite echelon of the Mile High City, which was again making a place for itself in history. The feverish gold-rush atmosphere had every developer and major oilman intoxicated with the possibilities of making fortunes overnight. Civic leaders were waging war on several fronts to maneuver Denver into a front-running position as the most progressive city of the future. City Hall, along with a well-oiled political machine, was pushing bond projects to underwrite every attractive civic amenity, from a new convention center to the largest airport facility in the world. Many business leaders participated in the various planning commissions to help build the city of the future, and many gave a lot of credit to Chris Welbourne for her vision.

Alex stepped off the elevator and turned right down the richly decorated hallway that led to Welbourne Enterprises. The name of the company was prominently displayed on the rich mahogany double doors; the sign for Aspen Development Partners had been ordered and was on its way. The glass corridor leading to the office offered a threatening sky.

"How are you, Jeff?" Alex had always been amazed at how few people were employed full-time by Welbourne Enterprises, a lean, efficient operation. Jeff Ashton miraculously handled all the follow-through for Chris, who created a wake of work that might easily have occupied the time of ten men. Chris would return from a meeting, exploding through the office entrance and rifling off the "must be done NOWs" while Jeff calmly noted every detail. He rarely missed a beat and was perhaps the best executor in the business, making him the perfect assistant for Chris Welbourne, who had her investment fingers in just about every piece of the Denver pie. He had once jokingly said to Alex that "working for C. D. Welbourne is like sweeping up behind a herd of elephants." Two secretarial support specialists assisted Jeff, and they made the whole team, save for a full-time CPA who spent his waking moments creating a paper trail of the myriad business transactions that took place every day.

"Well, that didn't take you very long." Jeff's deep voice rang out familiarly as Alex pushed through the heavy doors. Until they were ready to hire their own staffperson, Jeff's resources and organizational skills were on loan to Aspen Development Partners. He was a loyal and devoted member of the team. "You look ravishing."

The compliment missed its mark, sailing by unnoticed. Alex had heard his smooth way with women on many occasions. "Are there any messages?"

"Just these," he said, handing her several pink notes. Jeff Ashton stood right at six feet tall and had black hair and robin'segg-blue eyes. In the late afternoons a heavy beard shadowed his well-defined features and extended to the rim of a shirt collar where slight tufts of ebony hair escaped over its edge. His athletic frame was left over from college years when he played football on scholarship to get through the University of Colorado with a major in petroleum engineering. Fate had placed him at a drill site with Chris. He was thorough, intelligent, and motivated, which had impressed her. He was also drop-dead attractive.

The well they worked on had performed poorly, and Jeff was flat broke after several attempts to rework the site. When Chris called and asked him to consider joining her team, he had jumped at the opportunity. Jeff was approaching thirty, eight years Chris's junior, not that it mattered, and very single. Alex had been asked on more than one occasion about their relationship. Chris liked being flamboyant, and it amused her that people were so curious about Jeff's role in her bedroom as well as in the company. She had a way of surrounding herself with brilliant and handsome men, as if she were collecting fine art.

Chris came out of her spacious office upon hearing Alex's distinctive husky voice. There was a hint of strawberry in lustrous blonde hair that was thick like a horse's mane, falling just below her shoulder blades when unleashed. For business it was pulled back neatly with never a strand out of place. Her penetrating deep emerald-green eyes and perfectly sculpted Roman nose were offset by an ultrabright smile. High carved cheekbones proclaimed her Germanic ancestry. She wore a predictable business uniform that today took the form of a conservative Escada ensemble with matching scarf, handbag, and heels.

Chris leaned over to embrace Alex. "I can't wait to hear about your meeting this morning and your impression of Jake Winston."

The office was buzzing with activity. Phones blinked as fax machines ferried information across the country. Every inch of available wall space was covered with maps and charts.

"Fantastic! He is as captivating as you said he would be."

"Would you like some coffee?"

"No, thanks. I'm about to float away to Java."

"Pull the file on the airport project," Chris directed Jeff. Currently a raging debate had escalated about the issue of whether Denver would build the industrial airport of the future to complement Stapleton Airport and eventually Denver International Airport. Chris was in the middle of the fray. Members of the private sector were pressing for endorsement from the city and county governments. The concept was to combine light rail and trucking centers at a world-class industrial airport shipping facility which would serve as a distribution center for the world. Savings and loans had lined up in a frenzy to lend money to the promoters. They needed the support of the FAA to make it happen and to begin attracting business to Denver from around the globe. Billions of dollars were riding on the project. To make matters more complicated, the local political leaders were engaged in a tug-of-war between personal goals and a waning concern for their constituency.

Jeff returned with the file in hand. "The mayor is on line two." Chris had been escorted by the young Don Juan–style mayor on several occasions. Already he had left two unreturned messages which certainly had to do with the airport issue.

"Make a believable excuse. Tell him I'll be back in this afternoon." The mayor would have to wait! There were too many other pressing concerns. Besides, her sights were currently on the debonair senator, a longtime political friend, who had also called her about the new industrial airport. He was trying to secure federal matching funds for the project but wouldn't get anywhere until the local power brokers could settle on a location. It would mean millions for the landowners who won the lucky roll of the dice. Welbourne would be influential in massaging certain power players into cooperating—if she chose to do so.

Many believed the airport project offered untold opportunities for the city and county, not just certain influential landowners . . . but various interest groups were against the government's supporting a private business venture. It would have to be a joint venture for the airport to be a success. At the moment, the planners' pressing concern was to disarm a group of homeowners who were afraid the industrial project and its noise pollution might be too close to their neighborhoods. They would have to be appeased in some way so the project could pass the initial voting process. The actual location was still very much up in the air, and the senator was furious that a rumor of a selected location had made its way into the public arena. Chris closed the door to her office, the brain center of Aspen Development Partners. Jeff knew instinctively that she and Alex would want to talk privately.

The partners began talking simultaneously, as close friends will do. Then Alex looked her dear friend square in the eyes. "I have to ask you a question, okay?"

Chris looked puzzled.

"Why didn't you hook up with Jake Winston?" Alex asked.

"You know more than anyone else about our affair, Alex. It ended years ago, but we still care deeply for each other as friends. That's it." Chris let a sly smile steal across her face and she laughingly teased her alter ego. "I see you've been smitten by those haunting eyes and that sensitive smile he delivers so well."

"Smitten, no! Intrigued, maybe," Alex protested, but it was apparent that Chris thought otherwise. She wanted to know everything Alex thought about her old friend.

"In fact, I did consider marriage to Jake," Chris admitted, "but you know that walking down the aisle and cleaving 'til death do you part has always seemed like walking the plank to me!" She had found single life more comfortable, much less complicated, and more profitable.

Always independent, Chris was used to being alone in the world. She had lost her parents as a young woman when their plane went down over the North Atlantic. When the catastrophe was announced to the world, Chris's life had been forever changed. But Chris had turned the tragic event into gold. She buried herself in academic studies at a prestigious eastern university where she never looked up from her business books or at an intimate relationship. After graduation she returned to the Mile High City and, as if emerging from a cocoon, took the business community by storm. It was then that she had met Jake and fallen in love. But they had both eventually come to understand they were too much alike. They jointly recognized their own fierce independence, which was the source of their passion and eventually their pain. When it became too painful for them to continue being lovers, they decided to remain good friends and sometime business associates. Chris adored Jake, but she knew she would never be able to give up her independence to settle down with one man.

Born in São Paulo, Brazil, the daughter of European parents who later emigrated to the United States, she commingled the passion of the South American culture and the precision of the Germans. She was the kind of female powerful men lusted after and married women often hated. She knew all this and thrived on it. In stocking feet she stood five feet ten inches tall, but she preferred to wear heels. Her presence was electric. She made it her business to be every bit the professional woman with the caveat that she could wink a thousand miles across a boardroom table and have even the toughest man squirming in his seat. Silent authority oozed from every pore.

"Look, if you're trying to get my blessing to see Jake Winston, then you clearly have it. Why do you think I introduced you to him in the first place?"

"I thought he was supposed to help us with the oil company . . . or am I totally naïve?"

"Of course he could be helpful, if he chooses to be, but it did cross my devious mind that you two have a lot in common. If all you needed was his experience and feedback, you wouldn't need

Jake Winston. Colton Forrester, the engineer you are going to meet today, has done this work for twenty years. He has a darn good track record, and mine's not too bad, either. But Jake could be helpful . . . he's connected. He's got his ear to the ground, and we would do well to stay close to him so we can keep up with what is going on with restrictions on development."

Alex was silent for a moment. "He seems pretty . . . passionate about his cause. Didn't you say he himself was a developer in his early career? I don't quite understand his disdain . . . "

"Ha-ha, that man!" said Chris with a wicked smile. "Has he used the word 'vultures' yet? Please remember that he was an oil-and-gas-land man in his earlier years, and he did *quite* well for himself. Alex, he's like a reformed smoker!" Chris insisted, laughing. "Now that he's on the preservation side, he sometimes acts as if development ought to be outlawed altogether. As if developers are criminals!"

"He seems to have the greatest respect for you," Alex observed.

"Oh, we will always be great friends. I adore the man. And we often find ourselves on the same side of an issue. But I also believe there is plenty of room for developers to do what they want to do. Of course open-space planning is important, but there is plenty of room for growth, too. Jake and I don't always agree on the specifics of these issues. But we will always be friends . . . and I knew he would be quite taken with you!" Chris paused for a moment, then added a thought. "Just keep your radar up."

"Because? . . ." Alex asked.

"Remember when we were on the ski trip several years ago and we sat up talking about him most of the night?" Alex nodded, confirming her recollection of the evening. They had been in Aspen for a girls' weekend, and Chris had bent her ear trying to make sense of her own feelings about Jake. "Remember what I told you: he has a freeze-dried spot in his heart. Amorous excitement sets in, you think you're close to him, and then he retreats."

Kind of like the way you are with men? Alex thought to herself as she gazed at her dearest friend.

"At first I attributed it to his celebrity in business," Chris continued. "I thought he just needed privacy from the public. But it was much more than that. There is a painful private side to Jake I could never wrap my arms around. I knew I was leaving a lot on the table with Jake, and walking away from something I would possibly never find again," Chris said pensively. Then a grin spread across her face. "But I'm a loner, too!"

"Well, I wasn't going to say anything," Alex teased.

It was true. When things became too close for Chris, when any man became too needy for her love and attention, she pulled away. Sometimes she would question or regret the end of the warmth and intimacy of a relationship, suspecting these were feelings that most women desired on a permanent basis. But in Chris's experience, the newness and excitement of an affair inevitably turned to obligation and dependence, dousing the sparks that first ignited passion.

"I'll bet the two of you turned heads!"

Chris diverted the compliment. "So when are you planning to see him again?" she asked, flashing her grin.

"He asked me to come to Boulder tonight for a casual bite to eat and a tour of the local area."

"Ah, the plot thickens!"

"No it doesn't!" Alex protested. "It's just dinner, Chris!"

"That invitation is a tremendous compliment, Alex. From what I know about Jake's dating habits, he rarely if ever has women out to Boulder . . . unless he's changed."

"I think he still cares about you."

"Yeah, right," Chris said deprecatingly, winking at Alex. "The stars tell *me* that you and Jake are going to be very close friends. But don't forget, I told you he's very unusual. Being with him is like trying to hold onto gold dust in the wind. A part of him will stick with you forever, but the rest just can't be grasped. Of course, maybe you could break down some of his walls."

"Thanks for the words of encouragement, but I wasn't looking to break through anything. Something to augment hotel room service is more what I had in mind. An occasional dinner companion, someone I can bounce ideas off . . . "

"When he does decide to befriend someone, he's dedicated and loyal. He'll never let you down, Alex."

"I'll keep that in mind."

"Did he tell you about Colorado Land Preservation and the specifics of what they're doing?"

"Briefly. He plans on filling me in this afternoon during the drive. This morning's meeting was short because of an appointment he had with a lender. He said it was rather important."

"I'll bet! I know he's trying to arrange financing for a big acquisition. It's public knowledge that Colorado Land Preservation wants to buy the Custer Ranch, but so does one of my investment companies, Castle Creek Investors. It's a highly confidential project, so don't mention a word," she warned. The last thing Chris wanted to do was butt heads with Jake Winston over the ranch deal and get into a bidding war that would end up being slugged out in the local papers. "Did he tell you who he was meeting with?"

"I think he mentioned Rocky Mountain Savings and Loan."

Jeff Ashton buzzed in, interrupting the flow. "Schaeffer's on line four for Alex and says it's important."

"Put her through!"

Alex picked up the phone.

Chris, made enthusiastic by the tidbit of information about Jake's meeting, opened the file cabinet that housed her bulging Custer Ranch file. She was cautiously pleased that Jake had to work with Case Storm, chairman of Rocky Mountain, which somewhat lowered Jake's chances of acquiring the land for Colorado Land Preservation. Her cerebral wheels churned madly. She'd had enough exposure to the powerful lender to know he would enjoy jerking Jake Winston around. He would relish the opportunity to control the outcome of Winston's deal because he thrived on manipulating strong individuals. She hoped that would work in her favor. On the other hand, Storm was known for trying to get his S&L a piece of every good deal that came along, which could complicate things considerably. No land deal in Denver was simple these days.

"What did Schaeffer want?" Chris asked.

"She was just asking what the time frame is from her end. She's got investors chomping at the bit."

Chris put the file aside and turned her attention to Aspen Development Partners business.

"We need to set up our financing right away so we can move forward with the drilling," said Alex. "What do you think about using Rocky Mountain Savings and Loan? I've heard they're into some pretty risky stuff, so oil and gas exploration won't be a stretch for them." The young businesswoman eyed Chris from the edge of the mahogany desk where she perched with one slender leg thrown over the corner.

Chris gnawed on the end of a number-two pencil, pondering the issue, which was a murky one. She knew every local financial player on a first-name basis, as well as who got in on what deals, and the inside scoop on almost every major transaction— but she was still churning over what to do.

"I don't want to do business with that institution. The president, Case Storm, is a real asshole! They're growing too fast, and he's a power monger. Not long ago they acquired First Denver Savings."

"Weren't you on that board?"

"Yes, for a long time before they were acquired."

Alex read bad news between the lines on Chris's forehead.

"I don't want to do business with him under any circumstances. We've got the financials to go elsewhere, and I intend to go on avoiding that lowlife like the plague."

"What's the problem with him?" Alex asked warily. "I've

heard he's pretty charming."

Chris usually had few words for talking about other people, and when she used expletives it indicated a serious dislike. "It's a long story, but in a nutshell, he held a party at his home for the board of Rocky Mountain—at least for those of us he was trying to keep on his board after the merger. You would not believe his place—the art, the rugs, the Austrian crystal chandeliers. There's no way he's not buying some of that stuff with S&L funds."

"So he's enjoying the ripe fruits of everyone else's labor? There must be something more." Alex knew there had to be something more than that for Chris to carry such a personal grudge.

"I can't believe I was ever cornered like that!" Raw disgust hung on every word. Alex narrowed her dark eyes to piercing slits as she focused on the word *cornered*. "It must have been one of those moments. I had my guard down, thinking it was just a social event. He offered to show me the art collection and like an idiot I followed. Before I knew it, I was upstairs alone with him. Stupid! I was so stupid. I wasn't paying any attention at first. Then I realized he was talking about our going on a weekend on the corporate jet."

"You don't sound flattered?" Alex interjected.

"Flattered? A snake crawls on higher ground. He's so full of himself. He's with a different woman every time I see him."

"Methinks thou dost protest too much." Alex toyed with her partner's emotions.

"I can't believe he's so arrogant he would think I'd get in line for those sheets. Anyway, he came up behind me and put his arms around my shoulders and started to kiss me!" Chris looked as if she had swallowed curdled milk. "I was in shock! Petrified even! Like an idiot, I stood there frozen while he continued his talk of how we could take the financial world by storm."

Alex listened attentively, slightly amused by the rare story. It was really the first time she had seen Chris so flustered.

"Before I knew what had happened, he was pawing me and

I slapped him as hard as I could across the face. I didn't mean to cut him with my fingernails, but I didn't mind that it happened that way."

"You assaulted him?" Alex exclaimed smiling.

"A red handprint popped up on his face. Then it got really ugly. He called me a bitch, and I called him something unmentionable."

"I'm dying to hear. Try to remember!"

"You're enjoying this too much, Alex."

"It's hysterical. Did he file charges?" Alex doubled over on the edge of the desk, not trying to contain her laughter.

"I think 'egotistical son of a bitch' is what came out, and maybe 'transparent thieving climber.' But I really try not to think about that incident," Chris sniffed.

"I guess that explains why you resigned from the board."

"And I should have done more. I just can't believe I'm the only one who sees through that bastard. I wrote a scathing letter to let him know what I think about his whitewashed business deals and his inside slimeball maneuvers. And I told him just where he could stick the corporate jet. He was lucky I didn't report him to the regulators! The bad part is, he's gone all over town spreading the rumor that he let me go from the board, that he had to force my resignation."

"You don't really think anyone would listen to that kind of rumor about you?" Chris had an outstanding reputation in Denver, developed over many years of participation in the community.

"There are a lot of ears listening to him, no matter what I think."

"Good grounds for a slander suit."

"I wouldn't waste the time," Chris said dismissively, but it was obvious to Alex that Storm's rumors had stung more than Chris wanted to admit.

"So what charm school did this guy buy his diploma from?"

"He's a face man who can talk himself into bedrooms and boardrooms all over the country, a former bank clerk who made his way to the top of a small Denver thrift. He was in the right place at the right time, and now his institution is one of the biggest in the country. His voice may carry more weight than I first thought, but I'll guarantee you he's as crooked as the day is long."

Chris had a healthy hunch that the corrupt S&L chairman knew one hundred ways to twist a dollar into his own pocket. Storm had made his own luck, helping to influence federal regulators as they changed the laws governing S&Ls. In 1981, Congress in its wisdom allowed S&Ls to take leave of their traditional investment vehicles—home mortgages—and enter the world of high finance. S&Ls became major players in the speculative markets and so did Case Storm, whose maneuvers were buying more power by the day.

"So have you reported him?"

"No, his comments to me were all just innuendo. Besides, I'm waiting in ambush. You wouldn't believe the high-risk loans he's making to all of his friends. He's the type who will hang himself if you just keep feeding him more rope. But I did put him in his place!"

"And it sounds as if he didn't like it one bit."

"No, and to make matters worse, we both sit on the Greater Denver Economic Council, and I have to make a pretense of getting along. He also has an ambitious role with the new Industrial Airport Planning Committee—he's supposed to be the financial advisor, which is a complete conflict of interest."

"How do unethical schmucks manage to get into those positions? That's a prominent financial institution he's running," Alex observed.

"By playing with a stacked deck and by their own set of rules. There isn't a line out there he wouldn't redraw. Just mark my words, and I haven't been able to prove it yet, but I'm sure he's doing something fraudulent."

"What's your next move?" Alex inquired.

"I'll tell you more when it becomes clear. John Curry, a good friend from my days at First Denver Savings, still works for Storm, and together we're keeping our eyes open. We'll keep digging and sniffing around until we find the decay. Then I'll nail his slick ass to the wall."

Chris's phone buzzed, interrupting the conversation. "This is Chris," she said, flashing a smile at Alex. "How are you today, Senator?"

Alex turned her attention to a mountain of geological data.

"That would be just fine, Senator. I'll look forward to going over the details later this evening. No, dinner would be fine. Yes, Bill, I will look forward to seeing you later. Will you be attending the airport planning meeting this afternoon? Yes, I'll be there on behalf of the Greater Denver Economic Council, so I'll see you shortly."

The receiver landed gently in its cradle as an infectious smile spread across Chris's flushed cheeks. Senator Bridgeforth was a third-term senator from Colorado and chairman of the powerful finance committee. He was sending big ripples from the Rockies all the way to Washington, and Chris had been a supporter during his campaign. He was successfully supporting the preservation of critical open space and more stringent regulation on environmental pollutants, and was quietly lobbying the FAA for support of the new airport that would make Denver the transportation and distribution center of the twenty-first century.

"Don't you look like the cat who just swallowed the canary!" Alex teased.

"The senator wants to discuss the proposed new industrial airport distribution center that will be adjacent to the new international airport if any of it ever happens."

"And I suppose that is why you are blushing?"

"I think it's the thermostat." Chris pressed a hand to her cheek. "Is it that obvious?"

"Yes, to me, but not everyone knows you as well as I do."

"Thank goodness! He wants me to persuade the Greater

Denver Economic Council to back the decisions of the airport planning committee. And I can't make that promise. We all need to work together, but the industrial airport is a private venture commingled with the international airport, which will be funded by a municipal bond issue. Every time the papers mention municipal and county funding for the project, the constituents scream bloody murder."

"Yes, there was an article this morning. Someone from the school board was criticizing the project, saying that there isn't enough funding for education or low-income housing, much less a billion-dollar airport project."

"The senator's goal is to dance on the hot coals and somehow appease all the factions. He needs to secure civic support and federal matching funds for the project, but he won't get anywhere until the local power brokers settle on a location that could meet FAA approval. The senator needs all the help he can get, and he says he's counting on my support. But, well, I don't know . . ."

Although Senator Bridgeforth was married, Chris had noticed all the signs that said he was a player. She liked to steer clear of married men—she couldn't afford a scandal at this stage of her career, and sneaking around never had been her style. But a harmless flirtation with the attractive Senator Bridgeforth was almost irresistible, and United States Senators had a way of being very useful.

After the interruption, Alex and Chris returned to their business.

"I do have one question, Chris. Jake didn't just jump up and down over our consideration of Front Range Engineering. I'm meeting with them as soon as I leave here."

"I'll wait to hear your initial impression, but the odds are you'll like Colton Forrester."

"Did something happen between Front Range and Winston?"

"Colton and Jake got sideways on a deal some years back, but I think it was strictly one of those ego-driven pissing matches between a couple of strong male personalities. They were drill-ing a well, and everyone wanted to be the commander in chief. Jake had his nose pressed too hard to the glass, and Front Range walked off the job. Nothing serious."

"Good. I'd better get going."

"Please tell Jake hello for me tonight. It's been too long since we've had a good visit."

"Will do, and give my regards to *Bill*," Alex flung the arrow skillfully.

"He is very intriguing!"

CHAPTER 10

J ake Winston's Cherokee turned onto Colfax Avenue shortly
after his meeting with Alex Sheridan. He was pleasantly wondering how he had been so fortunate to meet Alex, but he had to
turn his mind to business—he was on his way to make a presentation to the Rocky Mountain Savings and Loan chairman,
requesting financial support for a new acquisition for Colorado
Land Preservation, Inc.

Colorado Land Preservation was the brainchild of a group
of visionary leaders in the Denver area, including the governor
and United States Senator William Bridgeforth. CLP had been
established to strategically preserve critical open space, and the
senator continued to sit on its board. The group's mission statement called for the protection of the beautiful environs from
suburban sprawl. Bridgeforth worked closely with Jake, CLP's
executive director, in recruiting other influential supporters from
around the state.

CLP was currently trying to save one of the last great ranches
near Denver, and an interim loan was a crucial part of the for-
mula. Heirs to the Custer Ranch, which lay in the shadow of the
mushrooming city, wanted to be cashed out immediately, and
CLP had to have the loan to pay them off. Once private-sector
investors were in place, CLP would repay the interim loan and
the ranch would be protected from the wolves who were nipping
at their heels with the intention of developing the land parcel.

This, of course, went against the very lifeblood of every
developer in the area, including Jake's old friend Chris
Welbourne, whose consortium's members, along with about half

a dozen other silent partners, were trying to get their hands on the spread. It was a prime location, very accessible to Denver. As the temperature began to plummet, rain hardened on the windshield wipers, and Alex Sheridan continued to be a distraction in Jake's head. It was much more pleasant to think about her than to think about business . . . but there were millions riding on the next hour's negotiations. Allowing thoughts of Alex Sheridan to divert his attention wasn't going to make it any easier. First things first. He had to negotiate successfully with Case Storm.

In the marble-and-granite atrium on the main level of the Rocky Mountain Savings and Loan building, busy employees and impatient customers were conducting business. Here a throng of people scrambled for loans from the West's rising-star financial institution. A life-sized full-body portrait of Case Storm hung on the central wall between the row of shiny copper-colored elevators that transported people as far as the twenty-fifth floor, where Storm resided in opulent splendor. The portrait was a good, if somewhat younger, likeness of the chairman, whom Denver now courted like a prophet of prosperity. With his movie-star looks and expensive tailored suits, he certainly looked the part.

After the deregulation of the S&L industry, Rocky Mountain took its newfound profits and went on a buying spree, growing with each merger and acquisition. Now it could compete with the banks on just about every level, offering pacesetting loans to every type of customer. Like so many other thrifts at the time, all of whom were clamoring for business, Rocky Mountain didn't scrutinize the financial data of most of its clients. Conservative low-interest-bearing notes had been abandoned for high-yielding investments that were potentially more lucrative, even for deals that were at best a crapshoot. But no one seemed to notice that the portfolio was rapidly moving from black to red. Churning fees made cash flow look great, and Storm figured they could write off the bad debts if necessary. He already had more "good-will" on his balance sheet than snowflakes in a Colorado blizzard. The better deals that came across his desk were perused for potential personal gain. When Storm made a loan to a close friend, he made sure he was going to be paid back down the line.

Jake ducked as he stepped out of the elevator, holding in his weathered hands a small file containing the guts of the Custer Ranch deal. His Stetson was slightly damp with melting snow. He combed his hair with his large fingers after catching a glimpse of it in the mirror behind the secretary's dust-free mahogany desktop. An inconspicuous sign read MISS COOLIDGE.

"Miss Coolidge? I'm Jake Winston here for a 10:30 appointment with Mr. Storm."

The woman looked inquisitively at him and then understood his mistake. "Oh, I am sorry, we haven't gotten a new nameplate yet. I'm Chairman Storm's new personal assistant, Mildred Choate. Miss Coolidge was transferred to a branch out south which was more convenient to where she lives. You know, the commute on I-25 is really a nightmare." She delivered all the information in one long whisper, as if an explanation were required. Miss Choate was obviously another fresh recruit brought up to the front lines to assist the demanding chairman, who ran through executive secretaries and personal assistants like scratchpads. The newest secretary had the demeanor of a frantic rabbit and large aquamarine eyes with glances that ricocheted around the room.

As the phone rang at the former desk of Miss Coolidge, Jake wondered what indiscretions Storm had perpetrated on the poor woman. At least she had escaped. At various CLP events, Jake had heard more than he wanted as Storm talked about his conquests as if they were notches on the butt of a gun.

Sexual harassment had just emerged on the business scene as a serious complaint, and Jake speculated it wouldn't be too much longer before just the right woman stepped up to the plate and handed Storm exactly what he deserved. But he wouldn't be placing any bets that it would be Miss Choate.

"Mr. Storm will see you now." Deep lines formed tracks between eyebrows that had spent far too much time frowning. The diminutive assistant chewed nervously on her left thumbnail and nodded in the direction of the executive offices.

Rich amber furnishings reflected Storm's extravagant taste. The Persian serape carpet blanketing the floor had to be over a hundred years old and must have cost at least seventy-five thousand dollars. Eighteenth-century chairs covered in French tapestries depicting hunt scenes had been placed on the authentic carpet. Opposite spacious floor-to-ceiling windows hung several notable art works, including an original Chagall. Behind the desk was a signed Degas—there was no telling what it had cost the institution. Small bronze statues accented the antique English end tables.

The room had been furnished by one of Denver's exclusive interior designers, Morgan Dulany. Storm had selected the designer, who owned Cherry Creek Interiors, after hearing she had been the interior decorator for the mansion of oil tycoon and movie mogul Marvin Davis. Dulany had furnished the entire office, all the way down to the bronze d'ore inkwell on Storm's French Empire desk. Jake had stumbled across this information over dinner with Morgan Dulany herself, a casual acquaintance. She had boasted about her budget while he absorbed every detail. If the shareholders and investors of the S&L had seen the price tag—in excess of five hundred thousand dollars—they would have gone ballistic. Dulany's boasting had only supported Jake's suspicions about Case Storm. As for the rubber-stamp board members, they were apparently puppets who danced in Storm's corner when close votes were taken. The man made sure that lavish perks went their way; in return, they kept him in the lifestyle to which he had become accustomed.

Storm didn't budge from behind his opulent center of command. He looked in the general direction of Jake Winston, neither welcoming nor acknowledging him directly, as he continued dictating into a small handheld recorder.

"How is business at Rocky Mountain?" Jake inquired, trying to be superficial and polite. He'd made up his mind to leave pride parked in Boulder for the morning and play Storm's power game. Not wanting his height to be an intimidating factor, he began to lower himself onto a small chair.

"Do you mind not sitting on the antique chaise? The tapestry is over a hundred and fifty years old," Storm said in a commanding tone. A barely repressed explosion was simmering between the two men, although Jake was unaware of the degree and the source of Storm's deeper resentments. The only explanation he had for Storm's behavior was the man's enormous ego.

Case Storm detested Jake Winston—a man who had earned the respect of the business community over a lifetime of legitimate and profitable deals. Though Storm had all the trappings of success, he still didn't have the respect Winston commanded from people like the Custers, one of Colorado's prominent families. Only one thing gave Storm leverage in the community, his title and lending power as chairman of a major financial institution. He controlled money, a position that had earned him influence with those in Denver who were swept up by the gold-rush mentality, and he had taken full advantage of that. From the wildly expensive corporate jet hangared at Stapleton Airport to the free rooms at the palatial hotels that Rocky Mountain financed, Storm had created a baron's lifestyle. And at the moment he relished the opportunity to have the legendary Jake Winston groveling for a favor.

Maybe Winston could bed Chris Welbourne, or so Storm had heard, but when it came to money, Storm held the upper hand. Like a gorilla on a putting green, Jake moved to an armchair. At the same time, Storm stood up to show who was in control, hands on his hips, legs spread in a condescending posture.

It wasn't Jake's style to cater to anyone, but being diplomatic was important to CLP. No one wanted to get even remotely close to the dark side of Case Storm, who was known for quietly ruining major deals, calling loans at disastrous times, or demanding increased collateral if people didn't cater to his egotistical whims. Rocky Mountain Savings and Loan was a big player, and Storm controlled the game.

Hostility hung in the air. Storm gazed at Jake with flat black eyes, making it clear that this was not a social gathering. "Am I correct in assuming you are here to discuss the Custer Ranch sale?" Storm had attended the previous CLP board meeting, when the decision had been made to make an offer to the Custer estate. He knew damn well why Jake Winston was in his office. "Before you make your presentation, I would like to reiterate my position."

Jake felt a lecture coming.

Storm talked on. "As you know, I wear many hats in this community. CLP is a significant civic organization that I wholeheartedly support by sitting on its board." Arrogance bounced off the fabric walls and Jake felt as if he were drowning in the bilge. "But my primary responsibility is to the board and stockholders of Rocky Mountain Savings and Loan."

And building your own personal empire, thought Jake, biting his tongue.

"We will consider the loan for the Custer Ranch no differently from how we consider any other proposal, as you well understand. So don't expect any special concessions!" he said with naked aggression.

Silence, slow and even, stood between them. Storm had the power to grant CLP the eighteen million dollars it needed, but the terms of the loan, especially the interest rate, were important. It was Jake's mission to get the lowest rate and favorable terms. His personal feelings and ego had to be shelved. If he were successful, CLP could close on the ranch, then turn around and close with the six private investors who would jointly own the ranch, and CLP would end up paying only one or two quarters' worth of interest. That was crucial. The interest rate of nineteen percent on eighteen million would eat their lunch if they couldn't raise the money to pay Rocky Mountain as soon as possible.

"How are you planning to repay the note?" Storm's blank eyes studied everything but Winston.

"It's structured like our other transactions. The property will be the collateral, naturally. Five of the six investors have signed letters of intent. The sixth won't be difficult to corral," Winston said persuasively. "It shouldn't take more than ninety days at the outside to raise the money and close the entire transaction."

"What's in it for Rocky Mountain Savings—" he paused for effect "—*if* we make this loan on the Custer Ranch?" The banker surveyed his meticulously manicured hands. He wanted Winston to beg, grovel a little. It was part of the game Storm played with almost everyone.

But Jake had a plan, and it didn't include a payoff to Storm. It was time to implement an important phase of his strategy. "Before I answer that, let me tell you a little about the Custers." Storm would be keenly interested in the famous family. He had an Achilles' heel for rich, famous families, which momentarily gave Jake the upper hand. "As you know, Seldon Custer is now in complete control of the ranch and the Custer estate. Like yourself, they are fine, unpretentious people who happen to be worth a great deal of money." Jake was surprised he didn't choke as he spoke these words. "You remember her contribution to CLP several years ago?"

"Yes, didn't she give a substantial long-term gift?"

"One million dollars a year for ten years." Jake reminded him of the numbers, knowing full well that Storm was aware of every penny of the contribution.

"Formidable," the chairman said. "I don't believe they do business with our institution."

Jake hopscotched the pitfall. "I was speaking with Seldon Custer regarding the sale of the ranch. She mentioned that it would be nice to meet you if Rocky Mountain Savings decides to finance the acquisition. I took the liberty of saying you would be pleased to meet her." Jake could see Storm falling into the trap as if he'd stepped off the edge of the Grand Canyon. Storm would sell his sister for the opportunity to schmooze Seldon Custer and try to get some of her business. Jake continued. "Dinner is probably the best choice considering everyone's busy schedule. I left it that we would call sometime after our meeting today to confirm the date and time—assuming you're interested in participating in the transaction?"

The question hung between them.

"Of course we want to help save the ranch . . . as long as the terms are satisfactory." Storm's greed and excitement were difficult to mask. He would be all over the millionairess like flies at a Texas barbecue. Storm craved acceptance by the inner circles of Denver's social establishment, who often needed his endorsement and financial support. "How soon do we need to make the arrangements for the loan?" he asked too anxiously.

"As soon as possible. I've heard rumors that Chris Welbourne's Castle Creek Investors is trying to buy the place out from under us," Jake said, not knowing he had pushed a hot button in his favor.

Storm's black pupils narrowed to pinheads at the mention of Chris Welbourne. "I thought you two were quite close?" He glared at the large man, measuring minuscule gestures. Jake's romance with the notorious Welbourne had not missed the jealous eyes of the lascivious financier. Of course Jake had no idea of the depths to which Storm would stoop to beat Chris Welbourne out of the ranch deal.

"We are old business associates," Jake said. "By making the loan, you and Rocky Mountain Savings will be participating in a historic piece of land preservation. Senator Bridgeforth will be pleased when he hears the news," Winston added, trying to bring the meeting to a close.

"Of course, it is the duty of Rocky Mountain Savings to help in transactions of this nature—loans that benefit the greater community." Storm was heaping one shovelful after another, all the while imagining Welbourne reading the headlines. "When can we arrange the dinner?"

The prospect of an evening with Storm was depressing, but if it would accomplish their goal of buying the ranch before one of the other suitors upped the stakes, then it would be a victory. "I'll call Ms. Choate and set it up. But first we need to discuss the structure of the loan."

"Make sure this happens, Winston!" Storm pointed a stiff finger at Jake. "I'll get more pleasure than you can imagine by helping CLP succeed," he said, leaving out *and beating Chris Welbourne.* Storm's grudge had grown since he had made the mistake of blatantly coming on to Christine Welbourne—she had responded to his advances as if she had smelled rotten meat and had threatened to call the regulators on him. He would never forget Welbourne's disgusted response or the sting of the cutting blow that had drawn more than blood. Welbourne had spurned him—something he could not tolerate from anyone. But he was a patient man. He would make her regret her actions. Even now he reveled in the idea of annihilating Chris Welbourne.

"We need a favorable interest rate on the eighteen million," Jake said, sensing he had the upper hand. "CLP needs one-half point below prime interest, with no penalty for a balloon payment." Jake dictated the terms while watching Storm's mind churn with the possibilities for personal glory. At the moment, the terms of the deal were of little interest to Storm, which was good for CLP. With interest rates at a decade-high, CLP didn't want its cash store gobbled up while Jake tied up loose ends with the ranch purchaser group.

"Send over a proposal detailing what you need. We'll make it work. Perhaps Senator Bridgeforth and I could announce the deal to the public in a press conference here at Rocky Mountain. This has great possibilities."

Storm dreamed of the glory as Jake made a quick exit.

∽

Jake hurried over to the CLP office where he tidied up some details, including a call to Seldon Custer.

"Is Mrs. Custer in today?" he asked the housekeeper. The Custer matriarch was rumored to be worth over four hundred million, not including her G3 private jet. Seldon Custer loved Colorado Land Preservation, Inc., but she also had an eagle's eye for money.

"May I tell her who is calling, please?"

"Jake Winston." He paused for a second, then added, "Please don't disturb her if she's busy." While he waited, Jake rummaged around on his desk for the number of The Brown Palace. He gave up, pulled out a file drawer that held the Denver phone book, and flipped to the Bs in the business pages. Then Seldon Custer's voice panted over the phone line into his ear.

"You sound as if you're running a marathon," Jake said.

"I was just finishing up running the barrels on our new gelding, Icebreaker. He's a fine animal. If I could ever entice you to come out here, you would love him. We could go out for a ride and survey CLP's latest acquisition."

"The opportunity to ride with you would be a real honor. I don't know if I could keep up, though," Jake teased.

"Well, you'll have to!"

"What about next week if the weather holds?"

"That would be wonderful. Now, how did your meeting go with . . ." She hesitated. "What was that man's name?"

"Case Storm turned a few handsprings at the prospect of meeting you personally. I think we are on the right track. With your permission, I would like to set up a dinner as soon as possible."

Jake was anxious to get Seldon Custer to sign on the dotted line before something happened to change her mind.

"Why don't you bring him to the ranch for dinner?"

"That's a generous offer."

"I'll have the cook prepare something special, and we'll give him a first-class tour."

"Irresistible!"

"Sometimes I can't bear the thought of selling this place, but I see Denver encroaching on the horizon, and I know it will be better for the family, especially if this airport really happens. I don't want the children and grandchildren circling like carrion crows over the place. Selling the ranch to CLP is a great choice. You're going to have to match the best offer, though. There's another investment group threatening to present a contract."

Jake tried to smooth over the somewhat caustic remark. "Thank you for giving CLP the opportunity to preserve the ranch. Rocky Mountain has committed to the loan, so we are very close to making an official offer. It will mean so much to future generations, Seldon. No one wants to see it turn into a concrete slab for an office park of the future."

"We're on the same page. But I have an obligation to the rest of the family to consider every option." It seemed an innocent comment, but an ominous thunderhead was forming over the deal. Jake was determined to prevent an all-out storm. "What kind of deal did you strike?" asked the astute matriarch.

"It's not finalized, but he indicated they would lend CLP the eighteen million we discussed. Over dinner we can beat him up for a lower interest rate."

They both laughed and agreed to confirm the details in the next few days. After hanging up and thanking Seldon Custer, Jake worried about the developers seeking to buy the ranch.

CHAPTER 11

"This is Alex Sheridan calling to confirm an 11:00 A.M. appointment with Colton Forrester."

"One moment, please," the receptionist murmured.

Alex listened to a crooning Garth Brooks as she wondered where in South Denver the offices were located.

"Mr. Forrester asked if it would be too much trouble for you to meet him downtown. He's been delayed at our downtown warehouse."

"Actually, that would be very helpful," Alex responded. "I'm at The Brown Palace now, and it would save a long drive in this weather." She looked out the window at the snow that was just beginning to fall over the city.

"It's on the North Side just under the I-70 overpass." Directions were given to the industrial section of downtown Denver.

Alex changed from her Yves St. Laurent suit into something more suitable for snow and ice. She cinched Levi's at the waist with a black leather Texas belt that had a silver buckle the size of a flattened Coors beer can, and pulled on black cowboy boots. Then she grabbed her only coat, a full-length black ranch mink, and headed to the lobby of The Brown. She had decided to ignore the difference in the dress code between her hometown, where ladies wore their furs for every occasion including trips to the grocery store, and Denver, where the movement to ban furs was just beginning to snowball.

Lafayette, The Brown Palace's doorman, held the driver's door open, warning Alex about the streets that were beginning to glisten with black ice. The temperature had dropped at least thirty degrees since breakfast, turning rain to ice, and there were no signs the precipitation would let up. As she headed in the direction of the industrial section of downtown, she noticed the dilapidated buildings encroaching on the mirrored elegance of the business district. Darkness stole the waning light, allowing neon beer signs to flash like mute sirens on the roadside. While passing under an old train trestle, Alex caught a glimpse of a cornered bundle huddling against the razor-sharp wind. It would be the first full night in the shelters, she thought.

After pulling under I-70, she spotted a restored 1950s-vintage green pickup truck with a door panel sign that read FRONT RANGE ENGINEERING. The mirror on the driver's side, almost decapitated, hung by a single slim wire, and in what had been the rear window was a large green garbage sack secured with silver duct tape. Alex bolted out of the car, then dodged through fresh falling snow into the frigid warehouse. Several old vehicles were parked randomly inside a loading area that looked like a mechanical graveyard. A solitary metal desk rested against the back wall, supporting a dusty multiline telephone. There were no signs of life. For an instant Alex wondered just what kind of company Colton Forrester operated.

"Hello?" No response. "Hello?" A little louder the second time, Alex's gravelly voice echoed in the emptiness. Was she in the right place? There was nothing. Then a back door in the far corner cracked open, spilling muted hazel light across the dirty concrete floor. "Is anyone here?" She went to investigate.

She pulled open the door and the light illuminated her animal-like frame and snowflake-dusted hair. She could see the lower two-thirds of a male torso lying in a jigsaw puzzle of tools and motorcycle parts.

The mechanic arched his neck from underneath a bulky Harley to focus on the intruder. "Could you slide that small wrench, the one next to your right boot, over here? This thing has been running like a tin can ever since a poor excuse of a mechanic got hold of her, so I have to give her some personal TLC. Can I help you, darlin'?"

Alex shoved the wrench toward the man with her boot. "I have an appointment with Colt Forrester," she said in her most businesslike tone, which had an edge as she stiffened to being called darlin'.

"You're looking at him. Who, may I ask, are you?"

Alex bristled. *This isn't going to be easy,* she thought. "Alex Sheridan with Aspen Development Partners. We're interviewing engineering firms to work with our new company."

She tried not to stare at the smudge-faced dusty blond figure in the pile of motor parts. He was naked above his faded jeans, and she had to admit his physique was remarkable.

"I thought Alex was a guy's name."

"It is!" she said.

"Well, I sure am happy to see you instead of some fat old hairy-legged oilman. Did anyone tell you what part of Denver you were coming to? You stand out like a bear in winter in this part of town," he remarked, looking at the fur coat.

"I was scheduled to meet you in South Denver, if you will remember." South Denver was a far more upscale part of the city.

"Yeah, I just didn't want to go way out there in this muck."

"I thought this part of town looked kinda rough myself," Alex said. "But it's nothing compared to some of the small border towns in Texas."

"I believe that!" He continued tinkering with the underbelly of the machine.

"Does Denver usually get this kind of snow? I haven't seen a storm like this except in the higher elevations." Alex noted the fine layer of sweat highlighting the man's well-developed muscles. A jagged scar made a seam over one beautifully sculpted shoulder.

"We get some pretty nasty stuff in here around late October, early November. You may have to downgrade your wardrobe," he said with an impish smile.

"At least I don't have to worry about getting cold," Alex said playfully. Instinct told her he was a good guy, an appealing cross section of oilmen she had known. Colton Forrester lurched up, offering a greasy paw then instantly retracted it. He stood over six feet but not much. His neat fur-covered chest converged into a fine streamline of hair that disappeared into the waist of his frayed jeans.

"Let me wash up a little," he said, looking disdainfully at his greasy fingers. "I don't know about you, but I could eat a horse, saddle and all."

"Some food would fit my bill," she agreed.

"Have you ever been to the Left Bank?"

"Not unless you're talking about the one in Paris."

"No, it's not the Tour d'Argent, if that's what you wanted, but they make a killer Reuben!" he said.

Hearing the name of the famous French restaurant, Alex made a mental note: *Not your everyday petroleum engineer.*

Alex reverted back to business.

"Have you drilled in this area before?"

"Yes, we are very experienced with the local formations."

Forrester surveyed the room, suddenly aware that it was chilly, and found a discarded rugby shirt resting in the corner. "What geology reports do you have?"

"Just prelim studies of the general area. You'll need more than what I can give you today."

"How many people will I be dealing with?" he asked cautiously. He pulled on the thick cotton jersey, finally concealing his strong, wide shoulders.

"Not a bunch of investors, if that's what you're asking. I'm the principal, so the buck stops here."

Alex trailed behind him as he grabbed the beckoning telephone. The tail of his shirt fought against being bridled into the snug thirty-four-inch waist. "Forrester. You'll have to set up an appointment for later. I'm in a meeting." He hung up quickly.

"What do you say, let's go eat?" he asked as he reached for his leather jacket. He took long strides toward the door in his mud-covered leather workboots. "I was out fooling with an uncooperative well at four o'clock this morning. I'm starved."

It hadn't been more than fifteen minutes, but Alex was intrigued and growing more confident with his style by the moment. "I hope you can go over the studies at your earliest convenience. I'm anxious to make a decision on this project. As I was saying, I'll be the primary contact with the responsibility of communicating with my partners."

"That sounds fair enough. How did you hear about us?"

"My partner, Chris Welbourne . . ."

"She's one hell of a woman!" His eyes narrowed as he scrutinized his potential customer. "Do you like motorcycles?"

Alex didn't know if his question was idle curiosity or an excuse to change the subject.

"I'm inclined to travel in heated vehicles in the snow. Have you looked outside lately?"

"Good! Let's see if this baby will start. The Left Bank is only a block, but I want to take her around the block to see how she purrs. You shouldn't be in too much danger."

He flashed an irresistible smile and handed her a leather flight jacket. Without arguing, Alex handed him her coat, and he hung it on a hook behind the utility-room door. Then he mounted the Harley and brought it sputtering to life.

Colton Forrester looked like a rugby player, tall and strong like iron with legs like a linebacker. Nature had chiseled character around the periphery of his brilliant eyes and the edges of his mouth, leaving footprints of sun and wind and the oil wells he had drilled. Fire danced from Montana sky-blue eyes that were hidden in the crinkles of a warm smile. Alex watched him try to rearrange an untidy mop of almost sandy hair. Sun stained the uncreased portions of his neck and traces of black gold lingered on his long, strong hands. It was obvious that Colton Forrester worked for a living.

Alex followed him to the motorcycle, trying not to stare at his hard, broad back. Her heart pounded. Worn Levi's covered in oil-well stains hugged all the right places. She felt herself sliding into the emotional zone. Parts of her left brain strained to take control while wild horses pulled from the right.

The snow pounded silently. Riding motorcycles without helmets was risky, very risky, but their destination was just around the corner and there wasn't a car in sight. Her rationality screamed, *Don't ride motorcycles in snowstorms with men who obviously walk on the reckless side of time.*

She reminded herself of Chris's comment, that he was the best in the business. She would study his proposals and if he was the right man to work with, she would make an offer. The fact that he was attractive would only make the business dealing more interesting. She would know when to ignore the attraction. Her all-business demeanor could be flipped on like a circuit breaker, and that ability had always been her ace in the hole. Unlike many women who could be overcome by emotion, Alex had mastered the art of compartmentalizing, and it was this that had allowed her to maneuver like polished glass through the male-dominated business world.

Over the screech of slightly muffled exhaust pipes, Colton screamed something about shooting pool. Reaching back to happy moments in Texas, Alex laughed to herself, silently remembering small, dingy pool halls, late-night cigarette smoke, and cold beer. It had been a long time. They pulled in front of the crusty tavern and dismounted the motorcycle.

"If I can't go to The Punch Bowl on Broadway, this is my favorite spot when we're working out of the downtown warehouse. I met the owner, Joe Leftwich, when he helped me out of a tight spot late one night after a rowdy group outnumbered me at the Buckhorn Exchange—that's another favorite hangout, not far from where you are staying. We've been friends ever since."

"You met this man in a barroom brawl?" Alex asked with amusement. She had seen it all in the oil business, from scuffles on rigs to all-out wars over leases. She smiled at the idea of this high-powered engineer fighting it out with his hands.

"Nothing serious, darlin', just a friendly scuffle on a Saturday night. I can't even remember what we were fightin' over. Probably a pretty little girl like you. The Buckhorn is Denver's oldest bar—but this is my favorite hole in the wall." He held the front door, ushering Alex into the tavern.

A large redheaded man, bearded from head to collar, sporting a soiled apron, and two-fisting chilled beer mugs, rolled through louvered bar doors from the kitchen, welcoming the two in what had to be his personal style. "Well, it goes to show you who your true friends are! As soon as they find a beautiful woman they forget about their old buddies . . . unless you brought along one of your girlfriends for Big Bad Joe!" he said to Alex. Sparks twinkled from tiny bloodshot eyes.

"Now, don't get pushy, Joe," Colton admonished. "This is a serious business prospect I'm trying to schmooze, not a dancer from the Kit Kat Klub, okay? We have to treat her right."

"Let *me* take care of the little lady! You gotta watch this Forrester guy like a hawk," he warned Alex.

"I can take care of myself just fine," she smiled.

"I'll bet you can," Joe said, sizing her up carefully.

"Alex Sheridan, meet Joe Leftwich, the meanest, ugliest bar owner on the North Side."

"I'll get even with you later, Forrester. It's my pleasure to meet you, Alex. What's a lovely lady like you doing with the likes of him?"

"I'm here to meet you!" she shot back.

"The only reason Alex is in here is because I blindfolded her before we left the warehouse so she wouldn't have to see this dive in the light of day," Colt explained.

Alex laughed at the show.

"He hasn't sunk a well in ten years, much less been out with a girl like you." Joe smiled daggers at what was obviously a fond friend.

"Joe, business is tough enough without a buddy like you. Don't you have some beans to stir or a pot to wash in the kitchen to keep you busy? Maybe someone could come up with a couple of sandwiches and pickles, if that's not asking too much."

Joe handed them the two beers in his left hand and barked an order in Spanish to the Mexican cook peeking out from the kitchen.

"Let's shoot a game of pool while we're waiting," Colt suggested.

Alex looked around at the cedar-paneled barroom's decor: neon beer lights, including a flashing COORS sign with the *S* burned out, ashtrays, and Marlboro Man posters. One of the posters looked too much like Jake Winston to be coincidence. Over the polished wood bar edged with a row of empty barstools, the local TV newsman was speculating about the upcoming Broncos game against the Chiefs.

"Would you like something else to drink, or is beer okay?" Colt inquired.

"The beer will be great, haven't had one since I don't know when."

"You should have it more often." A million-dollar wink pushed Alex one step closer into a blind spot in her mind. "Give me a tequila back, Joe, when you get a chance," Colt yelled to the bar owner. "I'm celebrating the snow." Alex felt him brush dangerously close as he moved around the pocketed green felt table. Then he deftly grabbed the rack, rolling and caressing the balls into place, alternating stripes and solids. "Do you know how to play eight ball?" he offered Alex a pool cue.

"Don't all good Texas girls know how to shoot pool? Do you know anything about drilling oil wells?" she retorted sarcastically.

His massive farmboy hands jumped up in objection. "Tell you what, I'll play you two out of three for beer and lunch. Deal?"

"You bet, but I get to break!" Alex challenged, hoping to start with the advantage. She confidently checked the cue for weight and balance and skillfully rubbed chalk over the tip. He watched her as if she were a favorite movie.

"Now, are we going to play pool, or talk about business all day long?" He placed the rack under the well-worn table.

"Okay, but I have one question. Can you move quickly on this job if we decide to work together?"

"As long as we've done all our homework. I'm a stickler for thorough prep. Greatly improves your odds for success. Break!"

She liked his response. He sounded like the type of guy who could put something on paper and make it happen, the kind of guy you could trust with your money.

Alex stretched across the table. She broke decisively, then sank three balls before finally missing and handing Colton the cue. The eight ball rested close to the left corner pocket. Alex grinned across the green felt at Colton Forrester, who was pleasantly surprised by her barroom acumen and even more thrilled by her lean shape.

"Have you always lived in Denver?" Alex asked as they continued to play a casual game.

"No, I'm an Iowa farmboy who fell off a corn truck trying to get to California. Just landed here by accident. It turned out to be a lucky fall."

With openness he told her of leaving a small Iowa farming town that offered little hope for a strapping adventurous soul. The choice to leave had been simple—the family farm guaranteed only backbreaking work before dawn, sweltering summers, and frozen-solid, socked-in winters. At the end of a dream San Diego sparkled like gold, but the journey's pause in Denver had become permanent. He still thought about a life in California when the wind blew through the plains in late winter, and sometimes he wondered how he had gotten off track. Then a news report of a windswept forest fire engulfing California hills, a red mudslide, or the inevitable earthquake would shake him back to satisfaction. Nowhere else would ever measure up to Colorado after all. It was a formidable place to live, work, and play, and there were oil wells. Occasionally his Iowa roots dragged him back on his motorcycle to ride through summer's dusty-sweet cornfields, but he always returned to the untamable Rocky Mountains.

"I guess home for me is Denver now," Alex offered wistfully, "more specifically, The Brown Palace Hotel. Dallas has always been my base, but we lived a vagabond's life because of my father's oil business."

"Is that how you learned so much about oil and gas development?"

"Yes, I can't remember a time that drilling oil wells wasn't a part of my life. My father drilled all over the world, but mostly in the Persian Gulf region."

"And you were on site with him?" Colt asked with astonishment.

"In the summers we lived wherever the wells were being drilled. Somalia, Saudi Arabia, Kuwait. If an area was too controversial, like parts of the region where women were still required to veil their faces, I would study in Paris or Geneva."

"Sounds glamorous."

"Not always. It was rather lonely when my father would stay on a drill site for months at a time."

"What was it like doing business with the Saudis?"

"Delicate! My diplomatic father had a knack for getting along with the temperamental Saudis." Another pair of frosty mugs filled with New Castle ale appeared like magic.

"And how did *you* get along with them?" he asked.

"Well, I've never looked good in black veils." More seriously she added, "I prefer doing business in our country where the government can't just nationalize any old oil field it takes a fancy to."

"That would add an extra twist to a business already filled with risk." Forrester took a deep draw of the cold brew.

"Once we had an associate who insisted on butting heads with the minister of oil."

"What happened?"

"He received a military escort straight to the nearest border. There was no warning, and he left with just the clothes on his back."

"Tough place to do business!"

"In all fairness, I think he was doing a little more than oil and he got caught with his pants around his knees with some young lady who literally belonged to someone else. Left corner pocket." She pointed at the target with the honey-colored pool cue. The eight ball hit its mark, ending the second game.

"Good shot. I think I'm in trouble," he said. "I guess the Saudis expect people to play by their rules."

"Exactly. To achieve success in a foreign country, an understanding of the culture and mores is crucial."

"Do you have any other family?" he asked.

"My mother died when I was quite young."

"I'm sorry."

"No need to be. It's part of my life," she said bluntly.

Forrester narrowed his gaze, trying to understand the woman who was becoming more unfathomable with every turn. He listened with his eyes, hoping she would offer more.

"It was the summer I turned ten and my father and I were on a rig in West Texas for the weekend—a barren place near Midland where the land goes flat as far as the eye can see."

"West Texas can be a raw, desolate place." Forrester studied her face as the story was told, one tiny piece of a jigsaw puzzle he was interested in putting together.

"There was a windstorm blowing into Dallas from the Panhandle and the commuter flight went down because of wind shear. No one survived."

"It can't be easy growing up female without a mother," he commented in a sympathetic tone, suggesting he had a modest understanding of the pain a child experiences when a parent dies.

"My father and I managed well." It was the pat answer she was accustomed to giving people she did not know. Besides, what the hell did he know about girls growing up without mothers? Her familiar defenses were rearing their heads. Then she pushed on through her conflicting feelings. For some reason, maybe it was the snow, or the beer, she felt safe to talk some more. "But yes, it had its bumpy spots. Never have I ever felt so alone. Until I got the call last year that my dad had died."

Why she was sharing this with him was a mystery to her. On the surface, he didn't look like the type who would give a flip about past problems, much less really empathize. But he held on to every word with intense deep eyes that begged her to continue.

"I guess that means you know how to take care of yourself," he said.

"I can survive anything . . . "

He wondered. It sounded good, but he sensed a soft spot in her defense. The intriguing oil woman was fiercely independent, yet, in an odd way, almost too alone and vulnerable.

Sandwiches arrived when the third game was well under way. Just in time to lighten the moment and stave off hunger. An equal number of stripes and solids resting precariously around the pockets. Luck and skill commingled, and Alex won the deciding game with a banked shot in the left corner pocket—definitely not a maneuver she would have learned at the country club. Colton watched closely as her lean, curved frame stretched adroitly across the table. He was curious about the fiery Texas lady who was appearing more complex with each shot. She wasn't the spoiled rich kid he had first envisioned. But while it certainly wasn't the first pool game she ever played, he guessed she was more accustomed to full-sized hand-carved tables that didn't take quarters.

The beer-hall atmosphere and company brought back a flood of memories for Alex, memories of a complicated upbringing. She operated with ease in diverse, challenging situations, deftly handling a myriad of people who crossed through her life. While learning the oil business from her father, she had been both skillful and comfortable mingling with wealthy investors and field men alike—but she was more comfortable when out on the drill sites with the crews. At night they would sit, fingers curled around their cold, sweaty long necks, and tell raucous stories, building legends as they went. Sometimes they would caravan in their dusty pickups to the closest small town, finding a pool hall and jukebox to dance away fantasies in slow smokes and tall tales. It was very different from the elite Petroleum Club events where she had also invested substantial amounts of time, enchanting the monied power brokers. Alex, the chameleon.

But when the fires were low at the end of the day, there was something comfortable and especially appealing about the men she met in the oil field, something more substantial than what she saw in the social glitz of Dallas. Colton Forrester was rekindling her old instincts. She devoured the playful afternoon, sipping slowly on beer and gradually letting Colt Forrester seep under her skin. A hand brushed here, a shoulder there. There was laughter. She felt soft strings being pulled in her heart, and every nerve in her body was attracted to this radiant oilman.

He told her about growing up a farmer's son with dreams as big as the rolling fields. Born on a farm outside Des Moines, he was a product of Midwest rural life, where the cows were milked at daybreak by little boys who went to work before they reached the age of six. Cornfields, like an ocean, stretched and rolled as far as the eye could see. In the summers, heat lightning danced across the sky like a symphony of light. Alex guessed there must be a raw, unique beauty to the farm life that seemed to produce bronze-hard men with clear convictions. It was disarmingly clear that Colton viewed the world through a black-and-white lens with little space for shades of gray. Honesty, hard work, and keeping one eye on his backside had served him well over the years. There was right, wrong, and not much in between except just plain fun.

He avoided unpleasant people unless they tried to push him around. He could stand up for himself in just about any situation and wasn't the least bit afraid to do so. This quality had earned him a broken nose on more than one occasion. Joe stopped by and described Colt as an overgrown pussycat who shouldn't be pushed in a corner, but the best friend a man could ever have. Alex was enchanted. She slipped another notch into the fire.

Sometime during the snowy afternoon, someone selected the Eagles on the jukebox, and "Desperado" played soulfully in the background.

"Do you want to cut your losses now or play for double or nothing?" she asked in a playful challenging tone. It was safe and dark in the old tavern, where for just a few hours her preoccupation with oil wells had been forgotten.

"I think you've got me deep enough in the hole—besides, we need to talk about when we're going to run the tests."

"The sooner the better."

∽

Play was fun, but there was serious business to be considered. Alex had to look at Colt Forrester and his company through a clear lens. She looked at her watch, then at the snow falling outside Joe's window. She remembered her appointment with Jake, and reality intruded on their ball like the stroke of midnight.

"Can I send the geology reports to your office, then we can have a more informed discussion?" Alex inquired professionally.

"You tell me when and where, and I'll be there." The look in his lively blue eyes blew through her soul. He had silently taken a step inside her private space, invading every part of her being.

The jukebox whined through the smoke and noise. Colt was so close she could inhale his scent of clean sweat and cold beer. He reached with his large, strong hands to cup her flushed cheeks. His eyes searched for understanding and Alex did not retreat.

The song continued in the background.

"I like you, Miss Sheridan."

The simple, clean, honest, straightforward words tumbled out of his throat. Speechless, she acknowledged the compliment with a simple nod. Alex didn't want to leave the afternoon. She felt it had taken her several steps down a path she had been aiming for and running from for most of her life. Silently she cursed the time that was rapidly escaping. "I need to get back to the hotel. I have an appointment there in forty-five minutes."

"That's a shame," he smiled.

"Do you mind if we leave now?"

He never removed his gaze, penetrating and silent. One strong hand brushed her face softly. "Only if you promise to come back." He threw out wadded cash on the table, grabbed the leather coat, and put it gently around Alex's slender shoulders, giving an affectionate squeeze. "Come on, baby, let's get out of here." He took her by the hand and escorted her to the door. For once she felt like following another's lead, not blazing a trail, not bushwhacking. Dry snow had piled up four inches on the seat of the black Harley. They brushed it to the ground before they mounted the motorcycle and sputtered into the white, empty streets. The city would sleep early this night.

Alex sat confidently behind Colton Forrester, pulsing with excitement. Warmth radiated through his shirt like brandy on a cold night. One hundred fantasies danced in Alex's head, and they had nothing to do with oil wells and bank presentations. Just an untamed oilman in a snowstorm in the Rockies. For the very first time the sputtering rumble of a Harley seemed like a song. Rolling slowly, they eased onto the snow-covered pavement, arms wrapped around belly, not drilling oil wells, not signing contracts, just doing an unplanned, Friday, middle-of-a-snowstorm kind of thing.

Alex held on tight, letting the warmth of Colton Forrester seep through her bones. Little daggers of ice crystals in the wind cut her cheeks, so she buried her face into him, hair dancing in a winter wonderland, wind cutting, heat burning. He reached down, gently squeezing her leg not far above the knee. It was a familiar, warm touch, like flannel in winter. Then they pulled up in front of the warehouse.

"Come in for a minute and warm up while I start your car." He reached for Alex's red ice-cube hands and led her into the warehouse. "You're freezing. Must be that southern blood."

"I'm okay. The keys are in my coat."

He grabbed the plastic key ring, tossing the coat across her lap as he dodged out into the bitter wind. Moments later he returned.

"I think you're out of luck. The lights were on, and it's not even turning over. I might have some jumper cables."

"No thanks, I need to get back right away—maybe I can take a cab and deal with the car tomorrow." The press of time had pushed her back into full-business mode. A compulsively punctual person, she was preoccupied with the need to get back to The Brown to meet Jake.

"Tell you what, I'll lock it up in the warehouse and I'll give you a ride on the motorcycle back to the hotel. If we can get the car started, I'll drop it off later."

"You don't need to do that, but thanks for the offer. I'll take care of it tomorrow." Imposing on anyone was never a part of Alex's life.

"Honey, we may be eighteen inches deep in this stuff by morning, and people will be digging their way home for two days. I'll take care of it! Let's get you to the hotel."

Alex usually recoiled at being called "darlin" or "baby" or "honey." But coming from this Iowa farmboy-turned-engineer, it felt warm and natural . . . and she really didn't have time to wait for an unpredictable taxi. She hiked up her fur coat, walked down the stairs, and climbed on the bike. Colt pulled thick warm gloves out of the leather jacket he was now wearing and handed them to Alex.

"You'll need these," he said with authority. "Watch the exhaust, it wasn't designed for fur."

Her arms coiled automatically around his hard stomach muscle, holding on for life. He covered her interlocking fingers with his hand, giving a warm squeeze. They cautiously motored the vacant streets, headed up Broadway past the Holy Ghost Cathedral, and pulled under the porte cochere at The Brown. Lafayette was wearing a hat, gloves, and a full-length navy blue wool coat. "Miss Sheridan, come in out of that storm! Have you gone daft riding around on that contraption in this weather?"

So he didn't approve of the motorcycle. Alex smiled at the doorman as she swung a leg off the bike.

"Thanks so much for the ride," she said to Colton. "I'll never forget it."

She started to walk away, and something pulled her back. She turned, stepping into the slush at the curb, and threw her arms around Forrester, placing a spontaneous kiss on his rugged stubbled cheek. "I'll call you about the car," she said.

"Thanks for the pool game. We'll talk once I've looked at some geological reports on your lease."

Colton Forrester seemed slightly taken aback by the kiss, but pleased. He gazed into her eyes as if searching for something. Then a warm smile penetrated the cold. "I'll be back," he said.

Alex's heart was light with Colton Forrester. But her mind was drawn to business and the desire to succeed, which was always playing in the foreground. A part of her wanted to stop him from pulling away into unknown dark snow. A million questions rained in her mind. The Harley revved into the storm, leaving "Desperado" reverberating like an old phonograph inside her head.

CHAPTER 12

2:25 P.M.

Chris Welbourne walked into the airport planning committee meeting on three-inch heels, looking drop-dead gorgeous in a tailored suit. Eyes stealthily ranged up and down, trying hard not to stare too much as she headed to her seat at the boardroom table. The mayor's office was the venue for the powerful meeting where they would discuss the location of the proposed industrial airport. The airport project offered great opportunities for the city and county, not to mention a few influential landowners. But certain interest groups were against the idea for many practical reasons. It was particularly hard for some of them to swallow the government's supporting a private business venture.

At the head of the table sat Senator Bridgeforth, flanked by Case Storm, who was trying to hide his frustration over Chris Welbourne's presence, and the mayor, who was trying to get the meeting under way.

"Thank you for coming, everyone," the mayor said. "Chris, we're glad you could make it! Let's get started." He directed his dancing eyes and a strong smile toward Chris—but she didn't see them, as she was trying to avoid the gaze of the senator who sat beside him. Ever since the campaign, she had felt a fire smoldering between her and Senator Bridgeforth. "First," continued the mayor, "it's crucial that we have a state-of-the-art industrial airport if Denver is going to be the city of the future."

Storm cleared his throat. "There are a lot of rumors floating around that a Texas group has plans to establish Dallas as the transportation distribution center of North America," he said. "I'll be damned if I'm going to let them make their move ahead of us.

We should spare no expense on this project. If we have the airport as well as the necessary distribution support systems, Denver will be on top."

Chris jumped in. "That's going to cost billions, and everyone here knows that whatever the projections are, they'll end up painfully far below the final price tag."

"That's not our concern," Storm said, cutting her off. "Bonds can be issued for the next hundred years if that's what it takes to make this happen. We must have the components of a major league city if we are going to compete in the global marketplace. What does matter is the timing. We must settle on a location as soon as possible so we can begin to work with the FAA. The location will have to meet a number of criteria, including access to rail lines and trucking."

The group worked through the tedious agenda, accomplishing little, which had been Chris's experience with most politically charged meetings. Issues went around and around with little resolution. The president of Colorado's largest trucking company was present, and a consultant for the FAA was paraded in to answer questions. Chris was the entrepreneurial voice, and the politicians hoped she would serve as a liaison to the business community. She had been asked to serve on many committees because she had a reputation for unshakable honesty and for the ability to separate her personal goals from what was best for the community.

But the discussion continued to spin in circles. Chris was frustrated by the entire committee, now stalled over the issue of offering subcontracts to minority-owned companies.

"I move we take a fifteen-minute recess," said Case Storm, who had been contemplating his manicure for the last twenty minutes. It was the first time Chris had agreed with him on anything.

During the break, she noticed the senator in private conversation with Storm. A ratchetlike vise in her stomach ground one notch tighter. She didn't like thinking the two men might be friends. All of Denver was trotting around behind Storm as if he were the Pied Piper, and she prayed Bridgeforth was not danc-ing to the tune.

Making sure no one was eavesdropping, Storm spoke to the senator in low, urgent tones. "It's vital that we secure the vote for the North airport location *today!* As far as the city is concerned, no one will really care where the damn thing is located, and this insane conversation about subcontractors is a waste of time. We need to get this meeting back on track before Chris Welbourne railroads the mayor. She's got his ear, you know. This means mil-lions to me—and it could to some others like yourself," he said.

"I want no part of this deal," the senator said quietly.

"Well, the next time you come around groveling for cam-paign contributions—"

"Things are different now."

"I remember a time when you were in serious need of cam-paign funds," Storm said with a chilly smile. "You were a little more interested in my help then."

"I didn't intend to be associated with anything disreputable."

Storm glared at the senator. "Wake up, buddy! This is how you do business in the big city! You owe me, remember? And all I want is to nail down the location so we can capitalize on the adja-cent properties. There's nothing for you to fear. There's nothing illegal going on here, and we can get the committee to rubber-stamp everything. In this world, you are either one of the haves or have-nots—make your choice!"

"I'm here strictly to serve as liaison to the FAA."

"Bullshit."

Over the years, the senator had emerged as a powerful politi-cal voice with a respectable track record and an admirable public reputation. But he had made some mistakes, too. One of his bad decisions had been made years earlier when he accepted an invita-tion from Storm to participate as a silent partner in some small limited partnerships—not because they weren't profitable, but because Storm and his questionable dealings would eventually become an anchor around his neck.

"You're here to better your own interests and get in position for a run for the presidency," Storm hissed. "It will help if you can take credit for a world-class airport and distribution center. And mark my words, the mayor wants this, too. If you just help locate the airport where I want it, we can all get what we came for!"

"I'll second your motion for the North location," the senator said fuming. He was in a trap of his own making. "Once this airport issue is over, you can consider the debt paid!"

Sometimes Storm felt as if he just couldn't dance fast enough. It was crucial that his land development company, Western Slope Development, capitalize on the escalating land prices that would result from an official announcement of an airport location. His own financial pyramid was built on shifting economic sands— some of his limited partnerships were insolvent, and the S&L was way below government requirements for cash reserves. This airport committee had to be manipulated. When the meeting resumed, he offered a stirring sales pitch for the North location—which would, coincidentally, be right in the backyard of the Custer Ranch.

"It is vital to the city and incumbent on us as good custodians of our municipality that the committee vote in support of the North airport location. It is, after all, the location most desirable to the FAA. And in case you need a reminder, the FAA makes or breaks this deal. After we get their approval we can begin to structure the financing." Storm was silver-smooth as he worked on persuading the committee.

Bill Bridgeforth picked up where Storm left off. "I feel certain we can receive the necessary federal approval and matching funds if we select this location. Of course, time is of the essence," he reminded the group.

The land was about twenty-five miles northeast of Denver, in the middle of rolling farmlands. As the committee began to sway, Storm was already counting the millions to be made in the sea of apartments, hotels, and commercial developments that would follow in the wake of the airport decision.

"Is there a motion in support of the North airport location?" the mayor asked.

"I so move," said Storm, glaring at Bridgeforth.

"Is there a second?"

Bridgeforth raised his hand. "Second."

He detested being manipulated and controlled like this, but it was necessary because of that time during the early years of his career. He and some others had wanted an extra piece of the financial pie; a few small deals and they all got a nice piece of cash. It had seemed inconsequential at the time, but it had turned into a noose—the more he tried to slither out of it, the more constricting it seemed to become.

"Is there any discussion?" Silence circled the table as the first real winter storm began to rage outside.

Chris Welbourne raised her hand as she stood to address her male colleagues. She was elegant and imposing in her striking pinstripe suit and upswept hairdo. "Gentlemen," she began in a hushed voice, "there are many possible reasons for selecting any of the proposed locations—some of them justifiable and a couple even commendable. But I think it most imprudent to make this important decision in haste." She hoped at least some of the men would hear her as a measured voice of reason.

She searched each member for support. Her eyes locked on the mayor—who for some reason would not look her in the eye. His gaze fell first on the blank yellow legal pad on the mahogany table and then on an empty spot somewhere on the wall. Then something clicked in her brain. *He's in on it too!* she suddenly realized. Everyone there seemed to have a hidden agenda driving his preference for the airport location. Even Bill Bridgeforth seemed to be uncomfortable in his expensive leather chair.

"I don't think anyone in this room is even remotely objective about this issue." With every carefully chosen word Chris stared into the eyes of the committee members, all of whom were tired of discussing the plan. No one wanted the real facts splayed open for all to see. They knew what they were there for and knew what they wanted, regardless of the consequences.

"There are many representatives of our city," she turned to the mayor. "Certainly the cries of the city council have not fallen on completely deaf ears. There are many who say that this location is not in the best interests of the community. Every preliminary study points to other site options. Our job is to meet the future demands of our constituency, period!" She glared at Case Storm, and silent sparks seemed to fly across the table. "There are serious financial viability concerns that need addressing. In case any of you haven't noticed, this economy is fractured to the core. Look at the vacancy figures. Look at the interest rates." She felt as if she were screaming into a hundred-mile-an-hour headwind. "I move that there be further consideration of the location before we decide."

It was irrelevant to Chris that a vote for the North location might help her in some small way—what was one deal?—when the city's future was riding on their actions. It sickened her that everyone at the table seemed to be putting his own short-term interests ahead of what was best for the economy and the city. She knew in her gut that if Storm wanted it, there had to be something truly malignant about the proposal.

A single rivulet of sweat ran down Senator Bridgeforth's back. Not once in his entire career had he met a more disarming woman. Even if she lost this one, a river of power seemed to flow through her veins. For him, it was the ultimate seduction.

Chris turned to the secretary. "I would like it recorded in the minutes that I strongly oppose making the final decision today, and I oppose the location presented by Mr. Storm. I believe more due diligence is necessary to make this multibillion-dollar decision." But she knew her voice was falling on ears filled with the ching-ching of money in padded pockets. Her gaze flickered over to Storm, who was obviously seething.

"Everyone here seems to be ignoring the turbulence of the market," she continued doggedly. "It's sensitive to so many outside factors, including the oil embargo against Iran that has oil prices at a precipitous high." This was nothing like the Gold Rush of the 1800s, it was the real estate-oil rush of the eighties. Chris Welbourne could feel the tidal wave pressing down on the entire industry. Too many were making money flying high without a net. "Why in the world did you ask me to sit on this committee anyway?" she asked the room at large. "You know I don't agree. I don't feel comfortable . . . There are too many conflicts . . . I myself . . . "

Storm started to open his mouth, but Bridgeforth spoke first, his voice smooth and persuasive. "We still need you to work with the business community, Chris. You lend a lot of credibility to this group."

Chris stared. She understood that Bridgeforth as a politician had to work with Storm, that he had a complex role in the whole process . . . but she was irritated that he expected her to go along with decisions whose sole purpose seemed to be to line the pockets of those seated at this table. They not only wanted her to agree with them, they wanted to use her credibility to justify their decisions. No one else seemed to be making an effort to look at the big picture. And she herself . . . if this decision was going to be forced through, she could be accused later if there were ever any kind of investigation: *"You had a development nearby . . ."*

"Frankly, I don't think any of you here have any right to make these decisions. There are way too many conflicts of interest, too many people in the room who have things to gain. I am involved in several deals myself, and I don't believe this group can look at this issue with an unbiased perspective. Think about the long-term ramifications to the city of Denver. I'm not going to stand here and put my name on what this group is suggesting—I see no other choice but to resign from the board."

Bridgeforth began to protest, but Storm interrupted, "We understand your decision, Chris, and respect your choice. Now, gentlemen, there is work to complete."

Chris reached for her leather briefcase. "Good day, gentlemen." She left the room elegantly, the mayor's voice in her ears as she walked through the door.

"Is there any more discussion?" the mayor asked. "Then let's have a vote. All in favor—"

It was done. Chris was certain that Case Storm had gained something from the vote that had just been taken, and she was annoyed by Bill Bridgeforth's acquiescence. But it would not be too hard to follow Storm's trail. Storm may have won the first round, but the game wasn't over.

While waiting for the elevator, Chris heard footsteps behind her. She turned to see Senator Bridgeforth approaching. "I'm looking forward to seeing you this evening," he said. "Your office at six-thirty?"

"How can you support this vote!" she demanded, not trying to hide her frustration.

His eyes pleaded for her understanding. "This will be good for the city."

"You don't really believe that, Bill!"

"Let's talk tonight. See you shortly." He smiled, squeezing her hand.

Downtown was emptying as Chris walked back to the Rocky Mountain Savings building to take a shower and change. She had just enough time to return the day's calls and dictate several pieces of correspondence before the senator arrived.

The outcome of the airport planning meeting had her waging an internal war. She still wanted to have dinner with the senator—he was an attractive man and an influential friend. But she was irritated with his compliance with Storm's proposal.

And not only that: he had to be aware that something more

than friendship had been growing between them. He had called too often to discuss trite business issues over cocktails. The attention was flattering but dangerous. She knew where it could lead, and she did not want to get deeply involved with Bridgeforth. He came with complicated circumstances. Everyone in Denver was aware that he was married, even though his wife was rarely seen in his company. There had been speculation of a future presidential campaign, which would bring a lot of media scrutiny. Even if she were inclined to break her personal rule about not getting involved with a married man, prudence called for giving the politician a wide berth. Being caught in the crossfire would be a fatal mistake.

The entrance to the Rocky Mountain Savings and Loan building was formidable: marble and granite accented with solid brass. A security guard was prowling the corridors nearby, but for the moment the entryway was deserted. Chris entered the elevator which took her to the twenty-third floor, where Jeff Ashton was preparing to leave for the day.

"Do I have any messages?" she asked.

"You look beat!"

"This airport deal's getting out of control. I'm talking billions, not millions!"

"John Curry asked that you call ASAP. He said he would wait to hear from you." Jeff flipped to another page of notes. "Seldon Custer left her number." He handed her the pink note. "Is there anything you need for tomorrow?"

"No, thanks. I'm going to do some correspondence later. Probably work late."

It was a good sign that Seldon Custer had responded to the proposal. Chris's heart picked up pace as she quickly dialed the number and pushed the memory of the distasteful airport meeting into its own mental compartment to be dealt with later.

Seldon Custer's rich Colorado voice rumbled across the line. "Hello, Chris. How are you?"

"Great! After getting the note that you called. We're anxious to hear your response to our proposal."

Chris's Castle Creek proposal set aside a parcel of the land for open space with parks and enhancements for the planned business community which would eventually be developed around it. To stroke the ego of the family, the preserved land would be named Custer Park with a plaque summarizing the history of the ranch and recognizing the family's contributions to the community. Chris hoped that the family would jump at the idea.

"Do you have any questions?" Chris asked.

"The offer is very attractive, except for the seventy-two-hour deadline."

"We are aware that other bidders are making offers, but we can't wait to see if they raise the necessary capital. This is a clean cash offer to you and your family of twenty-two million, not to mention the parcel of land that will be set aside for the community. We have the money and we're ready to deal." Chris had managed to negotiate a nonrecourse loan for Castle Creek without a personal guarantee. Their limited partnership was a financial powerhouse, but if the development didn't work, only the savings and loan would get hurt. In the hands of irresponsible people, this was a way of doing business in the eighties that eventually took down the industry. Chris was known for doing substantial deals that made profits for investors, and being irresponsible was not her way of operating. But there were a thousand others out there who would leave a financial institution and its investors hung out to dry and never look back.

"I'll let you know something as soon as possible. It will not make CLP and Jake Winston happy, but it is very attractive for my family, which is my first priority. I suppose I should tell him we are having second thoughts."

"Does that mean you are accepting our proposal?"

"I'll let you know as soon as I've made a final decision. Give me just a little more time. This is a huge decision for our family.

And I have to think about what I will tell Colorado Land Preservation. There might be another property we could give them."

"That would be a wonderful alternative, accomplishing multiple goals. Your family would receive financial security and the community would still benefit."

"I'll be back to you as soon as I make a definite decision."

"We want to make this happen for all parties," Chris said, feeling the deal closing in her favor.

"I'll confirm everything tomorrow." Then the wealthy matriarch said good-bye.

Chris danced a mental jig and happily slammed her fist on the desk. She reveled in thoughts of victory for a minute and then thought about Jake. He certainly wouldn't let this fish off the line without a fight. She had always known that she and Jake would end up on opposite sides of the negotiating table one day—and she was charged by the challenge. Now the heat was turned up. Business was tough, even unpleasant at times—there were always winners and losers. And Jake had a ferocious temper when he didn't get what he wanted. But Chris hadn't become a multimillionaire by worrying about hurt feelings.

Jeff heard the bang in Chris's office and peeked in. "Are we still in the running?" he asked excitedly.

He had every reason to be excited. As part of his compensation, Chris always cut Jeff in on a small piece of the action. Such a practice boosted loyalty and incentive to stay on top of business, especially when the hours in a week stretched into sixty and sometimes seventy. Jeff had a small but potentially lucrative percentage incentive if Castle Creek got the ranch.

"You bet—in fact, I think we've got a live one." Chris had shoved her frustration over the airport decision process to the back of her mind and allowed herself to feel ecstatic over the possibility of acquiring the Custer Ranch and the future of Aspen Development Partners. Now it looked as if it would be in the shadow of the new airport, possibly increasing the potential value of the property as much as tenfold. With its proximity to the airport location, the Aspen Development Partners property was going to be a gold mine, too, not even including the oil and gas potential.

"I wasn't going to mention this, but since the deal sounds pretty sure, do you think you could buy out my interest in advance." He studied the slightly surprised look on his employer's face, then saw the look quickly evaporate. Chris's negative feelings after the airport meeting had been eclipsed by the optimistic call from Seldon Custer. She was in a generous mood, even though it was against her rules to price-tag deals that hadn't closed. She'd seen a hundred sure things fall apart at closings. There was no such thing as a done deal.

"How much were you thinking?"

"I have a real opportunity," he said awkwardly. "Could you make it fifty thousand?" He crossed his fingers and said a silent prayer that she would come through for him. He was overextended again and in need of cash.

"Are you sure you want to take your money off this horse and put it into something else?" Chris inquired. There was a huge upside potential for Jeff if he hung in with their consortium until the development was complete.

She doesn't understand, he thought. She had long lines of credit and unlimited cash while he was always in the squeeze play. "I'd better cash out now," he said, trying to sound matter-of-fact.

It was against her policies, but Jeff was a loyal employee. She trusted him with every aspect of her business and he would do anything she asked for the company.

"I'll have a check for you in the morning, but I think you are leaving a lot of cash on the table, Jeff." She thought he was making a bad choice, but it was his life and his money. Chris's head was swimming with exciting possibilities as night descended over the frigid city.

CHAPTER 13

Thoughts of Alex floated back into Jake's mind. Through the high-rise windows of the Colorado Land Preservation office he could see heavy clouds dancing across a charcoal-dusted sky, evoking dreams of moon-colored firelight. He rocked back in his worn brown leather swivel chair and supported himself with a twice-resoled Justin boot wedged on the corner of an open file drawer. Thanks to the good fortune of its supporters, CLP had landed a spacious yet conservative office space in the heart of downtown in Denver's United Bank Tower, a glowing erection of steel and glass that was new in the evolving panoramic skyline.

Jake wanted to leave for Boulder before nightfall stole onto the prairie. He was actually looking forward to the onset of winter with its fat snowflakes and naked aspen trees. He hoped Alex was prepared for a harsh season in the Colorado Rockies. She certainly hadn't been dressed for it this morning.

Extreme weather was part of living in and around Denver, where bitter sub-degree cold could grip the city and its foothills. It never lasted long, but being caught in an autumn storm could be treacherous. Fall in the Rockies brought chilling wind and an awesome harsh beauty. Aspen trees would turn golden yellow before leaving bare white trunks to survive the long high-mountain winter season.

By 4:00 P.M. the view from the window in the CLP office was blowing horizontal snow in downtown Denver. Winston looked wistfully in the direction of The Brown Palace. He hoped Alex wouldn't cancel their dinner. His mind seesawed back and forth until he finally decided to leave a message at her hotel. He left his office number, then bit the bullet and decided to place the dreaded call to Chris Welbourne.

⟡

The intercom buzzed in Chris's spacious office and Jeff's voice came across the line. "Do you want to talk with Jake Winston?"

"Put him through." She glanced at the clock, thinking *right on time*. Jake's moods and reactions were familiar to her like the backstreets of a small hometown. But he knew her too, and that made the chess game they were beginning to play even more intriguing.

Jake Winston heard only a few seconds of classical music before the familiar voice came on the line.

"Hello, Jake Winston!" came her genuinely warm greeting. "What a welcome call. It's been too long." She hoped he would bring up his meeting with Alex first, not the Custer Ranch deal.

"I enjoyed meeting your attractive friend this morning. What did I do to deserve such good fortune?"

"I'm lucky to have an exceptional partner. She is very talented."

"I look forward to knowing her better."

Chris's protective maternal instinct came crisply across the wire. "Take it easy, Jake!"

"All I said is that I think she is very attractive!"

"I just know you both too well."

"Do I detect a note of jealousy?"

"Absolutely not!"

"Come on, Chris."

"I just don't want to see anyone get hurt."

"You've been trying to get us together for months, and I'm not doing anything except what I was asked to do: help a little with your new oil company!"

"Point taken," Chris said with a sigh. "And I do appreciate

your assistance. I just hope you won't get in over your head with Alex."

"She appeared to be quite capable of taking care of herself."

Chris chuckled. "I'm not worried about Alex . . . it's you I'm concerned about."

"Since when? For that matter, I don't remember asking for your help. Besides, I don't get hurt anymore!" It was a small jab, but they both felt the sting.

"Still got your walls up, huh, Jake? Well, you could be playing with fire here."

"Hm, who is throwing stones? . . ." The sarcasm darted across the wires.

"Okay, let's stick to business, but don't come crying to me with a broken heart."

"Thanks for the big-sisterly concern, Chris, and the introduction, but I can take care of myself. And from what I saw today, you don't need to be worrying yourself over Alex either. She's an exquisite young woman and very shrewd for her age."

"Alex is light years ahead of everyone I know. She's got a bird-dog's nose for business and more instinct than you and I put together. And more experience than most of the drilling operators running around Colorado. She's a product of a real Texas wildcatter."

"Very impressive!"

"Her father was legendary in the Persian Gulf. One of the only people who could work well with the Saudis. She spent her youth traveling to different oil field operations in remote areas around the world. Few seasoned veterans understand the complete range of the business as well as Alex does."

"She asked me to be a kind of mentor for the company. Can you give me some more background?"

"You can expect every *T* to be crossed. She's very straightforward and we mean to be a major player."

"I mean background on her, if people ask."

"She and I have much in common. She lost her mother in a plane crash when she was pretty young. I guess that's what initially drew us together. In the last couple of years she put together a string of home runs, making her investors wealthy almost overnight. She's incredibly street-smart, yet intuitive and sensitive at the same time. She has barrels of experience. I'll fax you a copy of an article on her you might find interesting. She reads people as if they're transparent, at a psychic level."

"I'm intrigued."

"Jake, Alex has left broken hearts strewn around the world."

"Point taken! Now, can I change the subject?"

"Sure, go ahead." Chris knew him well enough to know that he would not pay attention to her warning about Alex.

"I would like to discuss a piece of land we are trying to acquire."

"There are two lines holding, and I'm late for a meeting. Is this urgent?" Chris asked warily.

"Your name came up in a meeting this morning, and I thought you might be able to shed some light on the subject . . . but it can wait until later."

Now he had touched a nerve. She knew he had met with Storm. But why had her name come up? God, how she loathed that man! "I've got a minute—shoot."

"You probably read the article in the paper that the Custer family is considering selling their ranch to Colorado Land Preservation. This is a strategic piece of land that everyone on the board including Bill Bridgeforth wants to preserve. It is even more important to preserve it if the rumors about the airport location are even close."

Silence hung on the line. He was sending her a clear message to back off. If she wanted a duel over the property, he was ready to fight.

"I thought you might have inside info on the status of the airport project," he said.

"I'm not in a position to discuss the airport plans."

Jake would have to find out about the plans for the airport from someone else. This was business and business was war. Chris didn't want any lengthy conversations in which her friend Jake would try to corner her about the Custer Ranch. Besides, she figured he must be really squirming over the deal if he was dropping names like Bill Bridgeforth.

"So, how did you enjoy Mr. Storm?" she asked, hoping to find out just how her name had come up.

"He is a smarmy son of a bitch," Jake said, "but all of Denver seems to be missing it. Everywhere I go he keeps showing up like a bad case of flu."

Chris's ears perked up. At least she and Jake were in agreement when it came to Storm.

"You can't get away from him," Jake continued. "The other day I was at a closing for CLP. We were selling a piece of land in town that had been donated to us to raise funds for some other preservation purchases, and I'll be damned if Storm didn't get his grubby hands lined with cash. The land flipped twice at the closing from my buyer to Storm to another guy who sits with you two on one of those civic boards. Storm didn't do a damn thing but show up, and he walked away with over a hundred grand. I know land is flipping all over Denver like hotcakes, but this deal had payoff written all over it."

"Well, you know he's not on my private dinner list," Chris offered. She didn't miss Jake's sour-grapes tone, and she filed away the tidbit of information for a future conversation with John Curry. They were closing in on Storm. No doubt he would bury himself, and all she had to do was find the paper trail.

"Well, thanks, Chris. We'll talk in a couple of days. Do I need to call and let you know that Alex gets home safely?" he asked sarcastically.

"Try to just be friends for once."

"Have you seen what she looks like?" They both laughed before signing off.

Jake hadn't really expected any hints from Chris about the property or the airport plans. Chris never said any more than she wanted to say. Too many gallons of water had flowed under their bridge for him to expect anything different from this woman he had once loved.

No one knew more about the land business than Jake Winston, but it would be obvious even to a greenhorn that the Custer Ranch deal might be affected by the plans for the new industrial airport complex. If the ranch ended up being in close proximity to the proposed site, it would be a gold mine for developers. At the same time, it would make it an even greater priority to preserve it as open space. Jake knew that in all likelihood Chris was making her own play for the Custer Ranch, but he wasn't going to make anything easy for her. He would do everything necessary—including getting his board member, the senator, to put pressure on her to back off.

Chris was mildly concerned about the inevitable upcoming confrontation with Jake. They were friends. She envisioned how his fury would erupt if CLP lost out in the bidding process. They could be headed for a nasty confrontation. But in an impish way, she rather liked the jousting with Jake. It was a challenge. It added a layer of intrigue to play the game with an opponent who knew the inner workings of her mind. And such a worthy adversary he was. Business was the big game, and oh, how she loved the hunt.

The intercom buzzer sounded while she was touching up her makeup in preparation for the meeting with the senator.

"There's someone on line one inquiring about that property you and Alex have in Aspen Development Partners—do you want to speak with him?" Jeff Ashton asked.

"Take a message for Alex."

Chris was talking on her speakerphone in the elegant bathroom which had been designed by Denver's preeminent interior designer, Morgan Dulany. The office suite was her home away from home with a walk-in closet housing various ensembles: jeans for riding, a set of ski clothes for last-minute trips to the mountains, three black cocktail dresses of varying degrees of slinkiness and corresponding accessories, various office ensembles, at least twenty pairs of footwear in individual cubbyholes, along with matching handbags, two fur coats, and a jewelry vault.

The office design included an ornate-mirrored wall which reflected snowcapped mountains on clear days. A wet bar with the finest Verde granite countertops, a state-of-the-art sound system, and custom-built furnishings covered in hand-painted French fabrics accented with period porcelains and lamps gave the office a feeling of importance and femininity. The designer had consulted a custom security firm on the state-of-the-art alarm system, and had incorporated a Murphy-style bed that rotated out of the wall for those occasions when Chris worked late into the night.

When the office was completed, *Architectural Digest* had put in a request to photograph the interior design for a feature on executive lifestyles, but Welbourne Enterprises had declined the request. Chris treasured her privacy.

Jeff Ashton picked up line one, apologizing for the delay. "There's no one available at the moment. Can I take a message and have someone get back with you as soon as possible?"

"My name is Harris Smith, with Western Slope Development." Smith spoke with a slight British accent. "We were looking at land records and noticed C. D. Welbourne listed as the title holder on a small piece of land north of Denver. Our company is interested in making an offer to purchase the property."

"Alex Sheridan handles everything related to that property."

"Please ask her to call as soon as possible. We have an interesting proposal. We represent a foreign investor who is willing to make a very attractive offer for the land as well as mineral and oil rights."

"I'll give her the message you called."

Harris Smith left his phone number. Smith was a front man,

an implementer. With a passport from the Isle of Man, one of the world's income tax havens, he had become a valuable commodity to his sleazy clients. An accountant by trade, he didn't mind taking care of the ugly details that his clients didn't want to handle when making certain kinds of deals. In Case Storm, he had met his alter ego.

꙰

The intercom buzzed in Storm's office.

"Harris Smith is on line three. Do you want to speak with him?" Line three was a private line reserved for confidential calls.

"Put him through," Storm ordered. He picked up the receiver. "Do you have any news?"

"I planted the bait, but haven't heard back. There's a woman named Alex Sheridan who's the point person on the deal. I'll have to get through to her."

"Stay on it. I want to know what Chris is up to and what they know about what we're doing."

"What if she's on to you?"

"That bitch isn't going to interfere with me," he said contemptuously. "How dare she think she can control what goes on at my institution? This is my bank; we'll see who falls first."

Case Storm was excruciatingly aware that Chris Welbourne had been making loud rumblings about some of the less-than-ethical dealings going on in the industry. And he knew she had a strong relationship with the Federal Home Loan Bank Board that governed his industry. He wanted to make sure she didn't rattle the wrong cage.

"Call me with an update, and for God's sake, don't leave any messages!"

Storm had good reason to be cautious. He had so muddied the waters between his personal finances and the S&L's that it had become impossible to tell the difference. To protect himself he'd involved plenty of high-powered people in his deals, making sure money was thrown their way as insurance. He had padded many a political palm. Storm actually felt entitled to the money after watching hundreds of entrepreneurs make fortunes during the recent boom years in the real estate business. If it were not for the thrifts, many of those new dealmakers would be penniless. Drunk with his own perceived invincibility, he continued abusing his position as a leader in the financial community.

Harris Smith hung up. Storm would want to know more about Alex Sheridan. It was his job to make sure she wouldn't be an obstacle to their plans of buying every available parcel near the new airport.

CHAPTER 14

Thursday 4:30 P.M.

Alex checked out of the star-spangled afternoon and back into the everyday world. The hotel concierge approached her with a pile of pink notes. One had Jake Winston's name scribbled at the top. The large bronze lobby clock clanged the half-hour and she raced to her room, where she was welcomed by a red-blinking message light. Ignoring the signal, she moved into the bathroom, picked up the extension, and dialed the number. She noticed in the mirror that her cheeks were flushed pink.

"This is Alex Sheridan returning Mr. Winston's call," she said in her professional style.

"I thought we'd lost you in a drift," came Jake's voice. "Are you ready to go?"

No, she was not ready to go at all. She was not ready to let go of the storm of emotions stirred up by the engineer she'd just left downstairs. But Alex knew how to downshift and move on. She was just relieved she hadn't run into Jake Winston while sitting on the back of Forrester's Harley.

"I'll be downstairs . . . can you give me a few extra minutes?"

"Sure."

"Boots and jeans are okay?"

"Perfect!" he responded—but he was beginning to accept the idea that there was no chance they were going to make it out of the city. Silently he cursed the snow.

Alex brushed, powdered, lipsticked, and exchanged her turtleneck for one that smelled less like a beer hall and Colton Forrester. She embraced her coat and nuzzled her face deep into the soft animal skin, branding the afternoon permanently into her mind. A quiet masculine fragrance, perhaps fresh soap, lingered on the powdery soft fur.

Forrester's age had been hard to determine—less than forty but not much—an outdoor life had weathered his skin but had kept his physique young and hard. Inside her head the unforgettable music persisted. Traces of his smile lingered between the lyrics.

The elevator moved like sap running down the bark of a gnarled tree, a quaint amenity of the grand old hotel. Lafayette stood at the door in the foyer as Alex approached.

"No more motorcycles, Miss Sheridan?"

"Not for today, anyway, but never count me out!"

The massive man tipped his black hat as two well-dressed businessmen swept in from the cold, their gloved hands gripping bulging leather attaché cases. A gust of frigid air flooded the entry, raising chill bumps all the way down to Alex's toes. Afternoon tea was being served in the open lobby.

"Where are you going on this stormy afternoon?" Lafayette inquired, letting his southern roots land on the end of each syllable. Snow fought against the glass in the door.

"Boulder, how long do you think it will take?"

"Now I can't quite tell you," he paused, looking at the door—"seeing how it's snowing so hard." He watched the snow collecting in the empty, frozen streets. "It ain't none of my business, but this ain't the kinda weather to be out drivin' around in, first real storm of the season and all."

"You're probably right." But in a warm, safe way, she was drawn to Jake. Dinner with him would be enlightening and potentially beneficial to business, despite the threatening weather.

She talked with the doorman until Winston's ice-covered Cherokee pulled up. Jake wore a heavy sheepskin coat and dusty gray cowboy hat—his stiff suit had been exchanged for flannel and denim. Alex jumped into the passenger seat and Lafayette closed the door.

"Be careful, now."

After exchanging pleasantries, Jake and Alex pulled out from under the porte-cochere's protection into frosty twilight. Jake's heart was pounding, while eerie city lights reflecting against the low swollen clouds reminded Alex of foggy deserted London nights.

The large brim of the crusty cowboy hat cast a shadow over Jake's face. "I still want to show you Boulder, but I don't think this will be the night. The forecast is for blizzard conditions—we'd never make it back to Denver tonight."

"It does look ominous."

"If you don't mind, let's have an early dinner here downtown. Boulder will be much nicer in the sunshine."

For hours he had debated about canceling their evening plans. Finally he had accepted the hand the weather had dealt. But he was surprised by his strong disappointment.

Alex was trying to mask her relief. She did want to get to know Jake better—he seemed to be a trustworthy new friend—but the stormy afternoon and Forrester had dampened her enthusiasm for the idea of driving to Boulder. And with the weather alert, an evening in downtown Denver would be wiser.

"That sounds great. It was such a full day, I'm not sure I would be the best company."

"But you have to promise to come another time." The old four-wheel-drive circled around downtown with Jake pointing out the CLP office and several other historic sites. At the edge of downtown, the famous Tivoli Brewery had just been restored into a major attraction filled with popular restaurants.

"Do you like Italian?" he asked Alex, who was gazing at the diminishing sky and remembering the touch of Forrester's hand.

"I'm easy."

What she really wanted was to go back to the hotel and curl up under fresh, starched sheets and listen to the evening news. She hadn't read the *Wall Street Journal* in two days, and she could almost taste strong scotch slipping down her throat, warming every cell.

"How did your meeting go this morning?" she asked politely.

"Better than it might have. The deal will probably go through after a little more maneuvering. It's a substantial transaction," he said.

"Tell me more about your preservation organization. Chris gave me only a brief overview."

"This project is fairly typical for Colorado Land Preservation. We're in the process of acquiring a substantial ranch which will be preserved as open space—meaning it will never be commercially developed. We raise money from private investors who receive tax credits for helping purchase a property. In this particular case, we will need to borrow some capital for the purchase, which will buy the necessary time to solicit more investors. Either way, it remains a working ranch. CLP will manage the new ranch, working with a foreman and staff to care for common areas like roads, lakes, stables, and buildings. The deal is attractive to wealthy individuals because of the tax credit."

The Cherokee crept through the icy streets and into the lower downtown area, an eclectic part of the city that was just beginning its revival. Streetlights cast a yellow glow on the white streets. Jake searched for the restaurant. Alex thought about Chris's Castle Creek investor group and wondered if Winston knew Chris was a competitor on this deal.

"It sounds as if you have everything worked out."

"We haven't signed any papers, but we have a commitment for the loan, which is the first hurdle. The rest of the details should be pretty simple."

Jake was sure his comments would make their way back to Chris. He was in fact trying to send a message for her to keep her hands to herself.

Alex knew Chris Welbourne had other plans for the property and suspected the deal would be far more complicated than Jake imagined. She decided not to ask any more leading questions, hoping to stay well away from the middle of the inevitable fray.

Jake glanced occasionally at his young companion as they talked. Her tight jeans accentuated a muscular frame and her loose, dark hair tumbled around defined shoulders. She periodically ran her long fingers through the dark mane, sweeping the unruly locks away from an exquisite face. She looked relaxed as they pulled in front of the restaurant. It was a small contemporary Italian spot bustling with early-evening guests who were hoping to dine before the storm shut everything down. A standing-room-only bar filled with boisterous patrons drinking local beer was separate from the tiny dining room with its intimate, elegantly set tables. The evening specials were scribbled in white chalk on a greenboard near the entrance. The waitress directed the couple to a corner table with three pastel roses in a demure bud vase resting on crisp linen.

"So how'd you settle in Boulder?" Alex asked, though she knew much more about Jake than her question implied. Boulder was a beautiful little enclave community nestled at the base of the mountains. It had become a haven for the fledgling environmental movement as well as home to many types of interesting extremists.

The large man's frame was coiled in the diminutive soda chair. "After graduating from the University of Colorado, I just hung around. One year turned into fifteen." Jake was leaving out details of his basketball career and stormy marriage. "Wait until you see the town. I love the topography there. The Flat Irons, massive rock formations, jut sideways from the ground as if they've been spit out of the mouth of Mother Earth. It's a peaceful place to live."

It was also a place with ample opportunities for a young businessman on his way up in the world. Eons ago, it had been rewarding for Jake to see the growth and development of the area, but when the opportunity to establish and develop Colorado Land Preservation, Inc., came along, he saw a chance to reach out and do something that would leave a different kind of mark on the community. Since that time, he had been almost single-handedly responsible for acquiring and preserving the land around Boulder and Denver as open space in perpetuity. As far as the eye could see, the gentle rolling green grass meadows would stay untouched and undeveloped, thanks to his efforts.

Then Alex remembered the message light she had ignored in her rush to call Jake. "Please excuse me while I make a quick call."

"What would you like to drink?"

The beers with Forrester had left her with heavy eyelids, and she drove back a yawn. "Iced tea is fine."

The pay phone was in a small hallway too close to the bar, and the happy-hour customers were beginning to make a deafening din. Alex dug the receiver into her face, trying to drown out the noise.

"This is Miss Sheridan in room seventy-four. Do I have any messages?"

"Mr. Jake Win—"

She interrupted. "I have that one. Anything else?" Her tone was clipped and efficient.

"Yes, Jeff Ashton asked that you return his call as soon as possible. The number is—"

She interrupted again. "I have it, thank you! Anything else?"

"Oh, yes! Ms. Sheridan, flowers arrived at the front desk. We delivered them to the room."

"Thank you."

Curious and distracted, she hung up, wondering about the flowers. She dialed the offices of Welbourne Enterprises and was transferred to Jeff Ashton. "Hello, Jeff, I received your message."

"A call came in not long ago from the president of Front Range Engineering. I knew you had a meeting scheduled with them earlier, so I thought it might be important. A Mr. Colt Forrester left two numbers, office and home, and asked that you call at your earliest convenience."

Alex scribbled down the numbers and shoved the crumpled message into her pocket.

"Is everything okay?" Jake inquired when Alex bounced back to the table.

"Yes. Everything's great. I'm just eager to get started on our first well. I hate waiting."

Alex wanted to get started on the project. Real estate deals and oil and gas projects were turning like hotcakes. Timing was everything in a market like this one. Two weeks could seem like a lifetime. But due diligence was also important—nothing could be rushed. And she was the decision-maker everyone was counting on. Oil prices soared through the roof, and they weren't going to stay there forever.

"How many wells can your property make?" Jake asked while they studied the limited menu. He had removed his sheepskin coat and his athlete's frame was revealed through an old flannel shirt. His biceps were firm and hard but not bulging.

"We'll have to see what the reports show. It's right at three hundred acres, just to the north of here."

A scrawny, efficient young woman with three silver-looped earrings through the top of her right ear quickly took their orders.

"I think I know the area," Jake said between sips of a cold Perrier and lime. "A substantial amount of the acreage in the area is owned by several prominent Denver families—one of them the Custers, with whom we are closely acquainted."

"I suppose the new airport will affect everything in the vicinity! Chris said there is a lot of political pressure on the committee to pick the location because of some of the landowners."

"She's right. That's why it's imperative that we save this ranch from the ravenous developers. Once the airport comes, then the roads, hotels, apartments, and commercial developments will devour the land."

His conviction was appealing. He was determined to do what he believed was right for the land and future of the city. Having conquered financial mountains in his younger years, he could now pursue more altruistic causes.

"That's exactly what's happening in Dallas." Delicious steaming pasta in light cream sauce with a split Caesar salad arrived in just minutes.

"Did you settle on an engineering firm?" His searching gray eyes studied her like a hawk.

"We haven't made any final commitments, but it's more than likely we will use Front Range." Alex didn't want to discuss Colton Forrester with Jake, who was shamelessly admiring her figure. She pretty well knew where he stood, and discussing the engineer would only lead to a dead end. Fortunately the waitress came by to describe a list of unappealing desserts. Both Alex and Jake agreed that tiramisu was highly overrated, but discussing dessert gave her a chance to change the subject. After declining dessert, Alex asked Jake about a controversial article published by the *Post* about Rocky Mountain Savings.

"Case Storm can be rather difficult." Chris mentioned him in less-than-flattering terms. "It's amazing how guys like that get so far."

"You're right. But he's a board member of mine and I'm not at liberty to discuss him. I'm sure Chris can give you a clearer picture." Jake communicated his feelings about Storm with his eyes. It was obvious he wasn't a fan of the man, but neither was he going to criticize him openly. "But I'd really like to talk more about you. Chris told me just enough to scratch the surface."

"What part was that?" Alex directed a sparkling smile at him.

"It sounds as if you have some world-class experience in the oil fields."

"I was born lucky, the only daughter of an extraordinary maverick who convinced me that anything in the world is possible. From him I learned there are no limits on dreams."

"It sounds as if you've done a hell of a lot on your own."

"That may be true, but I wouldn't be here if it weren't for

my father. He took me all over the world and taught me everything he knew. Until he died."

"I'm sorry . . . I didn't realize."

"That's okay, he was doing what he loved best, drilling oil wells. He had a massive heart attack in Somalia a little over a year ago and was airlifted to the cardiac unit in Cairo. After several emergency surgeries, there was nothing more that could be done. It was hell getting the body out."

She spoke like a well-trained director of communications explaining a political event. But just underneath the smoke screen he could sense the loss and pain that she kept hidden.

"That must have been so hard for you." It was a hollow offering, but he didn't know what else to say. She was so strong and young and capable, and she didn't seem to need anyone. Alex was an uncharted island he wanted to explore, but he didn't know where to start.

"Chris and I had already been talking seriously about partnering, so after the funeral I gave her a call. His death was part of the reason I was ready to make a major change. Timing is everything in life and new frontiers were calling. It wasn't the same being in Dallas without him. I sold my company and moved up here."

Her father had been her mentor and confidante. In some small way, Jake reminded her of the father she had so admired and emulated. All her intuitive radar indicated he was someone she could trust. Their conversation flowed, and he radiated warm strength, which she soaked up like parched earth drinking in a spring rain. Jake listened attentively, feeling an aching compassion for his new friend. She was not superficial or evasive . . . just complicated. She was independent and alone, yet open and adventuresome. He wanted to be her confidante.

They finished dinner with a cup of thick, black coffee, then they ran out to the car. The unrelenting weather had caused visibility to drop to almost zero. Giant snowflakes frantically tried to escape the methodical swiping of the wipers which droned back and forth, and little else but flickering city lights could be seen through the thick sky. Alex wondered again about the flowers that had been delivered to her hotel room, then she put her mind on something else.

CHAPTER 15

The telephone rang several times at the Deegan private detective agency. It was a crummy little office that reeked of stale cigar smoke, but all calls were monitored by the most sophisticated electronic equipment. The agency specialized in following and documenting individuals in "compromising situations." For the right price, Deegan would handle almost any situation, and technology made it possible to eavesdrop on almost anyone. Deegan's state-of-the-art listening devices could pick up a normal conversation from a surveillance vehicle one hundred yards away.

The owner, Vinnie Deegan, was a two-bit private eye with a penchant for electronics that allowed him to service a less-than-respectable industry. It also enabled him to stay knee-deep in nose candy, which was really all that mattered to him. He had enough cash for his growing habit and plenty more for the skinny female addicts who would do anything for a fix.

A blonde receptionist with blood-red nails and matching lipstick answered the jangling phone.

"Mr. Deegan, please."

"May I ask who's calling?" the receptionist inquired, flipping on the device that recorded incoming calls.

"A client," the caller snapped. He wasn't stupid enough to give his name over a telephone line. Any idiot with some wires could listen in, and he didn't trust anyone.

"One moment, please."

"Deegan," the middle-aged snoop growled into the receiver. On his desk was a dog-eared *Penthouse* magazine. Several pages had been ripped out and taped to the wall next to the phone.

"Is this line secure?" asked a familiar voice. The two men had talked before and needed no introduction.

"Only if you can trust me. Where are you calling from?"

"A public phone on the Sixteenth Street Mall."

"You can't be too careful," Deegan observed. "A pay phone *is* your best choice. Don't ever use a cell phone," he added.

"Have you installed the equipment for Welbourne Enterprises?" the caller asked impatiently.

"It was completed last night! No hitches. The security guard was snoring in the lobby when we left."

"You're sure it's working?"

"Yes. We've already run a test. Everything is loud and clear. You know this is a lot more technical than the typical snoop job. We use far more sophisticated recording devices than the average Joe who's trying to catch his wife screwing some young buck."

"That's what you're paid for!" the caller snapped. "There's a lot of money riding on this deal. We want to know who she's talking to, who she's seeing, and what is said." He wasn't willing to give Deegan any more information about what he and his client wanted.

"We'll deliver an audio copy for each twenty-four-hour period."

"What kind of security system do they have?"

"Nothing we haven't seen before. Only the big corporations have the super high-tech stuff. What kind of business is this?"

"That's none of your affair," the voice replied.

"We need the payment. Have $10,000 delivered to our offices —today." The investigator was irritated with the caller's officious attitude. "Cash!"

"We want recordings of every conversation."

"You'll get what you want—just send the cash." Deegan didn't like his business, or his clients for that matter. But there was a market for his services, and it generated big money that wasn't seen by Uncle Sam.

"The money will be couriered immediately."

CHAPTER 16

Chris poured herself a scotch and soda, then moved to her large French mahogany desk. *Poor Jeff,* she thought. He was so talented at managing a business, but he was certainly no entrepreneur. She had seen his kind of hungry dream on a hundred different young faces. These were people who fancied themselves dealmakers, but the truth was that not everyone was cut out to be an entrepreneur. Jeff wanted so much to hit the big time, but his talent was in being a detail man, and she wished he would be happy with his own invaluable skills. She hoped he wasn't chasing rainbow deals he couldn't handle.

A Waterford clock, a gift from the governor for her efforts on behalf of his party, read five-thirty. Next to it, in a sterling silver frame, was a striking photo of Chris with the president and first lady in the Oval Office.

Chris dialed the Rocky Mountain Savings loan officer John Curry, hoping he had not yet left for the day.

"Thank you for returning my call, Chris." John Curry spoke in whispering words that could barely be distinguished. "I need to come see you—it's urgent!" Chris recognized fear in his voice and was not surprised by the call. Earlier in the month John had expressed some concerns about the institution. "Can you come now?" Chris asked. She would have just enough time to meet with the loan officer before the senator arrived.

John Curry was an average man with respectable dreams

who hated to see what was happening to his institution. After discreetly placing a file in an innocuous brown folder, he had taken his leave of the few colleagues remaining in the office. He now searched the lobby of the Rocky Mountain Savings and Loan building before heading to the elevator that would take him up to Chris's office on the twenty-third floor. He was carrying with him information that could bury Storm's empire.

"You sounded disturbed, John, what can I do?" Chris welcomed her old colleague with a reassuring smile.

Chris stood several inches taller than John, whose bland features could have been cut and pasted to almost any man. His clothes were from a middle-of-the-road men's department store and the tie was an inexpensive acrylic stripe. The tired loan officer tried to wipe fear from his visage as his eyes darted nervously around the room. "I don't want to hurt anyone, Chris, but I know you share my disdain for crooks like Storm. I have a family and a reputation to consider . . . and I think this S&L is going down."

"No need to justify anything to me," said Chris. "I am flattered that you choose to confide in me." She noticed his hands were trembling. Her heart sagged with the weight of his burden, and her loathing for Storm grew like fungus.

"I can no longer turn a blind eye to what is going on," John continued. "Things are out of control, and innocent people are going to be hurt."

Chris nodded. "Rocky Mountain Savings isn't the only savings and loan dancing on the edge of the table, John. Other arrogant idiots like Storm are making big mistakes, mistakes that will haunt the entire country. It's admirable that you are trying to do the right thing."

"There may be some gray areas where people are on the edges of ethical boundaries, but this is more serious. This is black." Curry smoothed his tie nervously. Puffy eyelids formed large bags around tired eyes. He handed the file to Chris.

"So what do we have, John?" she asked.

"Storm is blatantly using the S&L for his own profit. I have receipts in this file for purchases in excess of two million, all items at Storm's home. Art, rugs, antiques. Not to mention the plane and the jet fuel that he burns like lighter fluid. I've got loan documents and deposit slips for Storm's accounts that show a pattern I think will be very interesting to the federal government. Storm makes loan after loan with no collateral and little documentation. A few weeks after every closing, he happens to come into some large profits from land sales. Each time it seems he's able to buy and sell the land on the very same day."

"What a coincidence," murmured Chris. She studied the documents for a few minutes. "Thank you for trusting me with this information."

"I hope this won't turn around and bite me in the backside."

"Let me make a few discreet calls to some of my trusted associates. I will mention no names, of course. I have a close friend with the Federal Home Loan Bank Board who can direct us. After the board starts the ball rolling on an investigation, they will leave nothing unexamined. But until I make these inquiries, let's keep this close. I think it's important for us to find out who else is involved in Western Slope Development. Can you find out who else is profiting from these deals?"

"I will call you as soon as I know more. Until then, we need to be very cautious."

There was no more time to talk to John Curry about Storm; the senator was due at any moment, and Chris needed the loan officer out of sight. "Unfortunately, I have another pressing engagement in just a few minutes. Under the circumstances, it would be best that no one see you leave this office."

John Curry scurried out of the office, disappearing into the vacant hallway. For what seemed like an eternity, the nervous thrift officer danced from foot to foot as he waited for the elevator. He glanced at the watch on his wrist. All he really wanted was to get out from under the grinding press that was threatening his livelihood. He loathed Storm, and he feared him, too. Curry was a good numbers man, and he knew there was little jockeying that could be done to fortify the crumbling institution. The elevator bell finally rang, the doors slid open, and Curry stepped inside.

"Good afternoon, Mr. Curry." It was the ice-blue voice of Case Storm. Curry felt as if he were in slow motion as he tried to recover from the shock of seeing the S&L chairman's face just inches in front of his own.

CHAPTER 17

Senator Bridgeforth was reclining inside his chauffeured sedan with the *Wall Street Journal* and a cell phone. After listening to a long list of messages, he used the phone to give instructions to his loyal secretary.

"Please make my excuses to Mrs. Bridgeforth for this evening. I will be late." He never asked how the secretary handled covering for his indiscretions. Somehow it always seemed to work out. Susan Lovelace knew that protecting the senator's privacy was one of her top priorities. After hanging up, she pressed the speed dial for his home.

"Mrs. Bridgeforth?"

"Yes, Susan."

Catherine Bridgeforth and Susan Lovelace usually spoke several times a day. Susan coordinated all the Bridgeforth social functions; in fact, she managed the demanding lives of the family.

"The senator asked me to call. He will be tied up until late this evening."

"Do you know where he can be reached?"

"He was leaving an airport planning committee meeting for a subcommittee meeting of some kind that will take him through dinner," she lied. "That's all I know." It was part of her job, so she lied some more. "He said he was sorry he couldn't stop by the house first."

"Thanks, Susan." Catherine's disappointment hung like wet paint in the tropics.

Chris Welbourne heard a warm hello drift in from the outer hall, signaling the arrival of Senator Bridgeforth. The senator politely knocked as Chris opened the interior door to her private office. He took her hands in his and stood back, letting his gaze slowly span her sculpted features. His politician's façade wavered at the sight of her. There always seemed to be a dazzling aura around Chris Welbourne.

"You look wonderful, Chris. I could hardly take my eyes off you in the meeting."

Chris snorted. "Thank you. But you'd better be careful in those meetings. You can't always tell who your friends are."

"I'm sorry you felt you had to resign from the board, though of course I respect your reasons. I hope you are still my friend?" he inquired seductively, knowing she had been furious with the outcome of their earlier meeting.

"Yes, of course. But Bill, this airport is going to be more complicated than the committee realizes."

"I wish you had been with us! We have to make this happen," he said, back in his political mode. "The future depends on it. Most people can't appreciate the significance of an airport and distribution center like this one, but I know you've got the vision. We're not just looking at the benefits for Denver. This is a project that will have global ramifications."

"I'm afraid the future of some people may depend on it too much," she responded warily.

"Chris, you know your backing could make or break the deal with the business community. Your resignation doesn't have to mean you have nothing more to do with the project. It's imperative that I have your support."

It sounded a little bit like an order. Bill Bridgeforth wasn't a United States Senator by accident. When he chose to be, the senator was like liquid gold, leaving all in his path in smoldering warmth and glowing confidence. Chris wrestled with his seductive power.

"Sorry, there are too many unanswered questions," Chris said. "The city is growing in the opposite direction from where the committee voted to locate the airport. You know that, Bill! The location is not what the demographic survey recommended. And then there is the question of cost." Chris walked to the bar and selected two crystal tumblers. "Scotch and water?"

"Yes, thank you."

Chris picked up the decanter that sat on a round tray next to a silver ice bucket and poured Glenfiddich into the tumblers.

"Chris, the money isn't the issue. We must convince the community of the importance of a world-class industrial airport and export distribution center."

"But why there?"

"You know the answer as well as I do. Money and power talk." He was alluding to the wealthy landowners who had much to gain from locating the airport in the North. "They make the big political contributions that gave them a louder voice than unmonied constituents." His voice fell to a murmur. "I understand your group is looking at some property? . . . "

Chris silently marveled at this man's skill, that he was able to make a comment like that and not have it sound like an insult. She ignored the comment. He knew as well as she did that she did not place her personal interests above the public good. "We are entering a recession whether the business community chooses to believe it or not. Look at what's happening in Texas. The financial community is crumbling at its core. I'm not sure you can float enough bonds to make this happen. The savings and loans are already in a tenuous position."

"This project will bring desperately needed business to our area, bolstering the economy. Denver needs this project, and where it eventually is located really isn't the primary concern."

Chris handed the senator his glass. "Bill, you're starting to buy your own bullshit. Just tell me where the money will come from! There are more bad loans floating around than the entire city could finance. You know what the S&Ls are doing. If you look at their books, the only thing they have is goodwill. It's all smoke and mirrors; there's no cash."

"I'm not going to argue with you about that . . . but this *airport* is the future! It will bring real jobs into the economy."

"I'll have to see it to believe it."

"I know for sure there are people in Texas working on a plan for an airport there. They have the same goals we do. If this doesn't happen now in Denver, we'll be in a firm second place ten years from now, which to me means nowhere."

"That may be true, but we have pressing tangible issues here and they should be considered now."

"I respect your position on the financial issue," he said, "but I wish you could help us present a united front. Otherwise there might not be any airport at all." Bridgeforth was concerned by Chris's attitude. He wanted her support in the committee, even though she had resigned from the board. He found it fascinating that she was fighting so hard against something that could personally enrich her.

Chris didn't like his tone or the pressure. "Are you still considering running in the next election?" she asked, changing the subject.

"I have received a call from Washington. I can't say it's unappealing, but no official organization exists yet. What do you think, Chris?"

Chris made light of the subject. "I think you'd better get back to your office ASAP. You know what they do to the private lives of presidential candidates. You'll be tarred and feathered if you're seen with me outside a meeting."

The hard edges of just moments before were softened by her genuine, warm gaze. Bridgeforth moved closer, flashing an endearing smile.

"I don't care, and for now it's not important. Let's forget all those issues for now. By the way, what did you have on your mind earlier that was so secretive?"

"I had a very disturbing meeting today with a savings and loan officer who had an interesting story to tell. I won't tell you his name because I promised to keep it confidential until we can verify the allegations."

"What did this person allude to?"

"Basically, it sounds as if Rocky Mountain may be in some trouble."

The senator was immediately focused on the subject. "What do you mean?"

"There are some very suspicious loans being made and large profits coming Storm's way shortly afterward. It has all of the signs of kickbacks."

"But Storm's one of the most powerful leaders in the industry. He's the most powerful financier between here and Washington."

"I know."

"What's this person after?"

"Nothing!"

"And he's certain about these allegations?"

"He's very concerned, but again this was a quick, hushed conversation. My friend at Rocky Mountain has been documenting every transaction, and he brought me the file today. You know, I was a board member for many years at First Denver Savings, which Storm acquired, and I still feel some responsibility to those depositors. He's robbing them blind."

"You don't know that!" the senator said. "Where's the jury on this?"

"This is more than gossip, Bill. We're talking about fraud and embezzlement."

The senator looked very concerned, but Chris had no idea to what degree he was worried. "What do you plan to do with the information?" he asked.

"If it's warranted, I want to turn him in to the regulators and have him prosecuted—I think he's stealing. But I can assure you, nothing will happen unless it is thoroughly documented."

"Perhaps there is only a slight indiscretion," Bridgeforth protested. "It would be tragic to ruin a career over something trivial."

"I'm not speaking of trivia," said Chris.

"Maybe your associate doesn't know all the facts. I know you will tread carefully."

Again, it sounded like an order. "I just didn't want you to hear it after the fact," she said. "It will be a huge scandal."

Chris was surprised by Bridgeforth's response, but she tried to hide her reaction. She wished she had had time to read through Curry's file more thoroughly. Later she would certainly do it with full attention.

"Thank you for letting me know."

"What did you have in mind for this evening?" she asked, again changing the subject.

"Let's go to that small French restaurant down near the train station. They'll have a room where we can have some privacy." He moved closer to Chris, taking her drink and setting it on the coffee table. Taking her chin in hand, he kissed her passionately on the mouth. Her heart started pounding from both excitement and fear, and the sweet taste of forbidden fruit.

"That's much better than banking deals and airports, don't you think?" he murmured with a lightness of being that shone in his eyes.

Her gaze did not waver from the face of the dark, handsome senator. "I think we're playing on the edge . . . and you have much farther to fall than I do, Bill."

He dismissed her warning. "We're only associates having dinner to discuss business—that's all." He squeezed her forearms.

"If you say so. I'm famished." She tried to ignore the fact that her temperature rose with each touch of his hand and that this "harmless flirtation" certainly had a powerful effect on her.

"Ben's waiting for my call. Let me give him a buzz; he's just around the corner." He brushed his lips across her brow. "You're almost too much, Chris Welbourne."

"Let me just powder my nose!" In the low light of the dressing area, she applied a cinnamon lipstick. Her face was glowing with a natural flush. She wondered about the senator's cavalier attitude about being seen publicly with a single woman, especially one who was recognizable. He already had a less-than-stellar reputation when it came to women. She dismissed the thought, telling herself it was his career, and the rumors were probably exaggerations.

And she found it very hard not to be attracted to him.

Franco's restaurant was one of the many popular spots in LoDo, the trendy name for lower downtown Denver. Franco opened with eight tables, a superb chef, and an outstanding wine cellar. The half-French, half-Italian proprietor knew every patron by name and encouraged each to call at any time for special requests and treatment. Gracious gentility oozed from his pores. He kissed the ladies and sometimes even the men. The clients loved being fawned over, and his business flourished.

The restaurant was a remodeled brick warehouse just around the corner from the old Oxford Hotel, a Denver institution. The work on the warehouse had been painstaking, but Franco's diligence had paid off, creating a truly elegant French Bistro atmosphere. With low lights, white starched linens, Hungarian porcelain, and excellent service, it had grown into Denver's most posh restaurant.

Franco was waiting outside in the crisp air as the senator's limousine made the wide turn into the parking lot. The restaurateur was blessed with stunning European looks. He had a full head of steel-silver hair set off by a bronze tan on a more-than-adequate physique. Opening the door with a slight bow, he embraced the couple with kisses on both cheeks.

"I am soooo pleased to see you again, Mademoiselle Welbourne. It's been too long," he cooed in a heavy French accent. "The table is waiting in the private room with champagne . . . unless you prefer an apéritif?"

"Thank you, champagne will be delightful," Chris responded before Bill had a chance to speak. If the senator wanted to play games in public, then she wasn't going to be shy. Franco led them to the quaint candlelit bar.

Not a person in the entire restaurant had missed the arrival of the high-profile senator and his conspicuous companion. Chris felt a tap on her shoulder.

"Chris, I *thought* that was you," said Morgan Dulany, the designer who had decorated Chris's office.

"It's good to see you," Chris responded, hoping to avoid a lengthy conversation.

Bill turned and caught Morgan's studied visage.

"Are you having dinner?" the designer inquired.

"Yes, just trying to wrap up some unfinished business," Bridgeforth said.

"Good to see you, senator," Morgan said and then moved on to her table.

Franco fluttered around the room, falling all over his high-profile guests. Having the senator in for dinner was a coup. His patrons thrived on being seen around the rich and powerful, which made evenings like this one priceless. Later the town would be abuzz with gossip about the evening.

Franco went by the table to take their order. He arrived in time to see Chris firmly pushing away the senator's hand, giving him a look that clearly said: *Straighten up.*

"Can I have the chef prepare a special just for you, or perhaps you prefer something off the menu? Whatever your pleasure," he offered in his thick accent.

"I think we've decided on the rack of lamb, medium rare, but surprise us with a special appetizer and whatever the chef desires to go with the lamb. I always love the grilled portobello mushrooms with warm chevre and sun-dried tomatoes."

"Very good choice, sir. Shall I suggest a wine, or do you have a selection in mind?"

"A '92 Caymus Cabernet, please."

"Of course."

The proprietor hurried off in search of the wine, and the senator brought up the Storm issue again.

"I am quite disturbed over the allegations against Case Storm. Are you absolutely sure he has operated inappropriately?"

"Nothing is absolutely sure, but it looks very suspicious."

"Who is the character making the accusations?"

She ignored the sarcasm in the question. "I have known him for many years and I trust his position. Even at first glance, it seems pretty obvious that Storm is way out of bounds. He is supposed to be above reproach as a leader in the financial community and chairman of Rocky Mountain Savings and Loan. It's one of the largest institutions in our country, Bill. Confidential information of a highly sensitive nature is shared at our meetings, and if Storm is operating unethically, and possibly illegally, then it affects us all. I have a close friend in a powerful banking position who's making some discreet inquiries."

"Will you please keep me informed? And . . ." he paused and then said, "be careful."

At last he seemed to be giving her suspicions the attention they deserved. Storm was as crooked as a snake. She assured Bill that she would proceed with caution, and then he excused himself.

The private phone line rang at the home of Case Storm. His

Cherry Creek residence was decorated with the finest antiques, appearing as a more elaborate version of his office. The residence had been carefully selected in an attempt to purchase an established position in the community. Original artwork covered most of the walls, and sculpture was displayed throughout the house. Below ground, the wine cellar housed hundreds of vintages of investor-quality wines. Storm strode through his home office to take the call, a chilled vodka martini in one hand and Cuban cigar in the other.

"This is Bill Bridgeforth."

"Hello, Bill. We sure nailed Chris today—" he began in a victorious tone.

"Forget that!" Bridgeforth interrupted. "You're crossing the wrong woman!" He almost shouted. "I can talk for only a few moments. You're in deep trouble! Someone at your savings and loan is spilling his guts to Chris Welbourne, and she's about to share everything with the feds in Washington. You'd better do something fast and it better be good." The senator's halting, shaky voice was filled with fear.

"Don't get hysterical, Bill. How are they ever going to prove anything? All we're doing is some friendly back-scratching. By the way, I have an angle on a big deal that will put me on Easy Street if it pays off. Would you have any interest?" he asked, arrogantly ignoring the threatened exposure.

"I'm not interested in anything except keeping my name clean. If they start snooping into your records, they'll find more than I bargained for. We have to put a stop to this right away."

"They aren't going to find anything other than a couple of insolvent land development companies. We can plead poor judgment in making the loans, and that's as far as it will go! I'll call Harris Smith and make sure there's no way to trace any of the follow-up deals."

"You'd better take care of it *now*," the senator said loudly in a voice trembling with panic, and then hung up.

Bridgeforth was scared. Storm had once lent him money to invest in a few no-lose deals with the secret understanding that the nonrecourse loans would never be called. Bridgeforth had put his money in Case's land deal, and made a quick million while the thrift ate the loans.

Later Storm had gotten too greedy. He was making loans and profiting under the table at every turn. The pattern alone would be enough to convince a jury to convict if it ever went to trial.

Storm refilled his glass with straight vodka and paced, trying to decide what to do. Sirens exploded in his head. He had been preoccupied when he had seen John Curry on the elevator, but now he was putting two and two together. John had entered the elevator from the twenty-third floor. Storm had thought it curious at the time, but now the reason was clear: a visit to Welbourne Enterprises. Curry had been up there to nail him. The leak at the bank had to be stopped immediately.

He would have to get rid of Curry, buy him off or shut him up somehow. Every man had a price, he believed. Bridgeforth was right—Curry and Welbourne had to be stopped.

Senator Bridgeforth returned in emotional turmoil to the table that was now the topic of every conversation in the restaurant. In her mind, Chris was rehashing the conversation that had taken place with John Curry. She was anxiously anticipating returning to the office to draft a letter to her contact in Washington. It would be a good evening to stay at the office and get a jump on the next day's business, she thought. Besides, the snow was blanketing the city into what was turning into a whiteout. Bridgeforth and Welbourne avoided the subject of Storm as the two enjoyed the five-star delights produced by Denver's most renowned chef. After dessert, they thanked Franco for a fine evening—the food had been superb as always—and departed in the limousine.

In the rear of the sedan, behind smoky glass, the slightly inebriated civic leader inched closer to his enchanting companion. The embers had been there, gaining heat since their first encounter at a political fund-raiser several years earlier. It was time to breathe some air into the fire. Slipping a hand under hers, he pulled her close. The smell of champagne and perfume intensely aroused him.

"Shall we go back to your place for an after-dinner drink?" the senator boldly invited himself.

But Chris's mood had been destroyed by her whirling thoughts.

"You'll have to excuse me, Bill, but it was an exhausting day and tomorrow looks hectic. Besides, I don't think this is in either of our best interests."

"We don't have to end the evening." He nuzzled closer, blatantly showing his desire.

"Thank you for a lovely evening, Bill. Ben, I'll be going back to the office if you don't mind," she directed the driver.

"Yes, madam," the chauffeur responded.

The limousine silently pulled alongside the curb outside the main entrance to the Rocky Mountain Savings building that loomed like a ghost in the snow. A dark quiet pervaded the streets.

"I'll walk Ms. Welbourne upstairs, Ben. Why don't you drive around the block until I call."

She didn't want to have a drink, but she wouldn't coldly refuse his offer to walk her upstairs. Chris waved at the security guard, who smiled as they entered the elevator. It was nice having him patrol the building on late nights. They ascended on the elevator in silence to the twenty-third floor. Chris disarmed the security system, turned on a lamp, and continued to make excuses to Bill, never dreaming the conversation was being monitored.

"It's gotten so late, and I'm very tired. Thank you for a beautiful evening at Franco's."

"You made the evening beautiful," he moved closer.

"It's obviously one of your favorite haunts," she slipped in a little barb.

"I get the distinct feeling you want me to leave."

"We don't need the complication, Bill. The thought is intriguing, but we should remain business friends—just that. If we continue this, I can think of three people off the top of my head who are going to get hurt."

"Can I talk you out of a glass of water?"

"Sure, just a minute." She moved to the bar with Bill Bridgeforth trailing behind. He reached out, spinning her around and planting a passionate kiss, forcing his tongue in her mouth. He was handsome, strong, and powerful, but she used every bit of rational force not to give in to his romantic advances.

"Not now, Bill, not like this."

"Chris, I've never been with a woman like you," he protested. "I've never felt anything like what I feel for you."

"It is time to go home! We can talk later," she tried to reassure him. She handed him the Waterford glass, noticing a dejected look in his eyes that she hadn't ever seen before.

Too much alcohol was beginning to show. "It's not my style to be dismissed. You should be careful who you toy with!" he said playfully, alongside a deep disappointment that could not be missed.

"We're both tired, Bill," she said soothing the angered and rejected male ego. "Let's get together another time."

The tightness in his face faded as he walked out of the office. "You're right, I need to go home. Ben's waiting."

His ego was bruised a little, but she had managed nicely to maneuver him home. She placed a polite kiss lightly on his cheek. "Thank you again for an enjoyable dinner." She believed the evening had been salvaged.

"Chris, I've never been with a woman like you. I know it looks risky, but I want to see you again, and not as friends."

They awkwardly exchanged good-byes.

Silence and calm returned to the confines of Welbourne Enterprises, relieving the tensions of a long evening. Bill had been stimulating company and the tension between them had been hot. Their conversation was always enjoyable, and he was extremely attractive, but her level head had helped her elude a precarious situation.

Now that he was gone, she could turn her attention to the explosive file that needed a forensic audit. Storm had been arrogantly careless, and the paper trail pointed straight to him like the needle on a compass. She was confident they were close to nailing Case Storm's hide to the wall. She prayed there wouldn't be too many innocent people affected if the institution came crumbling down. As she disrobed for the night, her thoughts about John Curry rebounded. He was a hardworking man with a family who lived on a modest salary. He and other individuals like him would be affected by the prosecution of Storm. A thousand dominoes in one long, tight row.

CHAPTER 18

Jeff Ashton arrived at Welbourne Enterprises, so bundled up that he looked like a ski lift operator. Eighteen inches of snow in twelve hours had brought business to a halt. The white blanket of snow suffocated downtown Denver, bringing an unexpected holiday to the city. The few cars parked curbside for the night were buried in deep drifts, waiting for the penetrating sun or a tow truck, whichever came first. It would be days, not hours, before operations got back to normal. There was some movement in the streets from four-wheel-drive vehicles sporting chains and snow tires, and a few snowplows trying to find repositories for the mountains of snow.

Jeff had been prepared. His downtown loft had a heated parking garage where he kept two cars: a convertible red Porsche for fun and a Land Cruiser for necessity. Chris filled him in on the situation with John Curry and Storm. It wouldn't be long before word leaked out to the financial community. Storm's response would be unpredictable. Where there was smoke, one could usually count on fire, and this was just the beginning.

"Where is Alex?" Jeff asked when the briefing was completed.

"With this much snow, she's probably walking from the hotel."

Within minutes Alex came through the door of Welbourne Enterprises, covered up to her knees in melting snow.

"We thought we'd lost you in a snowdrift," Jeff said.

"Almost. I was lucky to get here. None of the cabs are running, and they've closed the airport."

"That'll just add energy to the cries for a new airport . . . as if anyone can control Mother Nature," Chris commented. She looked like a model for Ralph Lauren with her crisp white shirt, razor-sharp-creased jeans, and Sorrel snow boots.

Jeff left the two women alone in Chris's office.

"So how did you find our friend Jake Winston?" Chris asked Alex.

"He's everything you described and more intense. It was as if he could look right through me."

"The same's been said about you, Alex."

"Well, I'm afraid I wasn't at my best." Alex thought of the rental car and the engineering plans in the works with Colton Forrester. She quickly dialed Colton, hoping there would be good news about the car.

"Forrester!" he answered on the third ring, slightly shocking Alex. Because of the weather she hadn't actually expected anyone to be at the office.

"Hello. This is Alex Sheridan."

"Hey, hotshot!"

"Thank you for the beautiful yellow roses!"

"Just what a Texas girl like you deserves."

She had been delighted the night before to find a dozen soft-yellow roses waiting in her room—they were the color of a West Texas sunrise. "How are you?"

"Buried up to my ass in snow, excuse my French," he said.

"You certainly predicted the storm."

"Are you going to give me a chance to win back some money at pool?"

"I can do that! But I am concerned about the rental company. I think they want their vehicle returned, and preferably not filled with snow."

"If you'll let me buy you a beer tonight and maybe even a steak, I'll show you where the car is."

"That sounds like extortion. Would you consider giving me a hint as to its whereabouts?"

"Only if you promise not to tell anyone who works here."

"Promise! Why?"

"They'll accuse me of being a softy."

"Worse things than that could happen."

"Listen, it's taken a lifetime to cultivate this tough-guy reputation."

"I won't tell."

"It's at your hotel," he said, obviously pleased with himself.

"How did you manage that?"

"Magic, darlin'. We engineers have to be able to pull rabbits out of hats once in a while."

"Can you work some of that magic on a well?"

"It's been done before. So will you have dinner with me?"

"I'm the one who needs to buy you dinner."

"I'll take care of that. Just don't let word get out that I'm a nice guy." His voice was strong and confident. "Is six-thirty too early?"

"I'll be ready. There are some new developments on the property I mentioned to you yesterday. There's some unbelievable activity about to take place in that area. We can talk tonight."

"I'll look forward to hearing about the new developments. See you tonight, baby."

Alex's heart felt light and fluttery, just as it had when she had been on the back of the motorcycle. She tried to quiet her emotions, but her head was filled with confusion. Being with Colton was like dancing on wings in the wind. Jake, on the other hand, was deep and soulful and profound. Parts of her were drawn to each of them, and for now, that would be manageable. Alex had learned to trust her instincts. It was clear to her that Jake Winston had a grudge against Forrester. Their paths had crossed once, apparently at an unpleasant juncture, and fate was throwing them together again, with Alex as a catalyst. Both were extraordinary men in unique ways: Colton with his emotions out front like the horns of a Texas steer, and Jake with his analytical mysterious sensitivity. Alex believed there was a purpose and a place in her life for each man.

CHAPTER 19

"**M**r. Deegan, you have a call on line one."

"Put it through."

"What did you pick up last night on Welbourne?" the caller asked.

"There was an interesting conversation between Welbourne and *the* Senator Bridgeforth. You should have told me there was a man like him involved in this," the private detective chastised his client. "That changes everything! Messing with a United States Senator can be dangerous."

"We didn't know about that, I assure you. Just tell me what was said and we'll make it worth your time. Remember, we're interested in her, not the senator."

"It's going to be another five grand for us to continue."

"You've already been paid too much!"

"Five grand! Or we pull the plug. Remember, it's my ass on the line if we get caught."

"I'll deliver the money when we pick up the tape."

Deegan had reason to be concerned about snooping on the high-powered senator, especially since he didn't have a clue about the nature of the inquiry. Most of his work involved trying to catch philandering husbands and wives, not financial espionage. This felt like poking a rattlesnake. He needed to take extra precautions. He'd put a tail on the courier today and find out just who was at the other end of the money. He sure as hell knew it was someone more substantial than that Harris Smith fellow.

The Bridgeforth house, in elegant Cherry Creek, was tastefully decorated, not ostentatious. Morgan Dulany had assisted with the design, creating a charming residence. The senator's study was surrounded in Burr walnut paneling with spacious shelves containing strategically placed memorabilia of power politics. There were several photographs of presidents shaking hands with Bridgeforth, an autograph neatly signed across each photo.

The study was used for confidential conferences, but Bridgeforth also retreated here when he couldn't face his own bedroom. He returned late after the dinner at Franco's, crept quietly into the house, and sought refuge on the office couch, thinking about how desperately he wanted a divorce.

In the half-empty king-sized bed a world away, Catherine Bridgeforth tossed and turned throughout the night. He hadn't come to their bed in months. She felt control slipping from her grasp.

Finally the sun arrived. In her elaborate bathroom, a haggard woman stared back from the looking glass. It was 6:00 A.M. Catherine dressed quickly, trying to avoid her reflection, then entered the kitchen to prepare coffee. Her temper slowly began to rise. No matter how hard she tried, she could not pretend he had not come home late from some sordid rendezvous. But she wasn't some unwanted campaign volunteer he could just discard! She dreaded getting into another horrible fight, which would jeopardize her standing even further. After the fight she would hate herself for her lack of self-control. Sometimes she wondered why she couldn't just leave him alone and accept her role. Women had lived desperate lives of convenience for years. For her, Valium and vodka had become a way of coping with life.

She knew there would be an unpleasant encounter over coffee. She could feel it coming. Then she would beg him for forgiveness and end up repeatedly apologizing for her outbursts.

As the sun rose over the eastern Colorado plain, the senator lay on the large twill sofa, his eyes on a favorite photo of himself shaking hands with the Speaker of the House. He was putting off the impending coffee encounter. His thoughts drifted back to the Storm debacle as the political wheels turned inside his mind. He would have to do everything in his power to distance himself from Storm. He knew what Chris said about Storm was true. If the senator was ever traced to one of the business deals, he would feign complete ignorance, blaming Storm for everything. He had been used and set up . . . he could rationalize and rewrite history with the best of them. And he really did believe Storm deserved the blame—he had been preposterously greedy, always trying to do bigger and bigger deals.

When the aroma of black coffee became irresistible, he ventured into the kitchen. "Did you sleep well?" he asked, determined to be cordial.

"Not really. I had some things on my mind and couldn't rest." Apparently the Valium wasn't working.

"I'm sorry I couldn't stop by last night before dinner, but the airport meeting dragged on and on. I think we had quite a storm last night."

"Well, you should know, you were out in it until two this morning. A terribly important meeting?" Her tone was sarcastic, and anger darted from her bloodshot-blue eyes.

"All my appointments these days are important," he snapped back, not wanting to engage in an argument.

"You used to take me with you once in a while. Now you don't even bother to call me personally to say you're not coming home." She had slipped into her uncontrollable nagging tone.

"I'm not going to fight with you, Catherine. I had a long day yesterday and have an even tougher one planned for today. If you don't like the role anymore, then we should make some changes. One thing is certain—I'm not going to keep coming home to your complaining. You knew what you were getting into from the very beginning. The job of a politician's wife is not easy—

unfortunately, you are making us both miserable. Just look at yourself!" he said painfully.

Her tear-streaked faced was pinched and drawn, a sad, pathetic countenance. Dark circles ringed her aching, sleepless eyes. Inside she was dying, one lie at a time, and fear and depression were spreading like a cancer. But she had paid for him with her youth and beauty and her family's money, and she had to keep him, no matter the cost to her now.

"We just need to be together, Bill," she pleaded. "Everything will be okay if we can spend a little more time together. I'll come to some of the business dinners the way we used to." She moved closer to him, reaching out, but he caught her arms in mid-reach, rejecting the gesture. Her touch had become abhorrent to him. "If I move to Washington, we'll be able to spend time alone again. And I can help you politically," she continued futilely.

Now she was groveling. This was an old song he didn't want to hear. He couldn't even imagine them together in Washington.

"We have options, Catherine, but that's not one of them." His voice was crisp and clear. Since becoming a member of the United States Senate, he had maintained a separate life, keeping a small apartment in Washington. The separateness was his solace and his sanity. It helped him forget how much he sometimes hated himself for the decision he had made. His greed had seduced him into marrying Catherine. Her money had been an aphrodisiac, had blinded him to the signs that should have told him not to get involved with her family. He had grown to hate her a little bit more each day he was sucked deeper into the quicksand of her family's control. "I have to get back down to the office. We need to talk seriously, but it will have to be later." He hoped he was setting the tone for a frank discussion of divorce. Walking out of the kitchen, he said, "I'm sorry we couldn't make it work."

"What do you mean?" she wailed, running after him. She pulled at the lapels of his rumpled slept-in suit coat with shaky hands. "Of course we're making it. Look at us. You are a United

States Senator, and we have a chance at the White House. We just have to stick together." She tugged at his arm childishly, and he pulled away. "You can't just leave—my family made you everything you are!" Catherine switched to her attack mode.

"Let's not make this any uglier than it has to be," Bill said tersely. A fire smoldered inside every time she reminded him of how much he owed her family. He was indebted with his soul and she never let him forget it. He headed silently for the shower, wondering how miserable she was going to make the separation. He needed to get to the office and call Chris. She was all he could think of for the moment. He had to see her and explain his slightly inebriated aggressive behavior of the evening before. He had been angry and frustrated with her rejection, but her strength enchanted him, and just the thought of her aroused him. With her on his team, a run at the White House might be within reach. Chris's money, power, and influence would be the perfect combination to catapult him to the next level. He was determined to have her.

But first he had to get rid of some complications. After all, Chris didn't need *his* power or position. He was even more attracted than he had been before and equally more determined to conquer her. If she would just listen to his dreams.

CHAPTER 20

Saturday, One Week Later

$\mathbf{A}$lex stood staring out the office window at the latest in a series of persistent winter storms that were crippling the city and the front range. At her desk, Chris was poring over financial data on the Custer ranch acquisition. Intimate comrades, the women thrived on the excitement of business prospects and the thrill of the chase in their personal lives. The phones were dormant, as most businesses were closed due to the snow, so they brainstormed and dreamed about the future of the company and caught up on each other's lives.

Jeff Ashton had long gone, and the two women were deep in geological charts and financial projections for Aspen Development Partners, working on long-range planning for the company. The quiet was shattered by a call on Chris's personal line.

"I just knew you would be at the office!" The senator's voice was warm and seductive.

"Alex and I were just trying to get caught up."

"Are you always so dedicated, Chris?" he asked in a beguiling tone.

"It depends on the circumstances, Senator."

"Chris, I have something very serious and personal to discuss with you. Will you please see me tonight?" He was taking a risk and laying his heart and future at her feet, but there was only awkward silence on the line. "Chris, it's very important to me, to us."

Chris knew better. No real good could come of further involvement with the senator. But she was curious about what he had to say.

"I promise to leave whenever you give the word," he cajoled.

"Where do you want to meet?"

"Can I come to your office early in the evening, say about six?" His voice was deep and anxious.

It was better than being in public, and it would be on her own turf. For another moment silence hung between the two negotiators. "All right . . . I suppose."

"Thank you, Chris. I promise, it will be okay." He felt her anxiety and longed to ease her concerns.

"See you at six." Chris hung up and turned to Alex, her face flushed. "He wants to come here this evening and see me. It sounds serious." Chris's cheeks glowed with open anticipation. Fear was mingling with excitement over the rendezvous.

"What could be so urgent?" Alex inquired. A knot made a bed in the pit of Alex's stomach. Something wasn't right . . .

"It could be anything. Maybe his wife heard that we had dinner last week."

"Word travels fast!"

"Especially when you're a high-profile politician with the potential to be president. I saw several familiar faces at the restaurant the last time we were out, which means it's probably been broadcast all over town. He'll be lucky if it doesn't make CNN."

"I'll be sure to tune in."

"Bill took me there for a reason. Perhaps he wanted us to be seen together. Maybe he wants an incident."

"You're dancing on the edge of the table, dear," said Alex.

"I know, but I can keep it under control."

"Would you ever consider a relationship, something permanent?" They had covered the subject of matrimony before.

"Well, he's already married! So this conversation makes no sense. I don't know what to think, Alex. You know the word permanent has always made me cringe." They both laughed. "There are a million possible scenarios to his future, and I'm not one for being in the passenger seat."

"But he's got your attention in a big way," Alex said, knowing Chris like her own soul.

"If something were to develop naturally without scandal and complications, it could be the ride of a lifetime. But there's no way that could happen. Tonight is just business, I'm sure . . . "

Alex listened intently, studying the uncertainty in her partner's piercing green eyes. Business was far easier than issues of the heart.

"I'll listen to what he has to say," said Chris. "Our last encounter wasn't exactly ideal." Then she changed the subject. "What are your plans for the evening?"

"Colton Forrester asked me to grab an early bite to eat," Alex said, still sensing something was amiss about Chris's evening plans.

"Not that anyone's counting, but doesn't that make three nights this week?"

"It beats room service. Besides, he's very interested in our company," Alex countered.

"Right! Not to mention he's not hard to look at either."

"Whatever it takes to get the job done right. That's my motto." They both laughed.

"He helped me rework a well several years ago that was giving us trouble," Chris said, "the same well where I met Jeff Ashton."

"Yes, he mentioned it was a real challenge." Alex said in a more serious tone.

"He saved the project! And I'm not the only one who thinks he's the best in the industry. You ask anyone in Colorado. He's made more wells and more money than any other outfit in the area."

"That's quite an endorsement."

"He is probably blown away by you, Alex."

"From what little exposure I have had to the man, I would bet that little if anything blows him away. But I can't say he didn't throw *me* a fastball."

"How so?" Light danced in Chris's eyes as she tried to read Alex.

"I don't know . . . he just blindsided me like a rogue bronco. Like one that can't be broken. The one you always want to try to ride again." She decided to change the subject. "Did I tell you how odd Jake Winston behaved yesterday?"

"No, what happened?"

"We had lunch. We've gotten to be pretty good friends. I feel really comfortable with him. I can talk about things I rarely ever share. But he can go from being very tender and communicative to as cold as an iceberg—as if someone turned off a light switch. I know you told me he has a cold place in this heart, but the man was almost rude!"

"He has a tendency to run from what he loves," said Chris. "I'm sure he's more attracted than you realize. When he starts feeling vulnerable, he turns his back on his feelings."

"He brought me back to the hotel with hardly a good-bye."

"He probably found your openness very threatening. He asked for it, and you gave him what he wanted. Then he shut down. It could take a week for him to recover," Chris said with a smile. "It's the intimacy that throws him."

"I think we can become great friends. But since we're on the subject of being blown away . . . it's Forrester who haunts me. When I got home last night, I found another beautiful flower arrangement waiting for me with this note." Alex handed a small card in a plain envelope to Chris, gesturing for her to read what was inside.

Chris took the card and read the penned words.

I'm falling in love . . .
Forrester

"*Very Hot!*" Chris dropped the note as if it had scorched her. "*Now* what are you going to do?"

"I don't know . . . he's such a chameleon, rugged at one moment and then gentle like a teddy bear."

"I've never seen you so distracted! Do I detect a serious heartthrob here in this office too?"

"I've never responded to a man quite the way I have to Colt. It's as if there's some force pushing us together, something beyond reason or mere attraction, something more powerful." Alex believed in the mysteries of fate, and she felt it was as if a mystical daimon had taken hold of their lives and they were being guided into a future not of their own making. "He can get away with things I normally hate, like calling me 'baby.' I even like the way it sounds. I must be losing my edge!"

"I'll say! Get a grip and take a cold shower." Their laughter was genuine and fun.

"It must be the snow that's getting to me!" Alex said. "Will we ever get a break from these storms?"

"Don't fall too fast, dear! We have oil wells calling and land deals to make. We don't want some brokenhearted, love-torn man with shaky hands sinking our casing in the wrong hole. Besides, I don't think I can handle the phone calls from *two* aching hearts in my old age."

"Give me a break, Chris!" Alex scoffed.

"Look, I've already got Jake Winston calling and panting about you. I can just see it now—a duel for your honor. I'll be left with the bloodbath to clean up."

Thanks to the paralyzing snowstorm, they were both enjoying the pressure-free day.

"What time is The Senator coming?" Alex asked in a pompous tone.

"Early."

"Do you want me to hang around and work late?" she asked playfully.

"Maybe not this time." Chris stared into the distance. "I rarely vacillate the way I have with this man. I know better than to get involved, but he is so incredibly attractive . . . and he really has done a lot of public good. In spite of his reputation, I believe he is an extraordinary individual."

"Doesn't he put his pants on like every other man?"

"I can't tell you that quite yet!"

They broke into peals of laughter.

"Let me know when you find out," Alex shot back.

"I should have said I would see him somewhere else, but he asked to come here. I swear, if it had been anyone else I would have said no. But the call caught me off guard. It's pretty flattering to have him panting around like a schoolboy. This is one of those times I'd like to kick myself . . . but I'm sure everything will be okay."

"Just remember what you've preached to me, my wise, dear friend, they all want only one thing, it's just the package they want it wrapped in that's different."

Chris ignored Alex's teasing. "The thing I worry about is having him show up here and end up being photographed by some fool who works for a tabloid. My ultimate nightmare would be seeing my face splashed across some supermarket rag. I can see the headlines now—DENVER BUSINESSWOMAN TURNS HOME-WRECKER WITH U.S. SENATOR."

"Call him back and suggest a neutral location," Alex suggested more seriously.

"No, it's too late."

"Please be careful." Alex didn't know why she continued to feel uneasy about the situation. She shrugged off her apprehension. Chris was a big girl, and she could take care of herself. Besides, Colt was waiting. "Hey, it's getting late. I'd better head back to the hotel."

"Give Mr. Forrester my best and watch where you fling those arrows."

"I know, I know! Call if you need me."

The phone rang three times before Catherine Bridgeforth, in a Valium-induced stupor, answered it. Morgan Dulany was on her way for their afternoon appointment. This month's project was redecorating the dining room. Catherine Bridgeforth liked to keep Morgan busy.

"Are you all right, Catherine?" Morgan asked, noting the slur in her client's voice.

"Yes, I'm just a little tired. I tossed and turned all night." For days she had been stewing over her husband's words.

"I'm just around the corner, stuck in traffic in Cherry Creek."

Morgan knew why Catherine was tired. She was tired of having her husband openly philandering with beautiful women. And the combination of pills and wine was taking its ugly toll. The decorator had been appalled by the bravado the senator had shown the week before when he walked into Franco's with Chris Welbourne. It might have been business, except they had lingered at the restaurant in an enclave until after midnight. Dessert was being served as Morgan and her husband departed for home. During the week, she had picked up the telephone a dozen times to call Catherine. It had always been her policy to keep her mouth shut, as she worked in close circles. But this was different. She and Catherine were close personal friends. Someone needed to alert her to what was going on. She rang the doorbell apprehensively.

"Hello, Morgan. I'm so glad you're here." Desperation hung in the air.

"It will be fun to redecorate the dining room." Morgan tried to be light. Inside she was furious at what Bill was doing to this once-lovely woman.

"Would you like a glass of wine?"

They walked into the kitchen where a chilled bottle of Chardonnay waited. The decorator was still hesitant to mention the senator's evening. "Not yet." Morgan looked at her watch, thinking it was a bit early to drink wine, then asked, "How's Bill?"

"Things are very strained right now," Catherine confided.

"I happened to see him the other night at Franco's where my husband and I were having dinner." She waited for what seemed like a long time for Catherine's response.

"He's out a lot these days. Did you see who accompanied him?" Catherine knew before she asked that the answer was not going to be good news.

"I think he was with Chris Welbourne. They must work together. I did her office some time ago, and she's very involved in politics." She was offering a smoke screen for Bill's abominable behavior.

"Yes, I believe they sit on several boards together." Catherine's heart sank, and her face flushed as suspicion turned into fear. She believed she could not compete with Chris Welbourne.

Two glasses of wine helped bolster her confidence. Chris Welbourne had to be the reason Bill was hinting at divorce. She forced herself to continue the meeting with Dulany, further avoiding the subject of her husband. It was a sickening carcass in the road they both managed to drive around.

The snow day had turned into a bitterly cold evening with stars working to dominate a cobalt-blue sky. Hiding behind the white-topped mountain peaks were the remnants of the winter sunset. Alex hiked several blocks through the snow-piled sidewalks to The Brown, anticipating the evening ahead. Colton Forrester had gripped her senses.

The cold rapidly pushed her into the familiar confines of the hotel where Lafayette was a welcome sight. His hulk of a frame and perpetual white smile made Alex feel safe and warm.

She scampered in and went up to her room.

A long, hot shower, a dose of CNN, and a light scotch with chilled water renewed Alex's energy. She padded around in satin underwear, enjoying her solitude. It was a relief to relax quietly in her own room after the long week, which had been more intense than she had realized. Tonight would be more of the same— talk of oil wells and engineering reports one minute, holding hands and flirting the next. She couldn't seem to contain the excitement he dished up like ice cream. She wasn't sure whether she was more enthralled by the immense business possibilities that lay before her or the personal feelings stimulated by Forrester. They had been out to several well sites during the past week, and the line between business and pleasure was becoming blurred.

She looked around the room, wondering when and where home would ever be, then shook off the melancholy digression. Home was the business and her friends. Home was a state of mind, not a place. Home was where one feels safe. And if all that was true, then home for Alex was the office.

The phone rang. "Hello, Jake. I just got back to the hotel. Thank you for a nice lunch yesterday."

"Any time, Alex, but I feel I should apologize for being so abrupt. Something came over me. It's really impossible to explain." Jake Winston wanted to kick himself for the way he had recoiled from Alex. During the brief time he'd known her, he had felt himself coming unraveled. She was too alluring.

"That's okay. You know I always enjoy being with you."

"Will you give me another chance?"

"Sure."

"There's a dinner at Seldon Custer's ranch next week. Can you join us?"

"I would enjoy meeting her and seeing one of Colorado's old ranches. Thank you for the invitation."

"Oh, by the way, I've been asking around about your potential buyer, Harris Smith. Apparently he called Seldon, too, but didn't get anywhere. She didn't give him the time of day."

"What did he want?"

"He was interested in buying a parcel of land adjacent to the ranch."

"That would be in the same vicinity as our three hundred acres?"

"Very close."

"Thanks for making the inquiry. What do you think that's all about?"

"Probably nothing. Just another vulture trying to get in on a deal."

"I'll look forward to the dinner next week," she said, wanting to end the conversation and prepare for her evening with Colton.

Alex thought about Chris and the senator and a wave of apprehension rippled through her. Chris was capable of taking care of herself, but getting too close to the married senator would not be in her best interests.

The television news anchorperson diverted Alex and she turned her attention to the local highlights. "More rumors continue to leak out about the proposed Denver International Airport site. Our Channel Nine reporter is at the mayor's office for a firsthand update."

The scene changed to a reporter bundled in heavy clothing. "Another rumor has developed around the controversial airport site. Our sources now believe the airport will be located in the North Side of Denver, where many prominent real estate developers and investors own most of the property. A citizens' watch group is accusing the city leaders of selling out to wealthy, influential power brokers." A group of protesters were marching behind the reporter, waving signs in the frosty air. "Now let's look at tonight's weather."

Colt Forrester would give her grief about the fur coat, but she found their bantering engaging. Alex searched through her limited selection of clothes again: black leggings, black turtleneck, boots, large western belt. She would have preferred a more extensive selection, but living out of a suitcase had its limitations. Time and attention was redirected to her makeup and hair. She tried on a seductive black hat and played with her image in the mirror, tilting the hat forward, then back, then down over her eyes like a gangster. Not quite the look she wanted, so it was discarded. For the first time in years, she was plagued with indecision—most of the time dressing took only moments. Then she caught her own gaze in the mirror and couldn't avoid the truth. She saw a woman in love. Then like a shrill school bell the phone rang again, catapulting Alex from the edge of the bed.

"Hello, are you ready?" Colt asked from the house phone located in the lobby.

"I'm on my way down." Alex nearly ran to the elevator. She felt more alive than ever before. All of her dreams seemed to be within reach—home-run business deals, romance, no fences, no boundaries . . . unlimited opportunity. All things were possible!

As she emerged from the turn-of-the-century elevator, the expression on Colt's face was telling: eyes twinkling, eyebrows raised, and a large wide grin of pleasure mixed with surprise. They stared at each other for a moment and he mouthed a silent *wow!*

"Are you sure you're here to meet *me?*" he glanced around. "You look stunning."

He was genuinely in awe of this brilliant woman who stood before him, so different from the buttoned-up businesswoman she appeared to be most of the time. She continued to surprise and seduce him. Her knowledge of the oil business, shared during their tour of various well sites, was formidable. And tonight she was enchanting—dressed head to toe in black, and wearing a large silver squash-blossom necklace and matching earrings that she had purchased from a small boutique in Santa Fe. Her form-fitting turtleneck grabbed every curve.

"I was going to take you to one of my favorite dives to hear some blues, but you look too fabulous for that funky place." His eyes surveyed her from the hair to the boots and he shook his head. "Texas is looking better by the minute."

"Let's go where you had planned," she protested. "I've been looking forward to a casual, fun evening."

"No, you've inspired me. There's a very special French restaurant, one of Denver's finest. It's in LoDo. Franco's will be more your style."

She wondered what he thought about her style. Alex was the product of an eclectic upbringing, and at times her multifaceted goals and desires pulled like teams of mules in a tug-of-war. "Only if you promise we can shoot pool and listen to music afterward."

Alex had been to Franco's with Chris and was slightly surprised by the selection. She hadn't predicted Forrester as a formal French restaurant sort of guy. Maybe he had more dimensions than she had thought.

CHAPTER 21

The senator was seen exiting the elevator on the twenty-third floor of the Rocky Mountain Savings building and then entering the suite of Welbourne Enterprises. His watcher was huddled in a utility closet, listening to Frank Sinatra croon his most popular tunes through the headset of a Sony Walkman. This job required patience and stillness.

Looking like a radiant cut diamond with her shining upswept hair and slim champagne-colored suit, Chris ushered Bill Bridgeforth into her office for their cocktail rendezvous.

"Thank you for allowing me to come here, Chris. I have so much to tell you . . . there's a lot going on."

He had called persistently since their last dinner, but Chris had been elusive until today. He discarded his politician's blue suit jacket, loosened his white shirtsleeves, and rolled them to just below his elbows. He stood tall and lean before her. Chris thought she could see genuine pain in his expressive eyes surrounded by edges creased with paper-thin crow's feet. This time there was no hint of a show, just painful sincerity.

"Can we just stay here and relax awhile? It's bitter cold outside." He stared off at nothing in particular.

"I don't want to go out either."

"How about some Chinese food?"

"Great idea."

"I'll beep Ben."

Then he brought up the subject of Case Storm. "Chris, I've thought about your comments regarding Case. I believe you should trust your instincts." His eyes bored right through Chris. A light went on inside Chris' mind. Now she knew what was so urgent.

"I didn't want to hear what you were saying last week because, in truth, I have probably fallen prey to his manipulations. He used me when I was just beginning my career, and that is hard to admit."

In the low light between them, she believed every word. "You are a man of conviction," she said.

Chris's apprehension eased. She felt safe and confident on her own turf. Perhaps she could even let down her guard a little. They sipped Glenfiddich, held hands and talked politics. After a while their conversation trailed off and Bridgeforth gave her a long look that emanated from his soul.

"Chris, I am totally captivated by you. I can't keep my feelings where they are now, locked in a box. I want more," he said, squeezing her hand sensually, serious and sincere.

Her heart began to flutter, but she wasn't sure how much was from excitement and how much from apprehension. "I am flattered," she sighed.

"I want you in my life," he said.

Chris's eyes narrowed skeptically.

Instinctively reading her thoughts, he added, "I can't and wouldn't ask you to be my mistress. You deserve much more than that . . ."

"Thank you for the compliment, but . . . "

"Please let me continue," he interrupted her. "The reason I asked you to meet me tonight is to tell you I'm asking Catherine for a divorce. It will be ugly, but that's my problem."

"I'm sorry for you both." Rarely was she speechless, but in this case, she didn't know what to say. *Congratulations?* Or *I'm so sorry* or *Why are you telling me?* "Divorce is never peaceful." It was a weak response, but the best she could conjure up at the moment.

"I want you, Chris! I want us to marry." He squeezed her hand with determination. "I want to be with you."

Chris was shocked by the declaration. This was far from

what she expected. She stood up slowly and walked to the bar for more ice as she attempted to gather her confusion into some kind of order. She was gifted with a quick mind and a sharp tongue, but this time she thought, *Take your time and listen for once. Take two breaths and think before you talk.* The ice machine rattled as another load crunched into the bin. Bill Bridgeforth was waiting for a response.

"Are you sure that's what you want?" she asked.

"I'm falling in love with you, Chris."

"No, I mean the divorce. It could be very costly."

"What I want is to be with you!" he said. "I want you desperately." He stood and moved closer to the bar where Chris was buying time, thoughts churning from his revelation.

"I'm not used to being with anyone . . . we barely know each other," she said. "Make this decision for yourself, completely independent of me."

"Of course. It's time for me to make this choice . . . but I can't deny you are a strong influence."

"Bill, this is your life, not mine. If you want a divorce, do it! But do it for yourself. When it's over, we can play and have fun as long as it lasts. But I will make no promises. For God's sake, Bill, don't leave your marriage for me!"

Her words were pragmatic, but her emotions were explosive. She'd tried for too long to shut off her intense attraction to Bridgeforth. She saw pain in his eyes and wanted to reach out to him . . . but she certainly didn't want the weight of his marriage on her shoulders.

"We can make our relationship work, Chris."

"Think about what will happen to your life, Bill. To your career. Change your mind about a divorce and we can still be friends."

But the energy couldn't be contained. A storm was raging, driving them together. They were caught in a tidal wave, swept out of control.

Chris was the most alluring woman he'd ever met, including the influential women in Washington. She operated and reacted like a man although she had the sex appeal and charm of a seductress. Strong convictions ruled her and feelings rarely distorted her perspective. But at this precipitous moment she was faltering. The senator approached her deliberately and placed a sensual kiss on her mouth. She melted into a pool of emotions at his touch, passionately returning his embrace.

His disclosure and expression of caring had bridged the distance between them. She knew it was dangerous to get more involved with the dazzling senator, but at the moment she was unable to turn away. He was irresistibly seductive.

Chinese food arrived, wine flowed, and all business was forgotten in a maelstrom of emotions. For the moment the world could wait. The sunset had long disappeared behind the Rockies. Candles were lit, music played, and they danced slowly as an excuse to touch.

"Come with me to Washington, Chris. You and I can make anything happen. There are people who want me to consider the presidency, but I would not even think of it with Catherine. She just doesn't have what it takes. She doesn't understand the system. I've given her most of my life and I can't give anymore. If a divorce hurts my career, that's the way it will have to be. But I don't think it will. The public has a short memory. It will make headlines, then it will be forgotten."

"Just make sure whatever action you take, is your own. You don't want events and outside influences to control your plans. Think long and hard, then decide on a course."

"Chris, I've already made up my mind. Now it's just a matter of execution. I don't want you to be affected by the fallout, but it would be nice to know that you will be with me when it's all over."

"I'll support whatever decision you make ... but I can't make any long-term promises."

"Of course not, and you shouldn't be dragged into the mess. I love you too much to let that happen. This will be our night together. I won't ask you to see me again until the divorce is over."

"Let's not make any promises, Bill."

"I love you, Chris. I want you."

Chris was accustomed to long-range plans, not unexpected dreams. Bill Bridgeforth with his declaration was blowing her well-charted life right out of the water. They moved to the couch and kissed passionately while the music played into the night. She opened his shirt, running long manicured nails through matted black hair, longing to feel skin on skin. How long it had been since she'd let herself indulge in such intoxicating feelings. A CD of seductive romantic background music played as they moved to the Murphy bed. She extinguished the office lights and only the twinkling of the stars penetrated the room.

They discarded their clothes in random piles around the bed. The crisp sheets warmed quickly as they romped untethered by inexperience, driven by desire. They slowed the pace to explore the pleasure of never-before-touched skin. Chris felt him hard against her and drew a deep breath of anticipation. Bill Bridgeforth stroked her full breasts until his yearning became explosive, then gently pulled into her. Holding tightly to a handful of hair, he nuzzled her neck, devouring the sweet gentle smell of just-damp female skin. They rocked unconsciously to the motion of the music —touching, kissing, caressing—engulfing each other in passion. He was a passionate lover made of steel and fire. Finally he climbed out of their sweltering, mangled nest of sheets. One long slim bronze leg lay on the top sheet like artwork in the night shadows.

"More than anything in the world I want to stay," he said. "I detest having to leave, but I'm going to have to call Ben in a few minutes."

Chris pulled the sheets up around her face, watching the powerful, naked man standing in the ghostlike shadows of her office. "Yes, it's very late."

"Life is going to change now, Chris . . . "

"Let's not say any more," she interrupted. "I'm grateful that we had tonight. That's enough!"

For him it wasn't enough, and he would go home and tell Catherine he wanted a divorce. Chris directed him to the marble shower, then wrapped herself in a gold silk robe. The frozen night penetrated the huge glass windows, bringing an early-morning chill to the room. She decided to check on Bill, and a quick rinse turned into a passionate back-washing. Smooth, hot, clean skin mixed with feverish passion, and they again found themselves wet and entangled in the moonlight. Cradling her back, he pulled the exquisitely carved face to within a whisper's distance, then reconfirmed his desire. Love, want, and passion overlapped in a moment of total ecstasy. He was determined to have her.

Chris would believe the divorce when she saw it. They had had their tryst, which would clear the sexual tension and allow them to return to their respective realities—hers more appealing than his, she reflected as Bill collected his slightly rumpled belongings. It had been a spectacular evening, but reality screamed back with the approaching sunrise. She would welcome solitude to reflect on the past hours. Bill had talked about far-off fantasies commingling love, lust, and accomplishment—taking her to Washington, a bid for the presidency! Too much too fast, she thought. But it had been impossible to reign in his euphoria. The odds were, in her estimation, the divorce would become too destructive and Bill would eventually retreat from his decision. The line of least resistance was the politically correct way, and Bill Bridgeforth was the consummate politician.

He was stunning and vital in his Brooks Brothers blue suit and with still-wet dark-gray hair. Inside he was dying. As he prepared to leave, he cupped Chris's face in his large hands. She smelled her own soap on his palms. "I love you!" he said in a strong whisper. She started to protest, to explain why this was insanity. He placed a finger gently against her lips and kissed the top of her forehead. "Shhh . . . I love you." His mind was racing with the possibilities of an exciting future, one that would be enhanced, even made possible, by a woman like Chris.

They kissed goodnight, then he closed the door to the office and disappeared like a forgotten dream.

Chris hoped their relationship would escape scrutiny. As far as she knew there was nothing compromising about their public lives to this point. Their dinner at Franco's had been above reproach. To her knowledge, no one had seen them come and go from the office except during appropriate business hours. She prayed he would go unseen that night.

Physically exhausted and emotionally drained, she sank into her favorite burgundy leather armchair in front of the expansive windows. She was reflecting on both Storm and Bill Bridgeforth as she sipped the delicious remnants of her single malt whiskey. Storm would be furious when she made public her allegations. She was prepared for his political and personal attacks, and she was prepared to go the course to prove his guilt. She was glad that Bill had come around to her point of view on the subject of Case Storm, even if his new stance was a puzzling about-face.

After studying John Curry's file in detail, she decided to blow the whistle on Storm as a matter of principle. She had composed a letter and placed it on her desk to send to David Hazelhoff at the Federal Home Loan Bank Board. She would mail it overnight after she had a chance to call Storm and tell him what she was doing.

Storm was jeopardizing the security of every investor and depositor of the institution, she thought as her eyelids grew heavy. Many of those people had trusted Chris as a board member before their S&L was swallowed by Storm in one of his acquisitions. He was tougher than appearances would indicate, but so was she. She had tried to part amicably when she resigned from his board, but he had made friendship impossible. Now she was going to throw the first punch, and it wasn't going to be a stab in the back, even if it would be delightful to see him squirm. She was grateful the snow had closed the savings and loan, and it could all wait until Monday.

In the secure darkness of her office, she drifted into a deep and dreamless sleep.

⁓

Deegan was working the Welbourne case personally because of the subjects involved. He sat in a comfortable chair at his agency, listening to the sounds from Chris Welbourne's office. The transmitter picked up ninety-five percent of the conversation, most of which sounded rather uninteresting though steamy. There was no specific business information Deegan would be able to pass on to his client, but it was erotic listening in on the romantic liaison. There was no question what was going on between the two subjects. When the senator left, Deegan lost interest. The highly-sophisticated hidden recording device continued to record everything.

CHAPTER 22

Franco's was a perfect dinner location, a place that would give Alex and Colton opportunity to converse. She learned more about his Iowa roots and his farmboy-turned-oilman life. Their evening was humorous and light, supported by a cosmic attraction. From the moment they left the hotel, Alex felt magnetically drawn to the ease and confidence of her companion. He was a self-made, fiercely independent man with an electric personality. Their previous dinner conversations had covered politics, oil wells, and sports, but the atmosphere at Franco's drew them into more intimate subjects. They talked as if they had been friends for a lifetime.

"Do you think about a family?" she inquired.

"No, I tried marriage for a short time ages ago, but it didn't work. Too many changes were required and there was too much dependence. My wife was very, how do you say it?" He searched for the right word. "High-maintenance. I had to take care of everything. If it wasn't to her liking, then trouble started. It was best that I left. She could do things her way and I could do them mine."

"You didn't have any children?" Alex hoped she wasn't appearing too curious.

"No. Sometimes what you think will bring happiness is what society and culture dictate. But I found myself waking up with a perfectly nice person who was the last woman on earth I should have been with. It was my own doing, I know. I was briefly seduced by the glamour of Denver society . . . but when you take off your clothes, all that is left are the values, character, and passion of a person. In our case, our dreams didn't line up."

"That's too bad," Alex said.

"Not really—otherwise, I wouldn't be sitting here with you thinking these beautifully obscene thoughts."

Alex shook her head, struck by the realization that this man could get away with saying things that made her cringe when she heard them spoken by other men. Colt just made her laugh when he said these things.

Over coffee, Alex told him more about Texas and how she learned the oil business. "I guess I'm a raving vagabond when you get right down to it. But I come by it naturally because of the way my family lived."

Franco stopped by the table, offering Alex the opportunity to converse in French, an ability that was one of the fringe benefits of her education abroad. Then she said something in Italian that they both laughed about. The down-to-earth engineer was surprised by her ease with foreign languages.

"Do you miss your international life?"

"No, and you know, I can always go back to that. But I did truly relish living in France, especially the Mediterranean village of Cannes, which still feels like home . . . walking the Croisette and drinking Pernod in the Festival Bar. And of course, just being around the excitement of the film festival."

A mere stone's throw from the charming Italian Riviera towns and the infamous village country of Monte Carlo, Alex had learned to play keno at the famous casino where the guests sported black-tie and dinner jackets. On special occasions she would venture up to the ancient town of Eze to meander its narrow, medieval streets and dine at the world-renowned Côte d'Or restaurant. Each story offered Forrester another facet of his fascinating dinner partner's life.

"And now you live out of a suitcase in a hotel in Denver, Colorado, drilling oil wells with roughnecks like me?" he inquired, genuinely perplexed.

"I'm committed to this business and Colorado. It's quite different in some ways from Dallas."

"I've only been to Dallas once. Didn't really take to it."

"It's a fabulous city if you like beautiful new buildings and great nightlife."

"Maybe you could convince me," he said with a flirtatious smile.

"First-class private inside tour." Her dark eyes flashed seductively. "We could see the Cowboys play at Texas Stadium. If you want to see some real Texas ranches and oil wells, we can do that, too."

"It would be fun seeing it with you. How long do you plan on staying in Colorado?"

"I don't know. For a while, or until I'm drawn somewhere else."

Sometime during the dinner he had taken her hand, and he had yet to release his tender hold. They talked of their dreams and their desires to visit unexplored parts of the world. She told Colton more about meeting Chris and their close friendship. "She's an incredible woman. Not many people know the personal side of Chris. She is passionate about her privacy, yet so generous to her friends and the community. No one really knows how much money and time she has given to this city."

"I am aware that she has done well financially, but not to what degree," Colt remarked. "She was involved in several oil wells I drilled that luckily turned out to be big producers. If she's done as well with her other investments as she did with those, then she's got the golden touch."

"She's been an incredible friend to me. When we met in Dallas at the Petroleum Club some years back, we instantly connected at a spiritual level, as if we had known each other for fifty years. I had no idea how successful she really was. One thing led to another, and she suggested we think about doing a joint venture and that I come to Colorado and see her operation. The next thing I knew, we were at Dallas Love Field boarding her Lear Jet to head to Denver—and she was flying the plane. Of course she had her copilot along. Chris is very much a mentor to me. We have a lot in common. She lost her parents in a plane crash, so that is a bond we have."

Alex shared one of her dreams with Colt, her desire to one day fly with Chris, not as a passenger but as copilot. Then Colton probed a bit more into her personal life.

"What about a family? Most women eventually want children."

"I have some mountains to climb first. Besides, I still haven't met the right guy. I'm one of those pie-in-the-sky dreamers who believes in finding a soul mate."

"That may be tougher than striking oil," he said, smiling.

"Well, I'm willing to go for a gusher."

"I hope you find him somewhere. I understand it is a dodgy business—finding the right partner. I think it must happen by chance," he said. Colt's piercing blue eyes reflected the dancing lights of the restaurant as he gazed openly at Alex. A passion for life was smoldering just below his calm surface. She sensed he was made of something raw and hand-hewn, like a massive red-wood beam.

"Maybe souls just collide in a giant explosion?" she said with a smile.

"I like that theory, kind of a personal big bang. Maybe we can explore that idea over some good music?" he asked as the waiter placed the check on the table. Colt sandwiched two crisp hundred-dollar bills discreetly in the leather binder. He motioned for the server to keep the change.

"How about that rematch on the pool game?" Alex asked.

"I know just the place."

He helped Alex with her coat, took her small hand, and led her to the car, keys dangling in his left hand. The locked door stared back in the black silence. He turned to face Alex. In the frigid stillness he could feel his heart pounding through his chest. He moved closer, placing the keys back in his coat pocket. Raising both arms to her shoulders, he stepped inside the circle closer to her heart. Leaning against the driver door, he pulled her to him, beginning a slow smoldering kiss that penetrated to the marrow. He did not smother or trespass. It was an invitation into something eternally private, something raw and elusive. They hung in the balance between then and now, until he finally released his hold. Steamy apparitions escaped from their mouths into the cold night air. When they were safe in the truck, he leaned over and kissed her again, this time even more sensually exploring her mouth. Lips found skin soft like a pony's nose. It felt beyond control.

When they came up for air he said, "I'm glad we finally got that over with. I knew it would be wonderful." They laughed in unison. "Damn waste waiting all this time to have something that good!" The heat flushed her forehead and ran to the base of her stomach where confusion landed with a thud. Then the engine roared to life, throwing out a smokestack of steaming exhaust.

They pulled out of the parking lot into Larimer Square. Late night had chased away most people, leaving empty streets save for the wretched homeless who huddled under bridges and in shadowed alley doorways. Colt led her down the block to a hole-in-the-wall where they had a drink and played pool with light jazz filling in the background. Bonnie Raitt crooned a soulful number that ravaged the heart. Just down the street was the old Ice House building, a landmark that would eventually be converted into avant-garde commercial space. The business leaders of Denver were slowly revitalizing LoDo, and residential lofts in converted warehouses were the craze. Numerous old buildings were being salvaged and would eventually be converted for modern use, bringing excitement and vitality to the mining town-turned-business Mecca.

The pool game just added to Alex's and Colt's anticipation. It was a delay tactic for the inevitable. Alex stretched across the bald green felt table for a long shot, waist bent at the edge of the table, slightly on one toe. Colt approached from the rear, placing massive farmboy hands around her tiny waist.

"I'd like to take you home and do something more than play pool." He put one hand on her firm bottom and took the cue-stick with the other. Then he expertly sank the eight ball. "Let's go home and listen to some music at my place. The atmosphere there is much better." Holding both her hands, he looked down into bottomless misty eyes. They wordlessly walked out of the Oxford Hotel into a polar express of frigid wind that rounded the corner and threatened to carry them away. The car ferried them several blocks west, then turned into the rear of a large red-brick building and into a reserved parking place.

"You like living downtown?"

"It's a fine way to live for someone like me." He fumbled with his keys. "The security is quite adequate, and if I decide to leave spontaneously, all I have to do is lock the door and bolt."

"A rolling stone gathers no moss?"

"I try to stay free and flexible."

A tiny arrow zinged through a soft unarmored spot in her heart. Why did she care at all about his life with no harness, no weight to hold him back? That was her life he described, one with big dreams and few personal commitments except to her business partners. But there it was. The pang, the gnawing trepidation of getting within reach of feelings she longed for and feared. Had she loved before? Maybe . . . maybe not! The fun evening was turning intense, filled with tangled emotions she had only dreamed of. Now what was she going to do about it?

The avalanche had been escalating since their first meeting. The choice of a lifetime lay before her. She knew firsthand about loss and abandonment. *Damage control,* the thoughts flashed. *Run while you still can.*

Alex fought the emotion. She knew what she wanted and she wasn't going to let a little apprehension stand in her way. She was someone who shook hands with her fears. Some wells were gushers and some were blowouts. There were dry holes too, but they had to be drilled first to find out. Alex took a long, slow step onto the small elevator leading to the private life of Colton Forrester.

CHAPTER 23

The elevator stopped at the top floor and opened into a loft. Alex was unprepared for the picturesque scene. Enormous windows brought the night sky into a cavernous room, and the ceiling disappeared overhead. A section of the room had been partitioned off to make a kitchen; large copper pans hung above a butcher block next to a commercial-grade gas stove. The rest of the place was one expansive room with the moon and the mountains serving as an art exhibit. Hardwood floors finished in a light honey-golden stain were dressed with several old Hariz carpets, and a small bronze sculpture of an oil rig stood alone in the corner. *A minimalist,* she noted. There was no clutter in the room to detract from the spectacular view. A highly organized bookshelf served as an entertainment center housing a sound system. A raised platform had been erected in another corner, creating a loft bedroom with a teak ladder for access and a brass fire pole to exit. Under the loft bedroom was an ultramodern bathroom of marble and granite, illuminated with track lighting. A large steam shower accompanied a Jacuzzi tub made for two.

Colt picked up a remote control, activating the stereo system, which piped soft music throughout the loft. He lit a fire and offered Alex a drink.

"This is amazing. I love the views—everything." Alex devoured the surroundings. "I don't know what I was expecting, but for some reason I'm surprised."

"By what?"

"It's not the typical bachelor's pad, Colt."

"I live in such rough conditions out in the field that when

I'm home I like a bit more comfort and privacy."

The lights were dimmed, letting the night intrude. The furnishings were simple yet sophisticated. A pair of massive leather armchairs rested in front of the fire. The dining table, a large slice of asymmetrical beveled glass on an antique marble pedestal, was placed in front of the plate-glass windows, offering the Rocky Mountains and their majesty. It would be an incomparable dinner atmosphere. Alex stood motionless, drinking it all in.

"I like it that the elevator is large enough to bring up the bike." He gestured to the corner by the kitchen where the motorcycle sat on a moving-van blanket. "I don't like leaving it in the garage."

Colt lit several candles, then selected an Elton John tape. Alex moved to the floor and sat on a deerskin rug in front of the hearth. She lifted a log of aspen wood from an antique cast-iron kettle and added it to the fire. The melancholy music filled the room. Colt slid in next to her and they whispered lightly, holding hands, kissing quietly. The fire played and died as hidden dreams marched forth.

"I want to know every part of you, every square inch of your brain." He caressed her face with tender hands. "The hidden wishes of your heart, what makes you thrive. I want to understand it all." He stroked her face, running gentle working hands through the ferociously thick, black hair that now tumbled over her slender shoulders. His blue eyes burned beneath the surface, delving into every well-protected corner of her soul.

"Are you afraid of heights?" he asked.

"No, why?"

"Do you trust me?"

"Yes!" The instinct was sure and strong.

"Good, follow me." He took Alex by the hand, guiding her to the ladder leading to the loft bedroom. "Go first, just in case you slip." He was in complete control and Alex was glad. She felt no fear, no ambivalence. She was beginning a journey she had been moving toward for an eternity. They climbed over the edge.

Colt hinged a small safety gate. "I've always feared falling down the ladder in the middle of the night, so the gate was added as an afterthought."

"Do you get tired of climbing up and down to go to bed?"

"No, it's very convenient. I have everything programmed to work by remote control, including the blinds. It's the engineer in me—can't help it." With the press of a button, the blinds were lowered and rotated. "On a clear day the sun streams through the windows, bringing the temperature to the boiling point if I forget to close the blinds." Alex was impressed with the organization and technology. "I'll be right back," Colt said. "Don't move."

"And just where would I go?" she asked.

"Just wanted to make sure you didn't disappear." He planted a reassuring kiss on her mouth. Then he walked to the corner, wrapped his work-sculpted legs around the brass fire pole, and disappeared into the floor.

"Where are you going?" Alex squealed with delight.

"To the kitchen! Would you like a cappuccino or brandy?"

"That sounds delicious. Do you need a hand?" She marveled at this man who liked old trucks, state-of-the-art electronics, French cuisine, and fire poles.

"No, I'll send it up in the dumbwaiter." The small elevator-style box ran from the basement to the kitchen and up to the bedroom loft. It was a brilliant device that eliminated the need to carry cumbersome packages up the stairs. Colt returned quickly and they sipped on the steaming coffee, enjoying the expanse of night sky with the image of the fire dancing in the glass. It was a spectacular evening, a free fall into the unknown. All they could do was hang on tight to each other and enjoy the ride.

Colt pulled off Alex's black boots, placing them neatly by the bedside table. She lay back on the large down pillows, melting into powdery comfort. She felt no apprehension. Firelight competed with the shadows on the ceiling. The bed frame was part of a 1935 Ford truck bed with the wheels removed and the rear window and frame serving as a headboard. A down-covered custom futon fit neatly into the flatbed. The wheel wells served as small nightstands.

"Did you have this made?" Alex inquired

"Rebuilt would be a better description! It was one of my favorite trucks, but I never had time to restore it. Then the idea to transform it into a bed came to my mind. I had a designer adapt it." He peeled off and discarded his shirt, revealing a bare, muscular chest covered in a blanket of fine sandy hair. "It's like having an old friend around."

"I've never made out in the back of a pickup."

"It's never too late to give it a try." He shed an inviting smile that melted her bones, then moved toward her.

With each passing minute Forrester was becoming more complex, an enigma mushrooming before her eyes. They sipped on brandy, holding hands and talking about their lives, dazzling and intriguing acts from different plays, trying to understand life-long dreams in just a few short hours. Somewhere during the conversation, time was lost. Colt expertly removed her clothes, placing them carefully beside the truck. Tension pounded through every cell. Without shyness, blue jeans landed in a random pile on the floor. After he discarded the remainder of his clothes, they slipped in between pristine white sheets, beginning a sensuous journey from where Alex would never completely return. He lay nestled beside her, hidden under the covers, exploring every curve and satin-soft spot. She was soft like baby powder and fresh as leftover rain in early-morning sunshine. He stroked and loved her into an excruciating passion that only the mountains could hear. Every curve and muscle was explored. Her figure in her clothes had provided only a hint of what was to come. She was muscular and taut in a little boy's body with delicious supple breasts. They pressed every square inch of available skin together, flesh wrapped around legs and arms entwined like vines. Colt started slowly kissing around her mouth, and worked his way from the tip of her cool nose to the bottoms of her delicate feet. They were pulled to each other like two magnets. And the closer they came, the stronger the attraction.

Alex buried her face in thick, satiny chest fur, sighing with relief and contentedness. Every part of Colt was an unexpected pleasure, from his passionate touch to his gentle kisses. He slowly took Alex apart bit by bit and then brought her back together with his lovemaking. Rest came in brief revelations, then they dived back into a slow crescendo of ecstasy until Alex begged him to stop. She had never made love with a man who could be aroused time and time again.

They caressed for a while, basking in each other's joy. He stroked her face and head and neck, and then she felt him against her again like a rising tide coming back for more. He moved slowly into her, arms wrapped around slender shoulders, desperately trying not to crush her petite frame with his dominating form. Then he pulled her up to him, suspending her entire weight with his strong arms. Their eyes locked in unforgettable closeness and for one split second they both knew something had passed between them that could never be taken away. Alex wrapped her legs around his waist, arms locked behind his neck, and rested her forehead against his. They rubbed noses softly, rocking back and forth and savoring the moment, trying to capture it like the tail of a comet. It would never be exactly the same again. There was nothing like fresh unknown love.

When Colt was sure that Alex slept soundly, he pressed the remote control, closing the blinds. Like a gentle tide, her breath rose and fell. His heart ached for this part of him that he now recognized had been missing for so long. He knew Alex was meant to fill the void. He gently pushed a lock of dark hair out of peaceful love-worn eyes, wondering how long she might stay. At least until sunrise. He could predict no more, but for the first time he wanted to know the future and make it turn out his way. Drained, they slept into the deep crevices of the morning.

Sometime in the darkness, she awoke slightly chilled and nestled deeper into his warm protective arms. He responded to her movement with small wistful kisses on the back of her neck that eventually found their way to her breasts, now longing for his touch. She lay back, allowing him to gently glide his fingers over her, massaging her until she could stand no more. Then she pulled against him again, aching for his hard body to engulf her. She traced every feature of his rugged face until it was emblazoned in her heart. And they held on tight to keep the vagaries of life from creeping into their piece of heaven. This was how it was supposed to be, powerful and spontaneous, gentle and free.

Again, for a brief moment, sleep came.

CHAPTER 24

Saturday 3 P.M.

Forrester's truck pulled under the porte cochere of The Brown, depositing a forever transformed Alex. He kissed her lovingly good-bye, promising to call after he returned from a drill site on the Western Slope. He'd be out of pocket for about two weeks . . . She went hurriedly to her room to change. Solitude rekindled her preoccupation with business, and she again felt a gnawing unease surrounding Chris's meeting with the senator. Anxious to talk, she dialed the office. No one answered the phone, but Alex was certain Chris would be in her office bunker buried in paperwork. Saturdays were her treasured private hours when work was enveloped in welcome isolation. No phones, no employees.

An unexplainable tightness gripped Alex and dryness parched her throat and mouth. She thought her exuberance from the evening and morning with Colt must still be defaulting every circuit. She couldn't wait to tell Chris about her feelings for Colt and their ripe dreams. Finally the confirmation had come: there would be one uniquely special person for her, the other half of her soul. Over hot tea and rye toast they had spent the morning fantasizing about the future like two high-school sweethearts. He had professed his love and asked her to stay in Colorado forever. They could work together doing oil deals, drilling wells, and making love. They would get married in the wonderful stone-steepled church in Aspen, find a mountain cabin to hide away in together. In between, they could ski off the back side of Ajax Mountain into bottomless powder and brilliant sunshine. It was a bright and shiny dream.

"Chris? Chris?" Alex yelled, bursting through the unlocked doors of Welbourne Enterprises. She called out enthusiastically, unable to contain her excitement. There was no answer.

The afternoon light was beginning to wane. No lights were on in the office. The interior door to the private executive office was slightly ajar, and she burst through like a summer storm.

"Chris? Chris, you won't believe it—" she ran into their office. "You won't believe what is happening." Her emotional high was intoxicating.

Chris sat in her favorite chair, staring at the mountainous horizon. She did not respond. She was a frozen statue, motionless in the chair.

"Chris?"

Alex stopped in her tracks. She approached cautiously from the left side where a stranger might have mistaken Chris for sleeping. The chair faced the window. Alex moved forward until she could see all of Chris's silent face.

Red! A sea of red filled the familiar space. Grotesque reality stared back at Alex. The walls and windows were red, too—crimson covered the office.

Alex squinted and blinked hard. Focus. Air . . . her lungs seemed to freeze. Forms appeared out of the red haze. The outline of a desk came into view. Chris sat stiff and lifeless in the chair like a morbid mannequin, with a grisly distorted blood-streaked mask for a face. A sound resembling a scream, but far more primitive and painful, came from Alex. Her knees buckled and she hit the floor. Drying blood surrounded the chair, hardening into a brown glue. Blood splattered the window. Blood covered the right side of what was once Chris's head and destroyed the golden robe she wore. Alex reached out to touch her partner's left hand. Cold hard skin greeted warm flesh and she recoiled. Bile rose to the base of her throat and vomit muffled a guttural scream. She reacted to the horror in slow motion. Something ghastly and powerful had torn apart the lower right part of Chris's head. The exit wound.

Broken glass cut into Alex's knee where she had landed on the floor, and blood trickled down her leg unnoticed. Groping, she recoiled from the body, trying to get out of the office. She vomited over Jeff Ashton's desk, grasping at the phone receiver.

"I need the police," she numbly told the 911 operator.

All she could see was the blood, a scene that would play over and over again. The smell of death hung over the room like a thick malignant fog.

"Who's calling?"

A cross between a sob and a gasp came across the emergency line.

"Count to ten and try to calm down." The trained operator waited a few seconds, then asked, "Can you tell me where you are?"

"This is Alex Sheridan," she choked out. "I'm in the Rocky Mountain Savings building on the twenty-third floor. Someone's killed my partner, Chris Welbourne." That was all she could get out. She slumped into the chair.

"Don't touch anything. Someone will be there immediately. Can you tell me the phone number?" But Alex was silent, in a daze of shock. "What's the phone number?"

She recited the seven digits mechanically and dropped the receiver. Her mind raced. She would need help! Jeff Ashton? Like a stroke victim, she couldn't will movement. Then tremors ripped through every muscle and she dialed his number. No answer. She left a faint voice on the recorder: "Jeff, something horrible has happened at the office. Call me here. It's an emergency." Her voice trailed off. There were no words, no way to explain what had happened. Her mind seesawed.

Jake! Jake could help her. Directory assistance gave her the Boulder number. He was Chris's friend, he had loved her. He would understand how Alex felt. *God please let him be there*, she pleaded silently. Familiar rusty razor-cut feelings emerged from ages ago. The plane going down. Her mother dying in the inferno.

The pain was too familiar, as if her heart were being cut out with an old screwdriver. Then the unbearable feeling of aloneness.

"Please answer." Her voice was barely audible. She needed to talk to someone who knew Chris and could understand the fear and anguish that was beginning to set in like rigor mortis. Tears flowed down her hot red cheeks as she tried to speak to Jake. "It's Alex," she muttered.

"Alex? Are you hurt?" Patiently he waited, listening to her try to choke out words. Something traumatic had happened. She was incoherent. "Where are you?" he demanded, hoping the commanding tone might help Alex regain some control.

"The off . . . off . . . office."

"Take a deep breath," he coaxed. "Take your time," he said in a calm voice trying not to communicate the deep concern he felt.

"It's Chris. She's been shot!" Labored breathing came across the phone line.

"My God. How could—" he stopped himself. Alex needed help. "Don't move. I'm going to my car. Then I'll call right back on the cell phone. We'll talk until I can get there."

She hung up, and the phone rang again just a few seconds later from the car barreling down Sunshine Canyon.

"Alex, can you tell me what is happening?" His voice was strong and even.

"She's dead. I don't know. She's dead. Someone killed her." She repeated the words between guttural sobs.

"Breathe deeply and don't try to speak." Jake kept talking. "I'll be there as fast as I can, so hold on tight." He kept her on the line, offering words of support. "Have you called the police?"

"Yes." Trembling white, she held onto Jake Winston's words as he spoke.

"Just hold on tight until I get there."

The eerie calm was shattered when a phalanx of police and paramedics burst through the door.

An unimposing officer with a gentle voice and humble eyes approached her as if he were involved in an ordinary day's work. "Hello, I'm Detective Mike Carter with the Denver Police homicide unit. Are you the one who called?"

She shook her head up and down acknowledging cooperation, then said to Jake, "The police are here, I have to hang up!" Alex placed the phone down.

"She's in there!" Alex motioned toward the door to what had been their office. Carter quickly surveyed the scene. He entered their office and touched Chris's wrist perfunctorily. The once-vital body was stiff and cold. No pulse. No one could have survived that head wound.

Paramedics raced in with a stretcher.

"Don't go another step," yelled the commanding detective. "What the hell do you think you're doing?" Carter flashed his credentials. "You go in there and fuck with this crime scene and you'll have to answer to a lot more than just me."

Carter looked over the scene, careful not to step on or touch anything. A quarter of the right side of the head had been blown off at the point of exit. A small, barely distinguishable hole on the left side of the head behind and below the ear indicated the entrance path of what had to be a high-caliber bullet intended to do exactly what it had done: obliterate the brain stem and cause instant death. There was no life left to resurrect, and it was quite obvious a murder had taken place.

"We don't need you. Get that stretcher out of here," Carter barked. He turned his back before the paramedic could protest and gave another order to his subordinate. "Get 'em out of here, now!" he directed his assistant, a young man who could barely grow facial hair. "And call the coroner's office. Get a medical examiner over here ASAP."

"What is your full name?" he asked, returning to Alex. The

hardness in his eyes from moments before had disappeared.

Alex's dark hair hung in disheveled strands around her tear-streaked face. She responded to the standard questions, stating her name and address.

"Who is the victim?" The question was cold and flat, although he must have seen the well-known name on the large double doors when he entered the office. It was a name that was part of the power structure of the city. Alex gave the biographical information mechanically. "What were you doing here?" he asked firmly, eyes scanning the room for details. He stood in the entry between the murder scene and the outer office, shielding Alex from the sight of the grisly remains of her best friend. There was no condemnation and even a hint of sympathy from the slightly stooped, middle-aged detective. A trace of kindness remained in hardened blue eyes that had seen buckets of violence.

"Chris and I were business partners. We had a small company, one of many she was involved in. You must have known her name from the newspaper or television?"

He nodded.

"She was one of the most prominent people in the city," Alex added. But what was once the distinguished beauty was now a rigored body, soon to be ripped apart in an autopsy. "I was coming here to see Chris. We are, we were very close personal friends." Her head hung, eyes gazing at dust particles hanging in a stream of sunlight. A jackhammer worked on the inside of her head. Like a rerun, the scene at the hospital in Cairo came back. Brown hands working feverishly to put the life back in her father's heart . . . all the pain bled together. She noticed Carter looking at the blood on her black boots. She must have stepped in it by accident. Only in some movies death comes neatly, and in this moment of reality, it seemed that rivers of blood had flowed out of Chris.

Carter studied her closely, then the office surrounding them. On the walls, photographs of Chris hung like pages in an autobiography. In one photo she was receiving a plaque from the mayor. In another, she was flanked by the president and first lady. Their personal well wishes were penned across the classic shot. In another, Alex and Chris stood arm in arm at a Petroleum Club meeting.

Carter continued the questioning, undisturbed by the body positioned twenty feet away.

"Why did you think she was here on the weekend?"

"She usually works on Saturdays and Sundays. It's common for her to hibernate here and not take incoming calls. Weekends are the only time we can get any peace." *What an irony*, she thought.

"How did you get in?"

"The door was open, but I have a key, too," she said flatly. Irritated by the barrage of questions she added, "I told you, it's my office."

Two uniformed policemen arrived, responding to a request for backup.

"Excuse me," the detective said to Alex, and he turned his attention to the officers. "You two! Man the entry!" Carter barked the order without ceremony. "I don't want anyone in here, including the coroner, until I okay their credentials. Do I make myself clear?" Carter was an unassuming man who had a commanding presence that appeared when necessary.

"Yes, sir!"

"And get some guys downstairs. Close off these elevators and seal the place. If you have to yellow-tape the whole goddamn building, do it! I don't want this scene tampered with." Carter returned his attention to Alex, who sat in silence on the corner of Jeff Ashton's desk, watching a world blown away. Slowly and methodically, doors inside her heart were beginning to close. It would be unbearable to reenter her office with the remains of Chris resting in the chair where she had made so many dreams come true.

Carter flipped to his scratch pad of scribbled notes and the question came at her from miles away. "Was the door ajar or merely unlocked?"

Alex concentrated hard. She had to think for a minute. A heavy fog hung in her head. For the moment, life had turned into a Stephen King thriller. One more time in her relatively young life, she was blindsided by the sudden death of a loved one.

Carter watched twisted anxiety settle between Alex's dark eyes. And for one second he loathed his job.

She concentrated, trying to remember. How had she entered the office? She had been so excited about telling Chris about her precious time with Colton, she couldn't have been any higher. She had burst through the door with abandon. She thought she remembered turning the knob. "I think it was closed, but definitely unlocked."

Alex thought she would go mad with the detailed drilling from Carter, not realizing he was beginning to consider her a possible suspect. The evidence team arrived to back up the police homicide officers, who guarded the body in its horrid posture. They waited for the coroner, who would take charge of the body and pronounce the victim thoroughly and undeniably dead. *Any idiot could do that!* thought Alex. If she could just burrow a hole into oblivion and disappear. She wanted to get out and get away from the reality. Her instincts screamed: *Escape! Run and don't look back!*

An investigator from the coroner's office arrived with a small bag and a white sheet. She was a slight woman with translucent skin and thin hair and hands that looked as if they'd been in formaldehyde too long. Until the chief medical examiner arrived, she would be in charge of the body and all the evidence on the body. In a starched white lab coat, she circled the corpse that was now in full rigor, lying where it had been for at least twelve hours. Carter asked for a liver temperature to get a time of death as accurate as possible, although at best it would provide a reasonable estimation. Then he ordered his men to gather evidence methodically from every corner of the office except the one with the body.

The investigation began. Dust was covering every imaginable surface and filtering into every crevice. Fingerprints were lifted from doorknobs and desks. The investigator took out two brown lunch bags and covered each of Chris's hands, then bound them with masking tape to preserve any evidence.

The office would never be the same, thought Alex as she witnessed the destruction of their business world. Every part of her being felt violated. Helplessly, she thought about how much Chris guarded and treasured her privacy. *She would be so pissed,* thought Alex.

The photographer arrived from the homicide unit to take pictures of every item from a hundred angles. More prints were lifted. The place buzzed like a wrecked beehive. Another photographer from the coroner's office, arrived with video equipment. Cameras dangled from around his neck like cheap jewelry. Every detail was catalogued and recorded slowly and methodically. Police officers whispered among themselves about the juicy murder. The unmade bed served as a focal point. Every once in a while, a muffled chuckle could be heard.

Jake Winston arrived at a critical moment, offering Alex a brief respite from the inquisition. He introduced himself to the police investigators. The shock of the death hung over them like dark thunderheads. He offered Alex a reassuring embrace and she threw her arms around him, hoping to stop the pain.

"What happened, officer?"

"It's premature to speculate." Carter focused on Winston, suddenly recognizing the familiar face. "Weren't you with the mayor last week at City Hall?"

"Yes, there was a press conference."

"What's your business?"

"Colorado Land Preservation."

"Yeah, they had that news special on you guys last week." Another layer of anxiety was added to the case. As if it weren't bad enough that the dead lady was a prominent citizen, now he had people like Jake Winston to deal with. People who were connected always muddied an investigation by jerking on powerful strings.

"Was it a break-in?" Jake asked, trying to understand why someone would want to kill Chris.

"As far as we can tell, someone made an unforced entry, walked up behind her—there wasn't a struggle, so I would guess she never saw the intruder—then pop, pop. It looks as if she must have been in deep sleep. It also looks very professional, not your ordinary crime of passion." The detective let his eyes fall on the disheveled bed. "Although my bet's that something pretty steamy went on before she was shot." He took Jake's vital information along with the details of his association with the victim. One pile of complications after another.

"Was the victim married?"

"No."

"Then it wasn't a jealous husband. Did you have any dealings with Ms. Welbourne?"

"We frequently crossed paths in business circles. We sit on common boards, but we weren't working on any deals together." He declined mentioning the Custer Ranch. Seldon had called earlier that morning, setting off an eruption, and he had been seething ever since. She had been playing both sides against the middle, and CLP was losing ground. Several times he had tried to call Welbourne Enterprises, but the phone had only rung incessantly. He would not mention the situation to Carter. It didn't seem pertinent to the case, and now it seemed so unimportant in light of the tragedy.

The detective and his men combed every inch of the office. Alex became incensed when one of the young men riffling through Chris's private possessions made a lewd joke about a box of condoms in the bathroom drawer.

"She must have been one hot piece of ass," the rookie commented, picking up one of the photos that decorated the office. "She looks like the kind you want to stop late at night and frisk." Tasteless raucous laughter replaced deadly silence.

"What kind of animals are you?" Alex screamed. "Chris Welbourne was much more of a woman than you could ever handle. She'd chew you up and spit you out before you knew what happened."

Silence reverberated through the office. Detective Carter reprimanded the young cop for his insensitive comment. Then he turned to Alex. "You might want to have a lawyer. There are a lot more questions we need to ask."

"Why would I need a lawyer?" she asked.

"Because you found the body. Because you have a key. Because this wasn't a forced entry. It's routine, but if you want my advice, get a lawyer."

The nightmare grew darker and colder.

Jake stepped in. "Officer, Ms. Sheridan was Chris's closest friend." It took all his power to maintain control. How dare this guy accuse Alex of anything.

"Can you tell me where you were last night and this morning?" Carter asked Alex.

Alex's heart hit a new low. For a moment she just stared, unable to face either man. How could she possibly tell them where she had been?

"You'll have to tell us where you were, Ms. Sheridan."

"I must speak with a lawyer." Alex was furious and hurt. The intrusion into her private world terrified her. What had happened the night before with Colt was more personal than anything she had ever shared, and she wasn't about to try to explain it to some hardened stranger while Jake Winston witnessed the ordeal. Besides, no one would understand. Jake consoled her with a reassuring touch as Carter was beckoned into the office.

"We'll continue this at police headquarters tomorrow."

It was not an invitation. While carefully going through Chris's private business, Carter came across the file Chris and John Curry had assembled incriminating Storm along with the letter to the Federal Home Loan Bank. It didn't take a financial genius to see motive here. He turned to Alex.

"Do you know anything about this?" he held the file with a handkerchief.

"Yes, a little. She believed there was sufficient cause to alert the Federal Home Loan Bank Board to look into Mr. Storm's business affairs. But I don't know the details."

"He's the chairman of the savings and loan in this building?"

"Yes."

"I hope you can help us sort through some of this business mess. It looks very involved." Carter was proceeding on gut instinct and a lifetime of experience with murder investigations. He doubted that Alex Sheridan was his murderer. He needed her on his team. She knew the inside dealings of the victim's personal and financial life, and he didn't need to create an adversary. He tried to soften the hard question that had made her bristle. "It's a formality, but we will need to know where you've been the last twenty-four hours. There are a lot of other questions you might be able to help answer. That can all take place at headquarters tomorrow. When you have had more rest, it may be easier. It looks like she was involved in some pretty big deals."

It was late in the day, and Alex felt the walls closing in. She pushed each new wave of pain into a tiny black box in her heart.

"Yes, she was very concerned about Mr. Storm." Alex seethed inside, torn between what little she knew about Storm and what might have taken place with the senator. Chris had hated Storm and his unscrupulous principles . . . but the senator had been there in the office. Her head was spinning with doubt and confusion.

"Is there anyone you know who might have wanted her dead?" Carter asked.

"No, no one I can think of. She is one of the most well-respected people in Colorado." But the conversation about Case Storm loomed in her thoughts.

"What about her business? Not everyone is happy for someone with her kind of success." Carter remembered seeing the victim with the mayor on a recent television interview and wondered how complicated the investigation would become. She was connected, and that usually meant pressure for a quick arrest.

"She had intricate business involvements from minority stock positions in public companies to hundreds of real estate investments and who knows how many silent partnerships."

"Isn't she involved with the proposed airport?" Carter continued to violate Chris's desk, reading memos and scattered letters.

"Well, she was on the planning committee until she resigned last week."

"She was on the news last week with the mayor?"

"That's very possible." The banal response was drained and exhausted. How was she supposed to paint a picture of Chris's life for the detective? Chris was bigger than life. Carter would never get a grip on her complicated business dealings.

Jake sat next to Alex, holding her cold hand and patiently waiting for Carter to release them. The detective assured them it would not be too much longer, but reiterated that Alex would have to come down the next morning and give another statement.

"You aren't planning on leaving town?"

"No, why?"

"Don't—not unless you check with me."

Then the contract offering twenty-two million to Seldon Custer was found. The Custers were a household name in Colorado. Detective Carter could feel the complexities of the case mounting by the second. And where the hell was the chief medical examiner? The case was explosive, and he didn't need any mistakes with the body. If he weren't careful it could become a media free-for-all. This was a powerful woman with hundreds of business contacts and deals in the works. Whoever shot Chris Welbourne wanted her dead. The killer had used a large-caliber gun and placed the muzzle expertly under and behind the left ear—a strategy used to instantly obliterate life. No mistake.

Carter leafed through Chris's appointment book. It was a

small black leather book trimmed in peeling gold. He saw the airport planning meeting scheduled, then it was blank except for the initials *BB*. No hints. As he flipped back through the calendar, the initials appeared several more times.

Alex made the idle comment to Jake that they probably needed to call Senator Bridgeforth to let him know what happened. It was a thoughtless comment.

"Why?" Detective Carter jumped at the mention of the powerful senator. He didn't need any added political pressure.

"They were supposed to meet last night." When Alex saw the astonished look on the detective's weary face, she realized she had pried open a can of worms. The police weren't accustomed to this kind of world. She was probably the only one who knew about the friendship between the senator and Chris, and most surely, about the rendezvous that had been planned for the previous night. But there was no proof or certainty yet that he had been there or that he was the man Chris had slept with. But she knew Chris, and she had seen the look in her eyes and heard the edge in her voice the day before.

"Where?" he asked in total shock.

"I think they were supposed to meet here," Alex commented, hedging a little.

"Are you certain?"

"I can't say for sure they ever had the meeting. When I left around five, Chris was alone." Alex was backpedaling, wishing she could put the spilled words back in the bottle.

"Did she always work at night?"

Alex didn't like his sarcastic tone. "She worked all the time," she said sharply. "It was standard operating procedure."

"Well, was it also standard operating procedure for her to have sex with people in her office?" He wanted Alex's cooperation but he also needed to push a few buttons in an attempt to learn something while Alex's defenses were down and fatigue was in control.

"I wouldn't know."

"Because that's exactly what happened here last night before she was murdered."

In the background, the investigators were wrapping up the bedsheets that would go to the crime lab for DNA testing.

"Do you know the purpose of the meeting?"

"Not really."

"What time were they scheduled to meet?"

"Six-thirty, maybe?"

Alex was very concerned about dragging the senator deeper into this and possibly tarnishing reputations unnecessarily, especially Chris's public image. She didn't know or trust Carter. A blind man could see what had taken place in the wee hours of the morning. If word got out about the passionate tryst between the senator and Chris, everything good Chris stood for would explode in a scandalous puff of media smoke. Besides, Alex had some questions of her own. She wanted to talk to the senator herself and find out what on earth happened.

Detective Carter could feel the case gathering momentum. A United States Senator's involvement would complicate everything. Bridgeforth was a powerful man in Colorado, in control of many political appointments. His influence permeated the state, including the district attorney's office in Denver, which had been a hotly contested election. The senator's support had influenced votes, tipping the scale in favor of the current District Attorney, Bradley Germany, a man Carter would go to the ends of the earth to avoid. They would have to proceed with extra caution. Where the hell was the chief medical examiner?

Carter took meticulous notes. To keep Germany off their backs, it would be important to document every move the police department made. And he needed the chief medical examiner there. A botched autopsy and lost evidence, not to mention contamination and tampering, were a detective's ever-present nightmare. It didn't matter how good a case they could build if the evidence wasn't handled in a specific and methodical fashion.

"Be at police headquarters at 2:00 P.M. tomorrow and be sure not to discuss the case or scene with anyone, especially the press!" Carter directed Alex.

"What about the office? All my files?" Alex asked with astonishment.

"They'll have to wait."

"But my entire business is here." Her voice turned frantic. This was her world, her dreams . . . her life.

"It will have to wait."

"All my records, my financial inform—"

"It will have to wait!" he cut her off.

"But what am I supposed to do? The company can't—"

Carter interrupted again. "No one will have access to anything in this room until the investigation is over."

A damp darkness filled the spaces where her dreams had been. It was the end of a terrible day that had started like magic and shattered into a million razor-sharp shards of glass.

The head of the evidence team interrupted Carter. He was a short, fat man with trifocal black-framed glasses. Excitement danced on his ruddy face. "Someone was definitely here last night. There are enough fingerprints for a novel, and they all belong to the same two people except for what we found around the reception area."

"One set is the victim's?"

"You got it."

"Thanks, Ruddy. No mistakes on this one."

"We're on it."

"Are they through photographing?"

"Almost."

Alex didn't say another word to Carter, whose mind was churning with options. Carter hoped the prints would belong to someone other than the senator, but it wouldn't take a psychic to guess that was not going to be the case. Circumstantial evidence in the office pointed in his direction. The Waterford glasses, the remains of dinner for two, the bed. He looked at the power photos with Welbourne and a parade of political celebrities including the president. Then he made the phone call he had been avoiding for hours.

"Chief, it's Carter. We've got a mess down here."

"Yeah, I heard. Give me some details."

"I don't think you're going to like it. Looks like Welbourne had dinner and a special dessert with Senator Bill Bridgeforth right before she was knocked off. If I were him, I wouldn't want people nosing around this crime scene. He left some tracks, if you know what I mean."

"How do you know he was there?"

"His initials were in her appointment book. And her lady partner knew about the meeting. He was probably the last person who saw her alive."

"I'll call the D.A. They're tight as ticks. He can set up a meeting."

"You'd better make it in the next couple of hours because this could be all over the paper by morning. He's not going to want to read this cold over coffee and the morning paper."

Jake put a protective arm around Alex and walked her out of the former business sanctuary that had been her life. It was a long, silent ride in the elevator that took them to the lobby of Rocky Mountain Savings and Loan. When the doors opened, Alex's thoughts moved like a bullet train to Case Storm. The sight of his portrait in the lobby filled her with rage. He was the only real enemy Chris had ever mentioned. She wanted to make some sense out of the insane tragedy, and she believed that Storm had to be responsible. The lobby elevators were guarded by several more officers and surrounded by more yellow tape. A mob of reporters with cameras jumped at Alex and Jake like ravenous jackals. Word had leaked out and predators were circling, waiting for any choice morsel that might come their way. Cameras flashed as Jake tried to shield Alex from the swarming horde. Like a ghost, Jeff Ashton appeared, clean and freshly shaved.

"What's going on here?" he asked, bewildered by the small crowd and the guards at the elevator. "I tried to call earlier, but the lines have been busy."

Alex stuttered as she tried to find the right words.

"Where's Chris?"

"Something's happened, Jeff." Ashton's fine strong features melted into a tangle of fear. "We don't know how." Alex was trying to break the news when a greedy reporter jumped in, hoping to discover some details.

"Can you confirm that it was a suicide?" asked the skinny, rumpled young man.

"It was not a suicide!" Alex snapped, then wished she could inhale the words. That's exactly how they got their stories, by tricking you into talking. Alex prayed she hadn't let out a critical piece of information. There was no way the public knew how she died, and Carter wanted it that way. Now Alex had lost control and been sucked into telling this reporter it was not a suicide— which meant it was something else.

Ten voices attacked them at once.

"No comment."

Jake stepped between Alex and the hungry cameras, steering her away from the mob. Jeff stood dazed as the news sank in. "My God, Alex. What's happened? I was out of town for the weekend . . ."

"I don't know, Jeff. I found Chris around two. It was awful." Alex put her head in her hands, shaking it back and forth. Small sobs escaped as Jeff pulled her to him. The two closest friends Chris had in the world tried to comfort each other.

"I came as soon as I got your message."

"The police want to talk to you, Jeff."

"But how could someone kill Chris? Why?" he asked in disbelief.

"I don't know, Jeff, but I am going to find out if it kills me." Her dark eyes burned. "You can take those elevators by the police guard." She gestured with one hand at the only elevator in use, then wiped at the persistent tears she couldn't hold back. "Excuse me, Jake, I'm going to ride up with Jeff. Will you wait?" Her eyes pleaded.

"I'll be here."

Alex explained Jeff's relationship to the deceased, and the police allowed them into the elevator. Inside Jeff stared at the floor, shaking with the news.

"Why? Everyone adores her," he said, as much to himself as to Alex. "Was it a robbery?"

"I don't think so, but they don't know anything certain yet."

"What do I need to do?"

"Carter, the detective, just wants to ask you some questions. He'll probably want you to come to the police station later, too. I don't know. He doesn't seem too sophisticated about business matters. In fact, he doesn't have a clue. With all her companies and the deals they were doing, it could take them a year just to make sense of it."

"I'll call Chris's attorney."

Alex held the open button as Jeff entered the crime scene. The chief medical examiner had arrived and was taking charge of the body.

"I can't go back in right now. I'm sorry," said Alex.

"I'll be all right. Call me later."

In silence, the elevator carried her away from the promising future she had shared with Chris, a future that had just been erased into a blank page. At this moment, she knew she would never get it back.

CHAPTER 25

The last rays of afternoon sun had long disappeared over the Continental Divide. Jake led Alex to the Jeep and out of the scene that had become a dark play.

Not a word passed between them as they rumbled to the outskirts of Denver. Alex didn't know where they were going, and she didn't really care.

"You can stay in Boulder until we figure out what is going on here," Jake offered, breaking the silence.

"That's not necessary." It was a hollow protest—Alex didn't have the emotional energy to really argue. Only in morbid dreams could she have imagined the events that were unfolding. Numb to the bone, she stared at the approaching foothills. Jake drove home while the loss settled heavily on both their hearts.

"Lafayette is having your clothes packed and delivered to Boulder in the morning. By the way, he said to tell you he is very sorry."

Jake Winston was trying to pick up the pieces, and for that she was grateful. She needed him. The Jeep passed several abandoned tractor-trailers jackknifed in ditches along the highway, still uncleared from the storm. It was a dark, vacant expanse of highway angling toward the foothills.

Alex finally broke the heavy silence. "Chris always wanted me to see your house. She talked about how beautiful it is."

"It's my one-way mirror to the world."

"I don't want to be any trouble, but I'm so exhausted."

Jake felt a cold, wet blanket lift a little from his heart. He longed for more time with Alex Sheridan, to hear her voice and watch her dancing eyes laugh like angels in the wind. To see that radiant smile—no matter what the circumstances were.

"I have a private bath and guest room. It's simple, but you should be comfortable." Out of the depths of despair and the agony of Chris's death, Jake felt hope.

"Anything will be fine."

As they meandered up the canyon, he dreamed about what it would be like to smell her fresh scent in his spaces. The city lights abandoned them as darkness shrouded the canyon crevasses winding into the unknown. Fir trees swollen with frozen powder bordered the road. A deer stood bug-eyed and silent in the headlights next to a sign with faded letters that read WILDLIFE SANCTUARY.

∽

Detective Carter sat uncomfortably trying to digest Senator Bill Bridgeforth's elegant office surroundings. Next to him sat Chief Jack Chapman looking like a scared rabbit. Fortunately, the district attorney, Bradley Germany, had been successful in finding the senator at home on what was a quiet Sunday afternoon. The news of Chris Welbourne's death had landed like a Scud missile.

Steaming freshly ground coffee was served on a silver tray. The two officers artfully interrogated, trying to probe while attempting not to insinuate that Bridgeforth might be a suspect. This was not a man to be mishandled.

"Senator, I hate to have to ask you some personal questions, but they are a necessary part of the investigation," Carter said, feeling the weight of Washington on his shoulders. "We don't want any surprises!"

But Bridgeforth took the baton and ran with it. "Gentlemen, let's get on with this unpleasantness," he said, taking complete charge. "I want to help you, more than you'll ever know, and after you hear what I have to say, I think you'll understand my position and my interest in this case." He spoke in his most matter-of-fact tone in an attempt to hide his devastating fear. Carter started to interrupt, but Bridgeforth waved a silencing hand. "Bear with me while I tell you what happened. I'll be happy to answer any questions when I'm through explaining what I know."

This was a strategy he and the D.A. had concocted after the senator had admitted his compromising circumstances. The district attorney had promised he would handle the chief from his end and keep Bill Bridgeforth out of the line of fire. He assured the senator there was nothing to worry about, he would talk to the chief, and nothing concerning the senator would be recorded or written down.

Carter and the police chief sat mesmerized as the senator began to tell his story like a professional. One detail at a time, he brought the previous evening to life. He admitted everything to Carter and the police chief, man to man. The spectators listened intently. The only thing he hedged on was the time of his departure from Welbourne Enterprises.

"Had you been seeing Ms. Welbourne for some time?" the detective asked.

"No, not on a personal basis. We sat on the airport planning committee together until she resigned last week. Of course I have long known who she is. You must understand how difficult this is for me and my family," he added soberly. "I am not proud of being discovered in this delicate situation, but it is not easy to be in the public eye at all times. There is rarely such a thing as a private moment. It's like living in a fishbowl."

"We appreciate your position," said the chief. All the men nodded.

"The pressure becomes overwhelming, Jack," he said, directing his comments toward the chief. For the moment they were his peers and he was counting on their empathy and support. "Sometimes it leads to poor choices. I went by her office to discuss business, knowing full well it might turn out to be more than that. She had made it abundantly clear that she was interested in more than just business. One thing led to another. Certainly you know how these things can happen, particularly with such an attractive woman."

"I can imagine," the chief concurred. Carter never said a word.

"I know it's too soon to tell, but what are your leads?"

"There are a lot of loose ends in this deal," said the chief. "She was a powerful lady with her fingers in more pots than you can imagine. There are rabbit trails leading in ten different directions, not to mention the situation with you, senator. I've been trying to make sense of this for hours. It looks like she was about to turn in Case Storm, a big cheese in the financial community, for taking bribes in return for loans."

"Case Storm? My God, do you know who he is?"

"I've heard the name. He's chairman of Rocky Mountain Savings, a huge thrift."

"He's more than just chairman of an S&L—the financial community doesn't blink without his okay. Hell, he pulls strings from here to Washington."

For the first time the police chief, Jack Chapman, looked nervous. He was a man in the last stage of his career. All he wanted was a few more good years and his retirement benefit. He didn't need a sensational murder attracting every magnifying glass in the country into a study of his operation.

"Let me see that file," the chief said with a scowl. Then he asked Carter, "Do we have someone in white-collar crime we can put on this Storm fellow? Maybe he got wind of her meddling and decided to knock her off."

"I'll get someone on it right away. But if even one percent of this is accurate, we won't have to do much. The feds will have a heyday."

"It will be the end of his career," Bridgeforth offered.

"Hell, they'll bury him under the jail," the chief tossed the file back to Carter. "Make sure they assign someone who understands numbers, 'cause this is one convoluted bastard."

Carter looked at one of the crime scene photos of Welbourne and wondered if he could trust the smooth politician they were grilling.

The senator continued. "I don't want to sound pretentious, or make excuses, but some women come on to men in my position. I should not have been so vulnerable . . . but being a senator doesn't stop a man from having normal feelings and attractions." He smiled and they all chuckled. "Yes, we had some dinner, had a roll in the hay, and then I left. You can ask Ben, my driver—he took me home around 12:30."

"Can you give me his number?"

"Certainly, I'm at your complete disposal. Just remember, this stays inside this room." He sent an icy stare around the room and the air rippled. "I was never there! Do you understand, gentlemen?"

The two police officers understood more than they wanted to.

"It might have been immoral, but nothing illegal went on while I was there. Chris Welbourne was very much alive when I left. My wife probably heard me come in, if she looked at the clock."

"I don't suppose we could speak with her?" Carter interjected.

Jack Chapman wanted to choke Carter for posing the ridiculous question.

"I would appreciate it greatly if you can spare her the gory details of the evening. She doesn't need to know anything more than we were having a dinner meeting." He winked at Jack Chapman, who completely understood the gravity of the situation. The senator had everything to lose if the details came out, including a rumored bid for the presidency. He was working hard to be cavalier about his relationship with Welbourne, but the senator's veneer was transparent to Carter. His political career was at stake. If word were to leak out, Bridgeforth's chances for the Oval Office would be as dead as Chris Welbourne.

"We need to take your fingerprints," said Carter. "Just procedure. And a blood sample." Carter wanted the blood so the lab could run a thorough DNA test.

"Is that necessary?"

"I'm afraid so, sir. We can do it quickly here in your office. No one will have to know."

They took his prints, then moved down their list of questions, returning to Storm.

"Storm is a man you should look into." The senator stared into Carter's eyes, sending a clear message.

"In what way?" Carter asked, hoping for some sort of direction.

"Chris wouldn't make loose allegations. She was thorough and meticulous. There's something else you should know. I had some involvement with him on a number of boards. I even sat on the advisory board of his thrift. On one occasion, I was duped into an investment deal. With hindsight, and more experience in these matters, I now know that I was being set up and used."

"What happened to your investment?"

"I made money, of course, and so did Storm."

"Then why do you think he was setting you up?"

"He used my name to attract investors. I was foolish and naïve. I can't say for sure that he stole from the investors, but I wouldn't say it was a fair deal either. I'm telling you this because I believe Storm will be in deep trouble with the federal regulators and it could and probably will destroy him. You have to understand, I'm always in a delicate situation. I have to answer to all of my constituents, including the ones like Storm."

"Is Storm the kind of man who could kill someone?" Carter reached into the politician's eyes, trying to decipher the truth.

"Isn't every man capable of murder if pushed far enough?" The senator's eyes never wavered. A question answered with a question.

"I can't say. Could he have known that Chris Welbourne was about to turn him in?"

"That I don't know," the senator lied with aplomb. "It is

possible." He felt a knife in his heart. Of course Storm had known about Chris's discovery. He himself had called Storm to warn him about her. But how could he have known that the bastard would kill her? At the time, all he could think about was saving his own skin.

"Did you have other dealings with him?"

"Politically, because I had to. Part of my job is to work for improvements for the city and state, like lobbying for federal support for the new airport. I have to work on committees with people like Storm and Chris. It's my job to help them find compromise."

Carter was not one hundred percent snowed by the senator's innocence act. He hadn't made it to the United States Senate and into a Cherry Creek mansion by being a perfectly naïve fool with no personal agenda. On the other hand, he didn't strike Carter as the murdering breed. For the moment Carter could not see a motive, just a mountain of circumstantial evidence.

Only the sound of spitting tires against melting snow penetrated the car. A pulse thundered in Alex's abdomen. The world was out of control, spinning in a thousand different directions, and she couldn't contain it. Beginning with the night with Forrester, which might as well have been on another planet, she had felt the ground giving way. Now she was adrift without a sign of safe shore ahead.

Jake reached across the gulf between them and took her hand, feeling her transparent thoughts. He, too, was devastated by the grotesque tragedy. Chris had once been his lover and had become a treasured friend and respected business adversary. He choked back his feelings. Suddenly fate had dealt a terrible hand, and he and Alex were bonded in a strange ethereal way.

"You'll be safe at the house, Alex." His words were firm and reassuring, but Alex had her doubts. Life had proven to be about as stable as the California coastline.

But instinct drove her to trust Jake. "I'm grateful not to have to go back to the hotel."

The canyon road led them to a dirt path winding farther up the mountain. Through fir trees, lights twinkled and darted in the darkness. Denver sprawled like a horizontal light show below. Alex closed her eyes, but only the distorted, bloody face of Chris stared back. Maybe if she could just stay awake long enough the vision would recede.

A steep dirt-packed drive lead up to a charming stone house nestled in the Aspen trees.

"It's so beautiful." Warm light bled through the darkness, spilling toward them.

"I built most of it myself. It was one of only a few homes in the canyon at the time."

The afternoon's grotesque vision clung to Alex's mind's eye with gnarled fingers. She was alone in the darkness, detached from a part of her soul. She and Chris had become so much a part of each other that they thought the same thoughts; followed similar instincts. She was suddenly empty without her touchstone.

But she was with Jake at his home now. As they entered the house, he surveyed the spacious living room with proprietary eyes. Everything was in its place. An unwashed coffee cup sat undisturbed on a copy of Richard Bach's *A Bridge across Forever*. Nestled in massive bookcases between fantasy and fiction was a compact sound system tuned to an FM radio station.

"Can I look around?" she asked in an aimless voice.

"Make yourself at home," he said, and he meant it. "Your bedroom and bath are downstairs. It's my catchall area, so please excuse the mess. I'm not accustomed to houseguests."

Downstairs was cozy with a small bedroom and bath adjacent to a cluttered office. On the end table rested a small clock radio and an ashtray from the Jupiter Beach Club. A couple of old wood tennis rackets leaned in the corner waiting for a graceful burial along with a stack of dated magazines including *Sports Illustrated* and *Tennis USA.* One dog-eared *Field & Stream* with a trophy buck featured on the cover stood out of place. On the other end table was a lamp and a small cobalt-blue ceramic biplane. It had to be a special treasure.

She picked up the toylike airplane, caressing it gently. "I was just getting ready to start flying lessons with Chris." Her voice trailed off in the emptiness. "Do you like to fly?"

"No. The plane is just a simple sentimental thing. I bought it after being inspired by Richard Bach's book *Illusions.* It's a story of a barnstorming biplane pilot who turns out to be the messiah." If this didn't run her off, nothing would. He usually saved his reading interests for proven friendships. "You'd have to read it to understand."

"My favorite part of the story is the survival manual," she responded. They locked eyes and a wave of understanding passed between new friends. Never before had he met anyone who had read or liked the small book, one of his favorites. He wondered what else they would share in this lifetime, certain some profound experiences lay ahead.

After returning from the tour of downstairs, Jake excused himself for a moment, giving Alex time to snoop at a shelf of photographs and books. It was part of a nook in the living area, home to a large well-worn leather chair with ottoman, reading lamp, and telephone. *This must be where he lives,* she thought. A picture of a beautiful girl with familiar features rested by the phone.

"That's my daughter." He caught her by surprise, having changed into a comfortable sweatshirt.

"She's beautiful."

"Inside, too," he said proudly. "This was my son," he said, showing her a picture of a seven-year-old boy. "He died a long time ago."

"I'm sorry. Your daughter is lovely," she said figuring he would offer more about the child when he was ready. She was thankful for the distractions. Anything not to think about the events of the day. The horror would return soon enough.

The fire took only moments to build, and soon the large living room danced with a light show of orange and gold. It was several steps sunken below the entry, surrounded by immense glass windowpanes black with night save for the pinholes of light speckled in the distance. The towering ceilings and vaulted room entreated the night. A safe warm glow wrapped itself around the room.

"Could I clean up a bit and maybe borrow a T-shirt?" Alex longed for the hot steam and scalding water of a shower, though no amount of soap could wash away the wretched memory of blood.

He darted down a hallway and returned with a well-washed white cotton V-neck T-shirt. "I hope this won't be too big."

She held up the shirt, which could have been a large muumuu for her. And he thought he saw a tiny smile as she disappeared down the stairs.

⁓

In silence they let the warmth of the fire melt the pain of the day. Alex, draped only in the large T-shirt with her soaked black hair falling around her shoulders, sat mesmerized by the flames. Against house rules, Jake had run down to the local liquor store and bought a chilled bottle of French Chardonnay, the first liquor he'd purchased in eighteen years. Something for Alex to soften the sharp edges of her mind. She was a jumble of frayed emotions. Strong forces were pulling a fragile Alex toward the safety and strength Jake offered. But her heart was being ripped apart with the memories of her time with Colton Forrester. The intimate night with Colt now seemed part of a foggy dream.

"I don't know how to thank you. I just don't know where I would be tonight if it . . ." Quiet sobs spilled out of a heart that couldn't hold back the flood of emotions.

Jake reached for her, offering a safe heart and kind shoulder. Like a saint, he took over the conversation, rambling on, distracting her with the sound of his voice. He had grown up in California in a dysfunctional family before moving to Boulder. He rarely went back to where he came from. He told her about his alcoholism, divorce, and being in recovery. It had been a painful, but necessary growing experience.

"How long have you been divorced?"

"Forever!"

"That's a long time to be alone."

He wanted to know more about her, but not now, not tonight.

They sat on a throw rug in front of a roaring fire. Jake's long frame stretched across the hardwood floor that was spotted with Native-American throw rugs. Alex sipped the cool wine, staring into the heart of the flames. Her mind was black like the night. She didn't know what she was doing anymore, but she was grateful for Jake. Glad that he had made some decisions, thankful not to be at The Brown Palace alone. Jake's voice broke through her thoughts.

"Want to talk?" He moved closer and brushed away a wisp of dark hair. His dove-gray eyes locked onto hers, waiting for direction.

Her head shook back and forth. Jake had been given to her by Chris as if she had known what was coming. Alex reached out to him. Maybe if she held on tight enough it would all go away. His large hands stroked the back of her silken black hair.

"Chris was very special, Alex, someone we both loved in different ways."

Alex wiped a stray tear. "If it weren't for Chris, I wouldn't know you. For that I am eternally grateful."

"Do you think you can sleep for a while?"

Alex nodded. He pulled her head to his shoulder. As hard as she tried, she could not will away the bloody murder scene.

"Chris really loved you," he said. He pulled her closer, trying to absorb her pain. Willingly she lay in his massive arms, accepting his consolation.

"I should have been there for her!" she cried. Jake held on tight.

Finally the tremors subsided. She caught her breath and rested gently against his shoulder. "I think we will be very special friends," she said. There was something she wanted from Jake, something she needed, and safety was the only word that came to mind. There was no room for willful pride. She knew that she needed support to carry her through the unfolding tragedy.

Jake gave her another reassuring squeeze and snuggled her closer. Now that she felt secure, exhaustion took over.

Tenderly he laid her on the couch, shielding her from the cold with a throw blanket. A small light burned in the hallway. Jake retired to the master bedroom. Slipping into cold lonely sheets, he lay in the darkness, wishing for once the sun would not make its predictable journey and take Alex back to the other world.

The living room grew cold as the remnants of the fire lost their glow. Alex blinked, then focused for a few moments, gathering her senses. Maybe it was all a bad dream. Slipping quietly down the hall, wrapped in the blanket, she groped along the unfamiliar walls searching for the stairs. She crashed into an open door and hit her head. "Shit!"

"I heard that." A small light came on from the room behind a half-open door.

"Sorry. I woke up kind of turned around and cold."

"Come on in. It's freezing out there."

"Don't you have heat up here?" Her voice was a sexy deep nighttime rasp.

"Only for emergencies!"

Jake scooted over into the middle of the king-sized bed, vacating his warm spot and holding up the covers. "I promise to be a gentleman. It's much warmer if you snuggle."

Alex slid under the sheets and down comforter, giving a small shiver. Her cold feet brushed against muscular legs.

"Ouch! You feel like the abominable snow woman." He pulled her back up against his chest, enveloping her like a large bear. He placed a gentle kiss tenderly on the back of her black satin hair. "Let's get some sleep. It's just four."

Alex welcomed his warmth and protection, thinking about the stroke of fate that had brought her to this moment with this almost-stranger in the darkness. Chris was gone, their shared dreams imploding. Life had waved its black magic wand and, in an instant, she was lost somewhere in the mountains. But for the moment it felt as if she had known Jake Winston for a lifetime. And in peaceful comfort, consciousness gave up to the powers of the night.

She was safe.

CHAPTER 26

Denver, 1995, First Day

The airphone call went through to Jake Winston on the third attempt.

"Hello, Jake? It's Alex," she said with a voice that erased time. The satellite trembled.

"I've been expecting your call." The Rocky Mountains resonated in his rich voice. Her call was as predictable as night. The news had featured the break in the sensational case that was still veiled in mystery. He had known she would return. "How long has it been?" he asked rhetorically.

"I don't want to think about it. Way too long."

"I am so glad to hear your voice." Funny how the sound of her familiar voice could bring back a torrent of feelings. He remembered how different the house had seemed when she had returned to Texas. He could almost scent her mild traces of perfume that hung in the air like jasmine. Female tracks had permeated every corner—small footprints in the thick pile bedroom carpet, doodle notes on scratch pads by the phone, her special brand of shampoo left in the shower, the top ajar. He had a picture of her covered in mud planting red geraniums in terra-cotta pots on his deck. Each item remained like a tattoo on his soul.

"Will you please forgive me for not writing?"

"No apology is necessary. Where are you now?"

"On the plane."

"Can I meet you?" he asked hopefully.

Alex hesitated. "We're just about to land."

"You could come back to Boulder," he said tentatively. It was a silly suggestion, but a shred of hope remained. He thought about the T-shirt she had borrowed forever, the one that hung sideways just above her knees. In the early morning she would tuck her sculpted legs under her chin with the white T-shirt pulled down to her delicate ankles. The steam from hot black coffee would curl around her head like a halo while she immersed herself in her daily ritual of watching the rising sun.

"I'd better not. I have a reservation at The Brown. I thought it would be more convenient." But she couldn't even convince herself.

"You're old room is vacant, and we could talk, Alex. I'll bring you to Denver early in the morning," he persisted.

Alex wanted to go back to Boulder and sit by the fire, letting it work its spell for a while. For a brief moment, Boulder had felt almost like home. But now it was a forbidden memory. The fear and humiliation of her last encounter with Steve rushed her in an angry flash. At the same time, an oddly familiar power was beginning to smolder again. With every mile between her and her husband, feeling was returning to her paralyzed heart.

"Let me think about it," she said. "I'll call you from the taxi."

A flight attendant informed the passengers that the plane was beginning its descent into the Mile High City. Alex marveled at how the silent years had done little to change the intimacy of their relationship. She knew he understood it all, particularly the part between the lines.

After the murder they had become desperately close. Jake was her ally. He had been by her side through it all, even the time she told Carter where she had been on the night of the murder. Jake tenderly nurtured her without judgment. Even with the knowledge that she had been with Colt that night, he hadn't wavered. He had supported her throughout the painful funeral arrangements and media interviews. Above all, he stood by her side as the business she loved, Aspen Development Partners, unraveled with the weight of the investigation.

Once back in Dallas, far away from the scene of the tragedy,

Alex had clung to the lifeline of Jake's friendship through frequent conversations. Then the bloody nightmare set up house in her dreams . . . and each time they spoke, Jake's voice kept the nightmare alive. Time and distance eventually pulled them in different directions. Alex had Schaeffer to rely on in Dallas, and she pushed Denver thousands of miles into the past.

Steve Blake was her escape. She had had all the loss any one person should experience, and being with him allowed her to stay numb. She had grabbed the life rope not knowing where it would pull her. She threw herself into the Dallas Highland Park social world on the arm of a well-heeled civic leader who was determined to have her as a trophy wife. She rechanneled her hurt into a life of denial directed by Steve's goals for social prominence in the community. Employing mind over soul, she followed his plans by ferociously raising money for elite charities, relieved to bury herself in the details. She had begun to think that if she made him happy it would put the pieces of her shattered world back in place, and she couldn't get hurt again if she was with someone who didn't pose any risk to her heart.

Alex disembarked the jet to meet high-mountain blue skies and hailed a cab.

"Take me to the new airport complex," she requested.

"It isn't finished, lady . . . hell, who knows if they'll ever get it finished at this rate. Word I hear is it's gunna cost the taxpayers a billion more than they projected before it's through."

"Yes, but please just drive me as close as you can get to the area."

The cabbie rolled his eyes. "Whatever you say. It's your money." He turned the cab off Martin Luther King Boulevard, then picked up I-70 heading east away from downtown. The skeletal framework of the airport was beginning to take form in the distance. A million yards of concrete serrated the open rolling countryside where the ashes of her dreams had been scattered. She soaked up the immensity of the controversial building that sat like Stonehenge on the Wiltshire plain, and wondered what Chris would think. The vastness of the golden fields and craggy Rocky Mountains brought tears to the edges of dark eyes etched with antique grief. The power brokers had won. The sun was low in the sky, casting a golden-orange light onto the billowy white canopy that would distinguish one of the world's great transportation achievements. But there would be no industrial distribution system. That vision had died with Chris.

"Turn around!" she directed. "I've seen enough. Take me to Boulder."

Driving toward the mountains was like settling into a well-worn armchair, yet exhilarating at the same time. She was filled with the anticipation of seeing Winston, as well as the prospect of finding out more about what Detective Carter had uncovered. For the first time since she had left Colorado, Alex felt really alive. She was charged with excitement.

Things had changed little with time. It seemed to be a longer drive as they left the rolling fields behind. The impressive buildings of the Denver skyline were emerging in the distance, but no amount of time could markedly change the face of the Rockies. The Aspen Development Partners land was now part of the airport development. After a well-organized probate, the land had been sold for a nice profit, which was divided among the partners. Liquidation had been the best option for the company that had settled into the quicksands of the investigation. Dr. Gougon was out of the country most of the time, and Schaeffer and Alex had no heart to raise money for a new project without Chris.

Chris had generously left each of her close friends as well as her dedicated employee, Jeff Ashton, a sum of money, a million dollars each that came as a complete surprise. Jeff never missed a step. The senator hired him as a personal assistant of sorts to make sure there were no leaks about his dangerous liaison, and Jeff was reveling in the fast track of the Washington elite.

Schaeffer started her own independent company in Dallas,

and Jeanne went on to great accomplishments in breast cancer research. Life flowed on like the powerful Mississippi, moving forward with its unpredictable highs and lows. Oil prices plummeted, and overnight fortunes were wiped clean off the books. The government and the American people got stuck with a multibillion-dollar bailout of the savings and loan industry and thousands of innocent people lost their life savings.

The world turned, but for Alex life was never the same after Chris's death. An empty hole gaped where her friend's vibrant personality had presided and where their dreams had been born.

The proposed industrial distribution project had died, the energies and focus of the project scattered like dry sand in the wind. The senator focused his attention on distancing himself from the murder case, which left no time for anything but putting out fires. Thanks to Chris and the disclosure of the savings and loan documents compiled by John Curry, the feds got to Case Storm and deftly and methodically dismembered the paper tiger.

Riding in the taxi, Alex flipped through her old manila file that was brimming with newspaper clippings. The media had jumped on the Storm story, and the bureaucrats made him the perfect scapegoat for the problems that had come from boundless legislation that had given the industry more than enough rope to hang itself.

Storm's too-good-looking face on a tattered front page from the *Denver Post* awakened forgotten details. The press had peered into every angle to get the full story on Storm. People had thrived on the scandal as it took on a life of its own. Riding on the crest of the outcry for action, justice came down like a heavy hammer. Bill Bridgeforth prepared the way with a golden tongue, and John Curry testified brilliantly at a Congressional hearing, where Storm was drawn and quartered. Reporters speculated on the link between the murder and the financial leader, and readers hung on every rumor. Through Curry, Alex had her day in court, and Storm swung from the high gallows she helped erect. In a small way, Chris was avenged. Alex fingered the fragile papers, part of her wanting to leave the file in the tomb. But another part of her was awakening to the possibilities of a new life.

Despite all the publicity and innuendo, nothing had shed white light on the murder case. The district attorney had not had enough evidence to indict Storm for Chris's murder, so Alex personally made sure Storm paid where it hurt—with his reputation and money. She was the drive behind the efforts to ensure he was handed huge financial penalties that would wipe out the fortune he had not-so-secretly amassed during the glory years of the S&Ls. The once-invincible financial leader was brought to his knees. Bill Bridgeforth was her secret ally, though he covered his flank all the while. He schmoozed Carter and Chief Chapman and maintained total anonymity. In return they had his full and devoted cooperation. Eventually Storm went to jail for a long list of financial crimes, taking the last winds out of the industrial airport project that had once held such high hopes for Denver.

Deeper into the file, Alex found an article on the sale of the Custer Ranch. The pertinent quotations in the story were from Jake Winston. With Chris and Castle Creek Investors out of the picture, Winston had swiftly closed the Colorado Land Preservation deal with the Custer family. Without Chris's competitive offer, there was only one clear path for the Custers. His letter announcing the transaction was one of several Alex kept in the small safe back in Dallas. The deal preserved the entire ranch, now on the border of DIA.

The massive Denver International Airport construction site disappeared from the rearview mirror. A slight burnt-orange haze rested over the city with the Rockies as a backdrop, a sculpture of progress and development. The cabdriver grumbled about how great life was at the old Stapleton Airport and how he hoped they would never finish DIA. It was a financial catastrophe. The hotels were too far away. Nobody wanted it. He rambled on as Alex gazed out the open window. The dry crisp mountain air caressed her face. The taxi exited I-70 before it wound its way into the foothills, heading north toward Boulder.

Alex hastily checked her makeup, reapplying a little blush and lipstick. At that moment she realized the depth of the loneliness that dominated her life. Her friendship with Winston was a profound loving relationship, a part of her soul. Long ago he had helped repair what he could by giving her soul sanctuary and her body shelter. And she had unknowingly taught him about love.

She stepped out of the white city taxi, and the tall, strong form of Jake Winston stood like a Remington bronze before her. The familiar house framed his imposing figure. He reached out to embrace her reedlike frame, lifting her easily off the ground. They clung to each other for a long time before letting go and taking a long look. Alex held on tight with her eyes. Jake grabbed her few belongings, paid the taxi, and ushered her into the entryway.

Jake took the bulging briefcase and placed it in an overstuffed chair like an uninvited guest. He and Alex stared at each other for a speechless moment. Jake's gaze melted every layer.

"I've missed you terribly," she finally said.

"All these years I could always feel when you were thinking about me," Jake said. "There were many stormy days that you played over and over like a ballad in my head." He studied her discreetly. Thinner than he remembered, but even more enchanting. Age had enhanced her natural patina.

Alex devoured the room with hungry eyes, soaking in the familiar. Books were all in their places—even the schefflera plant had survived.

"How did things get to this point, Jake?"

"Life takes odd turns, and most of the time we never understand until later." He went to the refrigerator and pulled out two bottles of Perrier, then looked into her with haunting gray eyes. God, how he'd missed their conversations. They had shared the kind of long talks that meandered like a slow-moving stream, always winding up somewhere unexpected, then debated and argued opposing points just for fun.

"It has been unfair of me to shut out our friendship. I just didn't know how to incorporate it into my present life."

"It's been fermenting these last years."

"How could I think I could turn off my feelings and my friendships and my life like a faucet?" she asked as they moved to the comfortable living room. Jake settled into his favorite chair and Alex sat upon the ottoman . . . steps they had danced so many times.

Jake listened, radiating wisdom, then when Alex paused he interjected, "Alex, you closed our friendship away because you were trying to eliminate a part of the past."

"It didn't work." It was an honest admission to a safe friend.

"Maybe now you can embrace the good wonderful parts of your life here, the momentous joys you shared with Chris. Let the loss of Chris heal over."

She thought about the conversation she'd had with Jeanne and Schaeffer just before leaving Dallas. They all could see the truth. Why couldn't she?

"I'm trying, Jake." Her dark eyes focused on a crack in the floor. "Maybe if the mystery is solved . . ."

"Remember the fun and the exciting challenges you enjoyed? Chris would want it that way. Alex. Talk to Detective Carter. If they make an arrest, so be it—but if they don't, then let it go."

She perked up with curiosity. "You've talked to Carter?"

"Yes, he called several days ago to get your number, and he said they have a new significant lead. Could be a breakthrough, he said."

"Yes, that's all he would tell me. Did he mention anything else to you? My curiosity is driving me crazy."

"Carter just said that they were working on another case and an informant gave them a lead related to the Welbourne murder. He wouldn't say much else."

"Do you find it easier talking with him than before?" she asked, remembering early combative exchanges between Jake and the homicide detective.

"Yes, Carter is a good man, and time has a way of closing wounds." But not all wounds, he thought. His heart was as raw as the first day he had met Alex. Neither time nor distance had helped him stop caring for her.

"I hated having to defend my reputation to him." Shame dripped off every syllable. "That was the most difficult part after discovering Chris in the office. I thought I would break apart inside when he demanded an alibi for the time she was killed." Again Alex's gaze went to the floor.

"And with hindsight at this distance, it's easy to see he was just doing his job." Jake offered Alex a drink, then squeezed her hand in an intimate show of support.

"You're breaking house rules again," she said, knowing he didn't like serving alcohol. "But yes, I'd love one."

Jake opened a bottle of wine and offered her a glass. "You did nothing wrong, Alex." In the depths of his heart, he ached with her sadness and his own. He had never been able to take the risk and tell her how he truly felt. He knew too much about her dreams.

"I'll never forget the humiliation of having to get Colt Forrester to verify where I had been." The night in the loft was a million light years in the past, a thin shadow moment lost in the chaos. Jake hadn't been able to hide his disappointment over her affair, but he had never stumbled. They had forged an ironclad friendship. Jake protected Alex, holding her hand throughout the hours of inquisition from Detective Carter. Finally Carter became certain that she was not a suspect.

"Have you spoken with Colt?" Jake asked, tiptoeing on the delicate ground. It had always been a sensitive subject between them.

"No, I've not been able to anticipate where and how it would possibly fit in." She had been humiliated and defensive after the murder. Later, as their friendship matured, she had tried to explain to Jake the powerful love that had been exchanged with Forrester the night of the murder. She wanted to make him understand that it was more than just a fling.

"Think about it, Jake, I have a husband—who would kill me, by the way, if he knew I was here, much less if he knew about Colt! What am I supposed to do, introduce them and tell Steve, 'I'd like you to meet my one true love. This is Forrester, he's my soul mate, but I somehow got off track and married you in default at a weak moment'?" For just a second, a smile leaked out.

Despite the years, Jake still felt a sting. Her words cut into a part of him that could not be totally cordoned off, no matter how hard he tried. He always told himself that they were friends and that was all it could be, but the hope for more always lingered.

She still loved Forrester. Of this he was sure. And Jake still loved her. They were a triangle of incomplete pieces. He might not be able to have the mystery of her love in his life, but he could sure as hell try to help her out of the tangled web that wrapped around her in Dallas.

"Do you want to talk about it?" He understood far more than even she gave him credit for. He never believed for one moment that she would be able to keep her feelings for Forrester contained any more than he could turn off what he felt for her. That kind of love came along, if one was lucky, once in a lifetime, once in ten lifetimes. And he loved her enough to help her redis-cover it. He studied Alex's chiseled face, cherishing every tiny line and curve.

"I'm not sure what to think after so much time," she said wistfully.

"Stop thinking for once, Alex. Just feel for a few minutes. Use your gut, that intuition that has always been your guiding light. Try to sense what feels right. What does your heart tell you?" If he could only listen to his own wisdom.

"It's not just me. There's Steve to consider."

"Maybe if you explain it all to him . . . what it meant to lose the company and your dreams with Chris."

"Believe me, he's not the empathetic sort."

Alex thought about the loft, the music, Colt's touch, and the empty ache that dwelt within her. But the last time Alex had seen Colt was when he gave his statement corroborating Alex's alibi for the night of the murder. Afterward he had walked her to her car, begging her to come with him. But at that moment there was no light left in Alex. She had callously pushed him away, projecting her own hurt and anger onto him. What had burned between them was snuffed out by her all-consuming grief.

Later she had received a letter imploring her to let him into her life. First he called, and then he tried to give her space. Finally, he pleaded with her to let him back inside the caverns of her heart, to salvage the elusive fragment of love they possessed. But by then the stone walls were well erected. She had decided to stay at Jake's house. With Jake she was safe. Not in a place where she would risk her ravaged heart, not in a place where she would risk loving something death could take away. She remembered the lifeless sound in Colt's voice when she relayed the news. It reflected the dead space in her heart. The fantasies they had conjured together were obliterated by the realities of Chris's murder and later the Storm investigation, which had provided Alex with a consuming distraction. There was no room for love or Colt Forrester.

Alex punished herself for the loss of Chris. She irrationally blamed herself for Chris's death, thinking it could have been prevented in some way if she hadn't been making love with Colt at the time of the murder.

Tears began to brim from her eyes and Jake brushed them away, then handed Alex a red bandanna.

Alex kicked off her shoes aimlessly.

"Have you seen Colt?" she finally asked, not knowing what she wanted to hear. Life would be simpler if Colt Forrester had really vanished into thin air. Maybe she could finally give the haunting memory a proper burial.

"I saw him in a small bar, The Punch Bowl, about a year ago."

Alex's heart jumped. It was not what she expected to hear.

"Not your usual hangout?" Her eyebrows furrowed with curiosity.

"I was meeting a friend who was trying to come off the booze. Colt asked about you, but of course I didn't have any current news."

"How did he look?"

"The same I guess, a little more tired than I remember." Jake peered out the window, trying to find solutions to life's mysteries somewhere beyond the horizon.

"What about his business?" she asked, unable to hide the curiosity, the longing in her dark oval eyes.

"He was still in the oil business at the time, but I think things had slowed down considerably with the recession and all." Jake moved to the massive glass windows and adjusted the blinds, letting in the remainder of the sunset.

"I think about him." She could risk almost anything with Jake—her life and its closely held secrets. "It's like living in a subdivision of hell."

Jake listened with empathetic eyes and ears.

"It's best if I stay extremely focused," she added.

"Exceptional memories only grow in magnitude with time." It was an insightful offering from a man who understood loss. Jake shifted his large frame, throwing a long blue-jeaned leg over the upholstered arm of the oversized chair. His boots were as worn and dusty as his smile.

"When I let him pop into my brain out of the box he is stored in, it is unbearable." Alex sat sipping wine in a cross-legged position. Jake lit several candles as evening entered the room. A dark lock of satiny black hair framed her face. A free hand raked innocently through thick tresses. Jake couldn't take his eyes off her. "We had a moment of paradise," she said, unaware of her seductive appearance.

"Perhaps if you see him and put the memory into perspective, it would be helpful." His voice trailed off and a small voice inside him wanted to cry out: *Forget him! Come with me and let me love you.*

"I'm afraid of what I am sure to find." If Jake only knew the controlling emotional abuse she was enduring at home. "If Steve found out, it could be traumatic for everyone."

"Isn't it disrupting everyone's life the way it is now?"

"Yes, but Steve wouldn't understand. I married him in self-defense. Oh, God, I don't know why, for a hundred different useless reasons. I was numb. I was worn down. And I didn't have any emotional energy left. It was a rebound of sorts. I don't know, Jake, I know it was a mistake, but I've tried to do the best I can. I got more than I bargained for."

"Does he love you?" Jake inquired warily.

"Love isn't a word that comes to mind when I think of Steve. But no one put a gun to my head."

Jake waited for more.

"It was a disaster from the very beginning . . . but at least I didn't have to worry about him trying to pry into the private places in my heart. He's pretty self-absorbed."

More black hair tumbled around her shoulders as she ran long fingers through the unruly locks. Jake longed to touch her face and caress away the hurt that lingered below the surface. But it wasn't their time.

"People make mistakes . . ." Jake offered as he arranged a log on the fire.

"I was vulnerable and stupid—"

Jake felt her frustration, and he wondered why of all people Alex had ended up in such a painful situation. "You are awfully hard on yourself, Alex."

"I made the bed."

"Life doesn't have to be so black and white."

"It does in his world!" she snapped defensively. She was

angry with herself for walking into the snare and even angrier that she had been unable to see her way out. "His emotional needs are fed by power and acquisition. I'm a high-powered domestic executive. As long as everything rocks along with no interference to the polo schedule or the political agenda, he is satisfied. I am merely an accoutrement. I am of value because of my social and business skills."

Jake listened to the sadness and his heart ached. "It doesn't have to be this way, Alex."

"I had no idea what I was getting into. He's a vicious person. I was so blind."

"You can't hide from these feelings forever. You've run from the grief over Chris. You have tried to erase the memory of Colt. You are forcing yourself to live in a barren marriage. Look at me with a straight face and tell me if it has been successful."

The forlorn dark eyes that had once danced with vitality looked flat and hollow. "No, it is not the dream I wanted."

"So what are you going to do, Alex? Wallow in the misery forever?" It was not his style to push, but Jake wanted to help her take the plunge back into life's white waters. He longed to see her stretch and live again.

"Ending a marriage isn't like canceling lunch, you know. "

"Yes, Alex, but you've got Colt in your brain and your heart, so your marriage doesn't have a chance."

"Colt is probably married and living in who-knows-where Montana by now."

"You could at least find out."

"Then what?"

"Trust your heart again."

"What am I supposed to do, just call him and try to pick up where we left off?"

"What do you have to lose?"

"I'll think about it."

"I think he's still in love with you, but you have to swallow your pride and have the guts to contact him, Alex."

She had never been able to hide her feelings from Jake. Sometimes she wondered why they never hooked up together. Their intimacy was beyond anything she had ever imagined, yet sex was not part of the equation. After discovering Chris's body she had been in no emotional state to handle a relationship. She took the friendship Jake offered and gave hers in return, a gift that had altered the terrain of his life. Things were different now—more complicated, too complicated.

Steve Blake paced, watching the downtown Dallas skyline light up like a Christmas tree. In his left hand was an extra-dry vodka martini with a couple of imported Spanish olives. He took a long, slow gulp, then reread the memo from his secretary describing Alex's movements from Dallas to Denver to The Brown Palace. The vodka burned a warm path deep in his gut. Slowly the sedative spread from limb to limb. It had been easy monitoring her movements. American Airlines had cooperated fully once he threw out some big names. And it didn't take an anthropologist to figure out where she was staying. He had his secretary call the credit card company to verify the latest charges on her card, which led him directly to the hotel. She hadn't answered her phone all night. This enraged him.

A part of him was enjoying the game, the chase. But Alex had stepped over the boundaries this time. He seethed as he formulated a plan of action. Crystal, in a black garter belt and transparent bra, approached from behind and wrapped her arms around his bare waist, turning him to face her. He downed the remains of the vodka like medicine. Then he forced her to the floor. Alex burned in his mind like a deal gone bad.

"What time is your appointment with Carter?" Jake inquired, looking at the digital clock in his reading nook. It was almost 10:30 P.M., way beyond the boundaries of his routine, but he was holding on to every precious moment, knowing his time with Alex would end.

"10:00 A.M. tomorrow. Will you please come?"

"Yes, Carter kind of expected to see me. We can leave early and take you by the hotel."

"Thanks for always being here for me. I still think Storm had something to do with the murder."

"Yes, I know you do. But I'm not sure. He may have been a thief, but I don't think he had the balls for murder."

Alex pulled the thick file from her briefcase and slapped it on the coffee table in front of Jake. Bound with rubber bands, its rumpled edges showed signs of age. Contained in it was every newspaper article published on the murder and every reference made to Case Storm from the time of Chris's murder until Storm's release from prison. At a time of desolate loss, the dogged pursuit of Case Storm had given her life purpose. The file was her hard copy of several painful years of grieving. She had used all her connections to bring down the powerful financier, working from Dallas during times Steve was not around. Justice had been served, but Chris's murder was still unsolved.

"He could have hired someone."

"Someone probably did."

"Anyone with enough hate and the right connections could have orchestrated the killing."

Jake relived the familiar conversation, doing the old dance. They waltzed back and forth while Alex dug her teeth back into the case. "He had the most to lose, next to the senator."

"You're right, he could have hired someone, but there's still no evidence," Jake reminded her.

"Have you seen Senator Bridgeforth?"

"Only at official functions from time to time, but I think he's in Washington more than Denver. I saw his wife at a charity fund-raiser several months ago. She's rather attractive, but I'll never understand how he's stayed with her. Hundred bucks says she's got a serious chemical abuse problem."

"The real question ought to be, why did Catherine put up with him?"

"Power, prestige, position. That'll usually do the trick."

"I always wondered if she knew about Chris and her husband. No one should underestimate the rage of a wronged woman."

"I spoke to her only briefly that night. She was busy hob-nobbing with Jeff Ashton."

"Jeff Ashton? He's still working for the senator?" she asked with surprise.

"I guess so. They looked very tight."

Alex cocked her head curiously. "They make a very odd couple." But Jeff was like a cat, always landing on his feet. He had rolled right out of his deal with Chris and right into handling the senator's private affairs, keeping the senator's association with Chris away from the press. Jeff had worked miracles, and the public never got wind of the fact that Bridgeforth was the last person to see Chris alive.

"He had the top-ranking police officers eating out of his hand in a matter of hours. They guarded Bridgeforth like the crown jewels."

"The police chief and Jeff protected the son of a bitch." Rehashing the subject made her blood boil. The case was a muddy mess. Alex vacillated moment by moment, not knowing whom to trust. She wanted to believe the senator was above suspicion because of his professed love for Chris, but doubts remained like stagnant water. He had called her to his office after the murder and worked his charms. He would be on her team, doing everything he could to help her get Storm indicted. Alex did her best to believe the convincing portrait of a grieving lover, and Jeff assured her of the senator's honorable intentions. The senator had almost cried on her shoulder, sharing the loss. But she always wondered . . . was it real, or was he a brilliant actor who had killed his lover and her best friend in the world?

The cell phone in her bag rang for the third time, and she turned it off. She was certain it was Steve, but the caller ID was unknown. He would be desperately trying to locate her.

Alex felt uneasy. No one knew where she was but Jake.

"Are you all right?" asked Jake.

"Sure, I'm fine, why?"

"You just look a little rattled."

"It must have been a wrong number." But the tremor in her voice betrayed her.

The discourse continued into the night, taking the pair into the depths of the shadowy past. Like so many times before, they came up empty-handed. Jake reluctantly said goodnight in the small hours of the morning, and Alex retired to her old room filled with haunting memories and dreams of daimons and fire poles.

The sun was shining on another splendid day in the Rockies. Case Storm leaned back in a new leather swivel chair, two lines holding on his state-of-the-art multiline phone system, a setup he had purchased with the spoils he had amassed before going to prison. He was a man who knew how to hide money and hide it well—he had more money in foreign trust accounts than he could possibly keep up with, and he managed his affairs at arm's length through Smith. His plush downtown office was impressive, although not as ostentatious as his office in the glory days of the S&Ls, and his features were still frightfully handsome, but in a way that jail time had hardened.

Money was being made from thin air in the new offices. Case

Storm had climbed out of the bowels of despair and was in the process of amassing another empire as only reptilian dealmakers know how, men who have learned to maneuver through the governmental agencies and regulatory commissions like sharks in still, warm water. It had been easy seducing would-be entrepreneurs to join his team, young people who dreamed of making the big bucks he promised. His years in Washington had left him with a working knowledge of how to access funding from the government for almost any project. He knew the channels and the systems like a rat knows the sewer. It hadn't taken much time to right the sinking battleship of his life and get back to true North. The phone buzzed.

He pressed a button on the speaker. "Yes, Sandy?" he spoke to his assistant.

"I have a list of the charity organizations and their social agendas as you requested."

"Bring them in."

Sandy, a beautiful but hard-looking woman with just a little too much makeup and perfectly manicured candy-apple nails, came in with the list. Storm scanned it with keen eyes. He had a simple but well-thought-out strategy. Give enough money to the right social causes and to the right people and they'll forgive and forget anything.

"How much did we give to the Diabetes Foundation?"

"Five thousand."

"Call and tell them we want to be a lifetime patron."

"Yes, sir."

In a matter of several years he had managed, with the help of his old crony Smith, to reestablish a successful business. But it involved walking around the block to get where he wanted to go. It had been inconvenient being a convicted felon, but it only put a slight crimp in his business style. The government had a strict policy against lending money to criminals who had cost taxpayers billions, so Storm had set up Smith as the front man.

Smith was perfect. Storm could work him like a skilled puppeteer dictating every move, and Smith's innocuous name was on all the paperwork.

The latest fraudulent scheme had been easy to implement. The government was dying to lend money for day-care centers, and the demand was high. Tell them statistics they wanted to hear and they tripped over themselves to send the money. In turn, Storm and Smith built cheap day-care centers where you wouldn't want to leave a poisonous snake. Storm ran the operation behind the scenes, making sure the bare minimum was spent on the centers. Untrained employees were hired at minimum wage, and the profits flowed back to Storm with plenty of spillage left over for Smith. Professional managers were given kickbacks. Everyone made money. Never mind the horrid conditions and lack of care. They were a mother's worst nightmare, but for many families they were the only choice.

Storm was not concerned. He was playing with someone else's money—a game he knew well. He was even working on a scheme to take a day-care chain concept public.

Storm glanced at the morning paper in his orderly fashion. Business page first, followed by the front section, then local news worthy of mention. Sandy arrived with a fresh cup of coffee and a small stack of messages. Storm riffled through them.

"Deegan hasn't called yet?"

"No, sir."

"Okay. Interrupt me if he calls," he said. Something was very wrong.

"Yes, sir."

His eyes scanned the newsprint, then stopped dead. A wad of anguish settled in Storm's throat. A Detective Carter was quoted as saying there might be groundbreaking news on the Welbourne murder case. The small story on the inside pages of the local news section caught his attention like an atom bomb. An unidentified source had come forward with new information. Storm read the lines again in horror, letting the ramifications swarm in his head. There were no other comments in the article except that the police felt certain they were making progress in the sensational unsolved case that had caused them so much frustration.

The image of Alex Sheridan returned as if in a fever. How he loathed the woman. She and Chris Welbourne had cost him a piece of his life. At least Chris was dead. He intended to have the final say with Alex Sheridan.

Storm jerked the receiver off the cradle and dialed the too-familiar number. He had tried to call for days. The recording buzzed in his ear. "Please hang up and try your call again. This is not a working number." Sweat broke out on his forehead and ran under his arms. He loosened the tie that wrapped around his neck like a noose.

The phone rang, jolting him out of the chair. It was the direct line into his office.

"Storm," he snapped.

"You sound a little edgy." Vinnie Deegan's familiar voice came across the line.

"Where have you been?" Storm demanded of the man who had held a knife at his throat for too long.

"I ran into a little problem the other day . . . been sort of out-of-pocket you might say." The low-rent private eye–turned–drug dealer laughed vengefully from the pay phone at the Denver jail.

"I don't have time to play games," Storm said nervously.

"You may soon have lots of time," Deegan taunted.

"What do you mean?"

"I made a little mistake, and the boys in blue came down pretty hard. They have no sense of humor about selling crack around preschoolers."

"You idiot." Storm's palms grew moist as his thoughts spun out of control.

"You're not in a place to be calling names," Deegan sneered. Then he cleared his throat and spat on the floor of the jail.

"I saw the article in the paper."

"I was calling to do you a favor and give you a little warning."

"About what?"

"Well, they're real irritated with me right now and they want to fry my ass, so I'm going to have to give them some information."

Storm's noose tightened a notch. "You can't set me up, you fucking lowlife."

"I can do whatever I goddamn well please, and I sure as hell don't plan on going to jail for the next thirty years to protect your rotten ass."

"I've paid you a bloody fortune."

"Maybe you should have been paying Alex Sheridan."

"What the hell do you mean?"

"The cops mentioned that she was coming down here this morning. I'm sure she can't wait to see your ass fry!" Deegan cackled as the line went dead.

The ground was opening from beneath Storm's feet as his ultimate nightmare seemed to be coming to life. Not a day had gone by that he had not feared what Deegan could tell the police. The scum was capable of saying anything to save his hide. Terror hammered at Storm's temples. He could handle just about anything but more jail time. He had been in prison enough years to know his limits, and he was not about to go back inside a real prison for Welbourne's murder. His Judas, Deegan, wouldn't mind selling him for freedom. Storm could leave the country, change his identity, but he wasn't going back to jail, especially to a state prison for murder. He wouldn't last a day. Storm whimpered at his desk, cursing Deegan and Alex Sheridan. He had to find out what was going on.

CHAPTER 27

$\mathbf{V}$innie Deegan sat in a holding room on the fourth floor of the Denver Homicide Division, waiting for his attorney and sipping stale coffee. Under the circumstances, he should have been scared for his life . . . but this was a special case with special people. At the moment he was quite confident, even smug, that it would not be much longer before he would have a frosty brown bottle in his hand, followed by free sex with one of his cokehead girlfriends. He had already worked out most of the details of his negotiation. He was waiting for his attorney just so he could make sure he had missed nothing.

A small pile of cigarette butts grew in the rickety aluminum ashtray. The private investigator had been snatched in a big-time drug bust, and now he was up for real time. But he had the goods to buy his way out of hell.

Deegan liked dealing with desperate people. He'd seen mothers who would sell their daughters for a fix of crack. Tangible, reliable information was needed in the Welbourne case, and he had more than they could ever have hoped for.

❦

Carter entered the ten-by-twelve holding room, dominating the space with his presence. He had listened to hours of tape recordings Deegan had turned over as evidence, but it wasn't enough to crack the case unless there was something else he hadn't yet heard.

"Tell me again how you happened to be bugging the office of Welbourne Enterprises."

Deegan spat in the general direction of Carter's left shoe. "Like I told you before . . . we got this call from a client. Our job was to audiotape everything that went on at the office. I think the guy was looking for dirt on the broad. We put a sensitive microphone into a clock linked to a remote, voice-activated recording device. My specialty is keeping meticulous records," said Deegan, staring at Carter and looking smug. "On special occasions I keep copies of important recordings that I think might come in handy down the road. We gave the original tapes to a courier service that delivered them to the client. When she was blown away, that was the last we heard from the jerk who hired us."

"Okay, so what, Deegan. I've listened to the audio stuff. It's a bunch of garbage. You better pray that Alex Sheridan hears something useful or you're going nowhere."

"Trust me, I've got the goods."

"I wouldn't trust you with my cat," Carter observed.

"Touchy. I thought you'd be happy for a lead, seeing as how you guys haven't had much luck on this case." He was growing cockier with every word. Smoke poured from his flared nostrils.

"Fuck you," Carter said and turned toward the door.

"We should be friends."

"You're wasting my time." Carter called for a uniformed officer. "Take him back to—"

"Wait a minute, I—"

"No more bullshit."

"I just want to know the deal. I need a guarantee of—"

"There are no guarantees. You are going down on these drug charges if you don't start talking now!" Carter knew Deegan would walk, but he wanted to see the pissant drug dealer squirm.

"I was promised a deal."

"Then deal!" Carter cut him a look that was reserved for men who were about to hang. "Look, Deegan, the guys in vice don't give a shit about this case. They busted your ass and they want you to go away forever. So if you expect me to go to my buddies and tell them what a great guy you are and how we need to let you go because you're being so incredibly helpful, then I'm going to need more than the song and dance you're giving me right now." Carter bent over the flimsy metal table and got close to Deegan's face. He wanted to plant fear in Deegan before his attorney came in. Large hands grabbed the rumpled dirty collar of the drug dealer's black shirt. Carter pulled his face so close he could smell the stench of rotten tobacco. "I need details. Something we can use."

He let go and Deegan sank back in the chair. Carter was frustrated. He had people waiting to listen to hours of audiotapes, and time was pressing. The stifling room closed in on the adversaries. "Details now!" He slammed his fist on the metal table, sending tobacco ash and cigarette butts flying.

"Okay, okay." Deegan knew he was safe. The seasoned detective was wrinkled and tired. He'd been up half the night preparing for this day, and bags puffed under his red eyes. Carter desperately wanted to solve the case that was a black mark on his record.

An imposing officer with bulging biceps stuck his head into the interrogation room. "Mr. Deegan's attorney is out here waiting."

"Bring him in!"

A neat, slight, bespectacled man walked quietly into the room. No one shook hands. This was not a social meeting.

"Did you bring it?" Deegan asked his attorney.

The man patted his briefcase in affirmation. Anticipation hung in the air.

Carter perked up. More tapes? Maybe Deegan did have something more in his dirty bag of tricks. But Carter was a pro who could hold his poker face as long as necessary. "It's now or never, Deegan!" Carter said, pushing to the edge. "You've got twenty-five long years waiting to suck your life away."

Deegan looked at his attorney, then at Carter. "We put a hidden video surveillance camera with a wide-angle lens in a false bookend." He couldn't hide the smugness.

Carter's mouth gaped in a rare show of emotion. "And you have video recordings of—"

"The murder." The words hung in the air. Deegan looked as if he'd just delivered the crown jewels.

"You're lying."

"Show it to him!" Deegan ordered his attorney. "I'd be happy to let you guys take a look at it if you'll just get vice off my ass."

Carter reached for the tape.

"Not so fast. Do I have a deal?"

"It depends on what's on the tape."

"The murder. The whole thing is on the video."

Carter was silenced for a moment. This would change everything. If what the sewer rat said was true, the case would blow wide open. Carter quickly excused himself and went directly to the chief of police.

⁓

He returned with a plan. "You've got a deal, but we have questions."

"That's why I'm here." Deegan showed a crooked yellow smile.

"Why did you tape the office if you were only being paid to bug it?" Carter asked, curious about the sequence of events. Who knew what parts of the truth were being hidden?

"To cover my ass! And it looks like it's paying off." For the moment he had the upper hand. "I told you. I didn't like getting mixed up with listening in on a U.S. Senator. Hey, the feds are serious."

"When did you first view the videotape?" Carter continued, still shocked by the new development. He couldn't wait to see the film. But there was no way they would release this guy until they were sure the evidence he claimed was on the tape could be verified.

"A few days after the murder. The remote recorder was in the janitor's closet down the hall. We couldn't retrieve it immediately because the building was crawling with cops. When we finally picked it up, after you guys moved out, *voilà!* The whole murder was on tape."

"And you've been holding on to it all these years?" Carter asked in disbelief. "Why didn't you come to the police back then?"

"You guys haven't always been my best friends. Now let's talk about dropping the drug charges before we go any further. I'm a busy man, Detective!" Deegan lit another cigarette. Billowing gray smoke hung in the hot air.

"Who hired you?" Carter continued with the drilling. His eyes were bloodshot and tired.

"That you will know when I have a signed agreement and I walk out of this place a free man!"

"What were you specifically hired to do?" Carter asked, paying little attention to Deegan's continued stalling.

"Follow the broad, eavesdrop, snoop! Record and listen in on everything that took place in the office beginning a couple of days before the murder," Deegan responded, rolling scoffing eyes at the barren ceiling.

"What were you looking for?"

Deegan rearranged his emaciated form a little lower in the brown metal folding chair.

"Nothing," he responded flatly. "We were strictly gathering information and turning it over to the client. The only time we discussed the content was when the senator came into the picture. We were monitoring the office and suddenly Senator Bridgeforth showed up."

"Is Bridgeforth on the video?" Carter tried not to show any reaction to the mention of the senator, but he was beginning to get excited. If Deegan knew about the senator being there, this just might be legitimate.

"We weren't being hired or paid for that matter to listen in on the likes of a U.S. Senator. That's big-time shit. I told the client that wasn't our business. He told me they didn't know about the senator. Their subject was the lady, Chris Welbourne. Like I said, my guess is they were looking for dirt."

"What else did you discuss with this mysterious client?" Carter asked sarcastically.

"We doubled our fee and kept doing our job. Of course we didn't tell anybody about the video camera."

The small room illuminated by a single fluorescent light turned claustrophobic. Stagnant smoky air suffocated the chamber.

Deegan stared at the police detective. Tobacco spittle formed brown stains at the corners of his down-turned mouth. His deal was almost cut and it was only a matter of tying up loose ends before he was a free man. "I want out of here!"

"When were you first approached about snooping on Welbourne?"

"A week or so before the murder. We had to get someone in there in a hurry to set up the surveillance equipment."

"Tell me everything you can remember about the conversation, word for word," Carter demanded.

"I've answered all this crap!" he protested.

"You'll answer it a hundred times if I say so!" Carter glared at the drug pusher and chewed on the end of a flat plastic straw. He couldn't let Deegan know how desperately he wanted to break the Welbourne case. He still bore the scars of the failed investigation, and he had taken responsibility for the failure of the Denver Police Department. The media had eaten their lunch, picking apart the people and the system, blaming anyone associated with the case. Prime-time features on Chris Welbourne and biographical profiles had dominated television talk news shows for months, always ending with the unanswered questions: Why had this woman been gunned down, and why hadn't the police been able to find the murderer? With each televised segment, Carter had felt the sting. Now, finally, he had a chance . . . if Deegan really had what he said he did.

"When you're ready to see it and let me out of here, just tell me."

Carter stormed out of the interrogation chamber, slamming the door and rattling hinges up and down the halls. He didn't like Deegan, he didn't like drugs, and he hated being blackmailed. But breaking the Welbourne murder case was more important than one drug pusher. Still, Carter would have to convince the detectives in vice to buy into the deal. They didn't much like busting guys like Deegan and then letting them go for favors. Deegan was no small bust. The Denver Police had used a sophisticated sting operation to catch Deegan with several thousand pounds of crack cocaine ready to hit the streets of the Mile High City.

Carter walked back into the office of the police chief where the head of vice, Frank Steggo, a surly officer with more than twenty-five years on the force, waited impatiently. Captain Frank Steggo saw the toughest criminals come through the department, and any sympathy he once had for their humanity had been lost a thousand busts before. Mike Carter quickly explained the deal to Steggo and the chief, who reluctantly agreed they needed to see the tape.

Carter returned to the interrogation room, ready to negotiate with Deegan.

"You give us the name of the client and everything about him, along with the video. If it's legitimate, you get a deal for ten years probation. But if you so much as get near a kid with a candy stick, your ass will be buried so deep in the state pen they'll be looking for signs of life into the twenty-third century."

Deegan stood as if he were getting ready to leave. "Aren't you going to say thank you?" he asked sarcastically. "This might get you a big promotion."

"Just tell us who the client was and turn over the tape. After the chief sees it, you walk, but I'm warning you: if this is a bunch of junk, the deal's off."

"Trust me, this is juicy stuff. The senator's a real stud. You guys can sit around the precinct and get off together when you're not out harassing upstanding folks like me." Deegan laughed raucously. Carter slammed a metal chair against the wall instead of taking Deegan's head off.

"You're threatening my client," said the attorney, who had until this moment avoided the fray.

All they needed now was a civil rights violation, and Deegan would walk without having to turn over the tape.

Deegan flipped ashes on the dirty linoleum floor as Chief Chapman came in behind Steggo, who was almost purple with rage over the sequence of events.

Silence hung like pollution over Los Angeles as Deegan held his breath for effect. "So who hired you?" The three police veterans waited anxiously until Deegan lit the match that ignited the room.

"Case Storm."

Not a word was uttered in response as Carter's mind raced with the troubling news. Maybe, after all these years, Storm really was the one. He had motive, but they had never been able to make a close enough link between his white-collar crimes and the murder. Everything changed with this new revelation.

"Can you corroborate that with some kind of evidence?" the chief finally asked.

"Yep! I have everything you want, and you have everything I want." He stared at the chief and then at Carter.

Steggo left the room unceremoniously. The jerk was going to walk.

"How did you communicate?"

"Through a man named Smith. He was the guy who brought the money and picked up the tapes. After our last conversation, when I demanded the additional payment because of the senator, I had Smith followed. I don't like doing business with people unless I know who's paying the bills. He went straight to Storm to deliver the goods. We did our deal, and then bang, it was all over Channel 9 News that she was dead."

"Did he give any hint of why Storm wanted her office taped?" Carter probed.

"No. But I assumed it was about business. He might have said something about a business deal. I asked him if it was a domestic issue. He assured me that wasn't the interest. I remember that much," Deegan continued.

"Storm never contacted you again?"

"That's right."

"You didn't think that was more than a coincidence?" Carter asked pointedly.

"We're in a strange business in which it doesn't pay to speculate."

Deegan neglected to tell Carter about the little blackmailing scheme with which he'd been milking the senator and Storm for years. He didn't think there was any reason to muddy the turbulent water.

Carter mulled over the new evidence Deegan had provided, then they listened to a taped conversation between Storm and Smith. It sounded like the real thing. Carter tried not to get excited, but after many years they were on the brink of solving the biggest case in the history of the department.

"Let's get on with it." Carter was tired of interacting with the sleazy character and anxious to see the tape. Of course they knew the senator had been there. What they didn't know was what had happened after he supposedly left the office.

"Tell me when. I have things to do, places to go," smiled a confident Deegan.

CHAPTER 28

The phone rang at the residence of Senator William Bridgeforth, where Jeff Ashton was fielding a barrage of calls. The high-profile case that had dogged them for years had not gone away.

"The police chief wants to talk to you."

The senator took the call hesitantly, watching his past come back to life.

"The district attorney has informed you of the latest developments?" inquired Chief Chapman.

"Yes, there is some new evidence. He mentioned . . . tapes?"

"It sounds like this guy we've arrested has something substantial. He's just produced a video from a hidden camera that recorded everything that took place in Welbourne's office the night of the murder."

The police chief was confirming the news that Bridgeforth had already been wrestling with. "I want to see it. No one is to see that video before I do, do you understand?"

"You can see it as soon as you can get down here. There is a strong possibility that you are on the video."

"I'll be there this afternoon."

The chief looked at his watch, knowing they would all be on hold waiting for the powerful politician.

"The sooner the better. We have other people here who will need to see this, and I don't want to waste too much of their time."

"What people?" asked the senator, alarmed and horrified by the idea of more people knowing the extent of his involvement in the Chris Welbourne case. He cursed himself for the night of pleasure that had turned into a life-destroying event. His pursuit of Chris had cost him a career. The murder investigation was a black cloud hanging over his head.

"Alex Sheridan for one. She might recognize the killer. And Jeff Ashton is another person we would like to get help from. He was the person closest to her operation."

"Of course. They are good resources. But not until I see it and give the okay." He could control Ashton, but Alex Sheridan was another matter.

"I understand your concern. This is privileged information, but if there is a trial, it could become admissible evidence. If that happens, it will be beyond our control to keep you out of the case."

"Well, you sure as hell better do something! What went on between me and Miss Welbourne before the murder doesn't have a damn thing to do with the case!"

"We're doing everything we can, sir."

"I can assure you that nothing went on between the two of us except some raw sex, which, if I remember from law-school days, is still legal. So I expect you to use your judgment in handling this situation. I want to see the tape and I want any footage of my personal activities edited out. Do you understand?" he demanded. Bridgeforth hung up, angered and dazed. He had tried to put the case behind him, but the demonic murder haunted him at every turn. Deegan had been silently blackmailing him for years. He had already given up on the possibility of running for president. The scandal had been squelched, but a bid for president or even vice president would have been an invitation to the news media to look into every detail of his past. This skeleton was way too big. Now he was considering a bid for governor that would have to be put on hold. Chris's death had erased so many opportunities.

After the news sank in, the senator called in Ashton to warn him about the developments. "Be prepared for a new assault by the press. They'll dredge up old files and be all over us so fast your head will spin."

"The police chief mentioned that they might want me to listen to some audiotapes and possibly view a video. You never know, I might recognize something that could help the case." Curiosity gnawed at Ashton. He couldn't stand not seeing what had happened on that fateful night.

"I'm going down there this afternoon. Hopefully no one will have to see this grotesque scene but me." Deep lines furrowed the aging senator's craggy face. Time and secrets had not been his friends.

CHAPTER 29

Just before sunrise, Alex tiptoed up the stairs, stretched her arms wide, and opened the window shades. Like so many times before, she went to the small kitchen, found the coffee in its usual place, and ground the beans. The pink hint of sunrise against deep blue announced the coming of a near-perfect day, and the tail of the moon hung low in the western sky. While the coffee brewed, she sat, knees up, T-shirt pulled to her ankles, as if she'd never left. The old sleepshirt, one of her favorites, had been stored in the lower drawer by her bed, patiently waiting. Alex thought of mice and men and best-laid plans and wondered what on earth God had in mind for this strange day. Then Jake appeared, sleep still all over his face. For a few more moments they sipped coffee in their favorite places, but they both knew it was time to go. It was time to gather Alex and her belongings and head down the canyon to the hotel to face the business of the day.

∽

Jake and Alex pulled in front of The Brown Palace, a giant rusty triangle of a building, and Alex stepped out of the car.

"Welcome to The Brown Palace Hotel!" Lafayette stepped out from behind a glass door, top hat slightly off center, in his sweeping full-length black wool coat. He offered his welcome to what he thought was just another face that would pass through the revolving doors.

"Lafayette, it's Alex." She started to say Blake, then "Alex . . . Sheridan." The giant man moved closer while a wide grin splashed across his expressive face.

"I can't believe it!" he engulfed her in a spontaneous embrace. "Miss Sheridan, back after all these years!" In a single move he had all her luggage under one arm.

"I'm so happy to see you again," she exclaimed sincerely. "You're still here!"

"Where else would I be?" he asked playfully. "You're a sight for these old eyes! Where have you been for so many years?"

"Texas for way too long. I'm just glad that some things never change."

"You are even more beautiful than I remember, if that's possible."

Alex blushed. "You're prejudiced!"

"Discerning!" said the gentle man. "Very discerning." His eyes danced with delight. "You aren't still riding motorcycles in snowstorms, Miss Alex?" He chuckled as he followed her into the elaborate foyer. Her name sounded warm and familiar rolling off his Southern tongue. But his words brought back arid memories.

"No, not anymore. I'd better go check in."

Alex wondered if she could ever laugh again the way she had that day she and Colt had ridden through the snowy Denver streets. That easy laughter had been left behind years ago, stolen like a piece of her childhood.

"Will you be with us for a while?"

"I'm not really sure. Maybe a few days. We'll visit more later." She slipped a twenty-dollar bill into his cherry-pink palm, then squeezed the warm hand of her old friend.

The formal decor of the familiar hotel lobby was only slightly different from the way she remembered it. Rich dark fabrics, polished marble. She slipped back into the old elegance as memories floated around like ghosts. Alex asked Lafayette to put her things in a room. Then she hugged him, and told him she would see him again that afternoon.

Alex and Jake arrived at the Denver Police headquarters fifteen minutes ahead of schedule. It was her first morning in Denver in ten years, and a powder-blue sky welcomed her. Her anticipation had reached a feverish pitch—she was now back on the familiar emotional roller coaster. What could Carter have discovered?

"Hello, Alex, it's good of you to make the trip. One day we should get together for something simple like drinks," Carter said. Years had worn a few deep lines around the eyes and added what looked like ten pounds. Too many early mornings with doughnuts as the main course had taken their toll . . . but kindness still lingered behind his pale eyes. "Hello, Jake. Thank you for coming."

Alex hugged the old detective warmly. She had long ago forgiven him for making her answer too many painful questions. In a weird way, she was glad to see him again. Even the dingy police station felt oddly comforting.

"Let's go get some coffee." The old comrades headed to Carter's modest office.

"What exactly is going on?" Alex inquired, anxious to hear more about the new evidence.

"We have some startling new evidence, Alex. Audiotapes that an informant has turned over, of conversations that took place in your office about a week before the murder. I thought you might be able to make sense of the dialogue—more than anyone else except maybe Jeff Ashton. He has agreed to listen to the evidence, too." Carter went on to paint a complete picture of his morning with Deegan until he was interrupted by the police chief.

"Carter, can I speak with you a minute?"

Carter followed the chief out into the hallway. "What's up?"

"I want to put everything on hold until we've seen the videotape. It might tell us everything we need to know. And we can save a lot of everyone's time if we don't have to go through the audiotapes."

"Should we look at it now?"

"No, I talked to the senator and he wants to see it before anyone else."

"Oh, for Christ's sake. So we are all supposed to sit on our hands waiting for him?" Carter had been through the drill before with Bill Bridgeforth calling the shots, and he did nothing to hide his disdain.

"We'll get to see it this afternoon . . . besides, the fewer eyes that see it, the better. Just tell Ms. Sheridan there has been a new development. We might even want her to see the video—but not until the senator and I have taken a look. It could be very violent," he said ominously.

Carter went back to the office where Jake and Alex sat speculating. The detective was visibly agitated. "There is another development as of just moments ago. The informant has produced a videotape from a secret surveillance camera that recorded everything the night of the murder."

"Will we be seeing it this morning?" Alex asked, horrified at the idea of witnessing the atrocity which had taken place so many years before. Chris had meant everything to her—mother, sister, mentor, and partner all rolled into one. She was the one person Alex had confided in before she had been savagely ripped away.

"We hope you or someone will recognize the killer. But this will affect our plans for the day. We are going to postpone the tedious task of listening to the audiotapes until we have previewed the video. Then we may need for you to take a look at it. But that will be later. I'm sorry, but you'll have to wait until it's been previewed. It could be quite graphic."

"So the actual murder is recorded on the video?" Jake clarified.

"That's what we're led to believe."

Alex had anticipated reliving painful memories, but this had not been in her wildest dreams. She could not watch Chris murdered like a Saturday night at the movies. It was barbaric. *Why didn't they get some popcorn and make an evening of it,* she thought.

"Thank you for being patient with this change in plans. Since these things could drag on, it would be better for me to call you when we are ready rather than keeping you here all day waiting for the senator to show."

"So the senator gets to see everything first," Alex scoffed, picking up the piece of the story that had been deleted.

"He is supposed to be here shortly to preview the evidence in private along with the chief. They will look at it, and we'll take a statement from Bridgeforth. The rest of us will see it later . . . if the chief thinks we still need your help," Carter explained.

The word "if" hit Alex between the eyes. She exploded with frustration. "This is so typical of this case!" she exclaimed angrily. She had come all the way back to Denver, jumping back into the icy waters of the case, and she had no intention of stepping aside. She was determined to find out what was going on and be a part of the closure.

"I hope it won't be too much longer. I'm sorry for the delay. Alex, this frustrates me even more than you can imagine."

"Frustration I understand," she said emphatically.

"I need to finish up with the informant. I'll leave a message at the hotel about where and when we'll need you."

"I'll check my messages at the hotel."

"My guess is that we won't be seeing anything until tomorrow."

Carter didn't want to tell them about Storm. He was scrambling to put together a case against the high-flying entrepreneur before any word leaked out. Storm was a man with big money, and that meant mobility. The seasoned detective considered flight a strong possibility. The chief could hold the senator's hand and view the video while Carter worked with his team to put together a plan.

CHAPTER 30

After the tape debacle, Jake had to head back to Colorado Land Preservation, leaving Alex with unexpected free time. It was a clear, crisp winter day. The excitement of the morning had turned into disappointment, and Alex found herself pacing around her room like a caged animal. She decided to check in at home.

"Good morning, Fran, I just wanted to make sure you didn't need me."

"No, I've shuffled all your commitments and given out no information," she announced proudly.

"As usual, it sounds as if you haven't missed a trick." Alex stood in front of the spacious glass windows looking at snowcapped mountains. Out of habit, she checked her watch for the time. "Please make excuses for me for the next couple of days. It doesn't look like I'll be home."

With time suddenly on her hands, Steve was nagging in her head. She knew he would be upset. Even at this distance she could sense his outrage.

"Mr. Blake called. I might add he was most upset." Fran was given to understatement, and Alex got the message loud and clear. Steve was furious.

"What's new?"

"He mentioned that he would be at the polo club most of the time, and he expects you to call. The preliminary round of the polo tournament starts tomorrow, and he demanded that you come home."

"Demanded?" The hair stood up on the back of her neck. She was a thousand miles away, and oh, how that had changed her perspective.

"He also wanted to make sure you had taken care of all the arrangements for the governor's dinner at the end of the month. He wanted to know if you had already called the society editor to let the paper know about the dates, et cetera."

"Thanks for covering for me, Fran. I'll call as soon as possible." Alex had come to detest Steve's self-centered ways and suffocating control. He was a stark contrast to her dear friend Jake Winston.

"I understand," Fran responded loyally.

∽

11:30 A.M.

In the solitary hotel room, thoughts of Colt Forrester once again invaded Alex's brain. It wouldn't hurt to look up his number. She had found the phone book in the elegant mahogany bedside table, its weight heavy in her hands. Slowly, she opened the cumbersome pages. Nothing familiar jumped out of the business pages, so she tried the Yellow Pages. Her heart jumped. There it was, big as life: Front Range Engineering. The numbers leaped off the page. Slowly she began to dial the bold-faced numbers, but she hung up before completing the series.

Thoughts of Steve bounded in her head. What could she say, anyway, if Colt answered the phone? Carter could call at any time and tell her the case was solved and she'd be back in Dallas in the blink of an eye. Then what? She had been painfully disappointed by the aborted plans this morning, and she was not so bullish as she had been a mere twelve hours before when her world was coming alive with possibilities.

But the memories persisted. After hesitating once again, she dialed the number. In moments the line of the engineering company rang in her ear.

A female voice answered. "Front Range Engineering."

"Mr. Colt Forrester, please." Her sweaty hand was holding the phone tightly against her head.

"Let me put on someone who might be able to help you." Her heart teetered as another voice came on the line.

"This is Sam Gillespie. Can I help you?" offered a warm midwestern voice.

"I was trying to reach a Colt Forrester who once owned Front Range Engineering?"

"Yes, I bought him out about a year ago."

"Do you know if he's still in Denver, or where he might be reached?" Alex asked. The Pandora's box was now opened and she had to find Forrester.

"Not exactly. He kept a truck in the downtown warehouse until last summer. That was the last time we talked. It must have been five or six months ago. He was planning on doing some traveling after he sold the business, but again, I don't know where he went."

Suddenly her heart felt like an anvil. After all the miles of time, she longed for him now more than ever. The encouragement from Schaeffer and Jeanne coupled with seeing Jake had put a distant fantasy back on the front burner.

Gillespie continued. "I might have a number, but it would be at least six months old. Let me look in my Rolodex." There was a pause as he shuffled the cards. He must have sensed Alex's desperation. "We're not totally computerized around here. I guess the Rolodex is about to become a dinosaur. Anyway, here's the number."

"Thank you for your time." Alex hung up quickly after taking down the number. Now she was on a mission. She dialed the number, letting it ring four or five times before hanging up dejectedly. The chances of her path ever crossing with Colt's again were remote, but her instincts told her there were unrelenting forces at work here. Alex remembered the ethereal condominium that he had prized for its low maintenance. He could leave it locked up for months and go touring with no strings attached. What would she do if she saw him again? He probably had a brilliant woman in his life and only fragments of a fond memory of Alex in his heart. But being in Denver had taken her memory from a fantasy to a vivid possibility. Walking the familiar streets and interacting again with Jake and Detective Carter had mingled the past with the present. She tried the number again to no avail.

Frustrated and anxious to get out of the confining room, Alex decided to take a drive. She drove through the city, embracing its magnitude like a dear, estranged friend. New buildings dwarfed the façade of the old cow town, but its character and grace remained in the charming turn-of-the-century architectural legacies that were the heart and soul of lower downtown. Her car found its way down to Wazee and the Ice House and then to the Oxford Hotel, an old stone-front hotel that retained its historic charm. She soaked in the sights, then gave the car to the hotel's valet to park while she searched out a light lunch. It was a crisp Colorado winter day. Frost hung on the last edges of the morning, but intense sunshine felt warm on her face.

In the foyer of the hotel, huge antique-replica silver coffee urns rested on a period mahogany table. Old stained wood and period tiles had been restored to their former glory. A fire beckoned visitors to linger over newspapers and refreshments. Alex picked up a *Denver Post*, sipping steamy coffee and relishing the unshackled moment. She read the *Post* cover to cover, then picked up a section of the *New York Times*. Patrons, mostly downtown businesspeople, came and went.

There was nothing particularly special about the old hotel. But it was quaint and intimate. A good place for private meetings and uninterrupted solace.

Thoughts of Steve thundered in her head again. It had become her habit to agitate about him. Lately, all of her emotional energy had been directed toward keeping the peace or avoiding his rage.

It was not a peaceful way to live.

Alex stayed in her own world, unaware that Case Storm had come in through the side entrance. She was buried in the financial page, oblivious to the other patrons. In one second, Storm's eyes locked on the face that he loathed. He hadn't seen Alex since she'd attended the Congressional hearing to witness John Curry's testimony—but he had vowed they would have their moment.

Alex picked up the house phone, oblivious to her audience. "Carter, this is Alex. Do you have any idea yet when you will need me to come back down?"

"I still don't know, Alex. But you may have been right all along." She could hear the excitement rushing in his voice.

"What do you mean?"

"We have substantive evidence that Storm hired the private detective who was monitoring Chris's office. Between that and your statement, we may be able to get an indictment."

Alex was overwhelmed with hope. "You're sure about this?"

"We're never completely sure, but this looks tight, real tight."

"I always felt he was involved. You know I can testify that Chris was about to turn him in. There was real motive. He hated her."

"Why don't you just plan on coming down in the morning?"

"Sure. When will you indict Storm?

"We're working on it now. So keep this between us." After the debacle of the morning, Carter felt he owed it to Alex to keep her informed. "Thank you for being so loyal." It was his version of an apology.

Alex hung up the phone, and a wave of relief swept over her.

Just steps away, Storm fidgeted in the back hall, waiting for Smith, who finally showed up in a black-belted overcoat. Smith was a small, wiry man with slicked-back black hair and tinted glasses. Storm spoke to him in a hushed whisper. Then Smith left, heading to the police station.

Storm never took his eyes off his nemesis—the woman he had vowed to one day destroy. He retreated several steps back into the hall, seething and wondering what disfigured hand of fate had brought her to this place. It had to be the case. If she was in Denver and if Deegan was singing, then there had to be something serious coming down—and he didn't want it to be his life again. His throat tightened and his heart raced. The possibility of being turned in by Deegan blinded him with fear. He knew Alex would do anything to see him hang. She was like a bloodhound with his scent. She had always believed he was responsible for the murder. Now that he had the opportunity to face her, what would he do? Many days in prison had been filled with vengeful daydreams.

Carter's startling news dispelled all hunger. In a daze, and still oblivious to Storm's stalking eye, she paid for the half-eaten meal and asked the valet to bring her car. The morning had slipped away while she rehashed the case and pondered the change in plans. Pedestrians hurried up and down the busy street, all with places to go. Alex watched with a glassy-eyed stare. The case was finally coming to a crescendo, and she felt freer than she had in years. But it was a hollow freedom. Steve would never let her go.

It was just after noon when a vivid image of Chris entered her daydream. She was laughing freely and talking about a real estate acquisition they had made many years before. Happiness danced all over her face. *"Either the deal works or doesn't—you can't ever look back,"* Chris had said. It was as if Chris were trying to send her a message! For the first time since the murder, Alex thought of Chris without feeling gray. Maybe the trip to Denver was bringing some closure and she really could say good-bye.

Alex tipped the valet and pulled out into the street without a clear destination. Automatic pilot took hold as the rented car headed onto Wynkoop, then picked up Speer Boulevard in the direction of Cherry Creek. Wind rattled in from the mountains, gusting leaves into the crisp air as the car wound along the creek to Sixth Street then turned westward toward the foothills. Billowy white cumulous clouds mushroomed in a now-volatile sky. A force was moving her into the mountains, beyond control or understanding. On instinct alone, she found herself heading into the foothills, unaware of time and space. Once-familiar roads came back into focus. The instinct was powerful and she paid attention to the details.

The city, swollen with growth, sprawled toward the mountains. Alex enjoyed seeing the changes that time had etched into her favorite city. The town retreated in the rearview mirror. Finally her car came to a stop in the small village of Evergreen, about thirty miles outside Denver. She went into a tiny saloon for a rest stop.

An old cowboy sat comfortably at the end of a long, lacquered bar, with plenty of vacant barstools as companions. Alex found a comfortable seat and studied the dilapidated decor. "You been here before?" the cowboy inquired matter-of-factly.

She looked blank for a moment. "No," she said, slightly startled. Then she turned to the bartender who had appeared from thin air. "Can I have a New Castle please, and bring another Coors for the gentleman." The beers were produced instantly, along with a frosty mug. The bartender offered some popcorn and peanuts, and Alex thanked him, remembering her half-eaten lunch.

"Thanks for the beer," said the old-timer. He put a chokehold on the bottle and downed half its contents in one large gulp.

"You're welcome."

Alex looked around the low-ceilinged, musty place. An old saddle rested on the end of the bar, part of the Western motif.

She listened to the weathered cowboy ramble on about the rapid development of their precious mountain town.

"My name's Bill Sterling," he said, extending a scarred hand with knobby fingers. "You spend much time up here in Evergreen?"

"No, I was here once, many years ago." Alex looked at her watch. "In fact, I'm looking for an old ranch property. It used to belong to a friend of mine."

"Close to here?"

"It was somewhere not too far from here, but I'm damned if I can remember how to find it."

"I've been around these parts for a long time." He sucked in a lungful-and-a-half of his unfiltered Camel, etching another deep crevice into his stone-ground face. His fingernails were permanently stained black from hard work, oil fields, she guessed.

"The place belonged to Chris Welbourne. Does that name ring a bell?" Alex asked.

The man inhaled another black lungful, and like a picture of Hades emerged from a halo of murky smoke. "The property's still there. It's some kind of state park or something. Not too many people go there." He paused with a questioning squint in his eye.

"Why's that?"

"You know that lady who owned the ranch was murdered," he spoke in a low whisper as if there would be danger if the truth escaped. The predictable rumors surrounding Chris's murder had evolved into local folklore. It was fitting that Chris would be sensational even in death. Alex chuckled to herself, believing Chris would be pleased with the drama she was providing the provincial community.

Alex recognized this was part of her unfinished business. It was time to meet the painful memories head on and put them to rest. She knew she had to go up to the ranch for a final good-bye. "Do you know the way up there?"

"It's not too far from my place," responded the leathered old fellow.

"I thought I might drive up there and take a look around. They say it's quite pretty," she said, not wanting to arouse curiosity. Alex had been in a state of shock when Winston had escorted her to the small ranch so many years before. Chris's will had been explicit. She was cremated and her ashes spread in the wind over the ranch. An impressive stone memorial given by Alex, Schaeffer, and Jeanne was erected deep inside the boundaries of the spread. Only a handful of friends were present at the mournful dedication. Alex, Schaeffer, and Jeanne were the honorary pallbearers. There was no family.

Alex's reminiscence was interrupted when the stranger offered to show her the way. "I'm going that way if you want to follow me. There are a few unmarked turns that make it hard to find," he said.

"Thank you. I'd like to look around the property before it gets too late."

A changing sky greeted the pair as they exited the dark watering hole. Alex squinted against the harsh light and shivered as a cold wind cut through her thin fleece jacket. Sterling's rusty old pickup led the way out of Evergreen into the glowering mountains. Wheels rumbled on the rural roads. On the radio, Bonnie Raitt sang a song full of heartache. Twilight was encroaching on the afternoon sky as the mountains hastened to steal the last sunlight from the afternoon.

Alex reflected on Chris's last wishes in the will that had been meticulously detailed, a testament to Chris's organized business style. At her request, the ranch would be preserved through Colorado Land Preservation, which would maintain it as a wildlife sanctuary in perpetuity.

Alex followed Sterling turn for turn, and after twenty minutes of winding up the tree-lined roads, they emerged into a clearing. On the slightly sagging gate was a large iron brand: CDW. Everything was as it should be, just as she remembered. In a vision, she saw Chris's ashes thrown into the wind, then whoosh, Chris was gone forever.

"Thank you for leading me up here." Her firm hand shook gnarled callused fingers.

"It was a pleasure, ma'am. Should I wait?" he asked curiously. "There's not much to do this hour."

The sun sat low in the winter sky. "No, thank you. I just want to look around a little and enjoy the solitude." She was ready to be alone. "I won't have any trouble finding my way home." It was time to have a heart-to-heart with the hurt, anger, and hostility that had paralyzed her emotionally since the murder. It was time to bid a final farewell. Cold wind tousled her hair and cut through the lightweight clothing.

"My wife and I live only a couple of miles down the road if you need anything." He tipped his hat with a crooked finger.

"Thanks again for your help," she said politely. "I never would have found the ranch without a guide."

The 1978-model pickup lurched into the twilight, kicking up a fog of caliche dust into the approaching dusk. The view of Alex diminished in the rearview mirror. The truck ambled along at country speed, Sterling's weathered arm resting on the open window. The wind gusted, bringing a storm down from the high country. The old man's rural blood didn't like leaving the nice woman up there alone, but it was really none of his business. Of course, in a small town, everything is everyone's business. He checked the rearview mirror again and headed down the bumpy dirt road to his mountain cabin.

CHAPTER 31

It was two in the afternoon, and the chief asked an assistant to recheck the video recorder for the fourth time. The intercom buzzed.

"The senator is here."

"Send him in." The chief smoothed his thinning hair and glanced at his aging reflection in the mirror attached to the back of the office door. He was nervous, and for good reason. If he could continue to keep the senator's involvement in the case out of the jaws of the media, he still had a shot at hanging on for a few more years until retirement. If things became politically sticky, this could easily be the end of his career. The senator was powerful and manipulative. He had warned the chief on more than one occasion that if he were destroyed, there would be consequences for the people around him. No one would remain unscathed.

"Good morning, Chief." Senator Bridgeforth offered his political glass-bottom smile.

"It's nice to see you in Denver, Senator. I'm sorry about the inconvenient circumstances." The two men shook hands perfunctorily.

"No one has seen the tape?" the senator asked officiously.

"No, sir. It hasn't left my office."

"The only other person who has seen it is the private detective you arrested?" Bridgeforth had paid dearly to keep this tape out of the hands of the public. He didn't want it circulated among snickering police detectives.

"Yes, sir. Assuming he is telling the truth."

The senator had known he could never trust Deegan. Bill

Bridgeforth had received the first extortion call two weeks after the Welbourne murder. Deegan had introduced himself and described in exquisite detail the tryst with Chris. He had demanded hush money. Over the years the ill-suited pair developed a convenient silent partnership. Bridgeforth sent thousands of dollars, and Deegan kept quiet about the tape and its contents.

Now, in some ways Bridgeforth was relieved. Now that the tape was out, he would be through with Deegan and the insidious blackmail scheme that had cost him money and dreams. His final act of involvement with Deegan had been to foot the bill for a good attorney to represent the despicable character. The tables had turned. The senator agreed not to turn Deegan in for blackmail, and they would never speak of the incident again. The attorney would be helpful in keeping Deegan out of jail. If Deegan ever contacted the senator again, he would be turned in for extortion. Suddenly the senator had much less to lose than he had before. Time and bad choices had eclipsed his once-promising career.

"Did you get any new information from your informant?" Bridgeforth inquired.

"Yes, sir," Chief Chapman responded.

"And what did he say?" the senator asked, taking charge of the meeting.

"He told us he had been hired by Case Storm." The chief waited for a reaction. At the time of the murder, Senator Bridgeforth had been very tight with the thrift chairman. When Storm's problems hit the papers, the relationship had changed as quickly as a cold front moving across the plains.

"That certainly sheds a different light on the case." Bridgeforth's eyes never wavered. He remained as placid as stagnant water. He actually sighed as the veil of fear lifted. So Deegan hadn't said anything about their long-standing blackmail relationship. But that made sense. After all, blackmail was a crime.

That left one piece of unfinished business. The last piece of the puzzle would be to see the face of the murderer.

"Shall we go ahead and see the tape?" the chief inquired.

"Let's get on with it." Bridgeforth doubted he or anyone would recognize the killer. From the beginning it had seemed obvious that it had been a professional job.

The senator sat in the dark, clutching the sides of an old metal chair with sweaty palms. He dreaded seeing himself on the video, but in a matter of a few minutes, the nightmare would finally be over. The chief was kind enough to fast-forward through the copulating and the shower that followed once it was clear no one else was in the room except Chris and the senator. The tape slowed to normal speed with the senator saying goodnight to Chris. Their last farewell, he thought, fighting tears. Seeing Chris brought back long-forgotten feelings. His life had been shattered by her death and its aftermath. His political aspirations had died as he sank into a low profile for the first time in his life. Stuck in a hollow marriage, he was paying dearly for his short time with Chris—and not only to a blackmailer. He choked back his emotions, watching the beautiful image of his long-ago lover kiss him good-bye. His tears were as much for himself as for her. In the darkness of the police chief's office, he watched himself leave the twenty-third-floor office. It was exactly as he had told the police so many years before.

The video rolled, revealing only darkness as they waited to see for the first time what had actually happened in the violent minutes that occurred after his departure. The pulse in Bridgeforth's left eye throbbed uncontrollably. He loosened his tie. Only silence and the gentle, graceful movements of his former lover filled the room. Like an angel in the night, Chris moved from the bed to a chair by the massive windows. Her translucent golden robe flowed elegantly behind in a wake. They strained to see the faint images obscured by the low light. She delicately grasped a Waterford tumbler in her left hand. The sophisticated wide-angle lens had captured every corner of the office.

The senator could hear the heavy, labored breathing of the chief and the pounding of his own heart. For seven years he had racked his brain, trying to imagine what had transpired that night. Chris moved to the wingback chair facing the expansive plate-glass windows. Light from the bathroom was reflected in the glass. For a moment the camera lost her face, revealing only the back of her head above the leather chair, along with pieces of her reflection. Her form grew very still as she softly fell asleep. Bridgeforth's mouth felt as if it were filled with cotton, and his palms were wet and cold. The chair groaned with his agitation. Then the light changed.

A shadowy form entered the office. A silencer was clipped to the muzzle of what looked like a .44 semiautomatic, a deadly weapon. It was a simple entry. The dark figure wore night-vision glasses and scanned the room like a stealth fighter.

Bill Bridgeforth strained to see. In peaceful sleep, Chris rested with her head supported on the back of the chair. Mouth slightly open, her chest rose and fell effortlessly.

The senator leaned forward in his chair. The air in the room hung heavy with the odor of fresh sweat. The chief's chair grated under his shifting mass.

The form of a man was hidden in the shadows. He turned, silently searching for his prey. Like a shark on the scent of fresh blood, he maneuvered to the edge of the room where Chris slept. The light from the fixtures in the bathroom illuminated the unknown intruder. Bridgeforth's stomach muscles knotted, then recoiled with anxiety. He held his breath, searching for control. Something was familiar about the face, the form, the build. He wasn't sure where, but he knew he'd seen the man before. The pulse in his head thundered as he strained to recall. From the recesses of his memory, an image came to him piece by piece. Then he wanted to crawl in a hole and die. In the instant of the senator's recognition, the assassin raised the large handgun.

Bridgeforth gave a dry heave of nausea. "Please stop! I can't see this anymore. Stop this." Bent over, he cupped his face in his hands between his knees. "I can't see any more," he pleaded.

The tape rolled on as the killer's hands embraced the large-caliber pistol, warming the muzzle of the silencer to the temperature of living flesh so the cold wouldn't disturb his slumbering victim. He placed the muzzle on the edge of her neck, just below and behind the ear in an aim designed to annihilate the brain stem and cause instant death.

Two shots at point-blank range left Chris Welbourne lifeless in the chair. Blood and brains and skull fragments sprayed out the exit wound, obliterating her world. The half-empty Waterford glass crashed to the floor, shattering into a thousand tiny prisms on the polished marble. Crimson blood in black and white trickled down her face onto the chair in a small rivulet dripping persistently into a pool that congealed on the icy floor.

The mysterious killer systematically removed plastic gloves, rolled them inside out, and stuffed them neatly into his bulky overcoat. He exchanged for them a pair of men's ordinary black leather gloves. Bridgeforth looked up again and absorbed every feature. The face made of chiseled stone disappeared into the shadows. Closing the office door without looking back, the assassin made his exit.

The clock on the executive desk of Welbourne Enterprises read 2:41 A.M.

Chief Chapman put an empathetic hand on the senator's shoulder. "It's over now. Could you make anything out of the tape?" Maybe it would be over for the chief, too. He was tired of having his future tied with an umbilical cord to the life of the senator.

They did not speak for a long while. Late afternoon was approaching slowly. Bridgeforth tried to pull himself together. The chief pressed him again, probing into the wound. There could be no protocol for a moment like this. "Did you recognize the man?" the chief asked.

"No. Nothing," he lied. "Except that now you know that I

wasn't there, this is over for me."

It was a cavernous statement that reverberated through their lives.

"We'll get a composite of the assassin's face, then send it out to the FBI and every other police organization. This could be a good lead." Then, with compassion, he tried to offer consolation. "I'm sorry you had to see it this way."

"Well, make damn sure no one else sees me in it. Edit out the first half and just show the murderer coming in. It's obvious I had no part in the killing. And I'll stake my reputation on it that you'll never find that man."

"I'll keep the original locked up here with the other evidence. You can go now, Senator." For a flash second, just a normal man in agony sat in his office, not a United States Senator or an emblem of power, just another grieving soul.

A broken man left the chief's office. Whatever hopes he had harbored of the nightmare finally coming to an end had been destroyed.

CHAPTER 32

A shiver ran through Alex's body as an early moon danced from behind the shrouded charcoal sky. The fragrance of coming snow permeated the air like traces of perfume. Alex was trying to remember the way to the memorial site. With intuition leading the way, she headed in the general direction. A carpet of pine needles blanketed the forest floor, and crisp, dry twigs snapped underfoot. Pieces of her soul had been torn apart and scattered here as surely as Chris's ashes had been spread upon the wind. Alex picked up the pace, fearing nightfall. It had been so many years. It would be almost impossible to locate the small clearing if she didn't find it in the next few minutes.

As she walked quickly through blue spruce, she anticipated calling Schaeffer with the news about Storm. For a moment she let herself fantasize about leaving Steve and getting back into the oil business. There was a lightness in her step. She followed a well-worn trail traveled by deer and small woodland creatures. Seven years before, the memorial statue had been ferried deep into the woods in a slow drizzling rain for what felt like hours until they had emerged into the chapel-like clearing. This land had been Chris's favorite place to ride horses and have picnics by a rushing stream fed from the frozen remnants of the winter. It was a sanctuary. Alex breathed hard in the high elevation, pulling the zipper of her fleece jacket tight under her chin.

A large owl screeched a warning to the trespasser. Alex began to question her motive. She had thought that returning to the ranch would help her find closure with Chris, but she realized she wasn't really looking for Chris, she was searching for herself.

Determination drove her to continue on the journey she'd started.

Suddenly, a hundred yards ahead, the trees parted and the clearing appeared. It was the right place. Relieved, Alex approached the granite memorial and lowered herself gently to her knees. She held her breath, trying to slow the pounding heartbeat that thundered in her chest. In the eerie light she could still distinguish the chiseled epitaph that Chris had written many years before her death.

> CHRISTINE DUNNE WELBOURNE 1946–1984
> Dwell not on the fruits of tomorrow
> Answer only unto yourself
> Live life on the edges of the wind
> Give freely what you wish to share
> Love with the ever-changing passions of the sky
> Hold tight to your dreams
> Soar with the eagles in the heavens
> Regret not what is past

Alex read and reread the inscription as if for the first time. Her eyes squinted against the looming shadows. "Regret not what is past," she whispered. She wrote down the epitaph on a small pad and vowed to read it every day for the rest of her life. It was a gift Chris had left for her many years before, but until now Alex had not been ready to listen. As the faint light rested on the stone in the wind, Alex vowed to build a new future. "Thanks, Chris," she murmured. "I've got work to do."

With her life in Dallas a world away, she headed back to the car, leaving the crippling memories to rest. Even if the murder case was never solved, she was now on a clear path. Her mind skipped ahead, churning with new purpose. She would call Schaeffer as soon as she got back to the hotel to start talking about a concept for another company . . . but it would have to be a completely new venture. She wasn't interested in excavating the past. The sky lightened as she emerged from the wooded canopy. High above, wide-winged birds of prey floated on the wind.

Around a bend in the woods, she stopped dead in her tracks.

Not fifteen feet ahead of her stood the imposing figure of Case Storm. The financier was bundled against the cold in a black trench coat. Face to face, their eyes locked in the mutual distrust that had only grown over the years. His piercing black eyes burned through her. Instinctively, she stepped back and prepared to bolt. A gale whipped locks of her hair, tearing at her eyes.

"You are trying to frame me," he pointed a trembling finger and moved several paces toward Alex.

"You hired Deegan. You can't get off this time," Alex said with conviction. Like boxers in a ring, the two adversaries squared off.

"I didn't kill her," he said pleading. "She was going to turn me in, but I didn't kill her."

"They have hard evidence!" His life was a dictionary of manipulation and deceit. Why was he trying to sway her?

"You have to listen to me!" he begged with desperation as he moved closer.

Alex stood her ground. "Carter has a witness—" but she never completed the thought.

In a flash he was on her with his hands around her neck. "You can't set me up for this. I'm not going back to jail!" He had snapped under the torrential pressure of the investigation. He knew they were closing in. He knew Alex was driven to see him hang, and he was fighting for his life.

Alex struggled against his grip, sucking for air. But his rage was fierce and powerful. Alex fell to the ground, a sharp rock digging into the back of her head. His hands tightened their hold and her mind went black.

❦

Steve Blake popped the cork on the 1992 Dom Perignon,

ignoring the priceless golden bubbles spilling onto the antique Italian marble table he used for a temporary desk and office. He stood erect—just over six feet tall—lean and naked in front of the spacious glass windows, studying the twinkling skyline of downtown Dallas. He wondered how many billions had been made and lost that day and then turned his attention to the business at hand. Crystal lay on the bed recovering from an early evening session of hard, fast sex. He was her only client, and she was his toy. "All mine!" he thought. He paid dearly for this luxury, and she performed handstands if that was what he wanted.

Steve casually picked up the opaque forest-green bottle and poured a glassful of the liquid gold. He sipped a deep, silent throatful before dialing Fran.

"Alex Blake's residence," she answered officially.

"Haven't I told you to answer our main line 'Blake residence' —or are you confused about who pays your check?"

"No, sir."

"Do I make myself clear?"

"Perfectly!" Fran loathed Steve, but her loyalty to Alex kept her from seeking other work.

"Have you heard from Alex?" he demanded. Crystal shifted in the bed, motioning for champagne. She was a beautiful nymphlike creature who had been born into a family that had only drugs, alcoholism, and abuse in its gene pool to pass on to the next generation. To her, life as a plaything for rich men like Steve Blake wasn't so bad. She'd had other clients who were more coachable but not nearly as rich. Steve could do it upside-down for all she cared, as long as the money kept pouring in.

"Not since this morning, Mr. Blake," Fran replied mechanically.

"I'm at a late meeting. You should go home for the evening."

"Yes, sir. I'll set the alarm." Fran knew something was wrong. She felt the heat of conflict rising and worried about the bruises it might leave on her employer. "Will you want breakfast prepared for you in the morning?"

"No! And don't bother coming in until ten. I'll be leaving early."

Fran understood. Mr. Blake had a way of suspiciously disappearing, and just last week she had finally figured out the situation. Fran took care of all the details of the Blake's home, overseeing everything. She knew where every article of clothing was hung and was also aware when items were missing for days. It was by sheer accident that she discovered the whereabouts of Mr. Blake's missing wardrobe. While running an errand she had accidentally seen him at the exclusive Turtle Creek high-rise in one of the missing suits. She had been on the way to deliver a contribution check to a woman who occupied the penthouse. Fran stepped off the elevator on the wrong floor and saw Steve Blake standing in the hall, freshly showered and shaved, locking the door to an apartment. She recognized a suit of clothes that hadn't been in the house for at least a month. It all made sense. Steve Blake was maintaining a pied-à-terre, a love nest . . . She had planned on telling Alex after the cancer fund-raiser was over, but she had not had the opportunity before Alex left suddenly for Denver.

Steve hung up the phone, poured more champagne, and cursed both Alex and Fran. He didn't trust Fran. He didn't trust many people, especially people who knew too much. He ignored Crystal as his thoughts churned. Lightning flashed in the mirror-like glass, and Steve reflected on his hard physique. Things were going to change dramatically when Alex returned. But it wouldn't be easy. Alex was devoted to Fran. That was bothersome. They were far too close. Thinking about Alex reminded him to call the hotel in Denver. He dialed the number while sipping on champagne remnants and ogling the youthful, supple body of Crystal wallowed in the heap of satin sheets.

The flat was a small but elegant hideaway he had purchased long before marrying Alex. The downtown Dallas nightscape twinkled like a field of Christmas trees in the blackness. He had figured it was a matter of time before he would give up this last vestige of his single life. But the time had never been quite right. Stylish, educated women made outstanding mates, but he liked high-priced professional call girls in the bedroom. They did what he demanded and he liked the control. Every now and then he thought about giving up the prostitutes, but then the lustful fire would return even stronger.

The apartment, along with Crystal and her fringe benefits cost him approximately twenty thousand dollars a month, which he justified as a basic business expense. Business went better when he was happy. Crystal was allowed to come and go as long as she checked in with Steve's secretary and wore a beeper, a golden noose that followed her from elegant bistros to the boutiques of Highland Park. She belonged to him. Charge accounts at the best salons with the usual limits were maintained in her name. He paid all the bills and called all the shots.

The phone at The Brown Palace Hotel rang once as he ordered Crystal, "Get in the shower. I'm hungry."

"But you promised me some champagne first," she protested.

"—and be quiet!" he yelled.

She moved to his side, rubbing up against his hard frame, toying with and caressing his naked body.

"I'll bring it to you in the shower. Now be a good girl and shut up."

"Brown Palace, good evening," the receptionist announced.

"Alex Blake's room, please."

After several rings, a robotic voice automatically transferred him to voice mail.

He slammed the receiver down and cursed under his breath, "Where the hell is she?" He had just about had enough. And who did she think she was, just leaving, not asking his permission, not calling to check in, just getting on a fucking plane like she owned the world?

He headed into the large marble-and-glass shower to find Crystal. She knew just how to take the edge off his temper, and no one could enrage Steve Blake more than Alex.

He turned to Crystal, savagely kissing her. Grabbing a handful of wet blonde hair, he forced her down on her knees. His mind raged, and his body responded erotically to the anger. He faced the wall above her, his arms stretched above his head, supporting his angular frame on the marble walls. Hot water poured down her face as he began to lunge deep into her responsive mouth. Her jaws ached. He pushed her head back against the marble wall and held on to her head with his hands until he was wasted. "Get dressed," he ordered, leaving Crystal slumped on the floor of the shower. "I have to get to the airport."

CHAPTER 33

Bill Sterling and his brother Bubba heard the muffled scream as they approached Alex's rental car. They had come back up the mountain road to check on the beautiful stranger. It had been a good excuse to have a beer and relax in the early twilight before returning home for the evening.

Bill Sterling was an average-sized man, something that could not be said about his brother, who'd been a lumberjack for twenty-five years. Logging was laborious work, producing vigorous men of iron. Alex passed out just before Bubba Sterling threw a paralyzing right fist into the face of her attacker. The second blow split skin and lips, dislodging teeth and disfiguring Storm's face. Another blow knocked him out.

Sterling used the toe of his boot to roll the man off the tiny, still figure. With a massive tender hand, he brushed a smudge of dirt from Alex's cheek. He cradled the featherlight form in his arms, ferrying the parcel to the front seat of the Ford pickup. Then he returned for the motionless attacker, whom he hog-tied and tossed in the back of the flatbed like a sack of flour.

"What are we gonna do with her?" Bubba asked his brother as he stroked the dirt-smeared face. They were good countrymen trying to do the right thing.

"Here. Cover her with this," Bill removed his coat. "Her hands are like ice."

The mountainous man moved to the driver's side. "Let's get her to the house and call the doctor. Then we can call the sheriff."

The pickup lurched into gear and bounced along the unpaved mountain road with Alex sandwiched between the two large men.

The lopsided moon shone through a twinkling halo of stars.

Alex regained consciousness in the living room of Bill Sterling's cabin with Meredith Sterling applying cold compresses on her neck and face. The throbbing of her head brought back reality. Through the creaky screen door came an old, weathered man carrying a black bag.

"Where am I?" Alex searched the room to get her bearings. It was a well-worn room filled with rural knickknacks and an antique rocking chair. A mug with Elvis's photo sat in a pine bookcase packed with memorabilia.

Bill Sterling leaned over and took her small hand. "You're gonna be okay, honey, just real sore for a few days."

Electric shocks of pain ran through her with every twist and turn. The doctor gently examined her. He studied the cut on the back of her head and the bruises on her face.

"I feel like I've been hit by a truck." Alex rubbed the back of her head.

"You may have a slight concussion."

The doctor gave her a pill for the pain. She put up no argument.

"You won't have to worry about your attacker anymore. We have him tied up in the pickup," Bill Sterling offered confidently.

"Thank you," Alex managed to express in a meek voice.

"It's a good thing Bubba came along for the ride."

"How did you find me?" Alex's speech thickened and her eyelids felt like steel doors.

"We just wanted to go out for some fresh air and a beer. To tell you the truth, I just had a gut feeling something wasn't right, leaving you up at that remote place by yourself. We found your car and then heard you scream."

"Thank you." Alex repeated in a more audible voice.

Mrs. Sterling came in with her china service and offered Alex a steaming cup of hot tea.

The local sheriff pulled into the dusty drive to find Bubba standing guard over the assailant. The action was over, but in the small country town the story would be retold in a variety of versions for years to come.

"What happened?" Tommy Billings asked. Billings served as the local sheriff in a community that experienced little crime and no violence and word was out on the CB and half the people near the Sterling place had already heard the news that was being magnified over the gossip chain. Pickups jammed the driveway, and old men in overalls drank beer in the moonlight, enthralled by the drama.

"Bill showed this girl up to the old Welbourne place, but he was worried she'd get lost trying to find her way out," the lumberjack explained. "I went back out there with him, and we heard her scream. Then we found her tangled up with this man. He would have killed her sure as I'm sittin' here."

"How's the girl doing?" the sheriff demanded. Tommy Billings wasn't accustomed to the procedures dealing with violent crime. He had graduated from the local high school as one of the star football players and after earning a degree at a small Colorado college, returned home to the quiet community of Evergreen. The hardest part of his job was dealing with friends. Saturday nights brought the usual under-the-influence arrests, but for the most part, it was a sleepy mountain enclave with little challenge to law and order. He was glad Bubba had been there.

"She's in the house with Bill and Meredith. Looks to me like they'll need to give her a stitch or two. The doc's in there now. Go on in and see what you think, Sheriff."

The sheriff approached Bubba's prisoner and read him his rights. There was no response. Case Storm's head hung low but his eyes raged defiant and vengeful.

"Give me a hand here, Bubba. I want to cuff him and put him in the car."

Bubba manhandled the prisoner, transferring the belligerent load into the sheriff's truck. In the light, the sheriff took a closer look. Dirt covered the man from head to toe, but he was wearing an expensive suit. It was obvious he wasn't from around Evergreen.

The sheriff went in to find Alex sitting up on the Sterling's sofa, trying to call Detective Carter on her cell phone. She pressed "end" and looked up at the boyish-looking sheriff. Even with bruises and the early signs of swelling, he could tell she was an exotically beautiful woman. "I'm just as sorry as I can be, ma'am. This sort of thing just doesn't happen around here," he said. "What's your name?"

She gave her name and explained the bare essentials of her background.

"Have you ever before seen the man who attacked you?"

"His name is Case Storm, and he's wanted for murder," she said.

"Murder?" stammered the provincial law enforcement officer.

"Yes, murder. Detective Mike Carter with the Denver Police Department knows all about it."

"Can you come outside and officially ID him?" the sheriff asked in disbelief.

"I guess so." Alex rose on wobbly feet to confront her attacker. The sheriff offered a supporting hand.

The sheriff and Bill Sterling helped Alex walk outside. The three strangers, thrown together by fate, entered the dirt-packed driveway now enveloped in mountain darkness. The perimeter of fir trees and lack of city lights intensified the thickness of the night. The cold front had arrived and stars twinkled in the clear sky overhead. Bubba pulled the prisoner from the sheriff's vehicle, yanking his head back to expose his face. The sheriff shone a blinding light into Storm's eyes.

The captive didn't fight against the giant lumberjack's vise-like grip. He glared angrily at Alex. Bubba forced him back into the truck as the sheriff supported Alex by the shoulders. "You're sure you recognize him?"

"Yes," she stuttered. "I could never forget that face."

"What was the name again?"

"Storm. Case Storm." She turned to the once powerful and respected man. "I hope you rot in hell where you belong." She turned toward the cabin, pushed away the sheriff's supportive hold, and headed toward the warm kitchen to try calling the detective again.

Carter answered on the second ring.

"We've got Case Storm under arrest up here in Evergreen." Her voice was weak but in control as the epitaph from Chris's memorial resounded in her head.

"What are you talking about?" he demanded.

Alex quickly relayed the details of the afternoon excursion to the Welbourne retreat, providing just enough information to get his complete attention.

"Storm?" Carter asked in disbelief. "You're sure it's Storm?" he asked again, almost rhetorically.

Alex's nerves were tattered. Hot anger exploded to the surface before she could control it. "Dead sure. Look, the son of a bitch tried to kill me. Don't you think I would know whether it was him or not? Come see for yourself." Alex regretted losing her temper with Carter, but his predictable, measured emotions and controlled investigative style were sometimes irritating. Then she checked her anger.

"Who's the sheriff?"

"Tommy Billings. He's right here."

"Let me talk to him," Carter ordered. "Then we'll get you back here as soon as possible." Carter and the Denver police chief had just spent hours trying to determine how to proceed with the investigation of Case Storm. They had planned on delivering a warrant early in the morning. Now fate had done its dance and they had him with little effort. Alex, holding an icy towel against the back of her head, handed the phone to Billings.

Alex shivered, thinking of Storm. The adrenaline high had worn off and was replaced by the sinking letdown that comes after physical and emotional trauma. Back in the warm mountain cabin, she felt a wave of fatigue flood through her veins. The drugs were working their magic. Her mind grew thick. Fatigue distorted every detail. Her pounding head made it impossible to think, and her eyelids filled with lead as she waited for Detective Carter. The medication took hold, and Alex fell into a black sleep on the Sterlings' den sofa as her plaguing dream returned in a mutated form.

This time, like every other, the oil field crew mingled around a well in progress. Alex saw herself studying the latest geological reports. It was a familiar place. She had come to know it a hundred times or more. The wind blew steadily from the west. This time they were in Colorado, maybe the western slope, but she wasn't sure. A drilling rig creaked and groaned in the background. Workers went about their chores. Then Chris appeared from nowhere, wearing white slacks and a crisp white shirt that almost glowed. Oil field equipment lay scattered around the site like Tonka toys on a little boy's playground. The drilling equipment cranked and whined as the drill bit cut deeper into the zone they hoped would produce oil. Men scurried about like ants on a mission, but Alex sensed something was wrong. Pungent doom filled the air. The drilling was taking longer than expected. "How's the well coming?" Chris inquired. The field crew operator was yelling at men who had scattered in all directions. "She's showing water, but there's oil down there," Alex responded. "We just don't want to let it get away from us."

The chief engineer yelled for everyone to get back. From nowhere the rains came, and they were caught in a driving rainstorm. As always, Alex ran past the trailer that served as a makeshift headquarters as the gusher came in. Wind blasted sand. Skin burned. Oil spewed. They needed to keep the well under control and cap it without losing pressure. But it was blowing right out of the ground. Panic swarmed over the crew. "Get it under control!" Alex yelled. But an unwanted rain of oil spouted from the severed artery inside the earth.

Then from nowhere came the unexpected: an explosion. Fire erupted as if from the bowels of hell. Alex jumped up to join the chaos, but Chris held her back. "Trust our people. It's under control."

"For Christ's sake, Chris, somebody's going to get hurt," Alex pleaded.

Chris held her by the arm. The men worked the well like a trained army battalion while oil spewed uncontrollably into the sky. Out of the slick blackness, Colt Forrester appeared, and waves of relief flooded through her.

Forrester stared at the two women. "We saved the well and it's gonna be a big one," he announced as the gusher was reined in.

"What happened?" Alex asked. "It was going fine, then all I could see was fire."

"Someone sabotaged the well."

"Sabotage?" she asked shocked.

"Yes, but he died in the explosion."

Alex left Chris's side and joined Colt by the salvaged well. Mud caked up around her ankles. Lying facedown in the mud was a badly charred body. Colt Forrester rolled it over with his boot. The blank dead eyes of Steve Blake stared at them from the ground. Alex moaned, turning her head as Colt pulled her into his protective arms.

"Who is he?" Colt inquired innocently. But she didn't respond.

Trembling, Alex woke up to a torrent of emotions and a pounding heart. The dream had changed; for the first time in years it had taken a new course. Clearly there was a new road. Somewhere along the way she would have to cross paths with Colt Forrester. Even if it was only to bury the memory. One way or another, their unfinished business had to be laid to rest.

CHAPTER 34

Jake Winston blustered into the Colorado Land Preservation office trying to get his mind back on work and away from the murder case. He threw his weathered hat on the magazine-littered reception table and glanced at his watch—2:00 P.M.—there was a pile of business to dig out from under.

"Mr. Winston, there's a man who keeps calling, but he won't leave a number," said Jake's executive assistant as she placed a thick stack of pink notes in his massive hand. Ethel Ferman was a mature woman with short, silver hair and leathery mountain skin who protected Jake Winston like a mother bear.

"Did he leave a name?"

"Yes, sir, it's on the first slip." Two phone lines blinked furiously as Ethel juggled myriad duties. "He wouldn't leave a company name or number, but he insisted he would call back. It sounded important," she added. "CLP, can you hold, please?" she spoke into the phone.

Jake looked at the name, raised an eyebrow, then methodically thumbed through the rest of the papers. He knew Ethel was dying with curiosity to know what it was about, but on this tangled subject he could not oblige. Besides, history told him she would eventually find it all out on her own.

"Detective Carter's office called, and they won't need you before tomorrow," she said with a quizzical expression. Fine wrinkles characterized her face. "Everything is all right I hope?" she probed for a morsel of information. She knew Alex had come back and turned his life inside out again, and she didn't like what it did to him.

He gazed blankly at the mountains with their billowy, gray canopy of clouds suspended over craggy peaks. The old familiar pain returned like snow geese in winter. There could be no satisfactory explanation he could give Ethel, or anyone else for that matter. The phone buzzed persistently in the background.

"Colorado Land Preservation, this is Ethel, may I help you?"

Jake lingered outside his office while his mind traveled somewhere beyond the horizon. A high blanket of clouds moved, ferried by a runaway wind.

"Mr. Winston, do you want to take the call?" she interrupted his thoughts. "The gentleman I mentioned is on line one."

"Yes, please put it through to my office." He ambled into the office, and the illuminated line blinked at him like a caution signal.

"Hello, Colton," Jake said as casually as possible.

"How have you been, Jake? It's been a while."

At first Jake sat silent like heat lightning in a summer night. "Yes, it has been a long time." Another effective but unstaged pause landed between them. "What can I do for you?" Jake knew the answer, and he knew why Colt Forrester was calling, but the question bought precious time. In fact, he was surprised it had taken the engineer this long to contact him. In his heart, Winston knew a pivotal moment had come, a moment for which he had been trying to prepare. But his emotions nagged him to stall for a few more minutes. He had never stopped adoring the petite black-haired maverick who would never stop loving Colt Forrester. Jake had been her spiritual source of strength, her friend, and her mentor. But Colt possessed her heart and soul. Winston choked back visceral feelings. Their destinies had been commingled in a painful hold that was beginning to finally unravel. Forrester broke the silence.

"I read a small article in the *Denver Post* about the Welbourne case. I wondered if you might know something." The two rugged men were faces on the opposite sides of a coin, both loving a woman neither had been able to possess. "Have you heard from Alex?"

Jake's eyes closed and he saw a vision of Alex by the fire, legs crossed in faded jeans. The crossroads loomed in front of him. One small lie. All Jake had to say was "No," and Colt Forrester could disappear in a trail of smoke. Jake could go have dinner with Alex and never mention a word, and destiny could be erased with one sweep of a brushstroke. Winston drew a deep breath. "She flew in yesterday, Colt."

"Where is she?" Forrester's voice was hot and anxious. "I have to see her, just talk to her face to face." There was no pretense in the rugged engineer.

"At The Brown Palace," Jake responded flatly, but the tightly wound muscles in his shoulder blades and back began to relax. Finally he'd been able to face the moment he had privately rehearsed ever since Alex had phoned announcing her return.

"How is she?"

"She hasn't changed much, Colt, but there's a sadness in her eyes. My guess is that it has something to do with you."

"I have to see her," Colt persisted.

"We're having dinner at the Chop House at eight o'clock tonight if you want to come," Jake offered reluctantly.

"If I can't reach her before then, I'll be there."

"Alex deserves to be happy," Jake said, speaking more to himself than to Forrester.

Colt paused for a moment. "I still love her."

"I do, too, but at least I'm not in your shoes." Jake wasn't sure which one of the three of them had hurt the most. But at least one or two of the players should be happy.

"What do you mean?"

"I know Alex better than anyone, better than you. She's treading water in a marriage to a cold man, pretending to live, and loving you every minute. She's punishing herself for what happened to Chris. She's lost everyone she ever loved, and, in some ways, I think she is afraid that if she lets herself love you, you'll be tragically doomed. I shouldn't stick my nose into your business, but I'm doing it anyway. And I'm doing it for Alex. Either find a way to be in her life or get out of it permanently." It was a paternalistic lecture that emerged from his own repressed emotions.

"Don't you think I've tried to be in her life?" Colt countered fiercely. "You should know that no one will ever be able to control Alex or her feelings."

"For Christ's sake! Someone in this fairy tale needs to end up with some happily-ever-after! I suggest you try harder. This may be your last chance."

They hung up without saying good-bye. In the wake of their conversation, Jake buried himself in paperwork and proposals. Ethel became swamped under a barrage of dictation, a habit that helped him cope.

Periodically Winston dialed the hotel, wanting to break the news to Alex that Colt was trying to find her. He hoped she would arrive at the restaurant before Colt showed up.

Why was he so worried? Alex was a woman he longed to nurture and protect, but it was her life. Reluctantly he buried himself in the pile of work heaped on his cluttered desk. Mundane business occupied the rest of the afternoon as the sun slipped into the bronze nocturnal sky.

"The Brown Palace," the operator said.

"Alex Sheridan's room, please," Winston requested for the tenth time. After five rings the operator came back on the line.

"There is still no answer. Would you care to leave a message?"

"No, thank you. Can you tell if she has picked up any messages from earlier?"

"I'm sure she hasn't checked them. There have been quite a few calls."

"Thank you." Jake hung up, perplexed. He left the office and headed to the Denver Athletic Club for a workout before dinner, wondering where Alex could have gone.

At 7:45 P.M., still sweating from the workout and steamy shower, Jake called Alex for what seemed like the hundredth time. Her disappearance was driving him crazy. Half of him anxiously hoped Colt had found her, while the rest of him was grieving. Out of frustration, he called the police station.

"Detective Carter, please."

"One moment." The operator put him on a lengthy hold before Carter picked up.

"Hello, Mike, this is Jake."

"You must be psychic. Alex just hung up, she's trying to reach you."

"I've been trying to call her all afternoon. Is everything okay?" he asked. "I was a little worried," he added.

Carter inhaled deeply, trying to posture the news. The unbelievable day that had begun at 5:30 A.M. was showing no signs of coming to an end. Most of the department had vacated the police station, leaving a skeleton crew with Carter as the backbone.

"Where are you, Jake?"

"Downtown at the Athletic Club, why?"

"Can you come over right now?" he asked mysteriously.

"Yes. Is she all right?" Sweat instantly gathered in Jake's palms. "What's wrong?" he demanded.

"She's going to be just fine, but I think it would be good if you came over," Carter said in a less-than-convincing tone.

"I'll be right there."

Winston threw perspiration-drenched workout clothes in the rear of his vehicle and raced over to the police headquarters at fifty miles an hour on snowpacked streets. Something wasn't right with Alex! The Jeep lurched into a No Parking place just outside the police station. He pressed the emergency break to the floorboard ferociously and barreled out of the vehicle.

At night, the police station was an eerie fortress filled with frightening people. City lights reflected against the opaque sky. Jake wound his way through the entrails of the department to where Carter paced back and forth. There were no other officers in sight and the air was stale.

The two men shook hands unceremoniously. Carter had a new layer of bags under his eyes and the remnants of a Big Mac lay on the corner of the desk.

"Where's Alex?" Jake demanded.

"She's on her way back to Denver with the sheriff from Evergreen. They'll be here any moment." Detective Carter scrutinized scribbled notes on a yellow legal pad on the desk. There were still no answers.

"What was she doing up there?" Jake asked. The big man paced around the stifling room.

"Apparently she went up to pay respects to Chris at the memorial site and was assaulted."

Jake's mouth gaped open in astonishment. "Assaulted? Does she need a doctor?"

"I don't think it's serious, but she believes it's related to the murder case, and so do I."

Jake listened attentively as Carter told what he knew about the confrontation.

"The man who attacked her is Case Storm."

"Case Storm! How could he have known she was going up there?"

"That will be one of many questions we ask. We'll take a complete statement as soon as they arrive. Then she wants to get some rest. I think the ordeal was pretty frightening."

"The scum ought to hang!" Jake exclaimed in frustration.

"I think the injuries are superficial," Carter responded coolly. Over the years he had seen too many pints of blood spilled, and-if Alex wasn't coming back in an ambulance, he knew it didn't warrant too much concern. "She did sound pretty shaken up."

"I guess this changes the complexion of the case?" Jake was

pacing back and forth, holding the dusty, gray cowboy hat by its sweat-stained leather band. The heels of his boots clicked on the aging linoleum floor. His mind rolled over with the news; he felt desperately helpless. Carter didn't bother offering a chair.

"It certainly puts Storm under the microscope." A large file lay open on the cluttered desk. Carter flipped through papers, trying to find clues. A confluence of circumstantial evidence was flowing toward Storm.

"We still don't have a direct tie to the hit man. But this is more than we have ever had before." The detective was cautiously optimistic.

"There are too many coincidences for my liking," Jake said.

"Well, it's tough to get a conviction on coincidences, but I agree that it isn't looking very good for Mr. Storm." Carter moved around the congested desk that heaved under the weight of the investigation. Stacks of files cluttered the work surface. He read and reread notes that had haunted him in the night. Something still didn't add up to square. Storm was a numbers guy, a modern flimflam man, and murder wasn't quite his MO. If he was the one who hired the private investigator, he was probably trying to get the edge on a business deal. Who would want to bug an office if they were going to have a person killed? Carter ran the rake through his brain and again came up empty-handed.

"What about the video?"

"I saw it late today—after the senator had his private viewing."

"Did it offer any clues?"

"Yes, but vaguely. The face of the killer was obscured."

"But you saw a face?"

"The whole thing looked very professional. We're having some technical enhancements done to try to get a clearer image."

"Then what?"

"I want Alex and Jeff Ashton to see the image once it is doctored by the tech staff. They can do wonders with enhancement these days." Something in his gut told him Jeff might be able to help. He had talked to and seen almost every person in Chris's life. If there were any clues hidden in the video, Ashton might be the man to see it.

"Then we'll circulate the image throughout the criminal justice system," Carter continued. "The FBI has a database that will help, but it's still a needle in a haystack. And if he's the kind of pro I suspect he is, we'll never find him. He's probably a creature with a hundred identities that change like the faces on a deck of cards." Carter looked dejected. His hair was as rumpled as his polyester shirt. The phone rang at the desk that hadn't been organized in years. "Carter!" he barked into the receiver. Then, "Send them up." The receiver landed back in the cradle with a thud. "They're here."

"What can I do?"

"We'll take a statement from Alex; you can help by getting her out of here as soon as we get through with the paperwork."

"I'll make sure she gets back to the hotel safely." Jake said, relieved he could finally do something to help.

"I'm too old to do an all-nighter. Processing Storm will take hours. We'll hammer him for a while, give him a good scare, then let him stew overnight. The hard-core grilling will begin in the morning."

Colt Forrester sat at the end of the bar, anxiously watching the brass doors open and close at the entrance to the Chop House. It was eight-thirty and the place was alive with sprinting waiters and wall-to-wall imbibing patrons. For the thirtieth time in as many minutes, he nervously checked his watch and looked up at the large, glass entry doors swinging open. He approached the overwhelmed maître d', inquiring if Winston had checked in, but there was no record. Then a cute blonde waitress in a short black skirt approached him. "Can I help you?"

"I'm waiting for the Winston party. Can you tell me if they're here?"

She checked the registry. "No one by that name has checked in. Would you like a table?"

"No, thank you," he said, hoping his worst fears were not materializing. He had been prepared for the possibility that Alex might not want to see him. Too many years and tragedy had led their lives in opposite directions. The pendulum continued to swing to extremes. Hope to grief to excitement to fear—all in a matter of moments. He checked his watch again as if time would change anything. He tried to rationalize the situation. Maybe it wasn't meant to be. Perhaps seeing each other would only serve to deepen the unhealed wound. Time and distance diminished the pain, but nothing had successfully filled the void left in the wake of the passion he had shared with Alex. Their hearts and minds had locked in eternity, and time would never change that. Her disappearance had left an eternal emptiness, a consuming aching in his soul that cried to be filled by her warmth and passion. In the sea of happy mingling patrons, he felt more isolated than ever before.

A receptionist was fielding phone reservations and soothed demanding patrons. Guests packed in every crevice talked at an alcohol-induced roar, making it impossible to hear a page, much less have a real conversation.

"Chop House, good evening."

"My name is Winston, I have a reservation for three tonight, but I—"

"Could you please speak up?" The racket was deafening and there were more people waiting for tables than they could possibly accommodate.

"Yes, I need to get a message to a guest. Please page a Mr. Colt Forrester," Jake yelled at the top of his lungs to the young receptionist.

"It's a zoo around here, but I'll try." The receptionist put him on hold and called out the name over the anemic P.A. system. At that very moment, a man approached the stand.

"Is your name Forrester?" she screamed at the slightly inebriated man.

"It can be if that would make you happy," the man said flirtatiously to the receptionist, who was still trying to hear Winston.

"I'll be with you in just a moment," said the greenhorn hostess. "I'm sorry, he must not be here," she said loudly into the phone. The receiver clicked on the line, then the shift changed and a reinforcement stepped up to the front lines of the restaurant.

Colt studied his reflection in the amber ale. Huge stainless-steel vats dwarfed the bar. The laughter made a din inside his head. He asked the receptionist one last time for information on the Winston party, but all hopes were dashed. No one knew a thing. He was offered another glass of beer, but declined. His mind wandered through the past years while he downed the remnants of his half-flat beverage. Then he exited into the frigid night.

Twinkling lights dotted the sky as he pulled his leather coat tightly around flesh, blood, muscle, and frame. Hard physical exercise had become a release and it showed in his athletic carriage. A hundred paths beckoned him to follow. The mountains and the road, oil wells and the ocean. For a while he just wandered the shadowy streets. A couple walked arm in arm, braced against the cold wind, their intimate laughter cutting through the night.

Over the years he had coped with the void in his own way. He had stayed busy, consumed with business, constantly on the move. Finally he left Denver and traveled from town to town, seeking fun and distraction and never looking up from the self-imposed treadmill. After selling his business, he had come up for air, hoping for a realignment in the stars. But all the milky dreamways pointed toward a woman in Dallas, a few light years and a past lifetime away. He had locked the door to the condo, throttled the bike, and headed north. The motorcycle hammered the highway up to Casper, Wyoming, where he saw one of the big rodeos and hung around like the cowboy vagabonds. He stuck with the circuit to Cheyenne, then on to Cody, but his restlessness returned. He headed down to San Diego and the border towns where he developed a taste for tequila. It was warm in the winter, a respite from the pelting ice and snow that he left behind in Wyoming, but eventually the mild climate grew tiresome. When Colt wasn't moving, he worked out: running, lifting weights, trying to sweat out the emptiness. With nowhere else to turn, he had found himself back in Denver, and nothing had changed but time.

The familiar streets of Denver eventually guided Colt to the door of his loft. It was time to finish the race; to quit running and go home again. Alex hadn't come to dinner for a reason, and there was no way to make her do something if she didn't care to. The previous six months had given Colt time to clear his head and ponder the next chapter of his life. It was time to look into a new venture. He had more money than any decent man could ask for, more independence than he rightfully deserved, yet no Alex. God, how he'd tried to shake her memory. He'd even tried to rewrite history by telling himself lies like it would be easy to find someone else.

Emptiness welcomed him home. Colt walked into the receptive void, heading straight to the telephone, an ingrained habit of many years. All was as it should be. The message light blinked on the answering machine. It was one of life's necessities that he abhorred. He pressed the "play" button and Jake Winston's voice came on loud and clear. His heart jumped as he strained to hear every word. The pendulum lurched hard, jerking his hopes and his dreams 180 degrees. With another random message echoing from the recorder, Colt pulled on his leather jacket and headed back into the night.

CHAPTER 35

The Brown Palace Hotel lobby was quiet. A uniformed porter trying to contain a large yawn stood supported by the wall in an empty corner. It was late on a weeknight, and most of the hotel's guests had already retired for the evening. Two men in need of directions had Lafayette's full attention. An exhausted, bruised Alex said goodnight to Jake, who expressed concern about the injuries she had sustained. She assured him the doctor in Evergreen had done a thorough job examining her head. The emotional trauma would not be as easy to fix; Jake's concern here was justified.

"Let me take you up," he offered.

"No! I am fine. You have a long drive home and I'm going straight to bed." She brushed his cheek with cool lips and disappeared deeper into the old hotel.

As Alex waited for the ancient elevator, the concierge appeared with a message in a small sealed envelope. "Are you all right, Miss Blake?" The surprise on his face was impossible to hide.

"Yes, I was just in a little scrape." She softly touched the bruise on her cheek. Her head was thick with the painkillers and muscle relaxants the doctor had insisted she take. She didn't like drugs of any kind, but there had been no energy left to argue with the conscientious man. The dosage had helped her sleep all the way back from Evergreen.

"I was just about to take this up to slip under your door."

"Thank you," Alex replied blankly. She took the envelope and slipped it in her pocket. She was too tired even for curiosity. The conversation with Carter was a muddy memory, and the ride from the police station to the hotel was a blur. Giving the statement to the police had taken her last remaining energy.

"Would you like some help up to your room?" the concierge inquired, noting her unsteady posture.

"No, thank you. Goodnight."

Alex floated, ethereal, onto the elevator and down the long, open corridor. She tried with all her energy to focus, but the world was fuzzy and gray. In the corridor she heard music through the spaces under the heavy wooden door of her room. The maid must have left the radio on, she thought. She hoped for an extra chocolate on the pillow. She fumbled for the key, which caught on the lining of her pocket. Her fingertips stumbled across the envelope in her pocket, reminding her there was a message waiting. The vacant hall was cavernous. Finally the door creaked and groaned, and a triangle of hall light was deposited in the blackness of the room. She was relieved to be back to her temporary home.

A faint familiar scent hung in the air. Her heart raced as she reached for the light, fingers groping for the switch on the wall. The pounding in her chest increased to a roar. The scent did not belong.

In an instant nightmare the lamp on the corner table illuminated the stony face of Steve Blake.

"Surprise," he said, and the edges of his mouth curled in a disturbing grin.

Alex stood rigid and speechless. It was the second time in a matter of hours she had wanted to scream and run.

"Don't you have anything to say?" He glared from the chair where he had made himself at home. He turned off the radio.

Alex stood frozen. She could hear the slow drip, drip, drip of the faucet in the bathroom. Silence stood between them.

"Hello would do fine." His jagged voice sent her a million sharp messages. She had heard the tone before—it was meant for special occasions, for the times he used words to hurt her. A shudder rippled her skin like a cold, wet wind.

"You frightened me," she stuttered slightly. "How did you get in?" Her mind was racing, calculating, buying time. She was furious over the intrusion. She needed a diversion, and she needed it quickly. Steve Blake was as smart as he was mean. She would have to be smarter.

"I'm your husband, Alex!"—as if the simple comment could explain his presence. "What happened to your face?" he asked out of idle curiosity without a note of concern in his voice.

"I was assaulted!" she spat back sarcastically, unable to contain the anger that raged in her heart. "And what are you doing here? I don't appreciate being spied on like one of your business associates." His intrusion into her life in Denver had driven a stake through her heart.

"You can't just leave without asking. You are married to me, Alex!"

"You don't own me, Steve."

"I decide when and where you are going."

"Please, help me understand." Her fury and contempt were certain. "I'm supposed to tell you where I'm going, when you can drop off the radar screen for days at a time and I don't even know where to find you?"

"My secretary knows how to reach me any time."

"Then why don't you marry her?"

"I don't like your tone, Alex." He rose from the chair, moving like a predator. "Where the hell were you last night?"

"Here in Colorado," she shot back. Alex stood petrified by the bed like a cornered animal.

Steve seemed to ignore her response. "Why are all these people calling you? I especially want to hear about this Detective Carter with the Denver Police Department who called you in Dallas. By the way, you have quite a few messages, if you're curious." He was waving a taunting red flag.

"I just adore having my messages checked," she fumed. "Thank you for being so efficient."

"Somebody needs to check them. You certainly haven't been here to take *my* calls—or anyone else's, for that matter."

"I want you to go now, Steve."

"You're coming home with me!"

"I'll come back when I'm finished with my business here. Until then, I don't want to talk to you." Her hands trembled. She had to get control of her emotions. The conversation was escalating and she had to figure out a way to escape. The words fell like rain in the desert. She knew Steve Blake, and he had no intention of leaving without her.

"Who is Colt Forrester?" he asked flatly, ignoring her request that he leave.

Just the mention of his name caused Alex to quake. Her heart was pierced by his question. What could he know about Colt Forrester? Maybe there was a message on her voice mail, but how could Colt have found her? Jake had said something about Colt in the car but she had been nodding off in her drugged state and the comment hadn't registered.

"And why has this Winston fellow called so many times?"

Alex felt a moment's relief. Maybe he didn't know where she had been last night after all. "This has nothing to do with you, Steve."

He looked at her with astonishment. "You are my wife! You do as I say!"

Alex racked her brain. She curled sweaty fingers around the note buried deep in her pocket. She prayed for some light and some hope. "This is none of your business!" she said disdainfully.

Steve Blake sprang on her like a vicious cat. "You are my business!" he roared through clenched teeth, pushing her against the wall and digging his fingers into the flesh of her upper arms. She could smell the odor of his cologne and feel his heavy breathing. *This is how it started*, she thought as the pain triggered memories. At first it was just angry words and a talonlike grip. Then pushing and shoving. Finally, the night before she had left for Denver, he had hit her hard. It was an injury that couldn't be ignored.

"You do as I say!" he roared, pinning her so hard against the wall that she could barely breathe. "Where were you last night?" he demanded again.

His hand came down hard on the side of her ribs, stealing the air from her lungs. She glared defiantly back at him, trying not to give in to the excruciating pain. She knew she had never seen such terrible anger. If she blinked, she thought he might kill her. But her eyes never wavered, as she was determined to meet his rage head-on.

He released his grasp. Air rushed to her screaming lungs and she could breathe. Her body still ached from the trauma inflicted by Storm. She force-fed herself calmness. She stood her ground and defied his rage, buying precious time.

"Pack your things!" he ordered. "We're leaving tonight."

"Now?" She was horrified. She wasn't leaving now. She needed closure on the murder of her best friend, and she desperately wanted to talk to Colt Forrester, wherever he was. If she left now, there might not be another chance. "Oh, no, Steve, I can't." She had to talk him out of it. "I'm so tired. I just need to rest. Let's have a drink and start over." She slumped onto the bed, holding her aching side, looking as pathetic as possible.

He stepped back, rearranging his tie and smoothing his outraged appearance. Alex watched his mind devour the circumstances.

"I didn't mean to sound so upset about you being here. It just caught me off guard," she said, like a child hoping acquiescence would push the right button. "Really, the doctor told me to rest for at least a day." She was winging it, trying to do anything to placate him. "Please, I'll go with you in the morning and skip my meeting."

The digital clock read 11:40 P.M. The glare on his hardened face remained frozen.

"You're right," she said softly. "I should have stayed with you, not come here worrying about something that happened so long ago." She thought she saw the muscles in his jaw relax slightly. She had studied his every expression and mood for a long time. She watched her subservience melt the ice. He liked nothing more than to have her spirit broken.

Steve looked at his gold watch. It was almost midnight. Alex could see wheels turning in his head—his pilots would be asleep, and it would take several hours to get going. She would let him come to his own conclusion . . . let it be his idea.

"Do you think the airport is still open?" she asked, knowing it was way too late to file a flight plan.

"No, of course it's not open now," he said in a condescending tone. He might as well have called her an idiot.

Alex moved to the minibar as he paced around the room. There were four bottles of Chevas, several packages of peanuts, and one jar of cashews. She was starving.

"Let's just have a drink and start over," she implored. "Since it's too late anyway, we can stay here tonight, and leave on the plane first thing in the morning. I should have called you and I'm sorry. Please don't be angry." The lines on his face relaxed a fraction as the hurt-little-girl act assuaged his temper.

The small bottles made a loud snapping sound. She added a splash of water to the scotch which she had no intention of drinking. Steve took his neat—she poured him a double and handed him the glass like a dutiful wife. The red message light continued to blink in the corner of her eye. She ached to check the messages to hear what Steve had listened to. Curiosity could drive her mad. But she summoned every ounce of control. The adrenaline rush and confrontation with Steve had flushed the effects of the medication out of her system, leaving her cool and clearheaded.

"I suppose we will have to stay," he said, flipping on CNN and taking a gulp of scotch.

"I need to go the ladies' room," she said subserviently. He nodded his approval. Slowly she moved to the small bathroom. She rotated the door lock, turned on the water, and stared in the mirror at her haggard reflection. This round she would win. A cold washcloth soothed the aching bruises. After taking a few deep breaths to relax, she pulled the note out of her pocket. Colt Forrester's name jumped off the page. The time on the paper read 10:50 P.M. The standard pink form was filled in neatly. His unforgettable, distinctive script scrawled across the page.

I received a message from Jake and hope you are okay. I must see you, Alex. Please call as soon as you get the message. We have to talk. XXX, Colt.

Attached to it was his simple business card with the recognizable address. She pressed the message to her lips and remembered his touch as if it were last night.

Then she looked in the mirror again. The bruise below her eye was swollen and red. But somehow she knew Colt wouldn't care if she showed up looking like a chimney sweep. She longed to call him, to tell him not to give up. "Please let him wait," she prayed silently. She wanted to see him, to feel his support and strength, to tell him she had never stopped loving him. Quickly she tried to repair the damage to her face while a plan materialized in her mind.

CHAPTER 36

After viewing the videotape at police headquarters, the senator drove home in a trance. The tape had triggered too many crooked memories. Once at home, he greeted Catherine and Jeff Ashton calmly, and made an excuse—severe stomach pains—for not going to a reception at the governor's mansion. He asked Ashton to go in his place, to serve as his representative and, as Jeff would understand without being asked, to make sure Catherine didn't embarrass the senator by getting too drunk. In truth, his pains were not feigned—the reality of the videotape had made him violently ill.

Bill Bridgeforth, alone and disconsolate, walked through his perfectly appointed house into the large mirrored hallway. It was not only a reminder of the Morgan Dulany décor he detested, but a tarnished reflection of his own life. For the first time in his life he allowed himself to take a hard look at the truth, which was crashing in on his world, destroying the beautifully cultivated illusion in which he had lived.

The videotape of Chris's death played incessantly in his head. He saw the shadow again, then bits of Chris's skull blown into the darkness. He had lied after watching the tape. He had always lied, and he was living a lie with a woman he detested.

He was also a thief. He had weaseled away from the savings and loan scandal, letting Storm take the full blame and all of the consequences. Even though he was just as much a thief as Storm, the senator had walked away from the scandal scot-free. Millions had been rat-holed away by his kind while the S&L depositors and the rest of the American people paid for the industry's excesses. He had skillfully channeled his fortune into an illegal Antigen trust account, evading the federal government and avoiding all taxes.

But now he was paying a price in his own private prison, and his alcoholic wife and her scary father were the jailers. Every day cinched another knot in his entrails.

He wandered through the shadows to the formal living room, its plaster walls trimmed with hand-carved molding a century old. A painting of his wife hung lifeless over the mantel. She had been portrayed as a regal lady, blonde hair piled high upon her head, a color that had masked the original dark brown for decades. In her expensive elegant gown she looked like a member of a royal family. "Low-life Italian whore," he whispered, and his hatred burned like blue fire.

He loosened his collar and studied the portrait. It had been painted by an artist on the East Coast and had cost a small fortune. He approached it and removed it from the large hooks embedded in the wall. He raised the framed canvas over his head, then smashed it across the back of a Chippendale chair. A pair of white lovebirds in the corner of the room flitted frantically in their gilded cage. The canvas remained intact. He pulled staples from the frame, but he could not seem to damage the painting no matter how much he tore at it. His eyes searched the room. It looked like a movie set. A gold letter opener engraved with lies about his contributions to the state lay neatly on an eighteenth-century antique English sideboard. He felt tears running down his cheeks patterned with broken blood vessels as the video continued to replay in his memory. It would not stop. He saw the shadow again, and he saw the face as he revisited the past.

There had been a time when he still had hope. Soon after their wedding he and Catherine had gone to a family gathering in Pennsylvania, where they would meet some of Catherine's relatives from overseas—they wanted to meet Catherine's powerful politician husband, one of the youngest members of the Senate.

The day had been as unforgettable as the video he had just seen, clear in his memory as if it were projected on a screen. The family had gathered at his father-in-law's original restaurant in Pittsburgh. Bill had not really wanted to attend the event, as he intended to maintain his distance from the controversial family— old Italians with deep Mafia ties. It was a way of life for them, part of their heritage. Bill had already explained to Dominique Morroni that as a United States Senator he couldn't have any illegal associations. The old don had winked and slapped him on the back in a paternal gesture, assuring him the family would never dream of doing anything to jeopardize his future. They were here only to support him. How naïve Bill had been! Over the years he had accepted too much; too many favors and too much money.

He remembered every detail of the old restaurant, Dominique's Italian Kitchen. Red-checkered tablecloths draped over metal tables resting on a battered linoleum floor. Cheap wine bottles covered in volcanic candle wax stood between white plastic salt-and-pepper shakers. The taste of Chianti came back to him as he recalled the scene. The wine at that family gathering was much higher in quality than the Chianti Morroni had been able to afford when he first opened the restaurant, but the inexpensive surroundings pleased the family members as a reminder of the old don's "humble beginnings." All were raving about how far the don had come in his life.

Dominique's was a rough place where men played deadly games. Bill mingled with family members in the kitchen, making a show of enjoying the private family function. After all, he was their rising star. Bridgeforth talked with a few of his wife's cousins, pretending to be interested in the stories of their latest business ventures in Nevada.

It was in that desolate, previously underpopulated state that Don Morroni was expanding his operation, and it had begun to reward the whole family handsomely. In a matter of years their flourishing business would have a stronghold in Colorado, Nevada, and California. That night at Dominique's, someone asked Bill his opinion of the future of casino gambling, and he deflected the question neatly. He was meandering around the bowels of the restaurant kitchen when a tall, dark man in a long leather jacket entered quietly through a utility door leading from the alley.

The family and friends welcomed the intimidating character as if he were a celebrity. He wore a dark hat pulled down low over glassy eyes. His face was heavily pocked and scarred, and his thick, short hair was the texture of steel wool. Dominique appeared from nowhere and quickly ushered the man to a side room. From behind the door came angry muffled voices. Bill could not make out the words, but it had been impossible not to guess the nature of the discussion. His father-in-law emerged as quickly and discreetly as he had disappeared, but the mysterious guest must have left by a rear door. One of the cousins asked Dominique if everything was going well in the new territory. Bill remembered the silence and the ominous response: "It's all taken care of!"

"Who was that man who came in from the alley?" Bill inquired.

"You're a real smart kid, right?" The don glared at him with a crucifying stare.

"Yes, but—"

"Forget the fuck what you see around here, understand?" Like Jekyll and Hyde, Morroni's face had transformed from that of a jovial host to one of a vicious tyrant. "It's a family tradition: we don't ask questions. Questions can get people hurt!" He shoved a crooked finger in Bill's astonished face.

Bill Bridgeforth had never been able to forget the look of hatred that had crossed Morroni's usually friendly façade, although he had tried to bury memories of the evening. Over the years he became callused to the murderous talk that circled around his wife's notorious family. He heard tales of men buried in cement for their mistakes. He heard jokes about baseball bats crippling the knees of men who did business in the wrong territory. He tried to pretend it was all a joke. His own days were filled with passing legislation, important laws for civilized people to live by. Aside from receiving an occasional handout, he thought he had no reason to take much notice of his wife's family—until the day the imposing figure of the man who dealt death for a living appeared before him on a screen.

Bridgeforth clearly remembered the face he had seen many years before. The pieces of the dark jigsaw puzzle began to lodge into place. He left the portrait of Catherine lying on the living room floor and moved to his office. The house held no sounds of life. The phone rang once, and he did not answer. He thought about Catherine's desperation when he had told her he wanted a divorce. He remembered her pathetic pleas to reconcile and his own desperate longing for Chris Welbourne and the freedom she represented. He remembered his wife's rage. Was it rage enough to kill?

The police, even with his help, would never be able to prove anything. Catherine and her family wouldn't leave tracks. But Bridgeforth believed as sure as he was alive that Catherine was responsible for the murder of Christine Welbourne.

He fumbled through the drawer in the right side of his desk for a pack of cigarettes and set it on the desk.

He picked up a Tiffany crystal decanter of Jack Daniel's bourbon. He poured a double on the rocks and removed his constricting necktie. He winced when he caught a glimpse of himself peering back from an Edwardian mirror. There was a sick pallor on his once-taut, tanned skin. His distinguished gray hair now looked sparse and receding, and puffy red bags underscored his tired eyes. The amber-colored liquor ran hot into his body, dulled his senses.

He poured another Jack Daniel's, this time without measuring, and he thought about Case Storm. Storm had been the fall guy when the feds moved in on Rocky Mountain Savings and Loan, and Bridgeforth had enthusiastically helped Alex in her efforts to pile up evidence against him. The investigators had begun to examine the senator's tenuous participation in several deals, but a member of Catherine's family made some calls to powerful people, people who could make a middle-level investigation evaporate like smoke in high wind. Indiscretions were made to disappear, and the senator's associations were discreetly swept away.

It was easy. Money and power saved him, and not for the first time. He downed the warm golden liquid in one long gulp, then poured another as he sank lower into the chasm of depression.

He wasted three matches from an old matchbook taken from the Willard Hotel in Washington before he successfully lit a stale Marlboro. Gray smoke hung in wisps around his head. Political memorabilia stared from all four walls. These were pictorial records of his life, minus a large photo of himself with Storm and the Governor of Colorado that he had removed moments after the media began their crucifixion of the financier. He was the champion of the investigation into Storm's fraudulent business dealings. The cremation of Storm's career had been complete. He just hadn't realized his own political dreams were about to end, a priceless sum to pay, he thought, for what he now thought of as a frivolous night of passion. He rummaged through a file drawer looking for memories.

A damp cold settled in the study, but Bridgeforth was numb to every feeling except desperation. His *Titanic* was sinking straight to the bottom. He poured the last of the bourbon and reached for some personal stationery. He looked at the official senatorial seal of the stationery and felt utter disgust. To think that he was part of the elite who comprised the United States Senate! Washington was a morbid joke that had been played on the American people, he thought. He wrote his confession on plain bond paper.

The clock struck eight as the copier buzzed to life, discharging two perfect copies. He put one in an envelope he addressed to his father-in-law; another he addressed to Carter. He left the original on the desk for Catherine to discover. It was a way of getting even.

He placed a stamp on each envelope and walked outside to the blue mailbox at the end of the street. The heavy metal lid creaked as he slid the testimonials into the box. With that action a weight lifted from his mind.

He could just see the outline of the mountains in the night sky as he walked back to his house, returning to the deafening silence of his office. He could remember nothing that had been accomplished in his life without a profit motive. Even his desire for Chris had been driven by his lust for power, fame, and fortune. But it was still the closest thing to love he had ever felt.

Fueled by cigarettes and alcohol, the pulse in his temple pumped hot. He clenched the cumbersome pistol in his shaky hand. The video of Chris replayed in his head. One last time he felt her touch and warm embrace in the damp satin sheets. One last time he felt her wrapped around him in the darkness. Then he saw her image in front of the large windows. He saw and felt pieces of skull blown away.

CHAPTER 37

Jeff Ashton stepped out of the rattling red Porsche, a statement car that had new brakes and represented a self-made man, into the sparkling Colorado evening in front of the Bridgeforth's house. Smoothing his athletic frame in a preening gesture, he went around to the passenger side of the car to assist Catherine Bridgeforth, who was well on her way to post-party alcoholic oblivion.

Ashton had readily obliged the senator's request that he escort Mrs. Bridgeforth to the governor's reception. He had made the appropriate excuses for the ill senator, knowing full well that the senator was in fact reeling from the shock of viewing the video.

The deceitful pair approached the rambling Cherry Creek house, dark inside except for lights in the back study. Shadows cast from strategically located floodlights floated around the yard. A couple walking their terrier quietly passed by in the twilight. Somewhere a car door slammed. Jeff and Catherine approached the door to the Bridgeforth residence as they had on many other evenings. Jeff was glad the senator was home, which meant he would be able to leave quickly without having to listen to Catherine's protests. His disdain for her had grown with his dependence.

The mirror in the entry hall reflected the features of the pair. A deathly quiet pervaded the hall.

"Bill?" Catherine called out.

No answer.

"Senator Bridgeforth?" Jeff Ashton echoed. A strange, rich odor seeped into the hall. Light beckoned from the office refuge where the senator invested many hours. As they proceeded down the corridor, the familiar odor brought back memories Ashton could not quite place. He quickened his stride toward the study with Catherine wobbling at his heels. Too much Chardonnay had dulled her awareness. Jeff stopped just inside the doorway and looked on the office scene as if it were a stilled slide show.

"Don't come any farther." He put out a protective arm, barring Catherine's entry into the death chamber.

The senator sat dead in his chair, a gun dangling from his right hand. With one glance Jeff saw that a portion of his head was missing. Brain matter and bone covered the left side of the desk. Ashton grabbed a handkerchief and wiped his forehead. *Don't do anything rash,* he told himself. Surveying the scene more closely, he tried not to look directly into the gaping side of what had once been the senator's head.

Catherine let out a shriek. "My God!" She pushed past him defiantly, moving toward the desk.

"Don't touch anything!" Ashton warned, grabbing her shoulders and pulling her away from the bloody scene. His mind raced into overdrive. He was a crisis man, a man hired to field curveballs from all fronts and never stumble. But the scene they encountered was outside predictable boundaries.

Catherine moved for the telephone. "I have to call the ambulance," she said shaking.

"Don't touch anything!" he ordered again. This was not a moment to be reckless. "Half his head's gone, Catherine! There's nothing anyone can do."

Ashton offered her a handkerchief, in which she buried her tear-smudged face.

"How could he have done this?" she asked no one. She slumped in a chair reserved for visitors. He had ruined everything.

"Just shut up and let me handle this!" Jeff commanded, trying to force a plan of action. He noticed the neatly organized desk. The tidiness was particularly odd since the senator was known to be less-than-meticulous. In fact, the area was flawlessly arranged except for one letter sitting on the burgundy leather inlay. He moved closer to the desk, making sure not to touch any of the furniture, and read the note addressed to Carter, soaking in every word.

"Look at this!" he ordered, showing her the letter. Shock and fear had turned into opportunity.

Catherine leaned over his shoulder to read the note he held with a tissue.

Dear Detective Carter,

When you read this, I will not be available for discussion, so let me be as clear and concise as possible. I am certain the murderer on the videotape is a man I once saw in Pittsburgh. I have no concrete proof, but I am sure that this man was hired to kill Chris Welbourne by my wife, probably with the aid of her father, Dominique Morroni. I have seen them all together in the past.

My wife's family has strong underworld connections. I tried to distance my career and life from them, but I did accept their money.

I am making this statement for you to use as you see fit. As you know, I was having an affair with Ms. Welbourne at the time of her death. My wife knew I wanted a divorce. Within a very short time Chris was murdered. I believe that a professional assassin was hired to kill her as the price for my infidelity.

Dominique will be an impossible target for prosecution. But for those who have a need for closure and understanding in the mystery of Chris's death, perhaps it will ease their grief to know what happened. Christine Welbourne was guilty of nothing except associating with me. She made a poor choice.

Be careful where you step. The Morroni family has big money and power, more power than the government. Don't try to play hardball in their game. Trust me, you can't win.

Sincerely, Bill Bridgeforth

"My God! He's accused me. The filthy bastard. How dare he kill himself and frame me for her murder," she ranted hysterically as the enormity of the suicide note settled over her.

But in some way it made perfect sense. Ashton read it again, slowly letting the senator's conclusions sink in. Then he laid the letter back in the exact place he had found it.

"We have to destroy it. You have to help me, Jeff," she pleaded for support.

"We're not touching anything!" Jeff rasped as he moved around the desk. The large-caliber gun dangled in the senator's right hand.

"I didn't have anything to do with it!" she said in trembling desperation. "He must have been going insane to write that letter! What are you doing?" she asked helplessly.

"Shut up!" he ordered.

The lines between her eyes furrowed. "You can't possibly think I had her killed?"

"No, but with this letter everyone else will. *There's no fury like a woman scorned.* Everyone knows the rumors—it is common street talk that the senator was in love with Chris. And it's hard to argue with a dead man."

"But it's a lie! No one needs to know about the letter!" she said. "It can be our secret!"

"Don't touch it!" he ordered viciously. "This note confirms all the sordid gossip! It's my ticket out."

She moved toward the incriminating evidence.

"What do you mean?"

"Don't be so naïve, Catherine, you were just a pawn."

"I don't understand what you're talking about," she said, genuinely perplexed. "All I did was try to help you." Then a light came on. "I loved you, Jeff," she shrieked. "I wanted to help you. I lent you money."

"You were a fool."

"I introduced you to my family!"

"I needed more than the trifling pittance you gave me. Why do you think I wanted to meet your family? Don't you think your father knew about the senator and Chris? I was your dear friend watching out for you. He counted on me to keep him informed about the senator."

"My father would never—"

"Oh, for Christ's sake. Of course he didn't do anything, he just gave me the name of a man who can make problems like Chris go away. He was happy to help me because I was making your miserable life better." Jeff looked in the direction of the corpse of the once-powerful man. "I just gave him a little fuel here and there. I told him about the senator coming to Chris's office and their sordid little meetings. He appreciated my love for you. He told me how I could make my problems disappear." Ashton stopped, took a deep breath as if proud of his cunning maneuvers.

"I don't believe you!" Catherine said, astonished by the scorn in his eyes.

"I owed people money, Catherine." He said with contempt.

"But you didn't know she had named you in her will!" Catherine exclaimed. "You told me you did not expect it," she said, remembering Jeff's surprise at having been left money in Chris's will.

"She was a fool if she thought I didn't know everything that went on! I saw every document and knew every move she made. There was no other option."

"But I loaned you money . . . "

"Your dribbles didn't scratch the surface." His eyes sparkled with vengeance as he moved toward the motionless corpse.

"You don't have to tell the police anything, Jeff," she persuaded. "I have to convince them that Bill's letter is the ranting of a sick man. They'll never know about your hiring the gunman. I promise—we can just destroy the letter and no one will know a thing. Please, you have to help me."

"They'll close the case and never think to look at me,

Catherine. It's too good."

Quickly he moved behind the desk, trying to position himself directly behind the senator. He acted instinctively, driven by need. Carefully, using his handkerchief again, he removed the weapon from the senator's lifeless hand and turned it on Catherine. Deliberately he raised the gun, the barrel pointing at her heart.

"And now the senator can take you with him to hell, and I won't owe you anything anymore."

The .357 magnum discharged at close range, ripped into the abdomen of Catherine Bridgeforth and threw her to the floor.

Jeff Ashton stood motionless, the gun barrel warm to the touch. He stared at a woman on the declining side of youth. She had been pretty once, but it didn't really matter now as she lay bleeding on the ancient Persian rug. Her pleading eyes were filled with horror and pain. He and Catherine had been discreet with their liaison, but things had gotten out of control. He hadn't given enough thought to an exit plan from the long-running affair. Contemptuously, he studied the pathetic creature she had become.

Slowly he approached her motionless body, taking a limp wrist to feel for a pulse. He would have to call 911, but it could wait until she had more time to die.

The seduction had been so simple, he reflected. The lonely wife of a politician was easy prey. Catherine had been needy and vulnerable. A few sessions listening to her feelings, and he had hooked her. Playing on her emotions, he had shared his own set of problems to draw her in. He had talked about the humiliation that went with working for a powerful woman like Chris. He painted a picture of being stuck in a thankless job with a tyrannical employer. Catherine had listened raptly, too willing to empathize with his plight, feeding her own terror with his disturbing revelations. She had shared her secret fears about the senator's affair with Chris while he had listened with convincing empathy and compassion. They were on the same team, united in their mutual hatred of the powerful woman. Jeff's clandestine meetings with Catherine had turned into more than one erotic rendezvous. He shared his heart, his financial woes, and his body, and she took the bait. Before long she was lending him money. Then, on a trip to Las Vegas, she had proudly introduced him to her powerful father. He was her golden boy, and Don Morroni was only too happy to make introductions for the man who was making his only daughter smile again. Catherine had glowed with the attention.

Jeff Ashton's newly established money stream accelerated his gambling habit and the mounting debts. For brief periods he would get ahead, or at least be able to pay enough to keep his creditors at bay. Then his luck turned cold as a cadaver. Cornered by his own greed, he fell farther into a black hole. The tables turned like bad dice and the men he owed hundreds of thousands of dollars to wouldn't wait for his payback. One night he had called Don Morroni in desperation, explaining his deplorable position and begging for a way out. Morroni acknowledged nothing, feigning ignorance, but the following night an unidentified man had called Ashton. The contract on Chris's life was made. And just that simply she was gone, leaving Ashton a windfall that purchased his life back.

Ashton found himself no longer dependent on Catherine, a woman he had come to loathe. His first ticket out of a crisis had turned into a chain around his neck. Sleeping with Catherine had become an increasingly pricey obligation. His fear of her father kept him from severing their liaison. Now, with the senator's letter and the false assumptions that would follow, he would finally be free.

He bent over Catherine to watch the life oozing out of her veins. Blood flowed from her ravaged torso. She was a tragic character in a tragic comedy. For a moment her eyes opened and she longingly caught his gaze.

"Help me," she pleaded.

But he didn't make a move. Then her eyes closed as the life

seemed to bleed out the wound. Finally, she passed out.

He edged around the desk and placed the gun back in the senator's hand. The gun slipped out of the fingers. Again he put the pistol in the dead man's hand. His pulse ran hot as sweat bubbled down his forehead. The silence in the death chamber was suffocating. This time he curled the fingers around the gun stock and they cooperated. The wretched mangled head listed like a grotesque Halloween mask.

For five more minutes he watched as the second hand on his watch ticked methodically. Then he felt for Catherine's pulse. There was no obvious breathing and he couldn't detect a heartbeat. His partner in a dangerous liaison was dead, he thought with relief.

∽

The 911 operator answered on the first ring and immediately dispatched an ambulance to the neighborhood that hadn't experienced a shooting in many years. Ashton calculated it would be only minutes. He gathered his wits and composure. After several deep breaths, he made the necessary call to the police department. It would be too odd if he didn't call Carter immediately.

"Detective Carter, this is Jeff Ashton from Senator Bridgeforth's office."

"What can I do for you?" asked the exhausted Carter, who was trying to finalize details on the Storm indictment.

"You've got to come right away," he said his voice shaking with desperation. "There's been a shooting here at the Bridgeforths'." He convincingly delivered the urgent news.

"A shooting?" Carter repeated in total disbelief. What more could happen on this twisted day?

"Catherine's in bad shape. I called 911 right away."

"Don't touch anything." Carter reeled with the tragic news.

"I haven't," he lied.

"I'll be there immediately. What's the address?"

Jeff gave the street and number of the Bridgeforths' home. "God, I hope she lives. It doesn't look like there's much chance for the senator," he added.

"Suicide?"

"It looks like he shot her and then turned the gun on himself," Ashton explained with great sadness in his voice.

The dial tone buzzed in Ashton's ear. It was going to be interesting explaining this to Catherine's family, he thought to himself. A new sweat broke out, forming beads that ran down his forehead. His mind raced to an alibi. There were hundreds of people at the party who could swear he had been at the governor's mansion. There was nothing to be afraid of. The senator had tidied things up better than he could have dreamed.

Minutes crept by as he moved to the hall, looking out the front windows for the ambulance. The faint siren in the distance grew louder as his pulse rate increased. Like a bullet train, the siren screamed into the driveway and paramedics bolted toward the front door. Ashton greeted them, disheveled and anxious. He had removed his tie and tousled his hair, trying to look as traumatized as possible.

"Please come this way." Jeff motioned down the hall.

"Who are you?" the bulky paramedic demanded.

"Jeff Ashton, I work for the Bridgeforths." He led the two uniformed paramedics through the ornate residence. "I put a towel on Mrs. Bridgeforth's wound. She's bleeding badly. I don't think there's any hope for the senator."

"Stay out of the way while we work on her." A stretcher was laid next to the body of Catherine Bridgeforth. Her skin was pale white. Blood was beginning to mat the fibers of the oriental carpet. Jeff stood in a corner watching the paramedics, who checked for vital signs and then began to work on her, first cutting off her expensive evening suit.

In the squad car, Detective Carter radioed for backup assistance and tried to make sense of the phone call from Ashton. But all he could think about was the Chris Welbourne murder. Racing down Speer Boulevard, he remembered the scene with Chris's body slumped lifeless in the chair. The interview with Jeff Ashton replayed in his head. He had idolized Chris. They were close friends and associates. Ashton lived on the edge financially, he had later found out, but that was all. Carter tried to concentrate. Somehow this was all connected in a hideous cycle of death which he could not understand. Lights flooded the Cherry Creek neighborhood like the Fourth of July. Two squad cars with sirens blaring broke through the residential tranquillity while uniformed men surrounded the house with yellow crime scene tape.

Carter entered the house and took command, quickly assigning duties to his officers. Two men were sent to guard the door. Another was directed around to the rear of the house to prevent unauthorized entry by curiosity seekers or the inevitable overzealous reporters. Carter strode through the halls, entering the study as prepared as one can be for death. Despite all the deaths he'd handled, it still made him shudder to see the bloody mess. Ignoring the senator, he checked all around Catherine's body while the paramedics protested the delay. "I want her hands checked before you move her," he ordered, knowing there could be microscopic clues under the nails or powder residue that might be lost to them forever when she was taken from the room.

Then he moved on to the senator. From a cursory examination it looked as if the gun had been stuffed in his mouth at an angle. No two suicides were the same, except for their horrid legacy. When the medical examiner arrived they would know more. Carter moved to the desk and picked up the letter in his gloved hand, reading it twice. The accusations and conclusions made by the senator were immense. But it was a tenuous link that could fall apart in the courtroom unless they found the man behind the face. And with only the letter and no testimony from the senator, things would be difficult. *Why'd he have to go and shoot himself?* thought a frustrated Carter. The Denver homicide investigative team arrived, led by a cameraperson who began to shoot close footage.

Meanwhile, the paramedics worked feverishly, trying to restore life to the dying Catherine. They applied paddles to her chest to shock the life back into her. One man massaged her chest while another forced air into her lungs.

One of the paramedics yelled, "I think I have a pulse."

"Get her out of here and to the hospital!" Carter ordered.

An IV bottle was attached to what had moments ago appeared to be a lifeless corpse. Her designer suit lay lacerated in pieces on the floor, and she was now covered in a layer of cotton and blankets. A pale yet composed Jeff Ashton helped hold the door open as the stretcher was ferried down the hall. The medics carried out the limp body of Catherine Bridgeforth. Ashton's insides curdled as the still body rolled by.

"How is she?" he asked from the front porch, where he again propped open the door for the stretcher.

"I don't know."

"We've seen worse cases make it," one of the paramedics said. "She's still got a pulse."

"I think she's got a chance," said the other paramedic hopefully.

Ashton choked on the news.

Outside the boundary of yellow tape, curious neighbors stood talking in low tones. The house looked like a surreal gift, wrapped in yellow ribbon. The ambulance doors swung open, and the stretcher was hoisted inside, where more emergency measures would be taken to work miracles on the ravaged body.

Detective Carter approached the porch where Jeff Ashton stood nervously. "Do all the people you work for die so dramatically, Mr. Ashton?" Carter said sarcastically, catching Jeff by surprise.

"Apparently so. I don't like your attitude, Detective Carter."

"And I don't like the body count around you, Mr. Ashton."

Two more uniformed officers from homicide pushed past the confrontation and headed to the crime scene now guarded like a fortress.

"I don't have to tell you how careful you guys need to be," Carter yelled at the fingerprint team. "If you botch this one, you'll have the district attorney on your back before midnight."

"Yes, sir," one of the officers replied without turning around.

"I need a statement, Ashton. Follow me." They walked in through the entry hall and stood at the doorway leading into the senator's study where more people than necessary were milling around like frenzied ants.

Carter pulled a squatty uniformed man over and posted him by the door. "I don't want anyone in here unless you get my okay, understand?"

"Yes, sir."

"And tell that idiot over there to put out his cigarette. No smoking! No food anywhere, do you understand!" It was so easy to contaminate a crime scene. It happened more often than not. Too many officers trying to help, people touching evidence and leaving traces of materials that didn't belong in the scene. If he wasn't careful, they'd be following a million tainted rabbit trails.

"Yes, sir."

"So, what happened?" Carter demanded of Jeff Ashton, who was watching the investigation unfold. "Start from the beginning."

"I don't know. After seeing the video of Chris's murder, the Senator was so shaken he couldn't go to the reception. I thought he was upset, but nothing alarming, considering what he saw."

"What did he tell you about the videotape?" Carter asked, all the while watching the team of officers gathering evidence.

"Just that he had to relive Chris's murder. That he had to watch her die, something he hadn't ever thought he would go through. He said something about never getting over her. Then he asked if I could attend the governor's reception in his behalf and make sure Mrs. Bridgeforth got home safely, which I did."

"Did he say anything else about the video?"

"No, not that I recall."

"Did he always discuss his personal relationships with you, Mr. Ashton?"

"Yes, and I knew everything about his affair with Chris, if that's what you're driving at. That's part of the reason I got this job. He knew I could keep my mouth shut because of the way I handled Chris's affairs. Until the murder investigation, no one knew they had a relationship. Everything that took place at Chris's office was considered sacred. And the senator knew that I had protected her loyally. I suppose he trusted me more than anyone else," Jeff explained, skillfully painting an honorable self-portrait.

"Then what?" Carter asked skeptically.

"I dropped Mrs. Bridgeforth off at the door and headed home. I was almost at my place when I realized I'd forgotten to get an important file, so I went back to the house."

"Where do you live?"

"In the high-rise near—"

"Just write it down. And include all your phone numbers." Carter handed him a pen and pad.

Jeff obliged, providing complete and accurate details. "I guess it took me about thirty minutes or so round-trip," he continued his fabrication.

"You didn't go in the house when you brought her home?"

"No, that's how I forgot the file, I guess. It was a long day, and the reception was tedious. I was bushed," he added, trying to look as haggard as possible.

"What time was it when you left the party?" Carter maneuvered him toward the front steps and away from the house.

"I'm not exactly sure. Eight o'clock, maybe eight-thirty by the time we said our good-byes and got in the car."

"Where was the function?"

"At the governor's mansion. It's not more than ten minutes away," he said helpfully.

"And you dropped her off without going inside?"

"Yes. I walked her to the door and said goodnight."

"Do you have a key?"

"Yes, but Mrs. Bridgeforth used her key. When I came back, the door was unlocked and no one answered."

"So you came in?"

"Yes, but first I rang the bell several times. It was odd since it hadn't really been that long since I had left."

"Then what?"

"I called out, but there was no answer. I went back to the office to see if the senator was still working. That's when I found them. And you know the rest."

"Did you touch anything?"

"No! I was in shock. I ran down the hall and called from the kitchen. I couldn't stand to be in the room."

"So you just saw the bodies and then turned and ran?" Carter clarified.

"Exactly."

"What file were you picking up?"

"File?" Jeff hesitated.

"What was the important file you were coming back for in the middle of the night?" Carter asked. He carefully scrutinized Ashton's halted mannerisms and reactions.

"I don't know. Just some papers the senator had asked me to pick up after the reception."

"Did you get them?"

"Huh? No. I didn't even think to look for them after finding him."

"And you don't know what the file contained?" Carter continued to dig.

"No. I don't know."

Carter guided Ashton toward his car.

"I can't believe he would really kill himself," Jeff said half to himself. "But I guess he couldn't handle it anymore. Knowing his wife murdered Chris must have pushed him over the edge."

"Well, at least it answers some questions," Carter responded, incredulous at Ashton's slip. He hoped like hell that Catherine Bridgeforth could be saved.

"What if she lives?" Ashton continued.

"She'll be indicted for murder," Carter said, studying Jeff Ashton's face.

"I'm sorry."

"Thank you for your help. I'll have to ask you to stay outside while we proceed with the investigation. If I have any other questions, someone will come get you."

Inside, the evidence team had been joined by the medical examiner, who was slowly beginning the process of gathering samples. Carter pulled the lead investigator aside and handed him the pen and paper with Ashton's name and address.

"Dust these for prints immediately. I want a clear picture!" Then he barked at another idle officer, "Cordon off the kitchen and don't touch the phone, or anything else for that matter." Carter returned his attention to the investigator. "When you're through with the pad and pen, I want you to do an autopsy on that kitchen phone. I want every goddamn print you can pull!"

Murder should really be left to professionals, Carter thought, returning his attention to the grisly scene in the office. He had the note carefully protected in a plastic sealable bag. He circled around the desk, flanked by his best evidence team. They studied the gun and the position of the body. The photographer took four rolls of film, capturing the scene from one hundred different grotesque angles, including the blood spray on the senator's right hand and on the gun. Blood samples were taken from every location. Carter expertly removed the weapon and studied it for clues. There was no doubt that it could kill. More photos were taken. Meanwhile, the medical examiner bagged the senator's hands.

Carter called over his two top men. He held up the weapon

in the light. Small speckles of blood dotted the surface in a defined pattern.

"Do you notice anything odd about the blood spray?"

The other officers studied it in the light. There was definitely something wrong with the picture. "Dust for prints!" he directed.

"Hundred bucks says there's not just one set of prints."

"I want the lab guys on this yesterday."

"Well, you can be sure he didn't want to live. Anyone using a gun with this kind of explosive power wants to finish the job."

"Call headquarters and get the chief on the phone, and pray like hell Mrs. Bridgeforth makes it," Carter ordered. "And I want a surveillance team now!"

CHAPTER 38

Steve Blake sat staring at CNN, sipping his drink and fretting about being grounded in Denver for the night. The hotel room was stifling. Alex reappeared from the cupboard-sized black-and-white hotel bathroom. Steve looked less agitated and more resigned. The crisis had passed and his cosmic temper had abated. He reclined silently in the corner.

"I guess I'd better start packing if we are leaving in the morning?" Alex employed a light tone, dismissing the fact of their explosive confrontation. History had taught her to act as if nothing had happened. She didn't want to ignite another fight. Nonchalantly, she packed several articles of clothing in a small suitcase.

"I called the pilot while you were freshening up. He's filing the flight plan now and we are leaving at 7:00 A.M. sharp."

"I'll cancel my appointments in the morning. But first, I have a little female problem. I'll be right back," she said lightly.

"Where are you going?" he demanded, rising up in the chair in alarm.

"I just need some tampons. Would you rather go for me?" she asked, counting on his predictable answer. It was a bluff.

"No. Bring up a *New York Times* and don't be long, Alex!"

"I'll let the front desk know we'll be checking out in the morning. Then we can relax and go to bed," she said in a seductive voice. She smiled her sweetest smile. Picking up her purse, she turned to the door. "I'll be right back. Why don't you take a shower, darling?"

Steve, reconciled to spending the night in the hotel, was

absorbed in a news story about a major Wall Street acquisition. "I'll be in bed waiting," he said coldly. A wave of nausea hit Alex as if she'd smelled week-old, pungent garbage. He didn't care for her or anyone. Like one of the polo ponies he manhandled, she was just another possession. She looked at her watch as she slipped through the crack in the door, leaving Steve and her possessions behind.

⁓

Two officers in an unmarked car spotted the red Porsche on First Avenue just past Neiman Marcus and the Cherry Creek shopping center. Heading northwest down First, the sports car crossed University and picked up Speer Boulevard heading back toward Brooks Towers, the downtown high-rise where Jeff Ashton struggled with the monthly rent. The officers reported the maneuvers to a dispatcher who kept Carter informed every few minutes. Inside his sports car, Jeff Ashton trembled with fear. Bile gathered in his stomach as he thought about Catherine Bridgeforth lying in the hospital. There was no way she could live, he thought desperately as he pulled into the parking garage. One officer went stealthily around to the rear of the building to guard the exit while the driver kept surveillance on the entrance.

⁓

Alex ran down the open halls overlooking seven long floors below. The elevator was at least one hundred yards from their room, across the open atrium. She beat on the antique elevator, desperately hoping it wouldn't be its usual slow self. It was eleven-thirty, but if luck walked on Alex's side of the street, Lafayette would still be on duty in the lobby of the hotel.

"Hurry! God, please, hurry," she whispered to the doors, which miraculously opened. She glanced for the tenth time at her room door. It was still closed. After descending for an eternity, the elevator deposited its cargo at the lobby. Every nerve in her body was on fire. Like a POW escaping through enemy lines, she bolted into the lobby, almost knocking over the night concierge who was carrying a handful of envelopes.

"Good evening, Mrs. Blake," he greeted. The phone rang at his desk. "Are you all right?"

Time was running out. It wouldn't be long before Steve would come looking for her. Her eyes searched the foyer for Lafayette, who was nowhere to be seen.

"Yes. But I need Lafayette to help me. I can't explain. Can he give me a ride?"

"Of course, Mrs. Blake," the concierge said, noticing the desperation in her voice. "He just walked outside to leave for the night, and I'm sure he would be pleased to assist you."

She moved quickly toward the revolving doors. When she glanced up one final time, she saw Steve striding down the hall toward the elevator. His eyes caught her gaze as he broke into a full sprint toward the winding stairs heading to the lobby seven floors below. Alex bolted through the doors into the cold, fresh air, right into the warm arms of Lafayette.

"Please, I have to get out of here now. Do you have a car?" She was pulling the giant man by the sleeve and down the sidewalk.

"Yes, but I have to tell the night manager."

"He already knows. Just get us to your car and out of sight as fast as you can. I'll explain later!" They broke into a trot.

"What's wrong, Ms. Sheridan? Are you in some kind of trouble?"

"Yes, Lafayette. I'm in big trouble. Where is your car?"

"In the parking garage around the corner."

She grabbed his large hand, dragging him down the dark, frozen street. Lafayette huffed and puffed in the cold, thin air. The cold cut to the bone through Alex's thin cotton sweater, and she could feel Steve closing in. He was fit and mobile, and now driven by ego and rage. Steve didn't like to lose anything—especially his personal property. He would be able to move twice as fast as Lafayette.

"Who are you running from, and where is that nice husband of yours who arrived this evening?" Lafayette inquired.

"You met him?"

"Yes, he said he was here to surprise you, and I showed him up to the room."

Lafayette was panting from moving his large, bulky frame. His breath crystallized in the freeze-dried, mile-high air, and sweat popped out on the bridge of his massive ebony nose. His movements were steady and deliberate.

"He's not as nice as he looks, and I hope he hasn't gotten downstairs yet. Come on, Lafayette!" she implored. "We're only about a minute ahead of him."

They made it to the isolated parking garage and stopped in front of an old green Cadillac with wide whitewall tires and shiny hubcaps. Its pristine paint job gleamed in the darkness. Lafayette fumbled for the keys until they finally gained entry. Inside, Alex churned with the thought that Steve was only steps behind them. Lafayette methodically situated himself, patting his coat and adjusting the rearview mirror in an old man's nightly ritual. Alex's eyes darted around the concrete-and-steel garage. Most of the cars were gone for the night, and in the empty lot, they were sitting ducks. If Steve rounded the corner, they would surely be discovered.

"Lafayette, we have to get out of here! Now. You don't know what he will do if he catches us. He's shrewd and powerful and cruel."

The doorman slowly turned his powerful frame to face Alex in the darkness. "Miss Alex, I won't let nothin' happen to you." The ignition cranked and exploded into life. "I'd be more worried about him catchin' up to me if I was you." His words were simple, strong and direct. "Ain't right for any man to have you so scared."

The gearshift lurched into drive, and the old sedan pulled into the open night.

Lafayette surveyed the streets. The coast was, for the moment, clear. "Miss Alex, I made a mistake once, a bad mistake, the kind you pay for the rest of your life." The car turned onto a deserted side street as the old man told his story. "That was when I used to drink. Not good whiskey like they serve at The Brown, but homemade stuff. If it didn't kill you, it made you wish you was dead."

Alex forced her attention as they crept through the night.

"I didn't mean to do nothing wrong, I swear, but I got angry when I drank the stuff, crazed out of my mind. One night a man tried to rob me in a dice game, and I killed him—with my own two hands, no knife or bat, nothin'."

Alex wondered why the big man was making this confession. Lafayette looked down at hands that could palm a medicine ball.

"They say I just snapped his neck like a corncob. I don't really remember, but they said it was true. That's when things got hard."

"Turn down this side street," Alex said, hoping to stay out of sight.

"Then I did some bad time, I mean hard, bad time, in a place in the Arkansas Delta called Tucker. It ain't a place where they take kindly to black men. It's a living hell where hope isn't even a recollection. Now that is something to be afraid of! So don't you worry about your man. He's nothing for us to fear, and he won't ever lay a hand on you if I'm around."

Alex studied his gentle, ageless face as they slowly motored down the deserted street. "How old were you, Lafayette?" She glanced back and forth, searching the streets. Somehow just being with Lafayette was reassuring. At least for the moment she felt safe. She had Lafayette by her side, enough money to last a little while, and, most important, she had Colt Forrester's phone number in her pocket.

"Old enough to know better, but real bullheaded, like boys can be who mix bad liquor with raging hormones."

"How long were you there?" she asked, imagining the wretched conditions he must have endured.

"I did ten years from seventeen 'til twenty-seven. Then I floated around until I landed here when I was about thirty. That was about the year you were born, I'd guess."

"I'm sorry, Lafayette."

"You shouldn't be. What I did was dead wrong, and I deserved every day in that rotten hellhole. It shaved the edges off my meanness." The words poured out with conviction and determination. It was the voice of a man who had learned the distinct difference between right and wrong.

Together in the night, they eased down the streets. Alex searched the rearview mirror, but for the moment she had eluded Steve and his rage. She ducked down as the Cadillac eased around the corner onto Court Street. She lay under the glove compartment, then reemerged as the old Cadillac rolled onto Broadway.

"Where are we going?" the doorman finally asked.

Alex hadn't thought about much except leaving. Now she had to make some conscious choices. "Do you know where police headquarters is?" Alex inquired.

"Yes, ma'am, I'm afraid I do. There are a lot of guests who end up being picked up down there. They get into some trouble, and the hotel sends me to bail 'em out."

The old Cadillac pulled into the main parking lot of the Denver police station. They were in the heart of downtown and only blocks from the hotel. She wondered what direction Steve would choose, hoping he would not think to check with the police until morning.

Two officers exited the front door of the police station into a blast of cold night air. It was well past midnight, but the place was abuzz with night trade. A drunk in handcuffs argued with a young female officer who didn't look strong enough to do the job, but made up for it with presence and firepower.

"Do you mind coming in?" Alex requested.

"No, ma'am." Lafayette removed his felt hat as they approached the night-shift officer handling reception. The cavernous room of red brick was intimidating. A familiar smile greeted Lafayette.

"Are you here to bail out another one of your hifalutin' guests from The Brown?" The beautiful female officer winked familiarly at the large man, giving no notice to Alex. Café au lait skin set off by crimson lipstick complemented a snug uniform.

"Not tonight, Saundra, I'm just an escort. This is Ms. Sheridan." The two ladies shook hands as a prisoner being manhandled by two officers was taken past the desk to be booked. The place was cold and stale with the scent of urine. Two adolescent children were being taken back to juvenile where their shoes would be removed before they were thrown into solitary cells. They were high and scared and crying.

"I need to get in touch with Detective Mike Carter," Alex said, hoping they would call him despite the late hour.

"He's still here, I believe. In fact, he got back here just a little while ago."

The officer buzzed Carter and ushered them through to the elevators. Homicide was on the fourth floor along with vice—the death and drugs department. As they stepped off the elevator, two emaciated women in handcuffs were being escorted toward the elevators. They appeared to be wearing more nose rings than clothes. Alex wondered what they charged for their services and what unwelcome benefits came with the trip.

Haggard and rumpled, Carter greeted them in the dark, barren hallway. There were no extra resources for decorations. They walked past the main homicide desk. On the wall was a handwritten list of the homicide investigations in progress. Two names were unceremoniously crossed out, meaning the crime was solved. There were thirty names on the list. Alex scanned the names until she found Chris's near the bottom. The corridor wound around like a coiled snake until they came to Carter's modest desk. It was in a large rectangular room with a cluster of desks huddled together. Carter directed them into the claustrophobic video interview room.

"This is Lafayette Boudreaux, from The Brown. Meet Detective Carter." They shook hands formally.

"What's going on, Alex? I assume this isn't a social call."

"No." For the second time that day Alex was in his office trying to make sense of a perplexing situation. The incident with Storm had shaken her more than she realized. Physical and emotional fatigue was bearing down hard. And in the lateness of the evening, she felt weary and drained. The straw on top of this giant teetering waste pile was Steve.

"Mike, I have a problem," she said, unsure of how to paint the picture.

Carter looked exhausted but concerned. "What can I do?"

"It's my husband. He followed me here to Denver and tried to force me to return with him to Dallas. I've escaped for the moment, but he shouldn't be underestimated."

"Escaped!" Carter tried to focus with eyes that hadn't seen the back of their lids for eighteen hours. Real sleep hadn't been on the agenda in days.

"The confrontation at the hotel was pretty rough." Unconsciously, she rubbed the aching in her abdomen. Her eyes begged Carter to understand without too many details.

"I'm sorry," he said sincerely.

"I'm sure he will come looking for me here. He knows you called me in Dallas."

"It's none of my business, but why are you running from him anyway?"

"I know if he catches up with me, he will be in a rage. If I don't do what he wants, I really think my life is in danger."

Carter notice her trembling hands. "You are really scared,"

he commented with astonishment. Now he understood her reluctance about coming back to Denver. It had not made sense to him until now.

She let her eyes drop to the floor. "I always made excuses for him. I blamed myself for his rage. The anger escalated from words to pushing and shoving, and finally to where we are now. In the last few months he has become increasingly violent."

"Did he hurt you tonight?"

"For the last time," she said defiantly. Alex was through crying and accepting. Now it was time to act, to do something about the situation.

"Do you have somewhere safe to go?" Carter had witnessed similar scenes unfold too many times. And he ached for the hundreds of women who lived in fear for their safety. He hated Steve Blake, a man he hadn't even met.

"I think so . . ."

"I can arrange for a hotel room and a patrol car if you like."

"I'll take care of Miss Alex," Lafayette offered his support.

"Did Colt Forrester get in touch with you? He was here earlier looking for you."

"Here?" she was taken by surprise for what felt like the hundredth time that day.

"I directed him to the hotel," Carter informed her. "I guess I should have called first."

"No, that was fine." Alex embraced the precious pink note in her pocket. It had helped save her life.

"He was very concerned," Carter added

"Thank you. I must have just missed him. When I got to my room, Steve was there, waiting to surprise me."

"I should never have let him in," Lafayette said regretfully.

"Never mind. I got away, thanks to you," Alex touched the large man's arm reassuringly.

The light on Carter's phone blinked. Saundra the receptionist's voice came across the intercom line. "There's a Mr. Steve something Blake here who says he must see you immediately."

Alex's heart plummeted. He had found them too quickly.

"Tell him to wait. And don't mention who is with me!" Carter hung up, turning to Alex. "What do you want to do about Mr. Blake out there in the lobby?"

"Can you keep him busy for half an hour?" Alex looked at the wall clock, then at Lafayette. It was almost one in the morning. "I need some time to get away where he can't follow."

"No problem," he said, concerned for her well-being.

"How do we get out of here?"

"There's a side exit you can use. No one will see you, but before you go, there's one other thing. It's been a particularly active night for the Welbourne case, Alex, beginning with your call from Evergreen."

Alex waited for more information. "Something's happened?" she guessed.

"I have some sad news that complicates everything. Just after you left, Jeff Ashton called from the Bridgeforths' home. The senator was found dead of a self-inflicted gunshot. And his wife is severely wounded and in critical condition."

"My God—" Alex's mouth dropped. The news was staggering.

"We don't know who shot whom at this point, but there was a letter explaining Chris's death."

"What did it say, is Catherine—"

"We are trying to sort it out now," he interrupted. Carter explained the details of the letter to Alex, who sat devastated by the news. "The letter indicated that Bridgeforth recognized the face of the man in the video. I doubt we'll ever catch the actual murderer. But his supposition is that Catherine was behind the assassination."

"But Storm is—" Alex rebutted, not believing the twisted plot.

"Let me finish, Alex. Bridgeforth's wife was insanely jealous over his affair with Chris. I guess she couldn't stand it. She could have contracted for the murder. Love and hate do strange things to a person."

Alex sat dazed and baffled by the news as Steve Blake paced in the lobby of the Denver police station a floor below. Momentarily she had forgotten her own circumstances. "What about Storm?"

"This changes everything. We'll know more in the morning after he's worn down a bit."

"But he followed me for a reason?"

"All I could get out of him was that he saw you at the Oxford Hotel. He was terrified of Deegan, our informant, who was spilling his guts about Chris's murder. The circumstantial evidence was piling up against him, and you were just another force behind the momentum driving the case in his direction."

"But it still doesn't add up," she argued, not wanting to let go of her conviction.

"Maybe it does make sense, Alex! It explains why Storm was so desperate. He knew that all the evidence pointed toward him. But just maybe he is innocent."

"But he still assaulted me!"

"And we will prosecute him for that. I will contact you tomorrow when we know more."

Alex let the twists and turns of the volatile case settle in, but Steve was too close. Knowing he was just beyond the door had her adrenaline pumping hard and fast. "Let me call you from a safe place."

"Be careful and let me know when you're okay." He gave her his home number in case of emergency. "After what's happened today, I'd expect anything." He turned to Lafayette, who had been standing patiently. "Are you going to stay with her?"

"Yes, sir. As long as necessary."

"Good! Then you two had better go. I'm tired, and there is still someone waiting in the lobby to see me." Carter hugged Alex and showed them the back way out.

It was after one in the morning. Carter was on mile twenty-five of a marathon day. He had seen a murder on videotape. Alex had been assaulted by Storm, who was cooling in jail, and the senator was dead and his wife in critical condition. Just another day the job. The absurdity of the situation beckoned laughter or tears, but he was too tired for either. Carter said a silent prayer for Catherine Bridgeforth before calling downstairs.

∽

Steve Blake was brought through the maze of steel desks to Detective Carter's corner of the universe. They were alone in homicide with the city lights and foothills beyond them in the night.

"I'm Steve Harrington Blake, Alex Blake's husband," he said in an authoritative tone. He extended a firm hand toward Carter, who avoided the ceremony.

"Take a seat, Mr. Blake." Carter directed him to a metal chair. Exhaustion added to the detective's low opinion of his guest.

"I'd rather not," Steve countered. His usual flawless demeanor was slightly flustered.

"What can I do for you?" Detective Carter tried his best to appear ignorant and disinterested.

"It's Alex. She's missing! Just minutes ago, she disappeared from the hotel. I want some men sent out to find her now! I know she had some business here with you, so I thought you'd be happy to help me," he commanded while fishing for details.

"Why do you think she is missing?" Carter asked the man who was clearly used to giving orders. Carter had taken an instant dislike to Alex's arrogant husband.

"She left the room and never came back," he said a little too sarcastically.

"Alex didn't tell me you were coming to Denver," the detective offered casually.

"It was a surprise."

"Maybe she doesn't like surprises," Carter retorted sarcastically.

Steve turned purple. "I want you to help me find her immediately. File a missing person report or something." It was another command, but Steve wasn't getting anywhere with Carter, who hadn't slept in nineteen hours.

"I'm afraid that won't be as simple as it might seem, Mr. Blake. There is a regulation that requires a period of seventy-two hours to pass before we can file an MP. We don't even know if she's missing."

Steve Blake controlled the impulse to jump across the desk at Carter. "Look, goddammit, she's been up here doing your work, and now she's God-knows-where in Denver, and I expect you to put someone on the case to look for her!" he screamed at an unruffled Carter.

"I don't think I like you," Carter said.

"The feeling's mutual!"

"Why don't you calm down, Mr. Blake," he responded flatly.

The two men squared off across the metal desk.

"I can mention this around headquarters to the different guys on duty. If she doesn't contact you within seventy-two hours, then we'll take this seriously." Steve was smoldering with angry frustration. He played with a rubber band like worry beads and glared at Carter, who was doing his best to act the fool. The empty office grew stuffy as Blake pulled on the tie around his neck.

"Look, Carter, I need to find her," Steve said, trying an ameliorating approach. "We had a small lovers' quarrel about a personal subject, and I'm worried she could be in danger if she's out walking the streets in the middle of the night. I thought she might come here to talk to you," Steve said.

Carter noted how well he lied. "Is there any reason you can think of that would make Alex want to hide from you?" He looked squarely into Steve Blake's hollow eyes.

"She's my wife and I have a right to know where she is," Blake yelled, sensing that Carter knew more.

"I wish I could help you. She could be back at the hotel at this very moment. Why don't you go back there, Mr. Blake, and let me get some sleep?"

"Be careful Carter! I know a lot of powerful people all over the country."

"I'll ignore the threat, Mr. Blake."

"I wouldn't like to see a poor schmuck like you have a sudden career reversal. You know how hard it is to lose a pension." Losing just wasn't something Steve Blake did gracefully.

"You know, your wife doesn't deserve a guy like you," Carter said. This arrogant jerk had pushed him to the limit, and he knew how to tie Steve Blake up in knots all night if he wanted to. Carter excused himself for a moment and found a greenhorn officer working the graveyard shift. Quickly he explained the mission and the two men returned to join a steaming Steve Blake. "This is Officer Cleveland. He will need you to fill out some paperwork. We'll need some detailed descriptions including height and weight, and a recent photo." The paperwork would take hours per his instructions. "Now, if you don't mind, it's very late, and I haven't been home since the day before yesterday. Do you have any questions, Officer Cleveland?"

"No, sir!"

"We can't do anything until the paperwork is complete." Carter stood up, stretching and reaching for his rumpled coat. He left the two men filling out the papers which would be shredded the moment Blake made his exit. Carter headed like a zombie toward his car.

Home was barely a memory, a distant concept reserved for people with regular jobs and normal hours. Carter circled through Cherry Creek instead of taking the direct route to his empty apartment near Washington Park. The radio in his seven-year-old Chevy Plymouth blared the latest news. It made him think of the dreaded press that would be all over the department in the morning. He swung the car past the crime scene for one more look. With a hired killer, it was going to be difficult to make the murder stick on anyone. Yellow tape still surrounded the home. After staring into the night for a few minutes, he turned off the ignition. Maybe another look at the crime scene would rattle something in his foggy brain.

The bloody office smelled of stale body fluids. These carpets would never come clean. He wasn't that concerned about finding the man who had actually pulled the trigger, although they would give it their best. Professionals were their own vampirish breed, called upon to do the dirty work of the real killers. The suicide letter appeared to tie up a lot of loose ends. But for Carter it still didn't add up. Why was Ashton lying? He had obviously read the note, why didn't he just say so? The confusing forensics also gnawed at him. Maybe he was too close to the crime, but if his hunch was right and his plan worked, they would find out the truth.

A final wave of fatigue drove him to leave the ghostly residence. A starlit sky engulfed him as morning pressed. He had to get a few hours of sleep before returning to the chaos that would surely erupt the next day. His mind rambled with predictions. The chief would be hungry to close the case and bury the file that had been haunting them for seven years. A press conference would be called and the district attorney and police chief would handle the questions. No one would want to hear any of his doubts.

Carter made it up to the small efficiency apartment that was his home. He fumbled for the wall switch in the dark. Kojak, Carter's overfed sluggish Tabby cat, welcomed him with a long stretch and a race to the food bowl.

The retired lady next door tended to the pet when Carter was knee-deep in cases like the Welbourne murder. "Has Mrs. Goethe been taking good care of you, Kojak?" She'd never told him her first name, and it didn't matter. Kojak meowed at the food bowl. The litter box needed changing, and there was no people food. A half-loaf of white bread with just a trace of mold was salvageable. The message light on his answering machine blinked red. After fast-forwarding through old calls, he listened to a message from the officer he had dispatched to the hospital to watch Catherine Bridgeforth. Carter sighed. It would really screw things up good if she died before they could ask some questions.

A few city lights shined into the dark ninth-story window of the old Washington Park high-rise. Too tired to eat, Carter poured a glass of milk and hoped it wasn't spoiled. He ignored the small stack of dirty dishes that reminded him there was another life. Unable to simmer down, he chewed on the case. It had taken him all evening, but finally he had gotten through to the infamous Don Morroni. Carter had delivered the tragic news as tactfully as possible and at the same time strategically planted a few seeds for the shrewd businessman to reflect on. And Carter had gotten the tidbit he wanted.

Finally he called the hospital. The switchboard operator picked up after what seemed like fifty rings, but Carter was too tired to complain. Eventually he was transferred to a nurse who knew what was going on with the fragile patient. The report was ominous. The sympathetic nurse explained the patient's delicate condition. Catherine Bridgeforth was closer to death than life, although her condition had stabilized somewhat. Carter thanked the nurse and hung up. He would have to make something miraculous happen.

He picked up his notepad and flipped back several pages until he located the number Jeff Ashton had scrawled earlier. He dialed it quickly. The phone rang in slow motion in his ear. Carter looked at the clock. It was after two. A groggy voice answered after five or six rings.

"I'm sorry to disturb you, this is Detective Carter."

"That's okay." Ashton sat bolt upright in bed. "Is there a problem?" he asked calmly.

"It's Catherine Bridgeforth."

"She didn't make it?" Jeff guessed anxiously.

"No. It was a miracle, but the bullet missed her vital organs, and she's going to be just fine. In fact, they said she was sitting up just a while ago," Carter fabricated the report. "I'll be going down in just a while to get a statement."

"But I can't believe it!" Jeff stuttered, trying to recover from the news. He had seen the bullet wound. She had lost so much blood. There was no way she could survive, he thought. "That's wonderful news . . ."

"I knew you would want to know. Go back to sleep." Carter hung up, hoping he had pushed the right button.

CHAPTER 39

Lafayette followed Alex's instructions, and after circling the block twice to make sure they were at the correct building, he pulled the creaking Cadillac to the side parking lot of the building where Colt Forrester had lived. The once-vacant buildings that had dominated the area had been refurbished. Luxury cars filled the streets that were home to upscale retail vendors. Alex's fingers fumbled with the note stuffed deep in the pocket of her black pants. She wondered how badly Colt Forrester really wanted to see her. There was a difference between looking up an old girlfriend and having a woman you haven't seen in years arrive on your doorstep at 1:45 in the morning.

Alex hesitated in the old car. She studied the empty street, knowing Steve was out there somewhere searching. She wanted to be free . . . but she knew she shouldn't underestimate Steve Blake. Anger and humiliation were a deadly combination for him.

Lafayette waited in the parked car without questioning Alex. Time had taught him patience. Alex looked up, trying to remember which window was Forrester's. It had been so long. For a moment she thought about the night, the only night they had been together here.

Lafayette stepped into the clean, crisp air, heavy boots crunching in the snow as he made his way around to Alex's door. In a natural gentile gesture he offered a hand. Alex eased out into the crisp night air. Her neck was stiff from the encounter with Storm, and her ribs still throbbed where Steve had done his handiwork. But the night's activity, fed by adrenaline, had worked out some of the soreness.

"Do you know where you are going, Ms. Sheridan?" Lafayette inquired, noticing her ambivalence.

Where am I going, she repeated in her head. Silently she pondered the blind journey that lay ahead. "I hope so, Lafayette."

The small foyer of the old warehouse loft was warm and inviting. The entry was now finished with marble and rich hardwood. A row of numbered buttons lined the wall next to an interior door that separated the entry from the elevator and foyer. Alex read down the list of names until she came to Forrester. For a searing moment she hesitated, knowing that her decision to press the buzzer was taking her around another bend in the road, farther away from any chance of salvaging the life she had made in Dallas. There was no telling what would happen.

But what if he didn't want to see her? She fingered the note again. Lafayette read the anxiety on her face. Then his voice broke into her fear. "Is this the man who was looking for you at the hotel tonight?"

"Someone was looking for me?" she asked, narrowing her eyes.

"Yes, his name was Forest or something like that. I can't quite remember, but he wanted to see you something awful." The old man smiled a devilish smile.

"Thank you, Lafayette."

Alex pressed a buzzer that blared against the solitude. She took the step. This was a conscious choice that would change her life again. In what way she was not exactly sure. Her heart pounded as she waited for lifelong seconds. Now that she was here, she didn't know what to do or say. What if there was someone else in his life? The thought was certainly reasonable. It was presumptuous showing up in the middle of the night. Sure, the note said he wanted to see her. But he had a life. And she was dropping in unannounced. The debate in her heart raged on, waging war with her confidence.

A part of her wanted to bolt and run. This was the same

vulnerable part that had been cultivated by Steve. Alex bridled the uncertainty, refusing to play the game. The turbulence and chaos of the evening had shaken her, but she was determined to see Colt face to face no matter the outcome. It was all a huge unknown. Now she was standing on his threshold in the middle of the night.

Silence hung in the chilled night air. She hit the buzzer again.

A raspy sleep-ridden voice came across the intercom. "Who's there?"

Colt Forrester was lying naked in the old car bed, trying to get his bearings. He tried to focus his eyes, which offered a fuzzy view of the digits on the alarm clock. It was 1:50 A.M. He untangled his legs from the down comforter. The room was dark except for the intruding starlight.

"Colt . . . it's Alex."

"Alex, my God, you're here."

"I'm sorry it's so late."

"Don't move! I'll be right down." His voice was filled with awe and excitement.

"I'll be right here." Alex's heart lightened with his warm reception.

"Promise!"

Minutes crept by like hours as she waited. In the dimly lit foyer she contemplated what it would be like to see him again. How would he have changed with the years and miles?

Upstairs, a world away, Colt pulled on faded Levi's that lay across the foot of the bed, and swooshed down the fire pole to the elevator. Seconds later the door to the lobby jerked open. For a moment, a brief second, he stared at what had been an apparition of his night dreams. For so many years and so many nights he had dreamed of the moment she would return.

Alex stared at the perfectly fit body covered in soft hair. His shoulders were wide and strong, his hair was disheveled with sleep. Deep dimpled crevices framed his mouth and a few additional crinkles bordered the smoldering blue eyes. There were no other remarkable differences. A million dreams danced in her head.

"Hello, Alex." He reached out, drawing her to him affectionately, then introduced himself to her imposing companion. "Please come in." He pulled Alex closer under his arm, overcome by the cosmic moment. "You look like you've been in a barroom brawl, baby!" Two fingers brushed the bandaged cut over her brow. "What happened to your face?"

"Well, we have a lot of catching up to do." Alex glanced over her shoulder, still concerned about Steve. Her fear might seem irrational, but her egocentric husband was not an ordinary man. The need to find Alex would drive him like the devil. He couldn't stand losing control.

As they moved toward the small elevator, Lafayette paused, turning to Colt. "Will Ms. Sheridan be safe here?" It was an intimidating gaze. "She can't return to the hotel." His large, dark eyes never wavered from Colton's angular face.

"She will be safe here with me for as long as she wants to stay." Colton didn't want to think about the future or what to expect from Alex. For this second, for a moment in time, she was here with him. She had come of her own volition, and he knew she wanted to be here. He hoped it would be for longer than the last time.

"You better lay low for now," Lafayette directed authoritatively. "I'm going to rest in my car for a while just to make sure we weren't followed."

"Thank you, Lafayette." He shook the massive hand. "Why would anyone want to follow you?" Colt turned to face Alex. He could hardly believe she was really here, in his building, in his life.

"It's my husband," she said, hoping he would understand. "I'll try to explain everything when we get upstairs." Alex was anxious to get out of the spotlight of the foyer and into the safe confines of the loft.

"Ms. Alex, do you need anything from the hotel?"

She thought about it for a minute. A team of wild horses couldn't drag her back to the hotel. The limited personal effects, including clothes and makeup, could wait. They were all expendable. Colt Forrester was all she wanted in this world, and there would never be another now. Alex hugged Lafayette, thanking him for his help. "When things calm down, when Mr. Blake has gone, we'll come by the hotel and see you."

Lafayette tipped his fedora and slipped into the night.

The elevator emergency buzzer sounded as they held it against its will. Then the small capsule delivered them to Colt's hideaway. For the first time since she could remember, calm filled her heart, calm from the relief of coming home to something that had been calling to her for an eternity.

Large, gentle hands cupped her face while blue eyes probed the unknown. He brushed her face with the hands of an angel. "I don't want to see the person who did this to you. I wouldn't be able to control myself."

He had so many questions, but they could wait until the right moment, until Alex was ready to open the door and enlighten him. In the pristine loft they were surrounded by the silence of the night. The coffee grinder roared into the vast quiet and the aroma of rich French Roast permeated the room. The fireplace embers were almost spent, but as he stirred the last remaining traces and added a little kindling, life came back to the dying fire, splattering yellow shadows against the walls. Strong arms effortlessly pitched a few large logs, feeding the flames. His back was broad and lean, covered with hard muscle. Alex burrowed into an oversized armchair, soothed by a steaming mug of coffee and warm snifter of golden brandy.

"I can't believe I'm here. Thank you for the note. I don't know how you knew where to find me."

"Well, it wasn't easy," he smiled.

"I'm thankful you did."

"We can both thank Jake."

"If not for your note, I'm not exactly sure where I would have gone."

"Winston told me a little about what was going on."

"He has always been a loyal friend."

"He alerted me when you didn't show for dinner. He loves you, Alex. More than you'll ever know."

"I love him, too, but not the way—" But she didn't finish the sentence. In her mind she said, *not the way I love you.*

Alex saw a wistful cloud pass over the Colt's blue eyes, the eyes that could reach through her soul with just one glance.

"I think I understand."

"It's not what you might think, Colt. I stayed with Jake because it was safe. After the murder I had nothing to give anyone, especially you. I'm so sorry, for you, for us, for everything."

Colt listened attentively. "You don't have to apologize."

"I had lost everyone that I had ever loved or trusted. I just couldn't risk loving anyone again."

Colt slipped gently beside her, putting a strong arm around her shoulder.

"Jake provided a haven for me to mend and heal. It was safe because I didn't have to give anything back. But in some strange way, my being there gave him the pieces of a relationship he could handle. He could love me in his own way because he knew that I would always leave. That's because from the very beginning I told him about my feelings for you."

"When did you tell him about us?" So many questions and so much curiosity pulled at him. There had been a million doubts over the years. Was she really in love with Winston? Why wouldn't she let him love her and help her? Why did she marry so soon?

"I told him everything. That I had found someone I thought I could spend my life with. But I didn't want to drag you into the humiliating, sordid mess that my life had become. I was just too afraid to love someone and risk being hurt again."

"And that's why you wouldn't come be with me?"

"Jake was already involved in the mess because of his close ties to Chris, business and personal. You may not have known about it at the time, but there was a pretty big controversy over a prominent ranch. A lot of money was at stake, millions, and the police briefly considered Jake a suspect. I suppose that tied us together for a while. During that time, I was recouping emotionally and getting used to the idea that my business and my dreams were over."

"But you could have started over. You had all the experience and knowledge anyone could hope for."

"It was a dream Chris and I shared together. I lost part of myself when she was killed. It took the fire out of my drive."

"I still see fire in your eyes." Colt nestled closer, taking her hand. The flames threw yellow shadows across his face and desire smoldered between them in the shadows.

"I couldn't get away from the avalanche that had taken over my life. The murder investigation was suffocating. Finally I had to just leave, get far away from the ordeal. Both mentally and physically."

"So you thought you could move away and start over?"

"Yes, I believed I had to leave Denver and all the memories. Every time I thought about us, I thought about Chris and walking in on the murder scene. I just couldn't cope with it. I had the crazy idea I could run away and bury the past like a corpse."

"But you finally returned?" he said.

"Fate stepped in," she smiled. "Detective Carter pressured me into coming back. The fact of the matter is, I had to come back to put the past to bed. Since I left Denver, I've been plagued by nightmares on one hand and dreams of you on the other. No level of willfulness could get either out of my mind. I was somewhere I didn't belong."

"Thank God you are here now." Colt stroked her hand and

brushed satin lips across her cheek. He longed to hold her and wipe the years away. "I have dreamed about this moment a hundred times." Strong hands caressed her tenderly.

"Thank God Jake got a message to you or I might not be here. I will be indebted to him forever for so many reasons."

Colt nestled into the chair as if they had never been apart. "I showed up at the police station and found out about the terrible encounter up at Evergreen. But it was Winston who encouraged me to go find you."

"How much did Carter tell you?"

"Just that you had a confrontation up at Chris's ranch and that Storm had assaulted you and then been arrested. Then he had an emergency call and dashed out without saying a word. I've been frantic for hours, unable to reach you at the hotel."

"I'm fine now, just being with you."

"Storm did a nasty job on your face!"

"It's already feeling better." Alex smiled intimately at the man she had never been able to forget. "Did he fill you in on the Bridgeforths?" Alex queried, wondering how much Colt understood.

"After I couldn't find you at the hotel, I called Jake, and he told me the senator had shot himself and things were a mess. And he filled me in on the rest of the details about the video."

"The whole case just keeps getting bloodier. It's eerie, but almost everyone near Chris's murder is crumbling."

Colt snuggled close to her in the large chair. "I don't want to hurt you."

"You could never hurt me. Steve's the one I'm worried about."

Colt stiffened.

"He tracked me to Denver and talked his way into the room. He was waiting for me when I returned tonight, and he wasn't happy."

"He's looking for you now?"

"He threatened to take me back to Dallas tonight, but I escaped from the hotel with your note in my pocket."

"You are safe with me, Alex. He can't hurt you here." Colt poked the fire as he processed the information. His protective instincts had been awakened.

"Colt, he is calculating. He knows your name. He will find this place."

"He won't get near us, I promise." He tried to reassure her of their safety.

"He's dangerous, Colt." Alex had been on the receiving end of Steve's domestic terror. But she was determined that he would never hurt her again. She would do anything to stand up to him and drive him out of her life.

"He can't force you to do anything!" Colt said confidently, trying to soothe her.

"I made a mess of things, Colt. It would have been so much wiser to have stayed here."

"That was then. You did what you thought was best, what you needed to do at that time. Let's not manipulate history. Of course, I agree it was the wrong decision," he chided playfully.

"I don't know why I thought running back to Dallas would solve anything."

"Darlin', don't ever waste time trying to rewrite the past. It is part of life. Some events are not supposed to be understood, Alex, just accept it."

"I'll never go back. I'll get a restraining order in the morning."

"Then there is nothing more for us to worry about." Colt walked over and set the security alarm for good measure.

"There is nothing in Dallas for me now, nothing there that I want. All these years, the only thing I ever wanted was to be with you again."

He pulled her close to him, careful not to add to the hurt. "That's all I've dreamed of hearing, Alex." Softly and carefully he kissed her, with a tenderness that melted all the hurt, anger, and grief. "I don't know why it had to take so long, but you're finally here," he whispered in her ear, holding her closely. "I was certain that one day you would come back. That's part of the reason I never sold the loft. I didn't want to change anything you had touched, anything we had shared."

"I never gave up on us, Colt. I could never completely let go of our dreams."

"I listened to the music we made love to a thousand times and never gave up hope that somehow it would all fall into place one day."

"It was a long way back."

In front of the fire, Alex stared into his deep, blue eyes sending a thousand feelings with one penetrating glance. He ran his finger down the bridge of her nose, tracing her features, then continued down to her heart where he took their entwined hands and pulled them to his lips and then to his chest, trying to envelop her heart in his. Eternity collapsed. They leaned forward, a breath away from touching face to face and stared into parts of each other that were now commingled. He soaked in her scent and caressed her radiant skin, imprinting the memory to verify the longing and love and lust that had haunted him like a phantom. Slowly the fragile fibers of their being unwound, and the fire between them grew. They kissed deep and long, tracing lips with tender longing, trying to get deep within each other's space into a part of the mind that only heaven can touch. For that moment their hearts and minds and souls were home where they belonged, embedded in each other's passion. Each touch confirmed the memory.

Resting safely in Colt's arms, Alex tried unsuccessfully to sleep. The news of the senator's death and the revelation of Catherine Bridgeforth's involvement prevented any peace. The scenario of the day festered in her mind, magnified by the darkness and fatigue. If Catherine Bridgeforth was responsible for Chris's death, then she wanted to know it. She dozed off for what felt like a few moments, then her tired eyes opened to see Colt watching her in the soft firelight.

"You had a nice sleep?" he asked tenderly.

Alex rubbed her bloodshot eyes. "Did I doze off?"

"Do you want to go up to the bed and get some more rest?"

"No, I'm too restless. I still can't accept that Catherine Bridgeforth killed Chris. There's some piece that just isn't right." Alex stood up, stretching stiff muscles.

"The senator had to have suspected his wife before now . . ." Colt said.

"I guess he waited for her to return and then shot her. They were both found around nine o'clock this evening."

Colt could see the wheels turning faster in her head as she began to talk about the murder. The case was still part of her. There was still unfinished business. And she wanted to be part of the resolution.

"So you don't think it's over?" he asked, knowing the answer. He knew Alex too well. She would not rest until her questions were answered.

"I have to go the hospital, Colt. Will you help me?"

"Of course. I'll do anything for you. But for now you need to rest."

"I can't rest. I have to look Catherine Bridgeforth in the face. I want to see her eyes."

"Don't you think this should be left to the police?"

"It's not that simple. A cloud has hung over my life since Chris's death. I don't want any loose ends to lie between us and our future. I can put this tragedy behind us forever, but to do that I have to see Chris's killer face to face."

"Surely they have her under guard or in ICU."

"I don't care. I have to see her before she dies. It's the final, but most critical piece in the puzzle."

"Then let's get this over," he said reluctantly. He saw the need in her determined eyes. She was a formidable woman who faced poor odds head-on. He had to help her close the book and know the trial was over. It was the lack of closure on the catastrophic event that had gutted a large portion of her life. Colt grabbed the leather coat he had shared with Alex on the snowy night ten years earlier. His arms reached out, offering support and strength. He studied a face much wiser than the one he had known. In it were both beauty and pain, and he hoped he could eradicate the pain with just the right touch.

Their decision took the lovers away from the safety of the glowing fire and into the harsh predawn. A hazy streetlight and the halo of the city interfered with the stars. Morning was just over the horizon. As downtown slumbered, they stepped onto the sidewalk where snow was piled in the gutters. They took several paces, then turned behind the ancient red-brick building into the side parking lot that backed up to the alley. Forrester's four-wheel-drive sat dusted with a light, undisturbed white powder. Alex's sore, tired muscles throbbed. Lead filled her gut . . . but she knew this was the only choice. Doom loomed overhead in the darkness.

Steve appeared out of the shadows, like a vampire. He had stalked his prey like the cunning animal he was. At his side was his copilot who doubled as his bodyguard. The two men stood like sentries in the night. Alex froze in the darkness as Colt moved close to her side, only steps from the vehicle.

"You shouldn't have left, Alex." Steve broke the silence.

They were trapped. Colt stepped forward.

"I'm not going to be a part of your life anymore, Steve," Alex said defiantly.

"Don't be ridiculous. You knew I would find you! This was so simple." Disgust rolled off his tongue as he glared at Colt. After picking up Forrester's calls to the hotel, he had accessed the address easily through directory information.

Alex began, "Why don't you—"

"Shut up!" he interrupted.

Colt stepped forward, putting himself between Alex and the two intruders. In a commanding tone, one Alex had not heard before, he said, "Come on, Alex, we're leaving."

Steve and his intimidating partner moved closer. "Don't make another move!" Steve ordered in the tone she had grown to loathe. "She's my wife, and you're trespassing." Anger burned in hollow eyes as the chess moves were made.

"You don't deserve her," Colt said aggressively.

"Leave him out of this," Alex protested to Steve. "He doesn't have anything to do with us."

"I told you to shut up!" Steve Blake moved toward them. His steamy breath puffed into the frigid air.

"You're not my keeper," she said.

Colt backed toward Alex, gently pushing her toward the car. "Get in the car, Alex." Surreptitiously he palmed her the ignition key.

Alex retreated toward the driver's door as Steve Blake lunged toward Colt. Colt caught Steve with his fist just under the ribcage.

"Don't ever come near Alex again! Ever! Or I'll kill you." The second full-force swing caught Blake in the jaw. Steve's accomplice jumped into the fray, knocking Colt off balance with a blow to his left jaw. His head snapped back, but he didn't go down. It wasn't his first street fight. Colt played the game, letting Steve make the next move. Steve scrambled to his feet, gaining momentum as Colt hit the bodyguard in the gut. The bodyguard was big and slow, and he doubled over in pain. Colt returned his attention to Steve, who was coming at him with wild swings. Just in time, Colt ducked a punch. Colt countered the attack with a full blow to Blake's nose and mouth. Blood spurted from the wound, peppering the white dress shirt with ruby red.

"You fucking bastard!" Blake held his face and fell to his knees in agony, trying to stop the gushing blood. He wasn't accustomed to being on the receiving end of physical violence. "Get him!" Blake yelled to his companion, who was still immobilized on the frozen ground. The bodyguard made a halfhearted attempt to rise as Colt kicked him in his ribs.

Colt panted hard, searching for oxygen while backing away cautiously from the unwelcome pair. He leaned against the driver's door, then left them with a warning: "If you ever come near Alex again, I'll kill you, mark my words." At that moment he meant every word. Colt slowly moved to the passenger door, never taking his eyes off the attackers.

With blood still running down his face, Steve scrambled to his feet. Slowly he fumbled. In the early-morning darkness Colt saw the iron gleam of a short barrel leveled straight at him.

"Don't move, Forrester!" Steve threatened, pointing the .38 snubnose revolver. "She's my wife!" Fire shot through the night as an explosion devastated the silence. Colt stumbled with the impact, reeling against the car. Hot pain ripped through his left shoulder.

Alex screamed desperately, cranking the ignition as Steve moved toward her door with the injured bodyguard close behind. Colt was doubled over, holding his burning shoulder.

"You're coming with me," Steve growled as he jerked the driver's door open and grabbed Alex by the arm. It was the same snarelike grip he had used to hurt and threaten her into submission on past occasions.

The car started, but she couldn't get it in gear. "You can't do this!" Alex clawed and twisted, then kicked wildly, trying to escape his grasp.

Out of the darkness like an angel of mercy, Lafayette's huge, hulking form appeared.

"Let go of the lady!" he ordered in a wrenching baritone. He stood behind Steve, put a fierce chokehold on his neck, and buried an elbow between Steve's shoulder blades.

The bodyguard moved to aid Steve Blake. Lafayette released one hand just long enough to crack a nightstick on the side of the big man's knee, sending him to the ground. With his other massive arm he tightened the hold on Steve, almost breaking his neck.

"Let go! You're killing me!" Steve pleaded for mercy.

Lafayette loosened his grip and buried a huge fist in Steve's kidneys. Then he smashed the terrified coward against the side of the Bronco and wrenched the pistol from his hand.

"Don't ever come near her again! You understand what I mean?"

Steve's eyes filled with terror as Lafayette pressed the night-stick against his cheek.

"Don't cross me, asshole!" With that, Lafayette released his hold and straightened his rumpled coat. Steve Blake retreated from the big man like a whipped dog. Lafayette moved to the car door.

"Thank you for being here." Alex gave a grateful hug to her protector and friend.

"I promised to protect you, now get on out of here. These guys aren't goin' anywhere except to the police."

"Will you be able to handle them?"

"Call Saundra and have her send over a squad car."

"It's done," responded Alex as she reached for the mobile phone to make the call.

The engine roared as Colt hit the electric locks. In the rear-view mirror Alex could see Steve cowering in Lafayette's vise-like grip.

Squealing tires barreled over the curb and into the street. For infinite seconds they drove at breakneck speed, saying nothing, holding on for their lives. It was a narrow escape thanks to Lafayette, who had deftly corralled the ugly pair.

"I thought he was going to kill me—or you." Alex drove in stunned shock until she saw Colt's face wince with pain.

"I'm so sorry, Colt."

"It's not your fault, but he got me pretty good in the left arm." Colt put his right hand up to the wound and blood oozed through the spaces in his fingers.

"Oh, my God, we have to get you to the hospital." Her worst nightmare was unfolding. Steve had found them, and he had almost killed the only man she had ever really loved.

But she wasn't going to let him steal any more of her life. Not when they had come so close to shutting the door on the haunting past. Alex prayed Colt wouldn't lose too much blood before they reached Denver General.

"It's just a flesh wound."

"How do you know? If it hit an artery, you could bleed to death while they fill out the insurance forms."

"I'll be fine." He squeezed her hand in a reassuring gesture. But his blue eyes had turned to a deep gray.

"You need to keep pressure on the wound and stay still," Alex said.

She hit the accelerator and headed toward the massive hospital complex. She was coming back to her old self. The vital Alex that Colt had fallen in love with was no longer dormant. She shuddered in the darkness as she recalled Steve's vitriolic words. How she despised him, knowing he would sooner have her dead than with another man. But he would not win.

The truck turned onto Vannock Street and into the vacant emergency-room parking lot. The hospital was a massive old building on the edge of downtown. For the moment, the normally chaotic reception area was tranquil. A stout middle-aged woman saw Colt's blood-soaked hand and immediately checked the wound, which had stopped bleeding. On seeing that it had been inflicted by a gunshot, she launched into a barrage of questions. Gunshot wounds raised many questions and had to be reported to the police. Colt answered each question patiently. He looked forward to pressing charges against his assailants.

"I'm going to call Jake and see if he can get one of his doctor friends over here ASAP," Alex said, wanting to expedite the emergency-room treatment. A sea of people filled the waiting area.

"I can handle this," Colt tried to protest. But there was no point in fighting her.

"My husband just shot you, now let me help," she implored. "I want someone here who knows about gunshot wounds and joints."

He gave in as Alex commandeered the nurse's phone.

"Winston," Jake answered in a sleepy voice.

"It's Alex."

"What time is it?"

"Early, 5:30 A.M. Sorry to wake you, but I need some help."

"Name it." Urgency cleared the fog from his sleeping brain.

"I'll explain the details later, but Steve stalked me to Colton's and then jumped us. Colt's been shot, and we're at Denver General."

"How badly is he hurt?" Jake asked.

"He'll be all right. But he needs a good doctor. He was shot in the shoulder."

"I'll call Max Sullivan right away."

"Does he practice orthopedics?"

"No, he's chief of staff. He can get someone down there who knows what they're doing."

"Thanks for helping Colt."

"It's about time you two finally got together. That is the way it's supposed to be."

"I love you." And she meant it. She did love Jake fiercely. He was her stalwart supporter, confidante, and friend. She could count on him for anything, even to love her when she could not return the romantic feelings.

For a moment, Jake was quiet on the line. They had finally arrived at a peaceful place where the pieces of the triangle fit.

"I love you, too. Call back in the morning and let me know how you both are doing."

In the darkness of the lonely room, Jake felt genuine happiness for Alex, but it did nothing to abate the emptiness in his heart. He stumbled from the bed and wandered down the hall. He remembered Alex in the white T-shirt, knees tucked under her chin, and the sly smile. While coffee dripped, filling the early-morning chill with its aroma, Jake moved to his reading nook.

His eyes searched for the familiar. From a lower bookshelf he pulled a small album that was sandwiched in a clandestine cubby. His heart felt swollen. Slowly his fingers caressed the cover like a treasure. He did not open it for a time. When the coffee finished brewing, he poured a cup and returned to the sanctuary where he settled into his favorite chair. All his books were in order. They were his friends, his solace. Slowly he opened the album to the first page where the small boy smiled back angelically. His innocence would live forever. Jake's heart flooded with paternal warmth as he imagined the tiny angel scurrying up on his lap for warmth and consolation. The doctors had not been able to make him into a miracle. After a year and a lifetime at St. Jude's Children's Research Hospital, the boy's soul retreated to wherever souls go when children die, and a piece of Jake went with him.

After a few ancient moments, he turned the page to find Chris in her usual place. This album was like fine wine, getting better with age. He remembered the day the photograph had been taken high up in the mountains. He and Chris had played like schoolchildren until their hearts and bodies had lost control. In the shade of a small stand of aspen trees, he had made love to her . . . and thought he would never be the same again. He had been right. Touching and knowing Chris had altered everything.

After a few sips of coffee, he turned to an empty page. Then from the ledge of the bookshelf he found his favorite photo of Alex, the one when she was planting flowers on the deck. Her hair was tussled and she was covered in dirt, but oh, how her eyes twinkled. Slowly he caressed the snapshot memory. Then he slid it into the clear plastic slot. She was home now, he thought, where she belonged, in his own heart forever and, physically with the man she loved. With the photo in its proper place, Jake felt oddly content, somehow resigned to the mysterious circumstances of his life.

CHAPTER 40

Alex walked through the hallway that reeked of hygienic cleanser. The emergency room was buzzing with activity. Gurneys rattled up and down the halls. Colt sat in a small cubicle, patiently watching the nurse cleanse the wound.

"How bad is it?" Alex asked the serious uniformed woman.

"Another centimeter and he would have lost a lot of blood. You are a lucky man," the nurse said to Colt.

"The chief of staff is sending a specialist over right away," Alex reported, "so just sit tight until he gets here."

The nurse raised a penciled brow at the idea of Alex pulling rank on the system. "Our emergency-room physicians are some of the best in the country," said the short, thick lady.

Alex ignored the comment.

"I'll be back to check on you in a few minutes. Don't go anywhere," she said to Colt, sending him a devilish smile.

Detective Carter stood in the old green-tile shower, letting a river of hot water soothe his tired muscles. The tile smelled of encroaching mildew and needed regrouting. He cursed the dark lightbulb that had not been changed for over a week. Water poured over his face and down his stooped back, bringing life to tired bones that had only had two hours of sleep. He thought about Catherine Bridgeforth, still alive but not yet out of the woods. She had lost pints of blood but was hanging on.

As he toweled off in the chilly morning air, the telephone

rang. "Carter!" he barked. He listened to the surveillance officer's update and combed his thinning hair. "Stay on top of it! I'm on my way," he ordered, pressing the "OFF" button on the cordless phone.

Carter dressed hurriedly before strapping on his shoulder harness. Then he dead-bolted the apartment door, descended the elevator, and walked out to his squad car.

He thought about Storm and the senator's head and Catherine Bridgeforth lying comatose in the hospital bed, and wished he had time for a cup of coffee. It would have to wait. Could she really have had the guts to hire the professional killer to assassinate her husband's lover? He wasn't a psychologist, but years on the scene of many a murder had left him with a bloodhound's scent for a killer. If he had to bet right now, the senator was incorrect in his allegations. He had been distraught and emotional after viewing the videotape, and he could have easily jumped to the wrong conclusions. By the book, Storm was still a strong suspect. He had hired Deegan and tried to kill Alex. Carter sped through the night trying to make sense of the events.

Alex checked on Colt, who was being examined by a tall, imposing doctor in a white lab coat that had the name KEITH RICHARDSON embroidered across the pocket. The young doctor hung his stethoscope around his neck and continued with a string of questions while Colt continued to cooperate patiently. The same round nurse took copious notes.

"You are personal friends of the chief of staff?" he inquired casually.

"Sort of." Colt didn't feel like explaining. "How long will I be here?"

"We'll watch the bleeding and look at the x-rays. Maybe a couple of hours. We want to make sure you don't have nerve trauma."

"Thanks for coming at this hour. Is the bullet still lodged in there?"

"No, you're lucky, it went on through."

Alex discreetly retreated while the doctor detailed the nature of the bullet wound. Through a door that said NO ENTRY, she ducked into a corridor and found the staff elevator. She called the operator from a house phone.

"This is Shelley Bridgeforth. Can you please tell me what room my mother Catherine Bridgeforth is in?"

"I'm not supposed to give out any information about that patient."

"This is her daughter," Alex pleaded convincingly.

"Well, I guess it would be all right then." Alex listened to the information and thanked the receptionist.

The hospital was empty, a sterile waiting place between the living and the dead. She passed the doctors' lounge and continued down the corridor to the stairs, taking them two at a time to the sixth floor. The vacant stairwell was gray and cold. Alex peeked through the exit door, noting the nurses' station. A bored young woman was periodically checking monitors and chatting with a uniformed policeman who was pouring coffee. Their backs were turned to Alex. She darted down a corridor in search of the room.

The private room was at the end of the empty corridor. Alex paused at the heavy metal door, on which was mounted NO VISI-TORS sign. She listened at the door before quietly pushing through. The low lights in the hall cast an eerie glow.

Until now Alex had only dreamed of confronting Chris's killer—and suddenly on the edge of the precipice, she hesitated. What would she say? Somehow her rage was subsiding. The events of the last twenty-four hours had brought the past crashing into the present and her emotions were spent. The anger and fear were vaporizing.

There was only one real unanswered question. Alex wanted to see Catherine face to face and hear her say she had hired the killer. Silently she stepped into the room. A fragment of yellow light spilled onto the linoleum floor. Two steps and she was in the darkened private room.

Alex found herself staring at the sleeping Catherine Bridgeforth. IVs and tubes entangled the frail form like kudzu, and Catherine's chest rose and fell in a steady, gentle rhythm. A wince of empathy touched Alex's heart. She dashed it away and a sudden wave of nausea hit like a bomb. She raced for the bathroom with sweat pouring down her clammy temples. She splashed cold water on her face, bringing temporary relief. The combination of no sleep, painkillers, and brandy had left her feeling seasick. She stared into the mirror wondering what had happened to all the dreams.

She heard a door creak in the hospital room. Like a mime she froze, trapped in the tiny lavatory. How would she explain her presence? Quietly she stepped in the shower, pulling the curtain to shield her presence.

The door to the hall thudded closed. For seconds she waited. No sounds came from the patient's room. She ached to hear, but there was nothing more. Finally, after a deadly minute of utter stillness, she left her hiding place. Millimeter by millimeter she delicately applied pressure to the door, cracking it ever so slowly. She slipped back into the dim room through the narrow opening. Flat against the wall next to the bathroom, unable to see the patient, she inched forward. She could hear a faint rustling noise coming from the bed as she silently edged along the wall. She could just make out a form in the shadows.

A figure was stooping over the bed. In the darkness it looked vaguely familiar. She didn't know whether to run or stay. At first she thought it was the doctor—but the doctor would have turned on the light. Then she heard the sound of feeble choking and sputtering. As her eyes adjusted to the darkness, she recognized the familiar physique of Jeff Ashton standing over the fading body of Catherine Bridgeforth. Alex watched in horror as he pushed harder on the pillow he held over Catherine's face.

Alex lunged from the darkness. "What are you doing?" She threw every ounce of strength and power at Ashton. No matter what the woman had done, she shouldn't have to die like that. Alex caught Jeff totally off guard. Her blow pushed him aside, sweeping the pillow to the floor. Gathering his wits, Ashton stiff-armed Alex, slamming her into the wall next to the bed. She fought back, clawing at his face.

He was desperate to complete his mission. He was a free man as long as Catherine couldn't talk. Opening his mouth had turned into a deadly mistake that was spiraling out of control. Just as one lie leads to another, actions from long ago had led to this. The money Chris left him had been his freedom ride, but as long as her murder went unsolved he couldn't rest easy. And then he had become tied by a noose to Catherine just as he had been to Chris. He had been so elated by the brilliant circumstances set up by the senator . . . at last he could be through with the murder and Catherine all in one fell swoop. It had been intoxicating. But Catherine hadn't cooperated—she persisted in living.

Ashton slammed a sharp elbow, crushing Alex back into the wall and knocking over an IV bottle, which crashed to the floor, setting off an alarm at the nurses' station. Alex's head cracked against the hard tile.

Ashton grabbed the pillow again.

A commanding voice broke the spell. "STOP!" Carter was in the cocked-and-ready position, two steady hands wrapped around the butt of his pistol. He was flanked by two officers who stood just behind him. He lowered the steel barrel of the .40 revolver and sighted it on Ashton, who dropped the pillow and raised his arms. Their eyes engaged until Ashton dropped his shameful gaze.

"He was trying to kill her," Alex coughed, breaking the silence. The two uniformed policemen moved toward Ashton, who was backing away.

"Don't move," Carter ordered. "Cuff him!" Swiftly they bent

him over, forcing his hands behind his back and snapping the cuffs. "You're under arrest for the attempted murder of Catherine Bridgeforth." Then Carter read him his rights.

Ashton glared at Alex, who was rubbing her head.

"I loved her. I would never hurt her," he stammered, helplessly trying to build another lie.

"That's a lie!" Catherine whispered defiantly from the bed. She was pale and weak from loss of blood. In a voice that was barely audible, the dying Catherine Bridgeforth beckoned Carter and Alex closer to the bed. Desperation glowed in her pale eyes.

"He thought I would die. He told me he had Chris murdered. But I didn't die." Her eyes pleaded with Carter to believe her story.

"She's insane! She's the one who had Chris killed," Ashton insisted.

"We're on to you, Ashton. Your arrogance caught up with you this time," said Carter.

Alex stood by, astonished, as a nurse ran into the room in response to the alarm.

"You're also under arrest for the murder of Chris Welbourne," Carter continued.

Ashton shook his head in desperation. "You can't prove anything," he said pathetically.

"We've got Catherine Bridgeforth's testimony. And I can prove that the shot that injured her was fired after the senator was dead! You touched the gun. The blood spray was smeared. And when we get through testing you, I bet we'll find powder residue on you as well." Carter explained his hunch proudly.

Catherine Bridgeforth, driven by the instinct to survive and determined to explain her innocence, willed herself to speak. "We found Bill together," she said hoarsely.

"That's not true! She's trying to frame me," Ashton argued. His eyes darted from face to face, searching for believers. Sweat formed on his forehead as he pleaded for understanding. "She hated Chris and she knew Bill was going to divorce her."

"Oh my God, what Bill wrote about me was wrong." Catherine moved a trembling hand, clutching at Carter's arm.

The nurse moved to aid the fragile patient and took her blood pressure. The excitement was too taxing for Catherine; every ounce of energy had been expended trying to tell the truth. Her eyes closed as she caved in from the exertion.

"You will have to leave now," commanded the nurse. "She is too ill to talk."

Carter obliged, ushering the group into the hallway.

Jeff Ashton whimpered in the tightening grip of the two large policemen. "I did everything for the Bridgeforths . . . I want my attorney." Violence erupted in Jeff's normally placid eyes. "You can't prove anything!"

"Take him away," Carter directed the officers, confident that the missing pieces were finally falling into place. "We'll get a full statement later."

Carter and Alex moved into the hallway while the nurse attached a new IV to Catherine.

"Was Catherine part of a conspiracy?" Alex asked, trying to understand the chain of events. The lack of sleep showed in her eyes as she rubbed her head.

"I don't think so," Carter explained calmly. "He was just using her."

"How did you know he would come to the hospital?"

"You might say I gave him some encouragement," Carter said.

Alex looked quizzically at the exhausted but relieved detective. Hospital staff moved about, oblivious to the drama that had just taken place.

"But what about the senator's letter?" Alex asked.

"The senator was pretty distraught after seeing the video, and he jumped to the wrong conclusion."

"He blamed Catherine for Chris's murder."

"We'll get a full confession from Ashton later, but my guess is that he used his liaison with the Bridgeforths to get some introductions to some underworld characters." Carter's call to Catherine's father had confirmed his hunch that Ashton had been in desperate financial straits at the time of Chris's murder. "Once we got a close look at the crime scene, it was obvious that some things had been moved. His story about leaving Catherine at the house after the party was weak. His web of lies finally snared him. He slipped and said something about the suicide letter . . . that was the first real clue he was lying. When we took a closer look at the gun, it was obvious that it had been fired after the senator had killed himself. Jeff is the only one who could have tried to kill Catherine, and killing her would have closed the book on Chris's murder. I think he hired someone to kill Chris for the money."

"I remember how anxious Jeff was to get the will probated, but I can't believe he could do that to Chris. She did so much for him." Alex was stunned by the revelation, remembering the trust Chris had placed in Ashton.

"We'll need a statement from you, Alex, about what happened here this morning."

"Gladly!" she said. "I'm going to need to press charges against Steve, too. He assaulted me last night and shot Colt. The doctor is working on him now."

"Good God, Alex. I never dreamed it would escalate like this. You know it would be my pleasure to help you." Carter had black circles under his eyes. "I need to get down to the police station before this gets to the media." He was rumpled and tired. It had been a horrific twenty-four hours, but he was finally confident that the case was coming to a close.

The elevator descended, taking Alex and Carter to the main floor, where they parted company. Carter had a grueling interview ahead. He was certain a confession about Chris's murder was forthcoming. The threat of a lifetime in prison worked wonders when trying to get prisoners to talk. If Ashton cooperated, he might have a chance at parole in forty years. It would be better than the alternative. Carter prepared himself for the meeting with the chief and the district attorney and hoped the media jackals were still in bed.

∽

Alex found Colt sitting up in a chair with clean bandages and a shoulder sling.

"I thought you had left me again," he smiled.

"Not a chance! It just took a little longer to say good-bye to this ordeal than I had planned."

"Did you see her?" he asked.

"It is finally over, Colt! And we've got a lifetime to try to understand what happened."

"Let's go home."

With his good arm Colt nuzzled Alex, rebuffing the cold morning air. It was an interesting thought, the concept of home. But Alex knew home was really a state of mind, not a place. Right now she felt a sense of belonging, and she was as safe, warm, and secure as she had ever dreamed could be possible.

The charming LoDo loft was warm and inviting. Colt went to the kitchen while Alex left a message for Schaeffer about the closure on the case. When the recorded message came on, she gave a quick summary of what had transpired, then left her dear friend with a tantalizing thought. "I'm in the mood to drill oil wells if you think we still know how to do a deal?" She left Colt's phone number and said good-bye. She smelled fresh coffee brewing while the morning anchorperson greeted viewers with news of a hot breaking story.

"The police have confirmed the arrest of Jeff Ashton in the murder-for-hire case of the late Denver business magnate Christine Dunne Welbourne." At the conclusion of the story, Alex flipped off the remote. She'd heard more than enough. It was really over.

"Here's something I've been saving for you." Colt casually

handed Alex a leather notebook.

"Thank you," Alex said absently. "I'll look at them in just a while. Right now I'm too exhausted to think." Colt merely smiled.

She collapsed in relief with Colt next to her in the oversized chair that enveloped them like a womb. In the early morning with the sun peeking over the horizon, the world slowed to a comfortable pace. Softly, like the touch of an angel, Colt caressed her face, reaching inside her soul to recapture the parts of her that had been lost for so many years. He traced her features with searching tenderness. With each touch, feelings came back in a furious, exploding rush. The burning fire called to them. Petal-soft kisses brushed wet eyelids. They spoke in Braille, studying every line and every feature with searching hands. His fingers ran through thick black hair, pulling her closer, kissing away the years between them. For the precious moments that hung like spun gold, there was no Chris; there was no murder; there was no Steve.

Like lost children they clung to each other, gazing at the fire and listening to music melt their hearts. It was a moment where nothing existed but their souls. Alex coiled around Colt, trying to hold on, determined to keep the illusion from vanishing. And in the pristine moment new dreams were born. The healing waters of hope rushed through them like a swollen river. And it wasn't an illusion. Alex wasn't going anywhere, and nothing was going to rip apart their dream.

EPILOGUE

In the early hours of the dawn, Alex slipped from the loft to find the small notebook that Colt had given her. Remnants of firelight splashed the walls with shadows. For a moment she caressed the worn dark-green leather. Carefully she opened the treasured book. The title page read, NOTES FOR ALEX. Her heart throbbed. She slowly turned to the first page where she found what looked like a poem. As she flipped through the journal, she found page after page filled with poems and love letters Colt had written to her. Dates, times and places from across the years. She went to the last entry, which was dated just weeks before:

> *In the sunsets and the stars*
> *I feel your heart.*
> *In the wind and river*
> *I sense your touch.*
> *In time and eternity*
> *I touch your soul.*
> *In destiny we meet again. . .*